Terry McGee is a practising obstetrician who lives in Sydney with her husband and two children. She is currently working on her second novel.

Misconceptions

TERRY McGEE

MACMILLAN
Pan Macmillan Australia

First published 2003 in Macmillan by Pan Macmillan Australia Pty Limited
St Martins Tower, 31 Market Street, Sydney

National Library of Australia
cataloguing-in-publication data:

McGee, Terry, 1957– .
Misconceptions.

ISBN 0 7329 1170 2.

1. Obstetricians – Malpractice – Fiction. 2. Man–woman relationships – Fiction. I. Title.

A823.4

Typeset in 11/14 pt Palatino by Post Pre-press Group, Brisbane
Printed in Australia by McPherson's Printing Group

Cover photograph taken at the Bondi Icebergs

For Jim, Dan, Imogen and Mum.

Acknowledgements

This book wouldn't exist if it weren't for my friends.

My colleagues Elizabeth John, Meredith Wilson, Jane McDonald and Martin Kluckow guided me through specialised medical information; my friend Kylie Nomchong and my husband, Jim Nolan, answered my legal questions; my old school and university colleague Megan Keaney shared her expertise on medico-legal matters; while Susan Nielsen helped in more general ways.

A band of dear associates ploughed through the manuscript for me, some of them more than once, and a couple were even shamelessly subjected to the early unreadable drafts. Each improved the book in some way by their suggestions and, just as importantly, kept me going with their encouragement. Thanks to Mary-Ellen Bard, Margie Bryant, Rosemary Gallagher, Anne Karczub, Nuala Keating, Rosemary Marks, Annette Moran, Leonie Piper, Julia Robson and Paula Sharkey, as well as Elizabeth and Megan from above and of course, Jim and Mum. I don't have any friends left, but it doesn't matter. The manuscript is finished.

Finally, I could never have got the book to this stage without excellent editing from Louise Thurtell and Julia Stiles. Thanks also to Margaret O'Sullivan and copy-editor, Jo Jarrah. I am likewise very grateful to the people at Pan Macmillan, especially Cate Paterson and Simone Ford, for the careful and generous way they have nurtured my story.

Chapter 1

The phone on the bedside table was ringing. Semiconscious, Julia groaned and fumbled for it in the dark, knocking over the not-quite-empty coffee cup she knew she shouldn't have left there. If she hadn't been so tired, she'd have sworn. But she didn't give a damn about the cup. Or the mess. Or even the beautiful Turkish rug the coffee now dripped onto. All she cared about at this moment was staying in bed. It was two-fifteen in the morning.

'Dr Kent, it's Liz Ellison from Royal Eastside. Your Mrs Roberts has come in. This is her second baby and she's eight centimetres dilated. Her waters broke during the examination and she's very pushy. You'd better come straight away or you'll miss it.'

'Thanks, Liz. I'll be right there,' Julia mumbled, mostly to her pillow, restraining her frustration until the midwife hung up. Then she groaned like an animal in pain. Didn't anyone have a baby during the day any more? Despondently, she put the phone down, missing the cradle initially and wincing at the clatter. Her face sank back into the pillow. She waited a moment then tried to raise it again, but it wouldn't move. The muscles in her neck were paralysed. She was vaguely aware that her mouth, slightly open, drooled saliva down her cheek, but she couldn't close it. The tug of sleep was irresistible. She'd had to work three nights this week already.

Years of brutal self-discipline forced her legs over the edge of the bed onto the now damp, cool wool of the Turkish rug, and she lay, half-kneeling, for what seemed an eternity, desperately searching her being for the energy to make the next movement. Finally she lurched forward and tottered unsteadily towards the bathroom, where the tiny night-light threw its jaundiced beam over her form. She briefly acknowledged her ghostly reflection in the mirror; they'd have to stop meeting like this.

She twisted the tap and leant forward, submitting to its awakening powers. Gaining momentum, she dressed quickly, ran a comb through her hair, and hurried out the front door onto the porch, down the steps and into the carport. The wind was up and it was raining lightly, and the cool was a blessed relief from the mugginess of the last two days.

She reversed carefully along the drive, window down and head out as usual. The gateway was narrow and she regularly scraped one side of the car or the other on the posts. Especially in the middle of the night. She'd promised herself many times to have them moved but never got around to it. With all she'd paid to the panel-beater in recent years, she could have had the entire fence replaced.

This time she missed the gateposts but, forgetting to duck at the end of the drive, felt her head connect with the overhanging, very wet wisteria, sending a hard spray of cold water down the back of her neck. She nearly cried with the misery of it all, but at least she was awake. Anxiety began to percolate through her weariness. After all this effort, she was probably going to miss the delivery. And her patient, and more particularly her patient's husband, would wonder what they were paying her for.

Sometimes she wondered herself.

Wondered why she was hauling her aching limbs out of bed in the middle of the night, careening recklessly to the hospital, rushing into the maternity wing, and clambering up four flights of stairs to be so breathless by the time she got there, she almost needed oxygen. Why? To do what? To pretend that she was needed, when for the most part nature was perfectly capable of completing the task unassisted. For the most part.

That was the rub. That was why she was needed. Because no one ever knew when nature's way and the best way would diverge, when nature's choice would be the human equivalent of a tidal wave. Which was why those who could afford it, and a lot who couldn't, paid her to look after them while they were pregnant. And especially in labour. And why Claudia Roberts was expecting her there, right now, in the middle of the night.

Claudia had seen another doctor for the birth of her first child. She and her husband Russell were schoolteachers. They had read all the books, attended all the classes, done everything they could to prepare for their first experience of childbirth. And it had all gone wrong. Claudia had wished for a spontaneous labour after a good night's sleep a few days before full term. She'd hoped for about five hours of manageable pain followed by the delivery of a gorgeous, screaming infant with whom she immediately bonded. And she'd wanted no stitches.

Instead she went two weeks overdue and had to be induced. Her labour had been long and arduous, and the epidural hadn't worked properly. Ultimately she was too tired to push the baby out and it had been delivered by forceps with a big episiotomy. Almost predictably, the breastfeeding had been a nightmare as well. She'd given up after five days, her nipples cracked and bleeding, while a starving Benjamin had greedily gobbled his first bottle. Exhausted by the whole affair, she'd felt a failure as a woman and a mother.

With this pregnancy, she was setting her sights lower, hoping only to avoid the forceps, have fewer stitches and perhaps a better go at breastfeeding. She'd changed doctors as well. In fact, it turned out she'd wanted Julia for her first confinement but had phoned too late. This time she'd taken no chances, ringing as soon as the pregnancy test was positive, three days before she'd even missed her period.

For her part, having heard the story, Julia acknowledged she would have managed Claudia's previous delivery in exactly the same way as her colleague. 'Since Genesis, labour is supposed to be bloody awful, I'm afraid,' she said, a small smile softening her words. 'And it often is.'

Sally Stevens, one of the suite's most experienced midwives, was at the desk as Julia panted her way into the labour ward. 'I'm glad you're here, Dr Kent. Mrs Roberts keeps asking for you. She's very close but I think you're just going to make it.'

'From the sound of that screaming, *she* mightn't, poor thing!' Julia joked, delighted that she wasn't too late after all. She knew how much Claudia wanted her here for the birth of her baby. She slid open the door as Liz, the midwife, was gloving. Claudia was just one or two contractions away from delivery. There would be no forceps this time, thought Julia happily.

Despite her distress, Claudia registered her doctor's arrival. Her relief was immediate. 'Oh, Dr Kent, please help me!'

Julia put on her gown and gloves, and took her place at the bedside. She sent the labouring woman a look of warm encouragement. 'You don't need my help, Claudia, you're doing really well all by yourself. And it's nearly over. Just slow your breathing. Fill your lungs with oxygen and breathe deeply. I think the next contraction is starting to build up.' She looked at Liz, who nodded. Her hand gently on Claudia's abdomen, the midwife could feel the tightening of the uterine muscle. As the pain became intolerable, Claudia's face contorted once more. 'Get it out! Get it out!' she screamed.

'Pant, Claudia, don't push. Just pant,' coached Julia in a low voice, all the while controlling the baby's head with the fingers of her left hand as it eased nicely over the stretched perineal skin. She badly wanted Claudia to avoid the railway track of sutures she'd sat on for a month after her last delivery, and was pleased that, so far, there was no tearing. 'That's good, Claudia, good, the baby's sliding out beautifully. Keep panting, good, good. The baby's head's out now. That's the worst of it,' she cheered. 'Now take it easy while we wait for the last contraction.'

Julia rested briefly herself, glad for a break and sighing almost in unison with her patient. Although she'd not been here long, the heavy delivery gown and the bright labour-room lights made it hot, sweaty work.

Claudia turned slightly, seeking her husband Russell. He had been supporting her head and shoulders while she pushed, and had now stepped away from the bed to absorb his own emotions. Claudia beckoned him closer again. 'Ice, please,' she croaked. Russell held the cup to her lips but, as he did, the knowing look of terror took over her face again. She spat out the ice as the power of the contraction overwhelmed her once more.

'A small push now,' Julia directed calmly as the shoulders, arms and chest of the baby emerged, and Claudia exhaled as the pressure eased. Julia then turned to Russell. She knew he'd felt excluded from the last delivery because of the forceps and had hoped for the past nine months that she'd be able to make it up to him now. 'Come and help me with the last little bit,' she invited.

Russell was startled but not unwilling as Julia placed both of his hands around the baby's chest where it rested between his wife's legs. He looked up at Claudia, whose face was alight with anticipation. They hadn't expected this.

'Lift the baby up onto Claudia's tummy,' Julia instructed. The child was slippery, covered in the newborn grease known as vernix, and Russell's grip was uncertain. Julia helped him unobtrusively as, with growing amazement, he saw the abdomen, buttocks and legs of his new offspring appear. Claudia reached out eagerly to receive the bundle from him and, as everyone watched, the baby obligingly bawled on cue.

'What have you got?' asked the midwife, who could already see.

Russell inspected the baby's genitalia, always relatively larger in the newborn than later. His assessment was not assisted by the filmy layer collecting over his eyes. 'It's a girl, I think,' he said, turning to Julia, who nodded. He gave a small cry of joy, the tears now spilling and streaming. He looked for something to wipe his hands on before touching his daughter again, even though the blood and grease and water were hers.

'It's a girl, darling,' he sobbed to Claudia, who gazed in disbelief at the new life in her arms. Russell kissed his wife's damp forehead. 'Thank you, darling, thank you. I'm so proud of you!'

'And we're all proud of you too,' said Julia, feeling she might shed a tear as well. 'If you can cut the cord as professionally as you delivered the baby, I'll soon be out of a job.' Her eyes laughed as she handed him the scissors, holding the cord for him to divide. With this he was more confident, beaming with paternal pride. The midwife took a photo while everyone clapped, and his daughter, who had been briefly silent, started up her lusty cry again.

After the delivery of the placenta, Julia left her thrilled patients alone for a while and retreated to the relative passivity of paperwork. Nature's way and the best way had coincided, she thought contentedly. This was why she had become an obstetrician: nothing rivalled the seductive spectacle of birth.

She returned to the labour room to say goodbye and found Claudia propped up in bed, adoring shafts of love swaddling the little girl attached to her right breast. As they exchanged glances, Julia and her patient both knew there'd be no problem with the feeding this time. Russell leant over his family protectively as he proudly related the night's events to his mum and dad over the phone. Julia had not wished to interrupt, but Russell excused himself briefly to his parents in order to hug her. 'Thank you so much, Dr Kent, you were wonderful!'

'When you look back, I think you'll see that you did it all yourselves,' Julia said, enjoying his praise even so. 'Now you'll be thinking of a third! But have the next one during business hours, will you?'

It was after four when she finally arrived home. The sky wore a lighter cloak than when she'd left; even so, dawn was still an hour away. The gusty wind had dropped, but a gentle breeze remained and she welcomed its cooling touch. She entered the dark house and went quietly to her bedroom. Relieving herself of bag and keys, she cast an eye over the bed. It looked very enticing. On the other hand, it was futile to try and sleep so soon. She'd have thought, after all these years, that she'd know by now how to unwind quickly after a delivery, but she didn't; the physical challenge and emotional exhilaration always kept her awake for hours. Since she had to be up again shortly anyway, she might as well tackle some of the paperwork in her bulging briefcase.

That did it. Just the thought of paperwork knocked her swooning onto the cool white sheets and she was softly snoring almost immediately, succumbing to a tiredness so profound that even her normally restive mind could not counter it.

Fifteen minutes later the phone rang.

'Hello,' garbled Julia, barely able to form the word.

'Dr Kent, it's Lucy Burton, Eastside Labour Ward. Antenatal has just sent down Mrs Gina Vella. She's thirty-two weeks now and is bleeding.'

'Is she?' Julia roused only slowly. 'Gina bleeds every few days, Lucy. It always settles.'

The midwife knew this as well; she'd been on the last few times it had happened. But this time the bleeding was much worse. 'I don't think it's going to stop, Dr Kent.'

The midwife's words jolted Julia awake. 'Is theatre busy?'

Lucy had taken the precaution of letting the operating staff know they had a possible caesarean. A team would be ready to start at five. Luckily, an anaesthetist was free and was now on his way around to see Mrs Vella. 'I'm very worried about her, Dr Kent.'

Lucy's tone alarmed Julia. Poor Gina. They'd been waiting for this to happen, for bleeding so heavy it would bring the pregnancy to an end, but now it had started, Julia felt the tension come over her. Dressing while she spoke, she instructed Lucy to cross-match four units of packed cells, four units of plasma, and to let the blood bank know that they might need a lot more. And she meant a *lot*. Lucy was to ask the anaesthetist to take Gina around to theatre and to get the operating suite to call in another team so that they could start immediately. 'I'll be there in ten minutes. And thanks, Lucy.'

Gina Vella had three healthy boys, all caesarean deliveries. Although she'd recovered slowly from each birth, she was desperate for a daughter. She joked that she was prepared to keep trying until she got one. This pregnancy had been difficult from the start, and Gina was worn out even before it was discovered that there was a serious problem. The placenta was praevia, dangerously located at the bottom of the uterus over the cervix and in front of the baby, rather than being up higher, behind it. This had been revealed at her twenty-week ultrasound, and confirmed a fortnight later when Gina bled for the first time. Since then, there'd been a trickle every week or so. In the beginning it wasn't much, but over time, the frequency and amount of blood loss increased and Julia had put her in hospital. It was distressing for Gina to be away from her sons, but her maternal misgivings were exceeded by her fear.

Gina's final bleed was so heavy that she was lapsing into unconsciousness by the time they got her to the operating theatre. Once there, the young anaesthetist was fearful to put her to sleep. 'Blood pressure's in her boots.' He stared anxiously at Julia. 'I don't know that she'll survive the anaesthetic.'

Julia swung her eyes from him to the clock, and from there to an increasingly moribund Gina. She then looked at the anaesthetist again. For more than twelve minutes she'd been waiting to start the operation, making nervous small circuits across the theatre's lino, taking care not to contaminate her sterile gown, but unable to stand still. As the thirteenth minute passed, she knew she had to take charge. While she sympathised with his fears, she was more experienced. She'd been in this situation before. 'I understand your concern,' she said kindly. 'But she'll bleed to death if I don't get this haemorrhage under control. And I can't do that until you anaesthetise her.'

'I'd like to stabilise her first,' he persisted.

Julia shook her head. It was now fifteen minutes. 'I don't think you're going to be able to do that. She's losing ten times as much blood as you can possibly put into her arm. If we don't stop her bleeding, we'll never stabilise her.'

Just then the midwife held the Doppler over Gina's uterus to

8

pick up the baby's heartbeat. It was very slow. Julia looked at the young anaesthetist again. 'The baby's not coping well either. You must give the blood as fast as you can, but please, let's start.'

The tiny premature boy was in real distress when Julia got him out – flaccid, pale and slow to breathe. She tried to stop herself biting hard on her lower lip behind her mask as she watched the neonatal team begin their resuscitation. It was a habit she indulged in in moments of extreme stress, the smarting of her lip distracting her from greater pains. After a few minutes the tiny child kicked a leg and flailed an arm and gave a small whimper. The whole theatre sent up a cheer and Julia left her lip alone.

It would be months, of course, before the damage, if any, would be known, but for now, the odds were in his favour. After thanking the paediatricians and watching them wheel the trolley off to neonatal intensive care, Julia turned her attention back to her other patient, the one whose abdomen and uterus lay gaping after the exodus of her son.

Gina was not doing well.

A placenta praevia together with a history of three previous caesareans was an obstetric nightmare; sometimes it even required the emergency removal of the uterus. As well as being aberrantly located, the placenta was often tenaciously adherent. It could not be left behind but attempts to remove it sometimes tore open enormous blood vessels, causing uncontrollable haemorrhage.

This was what was happening with Gina Vella.

Julia had to control her panic as wells of red filled the pelvis. The hours slipped by in a blink as she frantically sewed and oversewed the massive veins in the placental bed, tied off the arteries which supplied the uterus, called for larger clamps, demanded even more sutures. Nothing helped. Her lip was taking a beating and she could taste blood in her mouth. It was only fitting, she supposed. There was blood everywhere else.

She turned away from the operating table for a minute to wipe the mist from her glasses and in that moment faced up to the realisation that her dear patient, someone she'd cared for during all her pregnancies over the past ten years, could actually die. Still under her care. As she reluctantly embarked upon a hysterectomy, she admitted to herself that she had tried too long to save the uterus, knowing that Gina dearly wanted a daughter. In so doing, she had put her patient's life at extra risk.

The young anaesthetist was on the phone ordering further blood while a more senior anaesthetist had arrived to assist with the crisis. By the time Julia completed the operation, over twenty units of blood had been given, but at least the bleeding had stopped. The surgical bleeding, that is. Once someone's own fresh blood was totally replaced by stored blood, the ability to clot properly was compromised, and the oozing started. From every injured surface. It was the sort of bleeding unresponsive to further stitching. Julia knew her job was complete and she had to step back and let nature take over the repair. If it could.

'I've finished,' she said to the anaesthetists as she ripped off her mask. 'The rest is up to you and your intensive care mates. Thanks very much for your help,' she added, nodding to the younger one in particular. She pulled off her gloves but fumbled with the back of her gown, suddenly in a great hurry to be out of it. The theatre nurse quickly stepped over to help her.

'Thanks, Karen. After spending three hours tying knots, I think I've lost the ability to untie them.' Her feeble joke fooled no one.

It was now eight o'clock, and Julia's shoulders sloped sharply at the thought of the full day ahead of her. She was often up all night but usually things went well and the psychological buzz saw her through. But when, on top of exhaustion, there was also dismay, the day was always hard. She made herself straighten up. One step at a time, that was all she could manage. Everyone except Gina Vella would have to wait.

She fell into the chair where the young anaesthetist had been sitting, vacant now while he woke the patient, and tried to write the operation report. But the pen hardly moved, each word was an effort. When it was finally done, she continued to sit, unable to get up. Newton's 'First Law of Motion' sprang unbidden to mind: a body remains at rest unless acted upon by an outside force. She looked around for the force and found none; it would have to come from within. Groaning, she heaved herself from the chair, but no one was listening.

Irresistibly, she was drawn towards the hospital exit, to leave behind this awful night, to snatch a few minutes to change and hopefully recharge before she embraced the morning. But she couldn't go anywhere until she had spoken to Mario Vella. He'd been called urgently in the middle of the night but, on arrival, had found he was too late. While Gina was in surgery, he'd sat for hours on his own, fearing the worst and desperately waiting to hear. He jumped up when he saw Julia, his eyes pleading so wretchedly for consolation that she failed to tread the fine line between alarm and reassurance. He was entitled to know that his wife could easily die in the next few hours, but Julia couldn't get the words out. She left Mario thinking that Gina had lost a little bit of blood, that her stay in intensive care was routine, and that the caesarean had been only slightly more difficult than normal. She couldn't honestly recall later whether Mario even understood what a hysterectomy was and what it meant.

The morning traffic swallowed her car as she made her way home. She turned on the radio but heard not a word, her senses welded to the woman now lying in intensive care. She blinked back the tears but nothing could muffle the fear that played over and over in her mind. That if Gina Vella died, it would be all her fault.

She should have insisted that the junior anaesthetist start sooner, called a more senior anaesthetist in right from the start, requested a more experienced surgical assistant when the operation proved to be exceptionally difficult. And proceeded to the hysterectomy earlier. Perhaps she should even have done the caesarean when Gina had last bled a week ago. At least she would have avoided the litres of blood lost before the operation even started.

The final thought was unreasonable; she could allow herself that one concession. Gina's last bleed had been small and quickly over and she'd only been thirty-one weeks, nine short of full term, too early to take the baby out if the pregnancy could be safely continued. Each week the baby stayed inside the uterus

11

increased its chances of survival. Especially survival without impairment.

Julia arrived home, drained and dispirited, to shower and dress and join the rest of the world as it stepped into the new day. The overnight rain and wind had gone, banished by the sun, and it was already twenty-four degrees. Julia sniffed the morning air. It was going to be another scorcher, a third day of unseasonable heat in the middle of spring. While many complained, and air-conditioners were turned to maximum, it was weather Julia loved. Glorious Sydney beach days and balmy seaside evenings were why she had bought her home near the ocean. Not that she had much time to enjoy them.

As she walked through the front door and heard the music, Julia felt her mood lift slightly. Emma was up. There was always music when her daughter was awake. She had played the piano for years and dabbled with the violin, and her tastes were eclectic, ranging from Mozart to Eminem as the feeling took her. This morning Julia was greeted by something fresh from Kasey Chambers.

She followed the smell of fried bacon into the kitchen. From there she could see Emma, sitting in the morning sun at the table on the deck, engrossed in the newspaper and still in her pyjamas. With an indulgent glimmer, Julia's eyes also registered that her daughter had once again done what she was always telling her not to: she had pushed her plate to the far end of the long table, where the crumbs of her bacon on toast were now providing breakfast for two seagulls.

'Hi, Mum. Long night?' asked Emma as Julia came out onto the deck. A light sleeper, she knew Julia had been gone for hours.

'Long and awful,' Julia replied.

Emma took in the bruised lip and doleful face and was surprised. Her mother was usually so upbeat about her work. She thrived on the dramas it threw up and thrilled at each new birth. 'What happened?'

'Someone nearly died.'

'But she's all right now?' Emma asked with a hopeful inflection.

Julia's voice thickened. 'I'm not sure. She could still die.'

Emma hesitated. 'Do you want to talk about it?'

Julia hugged her daughter gratefully. There was nothing she would have liked more in the whole world than to sit here all day with Emma. But it wasn't an option. And with respect to Gina Vella, it wouldn't really help. Only her not dying would help.

The shower soothed her a bit. She welcomed the water, willing it to seep through her dilated pores and cleanse her spirit. She submitted to its caress longer than she should, but found the benefit fleeting. Her hands gave up before her body was half-dried, while her arms and shoulders seemed not to know their role in the towelling of wet hair. Every muscle ached.

Her body hadn't always taken the knocks so badly, but at forty-three she couldn't expect to bounce back like she used to. Especially given her record of neglect. Ruefully, she recalled the brief, half-hearted and ultimately fruitless attempts she'd made over the years to regain some of the lost fitness of her youth. A couple of years back she'd joined a gym, but only gone once. A single session was sufficient to know that she saw enough half-naked, sweaty, grunting female bodies in her work not to want them peopling her leisure time as well. She'd then gone for something private and bought an exercise bike, but it had rusted from neglect. The treadmill met a similar fate a year later. At least the two kept each other company in the shed. Most recently she'd purchased an exercise video, but had decided to view it first from the comfort of the lounge. Falling asleep during the warm-up stretches, she'd never even bothered to rewind the tape.

That last effort was months ago and with it came the unwelcome realisation that, as long as she maintained her current lifestyle, what little energy she had left over was best spent on holding body and soul together, rather than shaking them apart.

She looked at herself in the mirror. An observer would have seen an attractive woman, younger than her years, with a head

of fine blonde hair shaped into an attractive bob. The observer
would have taken in a round face, small snub nose, fuller than
average lips and green eyes, the iris of one being slightly speck-
led at the outer edge. Short and a little plump, she had heavy
breasts, a full curve around the belly, and legs that were reasonably shapely.

What Julia saw was a pimple appearing on her chin, not far
from where a cold sore was resolving. Both nestled uncomfortably into her increasingly blemished, dry skin although today, at
least, they were overshadowed by the purple welt on her lower
lip. She saw flyaway hair that needed at least ten minutes with
the curling wand and half a can of spray to stay in place. Her
eyes were drawn to her sagging, pendulous breasts, five kilograms of extra lower-body fat, an enormous swollen abdomen,
flabby thighs, a cellulite bottom, and legs that had always been
too short, and now were streaked with veins as well.

At this moment, however, her appearance was the least of her
concerns. She turned away from the mirror and opened the
wardrobe. When she felt tired, it was important to take special
care in selecting her outfit. Something comfortable, certainly, but
also smart enough to lift her spirits and carry her through the
day. Surveying the cupboard, she cursed again the weight she'd
gained in the past few years, and its distribution mostly around
her middle and bottom.

There were days, especially before her period, when it looked
like a small beach ball had been blown up inside her. She'd given
up trying to fit into all the lovely trousers and skirts she'd worn
in the past, and had moved them reluctantly, one by one, into the
cupboard in the spare room. She had come to accept that the for-
ties were not to be size ten years. On one particularly frustrating
Saturday, when the zipper on her best trousers had torn out of
the fabric as she forced it up over her bulge, she'd gone out and
bought a whole new wardrobe in size twelve, together with two
pairs of light cotton trousers in size fourteen.

'A very small make,' the saleswoman had assured her. 'And
very smart on you, madam.'

It was one of these larger pairs in beige that she selected this morning, matching them with a long, fine, white linen shirt covered in a delicate filigree pattern. The untucked shirt was the telltale sign of the terrible tummy problem, but the effect was smart and quite slimming. She put on the heavy gold chain she'd bought herself when she turned forty, jesting at the time that there was no one to give her jewellery any more, and teamed it with a pair of gold and pearl earrings given to her by Emma a year later to prove her wrong. She paid special attention to her make-up, choosing a darker lipstick than usual. She then spent the requisite time with the curling wand before joining her daughter on the deck where the aroma of coffee and warm toast beckoned invitingly.

Emma admired the transformation. 'You look great, Mum. No one would know you've been up all night.'

'Thanks, Em. I'm wearing your earrings for luck.'

As Julia placed a clean towel on the seat to protect her pale trousers and sat down, she confessed her fear that delaying the hysterectomy had jeopardised Gina's life.

Emma was loyal. 'It seems you did all you could.'

Julia sighed sadly. She'd certainly thought she was doing the right thing at the time, but now she could see her mistakes. A wave of despair threatened, but she quelled it. This was not Emma's problem. She found a more cheerful face and asked about her daughter's plans for the day.

She was studying for her ancient history exam on Thursday, of course. Julia gave a knowing nod. That would take her till about ten-thirty.

'After that I *might* pop down to the beach for a little while,' Emma conceded. 'But then I'll come back and study all afternoon. I promise.'

Emma would be eighteen in February and was in the middle of her final high school examinations. She'd done most of the papers in the past two weeks and had only ancient history this week, and her favourite subject, art, the following week. She was then planning to work for three months before taking most of the next year off to travel to Europe and see some of the masterpieces she had studied.

She hadn't decided much beyond that, although she'd joked for years that her ultimate ambition was to train as a high school art teacher and then find work in a school that didn't take art all that seriously. She quoted unsourced 'international scientific research' which showed conclusively that such a job had the shortest hours, best conditions and least responsibility. And a life outside work.

What she didn't need to add was that her decision sprang from a lifetime of seeing her mother consumed by her job.

'And tonight, Em?' Julia asked.

The teenager's face lit up. They were having a jam at Jade's.

Emma and three friends had formed a band earlier in the year. With the exams nearly over, they were rehearsing in earnest, especially since their long-awaited first public appearance was this Saturday night. Although it was just a local teenage dance in a church hall, they were overcome with apprehension and excitement. Emma played keyboards, Jade lead guitar, Petra base guitar, while Lisa was on drums. At this stage they shared the vocals and mostly did covers of popular songs, but their ambitions extended to writing their own compositions.

'Would you like me to pick you up when you finish?' Julia asked hopefully. They'd had little time together over the past few weeks and she missed her daughter's easy company.

Emma told her not to worry. Jade was happy to drop her home. 'Besides, Mum, I could wait all night for you.'

Julia winced. It was true. She'd often had to leave Emma to make her way home by taxi or with friends from restaurants, school functions, movies. But what could a single parent in a job like hers do? She'd spent the seven years since her divorce from Tony anguishing over it, always coming back to the same three options. Give up her job. Give up her child. Or muddle through. Luckily she'd been blessed with the ideal child to muddle through with.

Emma was resourceful, relaxed and funny. While untidy and often careless with her things, she was kind and caring and a font of enormous common sense; an excellent message-taker, breakfast-maker, sounding board, ironing lady, and general hand. Julia couldn't have managed without her. Which was why it was such a pity she saw so little of her these days. As she stood to leave, she hid her hurt. 'Have a nice day, Em. But don't forget to study, okay? There are only two exams left, after all.'

'Sure.' Emma hugged her mother. 'And don't you worry too much about Mrs Vella. She'll be fine. Hardly anyone dies having a baby any more.' As she saw her mother pale, she appreciated her level of anguish. 'You don't really think she might?'

Julia suddenly crumpled. 'Oh, Em, I sincerely hope not.'

Chapter 2

Julia was running very late. By the time she did her rounds at St Agatha's Private Hospital and then ventured fearfully back to Royal Eastside, it was ten o'clock. She should have gone straight to her surgery, but knew she'd have no peace of mind until she personally reviewed the Vellas. As she drove into the hospital's senior doctors' car park, she realised with relief that it was Tuesday and her most experienced secretary would already be at work. The wonderful Marcia spent most of her days rearranging patients' appointments for the four busy obstetricians who shared the practice, and did it with such charm that the patients were often left feeling they'd requested the amended time themselves. Julia reached for her phone.

'Well, of course, your nine o'clock, Mrs Dubcik has been here for an hour,' said Marcia. 'She says she's happy to wait, while the nine-thirty says she's happy to rebook for next week. Unfortunately, your ten o'clock appointment won't be so accommodating. She specifically made an early appointment because you kept her so late last time. But don't worry, I'll sort her out. And good luck with Gina.'

Julia went first to the neonatal intensive care unit to see baby Vella. The paediatricians had just finished their rounds and Dr Julius Tong, the director of the unit, disengaged himself from the group and came over as she walked through the door.

'Hello, Julia. You look apprehensive,' he said, with a slight smile.

'Is it that obvious?' She knew it was. Camouflaging her emotions was not a skill she'd ever really mastered. She asked how the baby was. The paediatrician's manner gave her reason to hope, but she needed to hear.

They were really quite pleased with him, Dr Tong said. His oxygen requirements were down, his colour was good and, so far, his blood results were reasonable. He would have a head ultrasound later in the day to exclude haemorrhage into the brain but, since he'd not been irritable, they were hoping it would be normal.

Her anxiety now eased, Julia went over to the plastic crib where the littlest Vella lay silently, flat on his back, spread-eagled, and intubated. The nurses had already taken a couple of Polaroids of him, one of which Julia pocketed for Gina.

She then took the lift from the fourth to the eighth floor, from neonatal intensive care to adult intensive care. It was not a commonly made trip. The last time she'd had an adult patient in intensive care must have been three years ago now. At thirty-four weeks of pregnancy, a young woman had suffered a massive bleed into her brain as the result of a burst aneurysm. While tests confirmed she was brain dead, her unborn baby was unaffected by the catastrophe. The woman was therefore kept alive on a ventilator for a month until the baby was ready to be delivered. After the caesarean birth, the machine was turned off. And while her mother's life had quietly slipped away, the daughter's vigorous wail announced that hers had just begun.

Julia stepped out of the lift and nervously approached the security phone on the wall outside the entrance to the intensive care unit. She lifted the receiver and identified herself, but her words came out so softly, she was asked to repeat them. The door swung open to admit her. After the good news with baby

19

Vella, she had subliminally become more hopeful about Gina, but the nurse who came to join her was steely.

'We're very worried about her kidneys,' she said as they inspected the small amount of urine in the catheter bag. 'Her creatinine is going up. They're talking dialysis if the trend continues. Dr McGrath was just here and he asked me to fill you in. He's very concerned.'

Julia was sorry to have missed her old friend Giles McGrath, the director of ICU. Not that he could have reassured her much at the moment.

At the sound of Julia's voice, Gina's eyes opened. 'Have you seen him?' she whispered anxiously, looking at Julia.

Immediately Julia came closer. She'd just come from the baby, she explained slowly, letting Gina take in every word. He was doing really well, certainly better than expected at this stage. She handed over the photo. Gina gazed uncertainly at the scrawny form of her fourth son in his plastic box, barely visible among the spaghetti of tubes and lines which sprang from his tiny body. 'Thank you, Dr Kent,' she gasped, her energy rapidly ebbing. 'Thank you for saving him.'

Julia shifted her gaze from Gina to her medical chart and then back again. Neither was blooming. Gina's blood pressure was very low but at least it was no longer falling, while her pulse was high but not rising. The loss from the pelvic drain had slowed and it seemed that the risk of further haemorrhage had passed. But her low urinary output was a worry; the profound loss of blood had put the kidneys into shock. If they were to recover, the next few hours would be critical. If they didn't, ongoing dialysis would be necessary to clear the body's toxins.

Julia solemnly put the chart down. Things were not looking good.

It was nearly eleven when she finally trudged into the surgery. Five patients were already waiting for her and the day was fully booked. As well, there were two urgent and ten routine phone calls needing a reply. As she readied herself, she hoped no one could guess that,

20

behind her welcoming smile, she was actually summoning all her telepathic powers to induce an electricity blackout. The equipment, lights and phones would go down, everyone would be sent away and she would be free to find somewhere dark and cool to curl up and sleep. It didn't work. She called her first patient.

Predictably, the day was difficult.

No one seemed to have a straightforward problem and the image of Gina Vella struggling to cope with four small children and hours of unpleasant, expensive kidney dialysis intruded on every consultation. What if she ultimately needed a transplant and a lifetime of medication? It didn't bear thinking about. But still Julia couldn't stop.

As the day wore on she had to repeatedly re-ask questions of her patients, having paid no attention to the answer the first time. Twice she missed the second telling as well. In her distracted state she wrote her own name on a pap smear slide instead of the patient's. Luckily Marcia noticed, laughing as she amended it before putting it in the box for the courier.

'Taking your own pap smear these days, are you?'

'What?' Julia asked, shocked at her carelessness. 'Yes, of course. That's the only way I know it's been done properly.'

Just on six she was finished. With the patients, at least. There was a pile of correspondence and a list of phone calls to deal with but she simply couldn't face them. Not until she knew how Gina Vella was. She passed through the waiting room which was still full, overfull in fact. There were three other obstetricians in the practice, but two were absent this evening. Leo Steiner was in Europe on annual leave while Sylvie Berger was at Royal Eastside finishing a public clinic. The waiting-room crowd belonged to Stephen Mitchell, the founder of the group, who saw his antenatal patients on Tuesdays. His practice was very large and he would be here until nine or even later. His patients, with their husbands and children, not only filled the waiting area but spilled onto the front porch, and even the path. With the searing heat outside, the constant comings and goings made control of the temperature difficult. A clutch of small children played a splashing game near the water cooler, a row of pregnant women

21

watched their ankle bones slowly disappear, and the air-conditioner shuddered in protest.

The secretaries at the reception desk were busy, not only with the patients waiting to be seen, but in making the final adjustments to tomorrow's appointments. At the same time Erica, the practice midwife, was trying to help Stephen catch up on hours lost earlier in the afternoon with a delivery.

Julia skirted them all and ducked into the tea room at the back of the large house which served as their surgery. It was a beautiful airy room, made even lovelier by its view of the ocean. She let her body slide into one of the large comfortable armchairs which faced down to the water. Not that she looked out the window, instead staring with dread at the phone. Her glance then flicked to the sandwich she'd never eaten; she'd missed both breakfast and lunch today. Should be good for her weight at least. Her eyes moved on to the kettle. Desperate for a wash of tea, she was defeated by the effort of making it.

Instead, she turned back to the phone. For hours she'd wanted to ring and find out how Gina was; but she hadn't wanted to as well. She lifted the receiver from its cradle. At the sound of the dial tone, all moisture immediately left her mouth and she put the phone down. She'd be up at the hospital shortly anyway. That would be soon enough.

However, if she wanted to catch Giles McGrath before he finished for the day, she would have to call now. She lifted the receiver again.

Dr McGrath was with a patient, said the nurse, so Julia would have to hang on for a few moments. She lay her neck against the smooth cool leather of the chair and closed her eyes. The tension mounted in her body, beginning in her leaden legs, skating past the sick pit in her stomach, and ending as a vice around her ribs. The room was suddenly airless.

'Hi, Julia,' said Giles, finally coming to the phone. He sounded pleased to hear from her and asked how she was. She lied and told him she was fine and made herself ask about his wife. Susie was flat-out at the gallery most days, he said. Things were going really well for her. Julia murmured her pleasure.

22

His tone told her nothing about her patient. She would have to ask. 'Giles, I was wondering how Gina Vella is?' Her heart stopped.

'She's doing fine, Julia. We were concerned right up until the last few hours, but I think she's out of danger now. She seems to be turning the corner and is passing good quantities of urine. Her creatinine is down and we're hoping to transfer her out of intensive care and across to high-dependency in the morning.'

Julia felt the vice on her chest spring open and her heart pump freely again. Thank God she hadn't rung earlier. 'That's great, Giles. Thank you so much for your help.'

'You were worried about her, weren't you?'

She gave a selfconscious laugh. 'You know me, Giles, I worry about them all.'

'I don't know why, Julia. Your patients always do well. The anaesthetist told me you did a terrific job with Gina. Saved her life.'

Julia was humble. 'It didn't feel like that this morning, Giles.'

'Well, that's what Singh said. Anyway, we must catch up soon. I hardly ever see you.'

'I don't see anyone these days, Giles. That's an obstetrician's lot, I'm afraid. I hardly even see myself,' she joked, relief giving her an immediate high.

'Susie's thinking of having a Christmas party at the gallery and we'd love you to come. I'll let you know the details.'

'That would be great, Giles. Thanks again. ' She kidded herself she would go. Anything seemed possible at that moment.

Riding her wave of happiness down the road to the beach, Julia eschewed her usual news station and flipped through the dial until she could strum her steering wheel to the sounds of the seventies. Her thoughts quickly arrived at her closest friend, Angie Russell, who had recently secured an appointment as one of the senior cardiac anaesthetists at Royal Eastside Children's Hospital. Over the years Angie had done less demanding operating sessions there, biding her time, waiting for this particular list to become available. From now on, she would spend a day a week giving anaesthetics for the cardiac surgeons. Today was the first.

Julia and Angie had been friends for twenty years, ever since their fateful first year as junior resident accident and emergency doctors in a medium-sized country hospital. Their supervisor's drinking problem had left them to handle medical crises well beyond their level of experience. Alone, neither would have coped, but together they managed quite well. Angie would look up the textbook and read out the appropriate drugs to Julia, who would weigh the patient and calculate the accurate dosage. Angie would then put in the drip while Julia loaded the flask with medication. Both would read the cardiograph of heart attack victims, or the peak flow of severe asthma sufferers, and then bury their heads back in the textbook for guidance on interpretation. If someone needed stitching, Julia always offered, while Angie drew up the anaesthetic, their future careers already palely defining themselves. When one was too tired to continue, the other would carry both pagers and answer all calls. And when things were briefly quiet, they would talk.

After that first exhilarating year, they'd spent most of the next decade in different hospitals, sometimes in different countries, while they completed specialist training. But they'd always kept in contact and, for the last ten years, had organised things so that they were back together again, this time at Eastside. Angie now gave the anaesthetics for Julia's operating lists twice a week, they lived only a few kilometres apart and they spoke almost every day.

With her mind finally free of anxiety about Gina Vella, Julia could now concentrate on her friend's thrilling new operating session, the one she'd coveted for so long. The senior surgeon was Professor James Macfarlane, head of the entire department of surgery, who had revolutionised the practice of children's heart operations in his thirty years at the hospital. Angie had spent time as a student and resident under his tutelage and had adored him, so inspired she'd even briefly entertained the thought of becoming a surgeon herself. Although she had relinquished the idea in favour of a career in anaesthetics, she'd never given up the dream that one day she would be a cardiac anaesthetist. His anaesthetist.

What a shock it had been when the professor collapsed from a heart attack while doing postoperative ward rounds just a week after Angie's appointment last month and before she'd had the privilege of working with him. He was currently convalescing with the intention of returning to work in the new year. In the meantime, Angie would be gassing for one of the other cardiac surgeons.

Julia rang her friend's mobile. 'Where are you, Angie? It's nearly seven. I rang your home and Geoff said he wasn't sure where you were.'

Angie's voice conveyed her dejection. She was still in intensive care at the Children's Hospital. She asked Julia how her husband had sounded, and confessed what had happened that morning.

The previous evening, Angie had spent hours at the hospital seeing the children to be operated on today. She'd spoken to their parents at length, read and reread their entire medical records, reviewed their medications, and pored over their X-rays. Determined to leave nothing to chance, Angie had planned to go back early this morning to check everything one final time. But she hadn't counted on having a problem with Geoff.

She usually left for work at six-thirty on Mondays, Wednesdays and Thursdays, while her husband, an associate professor of history, stayed behind to get their two boys off to school. On Tuesdays and Fridays, Angie reciprocated. The system had worked well for years, but was thrown out by this new cardiac list which fell on a Tuesday and started promptly at eight o'clock. As the anaesthetist, Angie needed to be at the hospital before seven to ensure everything was ready. She had discussed the change to their routine with Geoff months ago, before she'd even applied for the job, and again more recently when the appointment was confirmed. His first lecture was never before ten and, even on Angie's mornings with the boys, he seldom left before they did. The change in plans had not seemed to present a problem to him. Until just a few minutes before she was to depart this morning. When he'd said he was leaving immediately for an early university fundraising breakfast and she'd have to see to Ben and Richie.

'Can you believe it, Julia? My first list, I'm nervous already and running later than I intended, and he springs *this* on me.'

'What did you do?'

'What could I do? There wasn't the time to argue so I did a runner. While he was in his study, I nicked out the front door.' Angie's tone slipped from exasperation to sadness. 'I didn't even say goodbye to the boys.'

Julia made no comment about Geoff, but comforted Angie about her sons; they probably hadn't even noticed. 'Now tell me, how did the operating list go?'

Angie was surprisingly glum. 'The rest of the day was even worse.'

While Professor Macfarlane convalesced, his patient load had been assigned to Adrian de Bruin, a surgeon in his late thirties who had been appointed to the hospital the previous year. For months there had been muffled rumours about him; the nurses were circumspect, but it seemed he was impatient, arrogant and not as technically proficient as he needed to be in the more difficult cases. Especially with the babies. And he'd apparently become more unbearable since being given Macfarlane's list, as if the mantle of the great man had been bestowed as well.

Angie had entered the operating theatre a few minutes after eight, initially relieved to find she was there before the surgeon. The relief became perplexity when he had still not arrived by nine. The six-month-old patient, fasted for his procedure, was becoming increasingly upset, and the staff and Angie with him. When Dr de Bruin finally arrived at nine-thirty he offered no explanation for his delay. He did not greet the theatre nurses or introduce himself to his new anaesthetist, but simply proceeded to the scrub bay, from where he emerged five minutes later, gowned and gloved and ready to commence the operation. Except he wasn't ready. He complained loudly about the 'outdated' surgical instruments, was impatient with the 'clumsy' registrar, and was rude to the 'slow' scrub nurse, who should have been able to anticipate what he would need next. Even though he didn't seem to know himself. Angie counted herself lucky to be spared his wrath.

Needless to say, the operations had not gone smoothly. Angie was particularly worried about one of the babies, little Jacob Newton. Three hours after his operation, the twelve-month-old was not doing well. Angie thought he must be bleeding internally. His pulse was up, his blood pressure down, and his heartbeat was very irregular.

'What does de Bruin think?'

The answer was a loud sigh from Angie. That was part of the problem. No one could find him. The hospital switchboard had tried every contact number without success.

Julia turned off her radio. What an awful thing to happen to Angie on her first day, a day she'd looked forward to for so long. After her own struggle with Gina Vella, she understood with painful clarity what her friend was going through. If only there was something she could do to help. Angie appreciated her offer; she knew Julia would be there like a shot if she asked her. But they both recognised there was little an obstetrician could offer in this situation.

'What are you going to do?' asked Julia quietly.

Angie let out another sigh. She wasn't sure. But she'd better do it soon. 'Otherwise this baby's going to die.'

Chapter 3

The sun was now low in the evening sky. Even so, it was still thirty degrees on this third day of an unexpected heat wave in late October. Last night's southerly had been half-hearted, its relief temporary, and the entire city was once again listless and irritable. The only respite was on the coast where a light breeze at least took the edge off the humidity, and the streets were full of pilgrims seeking that relief.

Julia walked up the stairs of the crowded, humming restaurant and saw that Patrick was already there, seated at a table by the window, his back to the room, his gaze absorbed by the unparalleled metropolitan oasis of Bondi Beach.

The maitre d' greeted her warmly as she entered. 'Good evening, Julia. Your guest is here, but the beautiful Emma is not coming?'

'Not tonight I'm afraid, Elio. She's rehearsing. They've got their first gig this weekend.'

'But it is not possible to make good music on an empty stomach,' Elio protested, a hint of a smile in his dark eyes.

'I think Pizza Hut is taking care of it,' Julia confided, to which the waiter dutifully produced his most shocked expression.

Walking slowly towards the table, she registered a quickening of her pulse. Her heart had been drawing attention to itself all day, racing, then stopping, then tearing away again, but at least this time it was a pleasant sensation. Her eyes traced Patrick's dark blond hair to where it brushed his collar and from there she took in his muscled arms and shoulders, outlined perfectly by his well-fitting shirt. Her pulse quickened further.

Patrick Whitfield was an architect, a partner in a small firm which specialised in sympathetic renovations of older houses. Julia had met him five years before when he'd designed the alterations on the Bondi cottage she'd bought after her divorce. After the woeful tales her friends had told, she was pleasantly surprised at how well her own renovations had gone, and readily acknowledged that it was almost entirely due to Patrick.

From the beginning, Julia had found him enormously attractive. She could have watched for hours as his eager face looked from drawing to structure, mesmerised by the transformation of his ideas into reality. Patrick had liked her as well, welcoming the way her quick mind took in what he described, gratified that she appreciated what he was trying to create, and stimulated by the thoughtful but uncritical suggestions she made about his design. They had become quite friendly at the time. Indeed, he and his wife, Genevieve, had been among the guests at the first dinner party Julia held once the house was finished.

Then, eighteen months ago, Genevieve and their eleven-year-old daughter, Miranda, had been killed in a car accident. Julia had been at a conference in Singapore at the time and didn't learn of the tragedy until weeks after the funeral. She was distraught for Patrick and sent a note when she heard. She also thought to call him, but on each occasion had hung up the phone before dialling, unable to find the right words. Likewise, she had driven past his house several times, but hadn't gone in. There were always visitors' cars in the drive and she'd felt too bashful to intrude. In fact, she did not see him for nearly a year and, when she did, she walked right past him, so altered had he become. Gaunt and ashen, his hair was longer than usual and his previously clean-shaven face was adorned with an unkempt beard, considerably greyer than his sandy hair. He had spoken her name as they passed, noticed her shock at his appearance, challenged her neglect of him, and invited her over for a drink. That had been six months ago, and they were now in the habit of dinner once a week.

Patrick turned as she reached the table. 'Hi,' he smiled, standing. 'You look lovely tonight.' He put his hand on her arm and kissed her cheek and she felt herself both flush at his praise and shiver at his touch.

'Thanks,' she said, regaining control of her temperature. She was still wearing the same clothes she'd worked in all day, but the joy of knowing Gina Vella was going to be all right fairly glowed from her being.

'I'm sorry I'm late. I had to go back to the hospital.'

'You've got someone in labour?' he asked, frowning. She'd had to rush off before.

'No, the coast's clear at the moment,' she assured him, hoping it was. Surely nothing more could happen today?

'Good.' He shot her a grin. 'It must be too hot to have a baby at the moment anyway.'

Taking her seat and smiling at his cheekiness, Julia silently acknowledged that these evenings with Patrick had become the high point of her week. She looked forward to them, and recalled them, with an animation which was starting to concern her; he was on her mind far more than she'd care to admit.

His mind, appropriately, was still on Genevieve and Miranda; almost every topic quickly bore reference to one or both of them and he was often in tears. Julia knew what such grief was like and understood that this state of intense focused sadness would lessen in time, but would never fully pass. For now, he must be encouraged to talk; she was more than willing to listen. At the same time, she was careful not to be too available. Not because she feared his attachment and dependence. Quite the opposite. It was awareness of her own vulnerability that held her back.

Her divorce and the time which followed had damaged her

badly. Her scars were still crimson and tender and she had no desire to have them reopened.

But it was more than that.

Patrick was almost conventionally good-looking with golden skin and aquamarine eyes, a youthful intelligent face, and an intellect as robust as his body. He was engaging and appealing and could have his choice of women, and Julia knew that. She'd avoided love for many years, and would never have deliberately sought a relationship with someone like him. But her feelings for him were happening by accident, creeping up on her. And she felt very exposed.

As they ate, Patrick bubbled with excitement about Ryan's school camp. They were leaving in the morning and would be gone for five days. He was looking forward to some time out of the city in the company of his son.

'If it's too hot to have a baby, surely it'll be murder going camping?' teased Julia.

'We've got a well-ventilated tent,' he assured her.

'Air-conditioned?'

'Not exactly,' he conceded with a deep laugh. 'But at least the campsite's on the river.'

Julia watched him as he spoke, his boyish confidence charming her as always. He'd never actually been camping before, but that was no impediment to someone like Patrick. And it was lovely that he had something new to share with his son.

They finished their meal and left early. Patrick had to collect Ryan and his friend at nine and finish their packing, while Julia was heading back to the surgery for an hour or so. Relieved and well-fed, she felt she could probably face her paperwork now. Patrick walked her to her car. The pavement was a jostle of sweaty humanity and he took her arm protectively. Every hair on her body screamed to attention. She tottered on her low shoes and he firmed his grip. Very carefully, she took a slow, controlled breath. But then found she couldn't expel it.

They arrived at the car and he released her arm, his manner hesitant. Julia sensed he wanted to say something and she had

31

to remind herself to breathe again. Then she saw him decide against it. Instead he leaned forward, kissed her softly on the cheek and bid her goodnight.

Julia always thought of Waratah House as a grand old dame who, though still elegant, had unfortunately lost her crinoline and petticoats. The stately mansion had been built early in the twentieth century, originally set in the midst of extensive grounds of waratahs. Over the years the land had been progressively sold off. While still beautifully maintained, the house now sat in a crowded untidy jumble of lesser dwellings, wearing a resigned air of truncated majesty.

It had been Julia's surgery for five years. She loved the large light-filled rooms and the vista of the ocean, while Stephen Mitchell, with whom she'd bought the house, thought its understated superiority reflected his own and that its location would yield a handsome capital gain.

The front porch, tiled in the original green, red and white, led to a magnificent timber doorway, flanked on both sides by leadlight windows depicting waratahs. A wide and high central hall gave off two large rooms on each side, one for each of the four doctors in the practice. Beyond these, the hall spread into a broad comfortable space which served as the patient waiting area, off which was the practice midwife's room. At the distant end of the waiting area was the reception desk, and beyond that the private staff areas at the rear of the house.

Tingling from her evening with Patrick, Julia strolled contentedly back into the surgery and found Stephen, Erica the midwife, and Justine the junior secretary, all still hard at work. As Julia came to the desk, Justine was making an appointment for a departing patient, a heavily pregnant woman a day overdue with twins, still smiling bravely despite her discomfort.

'Dr Mitchell said to come back on Monday,' said the woman, handing over her card.

Justine hesitated, her eyes hovering between the appointment book and the patient's enormous abdomen, probably the largest she had seen in her six months in the job. 'Do you think you'll last till then?'

The patient was philosophical. 'Who knows? But if we assume that I won't need an appointment, then I probably will, so hopefully, if you give me one, I won't need it.'

'Seems logical,' said the young secretary doubtfully as Julia laughed.

Collecting her in-tray from the shelf behind the reception desk, Julia realised that her weariness could not be ignored for much longer; the relief about Gina Vella, and the buzz from Patrick's touch, would see her through for about an hour. Snatches of the new Taxiride hit that Emma had favoured all week played in her mind, and she hummed happily as she walked through the near-empty waiting room, past Stephen's closed door, and into her office.

Sitting down, she first dialled Angie, whose crisis had been at the back of her mind all evening. Angie's phone diverted to her message bank and not her home; she must be in the operating theatre, thought Julia grimly, offering an agnostic prayer for the little boy. And for her friend. Once again she wished there was something practical she could do to help. She left some words of encouragement.

She forced her attention to the bulging tray on her desk. She knew that some of her colleagues hated this part of the job, but she'd always quite enjoyed its leisurely pace and salve to curiosity. Every test and referral she ordered had a purpose and she was always impatient to learn the outcome.

The tray overflowed, results and reports and correspondence poking out at all angles. She dealt with them as they came and gave a small whoop of delight when she saw that Ayse Ozdemir's amniocentesis and ultrasound results were normal. She sent up another agnostic prayer, this time of thanks. Ayse's last pregnancy had been terminated because the foetus had multiple abnormalities. Devastated, she'd declared she wasn't going to try again and it had taken months of Julia's patient reassurance to change her mind. She phoned the good news through immediately.

Not so happy was the report from Wendy Dunstan's psychiatrist. Her postnatal depression had taken a psychotic turn and she'd been hospitalised. Julia phoned Matt, Wendy's husband. He was on extended leave from work to care for the baby and was managing reasonably well, although he was worried sick about his wife and dismayed at the unexpected dark underbelly of childbirth.

With a start, Julia noticed that the old house was completely still. She'd been at her desk for nearly two hours and everyone else had gone. Too late now to make phone calls, she set aside a handful of messages for tomorrow. There were only a few papers left. Her weariness threatened to overtake her and she was tempted to call it a day. But it was not in her nature to leave things unfinished so close to the end.

A sudden shard of panic speared her heart as she opened the final bulky envelope and saw the solicitor's documents: *Brendan Peter Edwards and Tracey Louise Edwards v Dr Julia Kent.*

Her chest tightened. Dizziness and nausea built. She tried to steady herself but couldn't. Standing up, she was uncertain what to do; then suddenly she knew. Stumbling, she jerked open the door and reeled down the corridor. And emptied the contents of her stomach into the toilet.

It all came flooding back. The horror of her ex-husband, Tony's, trial before the Medical Tribunal. The torment. The humiliation. The relentless publicity. It had destroyed their marriage and changed their lives forever.

'Not again,' Julia cried out to herself. 'Not again.'

Chapter 4

Julia Kent had fallen in love with Tony Cabrini when both were registrars at the Wentworth Hospital in outer-western Sydney in the mid-eighties. She was twenty-five and in the first year of her training to be a specialist obstetrician, while he was thirty and in the last year of his training to become a psychiatrist. They had actually met the previous year at a party, where they'd spoken briefly before being reclaimed by their respective partners. It was long enough for Julia. When they started working together, it took her just a week to know that she wanted Tony Cabrini. Forever.

He was different from the men she usually liked, more measured and quieter, with beautiful Mediterranean skin and unruly black hair. He was not overtly handsome but there was something special about him. It was partly his broad mouth of nearly perfect teeth, but mostly it was his large, heavy-lidded, black eyes, with their thick straight lashes that touched his cheeks when they closed.

Tony did not talk much, a precious trait in a psychiatrist, but when he chose to speak, what he said was worthwhile. Julia found him intelligent and insightful, kind-hearted and amusing. Now happily unattached, she soon adored everything about him.

Things were a little more complicated for Tony. He had just come out of a long-term relationship with Sybilla Ramsey, a fellow psychiatric registrar. They had come down together from Brisbane the previous year to further their training but, a few months ago, Sybilla had met someone new and ended the relationship. Moving out of the flat they shared, and living in hospital accommodation, Tony was bruised and wary and thinking of returning to Queensland, to his large Italian family. His father was dead, but his mother, four brothers and two sisters all lived in Brisbane, and he missed them.

When Julia learned that his relationship with Sybilla was over, she tried to orchestrate encounters with him in the cafeteria or the library or at clinical meetings. But while he was gracious and friendly, he did not seem interested. She was finally galvanised into action when she overheard a group of young nurses rating the new male doctors on their marriageability.

'Dr Grenville is very cute,' said one.

'But Dr Nguyen has a better body,' countered another.

'Give me Dr Cabrini any day,' said the prettiest in the group. 'He's so nice to his patients, and when he looks at me with those eyes, I just want to melt into the floor. I've given myself a month to get him.' She smiled confidently.

A few days later, Julia left a ticket to the Sydney Theatre Company production of *Cyrano de Bergerac* in Tony's pigeonhole. She had been going to the play with Angie who now had to work on Saturday.

Arriving early at the theatre, Julia found Tony already in his seat. She was surprised. If it had been her, she would have lingered in the wings to identify her secret benefactor, and then decided whether to stay. Her nervousness increased at his brave action and she thought to leave. Finally she approached. She hoped he would turn around and greet her, but he was engrossed in his program. She sat beside him. He still didn't move.

'Couldn't he come?' he asked eventually.

'Who?'

'Dr Russell.' He'd checked with the box office about the owner of the ticket.

'Dr Russell's a she.'

'Oh,' he smiled. He already knew.

Within weeks they were lovers. Each passing day found Julia liking him even more, and he seemed just as taken with her. She was in raptures, her happiness overwhelming, despite the rigours of her obstetric training program which kept her from him so much.

The working day was eight to six. As well, obstetric registrars did overtime all night twice a week, and all weekend at least once a month. On top of this they provided regular clinical presentations which took days to prepare, undertook two massive original research projects, and studied for examinations which took place in the fourth year. Fifty percent failed the examination on the first attempt. Fail twice and you were out of a job.

Julia was only months into both the first year of specialist training and the relationship with Tony when, after some momentary nausea, she realised she had missed her period. She was stunned. The days and nights which ran into each other, week after week, had thrown out her cycle, and caused her to miscalculate. For the first few days, she was in denial. Then, as the nausea increased, she moved into a state of indecision. She couldn't even tell Tony.

Their relationship was new and, while she thought he cared about her, they were just feeling their way. He might still be returning to Brisbane at the end of the year. And her obstetric training program was utterly incompatible with having a baby. The choice should have been easy.

Even so, she found herself considering the option of continuing with her pregnancy. Daily surrounded by tiny newborns, soft and dependent, with their small, jerky movements and their endearing facial expressions, she was torn.

'I was wondering when you were going to tell me,' Tony said when she finally summoned up the courage to speak to him about it.

'You knew?'

'Julia, you're hardly eating, you're always exhausted, and you're cranky as hell.'

'And I'm a first year obstetric registrar, completely run off my feet. That could explain those symptoms.'

'Well, there was one other thing.'

'What?'

'Your breasts have doubled in size.'

Julia smiled in spite of herself. 'I should have known you'd notice that.'

He put his arm around her. 'Darling, I notice everything about you.'

Which was true. It was one of the many things she loved about him. She asked what he thought they should do. He said it was her call. Whatever she decided, he would support her.

'Don't you have an opinion?' she asked desperately.

'Of course I do. In fact I have two. The first is what I think we should do. And the second is that it is the woman's opinion which really matters in a situation like this.'

'Do you think that our opinions might coincide?'

'It would probably be better for us if they did.' But he would say no more.

There followed another week in which she still could not make up her mind. She was not helped by Tony's persistent refusal to confide what the decision would be if it were his to make. She tried to second-guess him.

He did not seem overly interested in other people's children, but was from a large family and his nieces and nephews rang often and seemed to love him. He did not profess any particular religious beliefs, but had been brought up a Catholic. He had nearly finished his psychiatric training and was now thirty, but it wouldn't be his career that would be affected. Julia gave up. She couldn't decide for him, and she couldn't decide for herself.

In the end, Harold Bryant, the head of obstetrics at the Wentworth Hospital, decided for them both. A popular, caring professor who took a great interest in the careers of his trainees, he summoned Julia to a meeting in his office. There was something he wanted to discuss with her. First, he asked how she was finding life as a new registrar.

She said that it was good. Even with someone as approachable as Professor Bryant, it probably wasn't wise to tell the truth.

'It's hard, isn't it?' he asked, knowing it was. Which was why he wanted to talk to her. He wanted to introduce part-time training in order to increase the number of women doctors choosing to specialise in obstetrics. He felt it was a natural field for women. But while half the medical graduates were female, only a handful became obstetricians, most preferring the shorter and more flexible hours of general practice. A major reason was that specialist training occurred in the late twenties and early thirties, the key reproductive years. He outlined his plan. 'Do you think that there would be support for part-time training, Julia?'

She grinned. 'It would be just like working full-time in any other job.'

'Well, it would, I suppose.' He was mildly crestfallen. 'But it would at least be better than what we have to offer now, wouldn't it?'

Julia realised that she had upset him. She also began to see what his plan might mean for her.

Tony was over the moon at her decision to go ahead with the pregnancy; he could think of nothing nicer than having a child with her. They married the following month and their beautiful baby girl was born in February. For the next few years, Julia worked part-time and bloomed with the joy of her life. She told anyone who would listen that she couldn't believe her luck – a wonderful husband, a beautiful daughter, *and* the career she'd always wanted.

After she passed her exam in the fourth year, they went to London for two years, Julia to do further training while Tony secured a job as a hospital psychiatrist. Julia still kept in touch with Angie, who'd finally married the charming and gregarious Geoff Summers she'd gone out with for most of her time at university. They'd broken up by the time Julia met Angie because

Angie had discovered he was sleeping with one of her friends. He'd begged her to reconsider; the other woman had been a mistake, a fling, but Angie, wounded and proud, had withdrawn from him completely. She'd never really gotten over him, however, despite a drove of men who sought her company and, when she ran into him a few years later, had allowed the relationship to rekindle before there was time to remember how badly he'd hurt her before.

It was Angie, now at Royal Eastside, who suggested that Julia apply to the hospital for her final year of training after London. The senior registrar year was enormously important, leading as it did to the consultant opportunities for the rest of a specialist's career. Eastside was already attractive to Julia. Stephen Mitchell, one of her colleagues from the Wentworth Hospital days, had a private practice in the area and had asked her to join him once she completed her training.

On their return, Julia and Tony bought a small house in the eastern Sydney suburb of Coogee, less than a kilometre from the beach. It was close to Royal Eastside and Tony's new practice in Bondi Junction, and only a few minutes from Angie. There was also a school for their lively six-year-old daughter just around the corner.

'How long are we going to stay here, Daddy?' asked Emma the day they moved in. She had been from western Sydney to London and now to beachside Coogee, and was at the age when losing friends mattered.

Tony knew what she meant. He told her that they were finished with moving around. They were going to stay in Coogee for a long while. 'Maybe even forever,' he laughed, picking her up and swinging her around.

'Can I have a baby brother now?' It was something Emma asked often.

Tony glanced at Julia, who looked away. 'We hope so, darling.'

Chapter 5

'**M**um, Mum, wake up.' Emma touched Julia lightly, catapulting her into consciousness.

For a few seconds, disorientation held her. She tried to sit up but the bedclothes were tangled; she'd been fighting them. Her hair was matted with sweat, her eyes sticky and swollen. 'What's up?' she croaked, groggy and alarmed. It was still dark.

'Nothing, Mum, nothing,' Emma reassured her. 'You were having a nightmare, shouting out.'

'Was I? Oh, sorry, Em. Sorry.' Julia blinked her gritty eyes and glanced at the clock. It was nearly five. She sighed and fell back onto the pillows. 'Go back to bed. Sorry for waking you, darling.'

Emma sat on the edge of the bed and grimaced. 'Actually, Mum, I was already awake, working on the chorus.' Despite her own confusion, Julia read her daughter's disappointment; the new song she'd been writing for months wasn't going to be ready by Saturday.

'I thought you had it finished.'

'I did. And then I scrapped the last four lines of the chorus – they were terrible. Anyway, would you like a cup of tea?'

'Thanks, tea would be lovely.'

As she untangled her sheets and plumped up her pillows, Julia couldn't remember what the dream was about. Even the residual uneasy feeling which can persist for hours after a nightmare was receding quickly. For a few moments she was restful, musing on nothing in particular, vaguely contemplating her day.

Then suddenly it hit her. Brendan Edwards. That was her nightmare.

Julia pulled into one of the parking spots reserved for the staff at the back of the surgery; she turned off the ignition, but otherwise did not move. Dread filled her being. She couldn't face her office, simply couldn't, not with the accusatory solicitor's documents, the Statement of Claim, abandoned on her desk. Just the memory of them made her shudder.

Today should have been a *good* day, she thought resentfully. Especially after the misery of yesterday. Gina Vella and her baby were both doing better than expected. Gina would be taken to see her fourth son as soon as she was able to sit in a wheelchair, but in the meantime had been cheered by her husband's reports and some less alarming photos. She'd been transferred to high-dependency, a step down from intensive care, and had even been bright enough to quip to Julia this morning that it sounded like a place for drug addicts.

Reluctantly, Julia released her seat belt and leant down to pick up her handbag. There was a tap on the car window. Her colleague, Stephen Mitchell, was grinning at her. She opened the door.

'Not thinking of attaching a hose to the exhaust, were you?'

'What?' she asked, slow to catch on.

'You pulled in as I was walking up to the office ten minutes ago. And you're still here. I wondered if you were going to end it all.'

'Not today,' she replied quickly, amazed at his uncharacteristic intuition. Stephen's focus was usually on himself. 'Not yet anyway.'

A man at the shorter end of medium height, Stephen Mitchell had dark red hair, still vibrant in colour but thinning on top. His pale, lightly freckled face held a pair of captivating blue eyes which disappeared into tiny slits when he laughed, which he did often. As a younger man, he had developed a fine, well-muscled physique, but at forty-four, and after a couple of decades of ninety-hour weeks, he'd been stripped of it and left instead with a sizeable paunch.

He was easily the busiest, most popular obstetrician in the eastern suburbs. He was also the most expensive, which in some quarters only served to make him more desirable. Julia had joined his practice ten years ago. With consultant appointments at the same hospitals, it made sense for them to share expenses. It also suited Julia, and their subsequent partners, to share the after-hour cover for deliveries and emergencies, although this did not work so well for Stephen. He was defeated by his competitive personality and by the nature of the exclusive private practice he was trying to establish. Unfortunately, the money had become more important to him than the medicine.

Right from the beginning he charged more for his private work than any other obstetrician in the area. It was a deliberate decision to target what he saw as the better end of the market. But it created a problem for his after-hour cover plans. If you charged a lot more because you and your patients thought you were the best, it followed that if you were not actually there for the delivery, the patient might be left thinking that she had paid for the best but got something else.

So it happened that, while Julia and the other partners covered each other on weekends, Stephen usually remained available for his patients. He even holidayed in Sydney, albeit at glorious Whale Beach, so that he could be there when his patients needed him.

Julia gingerly accompanied her cheerful colleague through the back door of the surgery. The phones were already ringing and they could hear the calm tones of the secretaries as they

43

juggled the patients milling at the reception desk with the invisible, but no less important, ones on the line. Julia and Stephen were in the office on a Wednesday morning, while Sylvie was at the hospital. If Leo had been back from leave, he would have been operating at the private hospital, St Agatha's.

There were seven support staff in the four-doctor practice, all women, who worked an assortment of flexible hours. The three secretaries, Marcia, Cynthia and Justine, mostly dealt with appointments and phone calls. There were also two typists for the hundreds of letters generated each week, as well as Patricia the practice manager, and Erica the midwife.

Of these, it was Marcia, an efficient motherly woman in her late fifties, who principally took care of Julia's practice. She had in fact worked exclusively for Julia until the number of doctors expanded, at which point such exclusivity became impractical. Nevertheless, she still treated Julia as her first consideration. For her part, Julia admitted that without her wonderful secretary, she wouldn't get through the first hour of the week.

Stephen immediately strode to the reception area to learn of any changes to his day, but Julia found she couldn't face them, not yet anyway. Instead, she slipped into the empty tea room. Once there, however, she had nothing to occupy herself. She couldn't stomach a drink, didn't care about the newspaper, and found the glare of the ocean's shimmer too much for her bloodshot eyes. Grudgingly, she forced herself out to reception and beyond, towards her office. Swallowing hard, she peered anxiously through the door. It was still there. Stumbling, she fell into her chair, mesmerised by the document, as nausea threatened to overcome her again. For a long time, she just sat staring. Eventually she grabbed the papers and shoved them into the bottom drawer of her desk.

The phone rang. It was Marcia, wondering if Julia would like her to cancel a few of the morning's patients. She could tell them an emergency had come up. There were several vacancies next week that could be used. Agreeing, Julia choked back her grateful tears. It had taken her secretary less than five minutes to register that something was wrong. Not that she would ever ask. But Julia would tell her. She always did.

The first patient of the morning was Asuncion, a Filipina of nearly sixty who spoke limited English, and who had recently come to live with her daughter in Sydney. Her nine children had been born at home, attended by her sisters and the village midwife. Her periods had finished ten years before but recently she had started to bleed again. She'd tried to conceal the problem but her daughter Maria, wondering why her mother had taken to washing her own underwear, had prised the story from her.

Asuncion had never had a pap smear or a pelvic examination. Her husband had died five years ago and she had not been sexually active since. Nevertheless she submitted to the examination without complaint.

Julia was not surprised at what she found; the odour was distinctive. An ulcerative, bloody, cancerous mass had replaced the cervix and was growing down the vagina. It was at least Stage 3B and inoperable. But it might be responsive to radiotherapy. 'Asuncion,' she said slowly, looking up from the speculum to the dignified but frightened face of her patient. 'There seems to be something on your cervix. I will need to take a little piece of tissue to send for testing.'

Julia waited while Maria explained to her mother what the older woman already knew. 'I don't think it will hurt much,' Julia said confidently. Indeed the cervix was so friable that a large rotten chunk painlessly fell off as the biopsy forceps grazed it. Julia transferred the lump of cancerous tissue to the specimen jar, where it sank in the formalin.

'I would now like to have a feel inside the vagina,' she said, removing the speculum, at which point a large clot of blood fell out onto the waterproof sheet between Asuncion's legs. Surprised at its size, Julia looked up and realised for the first time how pale her patient was. Her darker complexion had disguised the pallor, but the signs of anaemia were obvious. The poor woman must have been passing clots like this for months.

After Maria had explained to her mother what was to happen next, Julia gently reached inside the vagina with the gloved index and middle finger of her right hand, then placed her left hand on the lower abdomen and pressed the two towards each other. The usually soft and mobile uterus was frozen in place, held hard and fixed by the tumour. The pelvis was full of it.

With Asuncion dressed, the three of them sat at the desk. Sadly, Julia had nothing surgical to offer. This tumour required radiotherapy and even then, Asuncion would probably die. But while she must tell her patient the truth, it was always necessary to maintain hope.

She explained what she had found and the treatments available. She recommended radiation treatment rather than surgery.

'Do you understand what radiation treatment is?'

Maria did. Her neighbour had had radiation for breast cancer.

Julia explained that it usually occurred in daily treatments, five days a week, for six weeks.

Maria nodded, then asked, 'Why can't the cancer just be removed?'

This was the hard part. Julia explained that the cancer had spread beyond the cervix and into the lymph glands. It wasn't possible to remove it all with surgery. She looked kindly at the distressed daughter. 'Radiotherapy gives Asuncion the best chance of beating this tumour.'

'But, Doctor, couldn't you remove as much as you can and then do radiotherapy?'

'That's a good suggestion, Maria, and in the past it's exactly what we did. But now we know that the complications of radiotherapy are a lot worse if there has been surgery as well, while the survival prospects are no better than with radiotherapy alone.'

Just then the phone rang. Julia took the call while Maria related the details to her mother. As she hung up the phone, the younger woman turned to Julia. 'Mum says that she would prefer to have the cancer completely removed and skip the radiotherapy.'

Julia patiently explained again the reasons for her recommendation, but still the older woman shook her head.

'What if we pay?' asked Maria.

Julia was momentarily shocked. Her patient thought she was being offered second-class treatment because she had no hospital insurance. 'Believe me, Maria, six weeks of radiotherapy is

46

vastly more expensive than an operation in this situation. What I'm suggesting for your mother is the best – and the most expensive – option.'

Disturbed by memories of Brendan Edwards, and heavy with sadness about Asuncion, Julia struggled through her morning. As she prepared to leave for her hospital clinic, she glanced at the desk drawer and trembled once more. She would leave the documents there, out of sight. For now at least. Gathering her things, she took a moment to read Leo's latest postcard, this time from Prague, which Marcia had brought in a few moments before.

Leo Steiner was in his sixties and had been in private practice as an obstetrician in the eastern suburbs for over thirty years. He was highly respected for his wisdom and experience. Five years ago, when Stephen and Julia moved their surgery to Waratah House and were looking for a third partner, Leo had been the perfect choice. Keen to keep working, he no longer wanted the worries of running his own business.

Julia's reasons for wanting Leo were not only professional. He and his wife Sandra were dear friends who had showered exceptional kindness on her during Tony's trial, publicly taking her side when others turned away in embarrassment. They'd invited her for meals and, while her own family was falling apart, they'd included her in theirs. Leo had also covered much of her work, even though he was not yet her associate and was busy himself. His unselfishness had enabled her to take leave at that time without overburdening Stephen too much.

Having the older obstetrician join their practice had worked well for the three of them. Stephen was pleased to divide the practice costs by one more, while Julia was glad to have another doctor to share the weekend load. Especially someone as wonderful as Leo.

He and Sandra were at the end of four weeks' well-earned leave; he was due back on Monday. It was the longest break Leo had had for years and, if the outrageous postcards he sent to the surgery were any guide, he was enjoying himself enormously. Julia giggled as she looked at the latest one. She had missed his agreeable presence over the past month; it would be good to have him back.

Chapter 6

Julia waited at the lift well on the ground floor of Royal East-side Hospital. Her clinic was only on the first floor, but she couldn't be bothered with the stairs. Not today. She was absorbed in a grubby mark on her left shoe which she knew she should bend down and wipe away, when a familiar voice greeted her. She stared at Angie in surprise. 'What are you doing here? It's still Wednesday, isn't it?' Wednesday was Angie's afternoon off.

Angie had been sabotaged. She should have known that booking a hair appointment was asking for trouble, but she'd gone ahead and done it anyway. The gods refused to let her get away with it and so here she was. The labour ward anaesthetist had gone home sick and Angie was now on her way to give the anaesthetic for an emergency caesarean.

Julia commiserated. 'Your hair looks fine, anyway.'

Angie laughed. 'There's no need to humour me, Julia. I know the grey is running amok.'

Julia *was* humouring her but, in fact, Angie's hair looked not much worse than it usually did; she wore it in an unflattering, shoulder-length style, the grey almost a highlight. It was a pity since she had a truly lovely face, with the large eyes, prominent cheekbones and beautiful olive skin of her European forebears. Not that Angie cared. She was the least vain person Julia knew; she probably didn't even own a mirror.

Angie was now forlorn. 'It wasn't just the hair. I needed someone to pamper me for a few hours.'

Julia guessed her meaning. 'That baby you were worried about last night?'

Anguish suffused Angie's face. 'He died, Julia. I wasted valuable time trying to find Adrian de Bruin and I never did. Eventually I had to call in Simon Littlewood, the other cardiac surgeon. But it was too late. It was a terrible end to an awful day.' Angie dismally began to fill Julia in on the details but just then the lift arrived and they were no longer alone. 'I'll tell you the rest tomorrow in theatre,' she whispered.

Walking towards the outpatients department, Julia's mind was full of little Jacob Newton. She could readily picture his distraught parents, their disbelief the only thing shielding them from the full assault of grief. And then there was poor Angie, such a careful doctor, always thinking ahead, constantly double-checking, preparing for any eventuality. It must have nearly killed her to stand by and watch little Jacob Newton bleed to death.

Julia's thoughts were curtailed by the sudden decibel increase that signalled her arrival at her antenatal clinic. Such clinics were held every morning and afternoon at Royal Eastside for patients without insurance to cover a private obstetrician, but Julia's had a special feature. It was devoted to pregnant women who were drug or alcohol dependent.

There were a large number of them, several hundred each year, enough to warrant their own clinic. Whilst a few were alcoholic, the vast majority were heroin addicts in varying stages of recovery and relapse. Many were multi-drug users, mixing heroin, cocaine, sedatives, speed, dope and booze, whatever they could get their hands on really. It made their pregnancies unpredictable and hazardous.

Julia quite enjoyed the clinic. While a few of the patients were unreliable and required hours of telephone follow-up, it did seem that the medical care and social work support made a difference to the lives of at least some of the women. It was often the only time their health was checked, their pap smear collected, their concerns listened to.

The midwife showed Cindy Smithers into Julia's consultation room. This was her fourth baby and, although well into the last months of pregnancy, she was only now booking in. This did not surprise Julia, who knew Cindy and had last seen her the previous year at the gynaecology clinic in the women's prison. Cindy spent a lot of time in prison for crimes related to her drug habit. Her other three children, none of whose fathers were known, were in foster care and rarely saw their mother. Cindy kept forgetting where they were.

Deep down Julia thought they were probably wasting their time seeing her. She knew that Cindy wouldn't cut down her smoking or other drug usage, wouldn't attend for any of the tests that they ordered, and probably wouldn't even come for another visit, simply turning up when she was in labour. And maybe not even turning up here. She lived such an itinerant life, she could turn up at any hospital in the state. If she wasn't back in prison by the time the baby arrived.

Julia greeted her. 'Good afternoon, Cindy.'

'Hi, Dr Kent,' replied her patient cheerfully, her pinpoint pupils suggesting that it was indeed a good one. It was a disadvantage of having so many junkies in one place at one time – someone was always dealing.

'I see you're pregnant again.'

'Looks like it, eh?' Cindy giggled.

'Do you have any idea when you got pregnant?'

'I've thought about it a bit, Dr Kent, and I reckon it's got to be some time between February and June.'

'Well, that narrows it down. Would you like me to have a look at the baby for you?'

It was always hard to be sure of the exact gestation of a patient who was seen for the first time in late pregnancy. A big

51

twenty-eight weeker felt much the same as a small thirty-two weeker but, given the small size of Cindy's previous babies, Julia estimated that she was probably close to thirty-four weeks. 'Will you be coming every week for a visit from now?'

'I reckon I might, Dr Kent. I want to get back on the methadone program.'

'Great,' said Julia, more positively than she felt.

'Yeah. I know I made a mistake last time, but I was wondering if you could get me back on.'

While it was easier to qualify for inclusion on the methadone program in pregnancy, Cindy had been expelled twice before in earlier pregnancies, making it unlikely she would be considered again. The first time was when consecutive urine samples showed continued heroin use despite a high dose of methadone, and the next was when she was caught trading her free methadone for speed while waiting for her antenatal visit.

'I think we should see first how committed you are to attending for the rest of your pregnancy. If you can manage that, we might see about another go on the program.'

'I'll do my best.'

'That'll have to do,' replied Julia, familiar with Cindy's best.

Back in the office at six, Julia knew she wouldn't be able to put it off much longer. She would have to confront the wretched Statement of Claim. But, procrastination still dominant, she decided to get a cup of tea first. Sylvie Berger, the fourth doctor in the practice, was in her office as Julia walked past, engrossed in a magazine article about Brad and Jennifer and feasting on a large slice of Black Forest cake.

Sylvie had joined their group two years before, at the age of thirty-four. Originally from Melbourne, she'd spent two years in Scotland before coming to Eastside as a senior registrar. She'd then returned to Melbourne with a view to finding a consultant's appointment. But, she'd told Julia, it had taken her less than a month to remember why she'd spent the previous three years away. Her mother.

Sylvie was the second child of Gerda and Otto Berger, who had come to Melbourne from Germany in the fifties, looking for a better life. Her parents' relationship had always been difficult, she said, mainly because of her mother's perennial disappointment. Disappointment at her husband's enduring roughness which her genteel influence had failed to correct. Disappointment at the small, dark house in outer Melbourne which was all he could afford. Disappointment in her adopted country, and its lack of music and culture, especially in comparison to her much-referred-to dazzling childhood in Europe.

And finally, disappointment in her children.

Sylvie thought that her mother had probably never wanted children, but they were still, at that time, a mostly unavoidable part of the package of marriage. As a result, Friedrich and Sylvie were born, two years apart. Both looked like their father, tall, heavy-set, coarse-featured and somewhat awkward in demeanour. And, as well as being physically graceless, neither was musical. It was a double disappointment for Gerda.

Sylvie turned out to be particularly bright. So bright she probably could have won a full academic scholarship to any one of a number of exclusive private schools, had her parents known such things existed. As it was, a particularly attentive teacher made sure she was accepted at an academically selective public high school. She had gone on to complete her high school, university and specialist training with distinction, but her mother remained disappointed.

'I just couldn't live with it any longer,' she'd explained to Julia after accepting the offer to join the practice.

With new awareness of her younger colleague's fundamental insecurity, Julia had made sure she conveyed to Sylvie her delight that she could join them, telling her how impressed she'd been with her as senior registrar. She was the sort of careful, thorough obstetrician Julia felt confident entrusting her patients to. And she knew Stephen and Leo felt the same.

In actual fact, neither of her male colleagues had felt any great need for a fourth member of the practice. But they were men. Julia had first mildly suggested, and then actively pushed for a

53

fourth partner, another woman, twelve months before Sylvie joined them. The nature of medical practice was changing and, with many more female doctors in general practice, patients expected to be able to see a female obstetrician as well. The demand had increased dramatically, but there remained only a handful in Sydney. Despite the innovations of people like Professor Bryant, it was still the case that few women doctors were attracted to the hours, the responsibility and, more recently, the escalating litigation associated with obstetric practice. Only twenty percent of obstetricians were women and, after a few years in practice, many stopped obstetrics and concentrated on gynaecology. This allowed them to drop from eighty to fifty hours a week, to plan their lives with greater predictability, and to stay in bed at night. Although they missed the excitement and joy of obstetrics, not one missed the lifestyle.

Julia herself had never seriously contemplated stopping obstetrics. Occasionally, after a run of bad nights, the idea would cross her mind, but the thought of doing gynaecology alone filled her with dismay. The appeal of her job was the thrill of labour and delivery, the exhilaration of each new birth.

She sat down in the chair beside Sylvie's desk. 'Have you finished?'

'The cake or the patients?'

Julia laughed. 'The patients, of course.'

Sylvie had seen all of hers but still had a few of Leo's to go. She was about an hour behind, but couldn't continue a minute longer without a break. Erica was looking after them for her, showing them a video about breastfeeding. Or was it caesareans?

As she spoke, Julia thought Sylvie sounded tired, and she was right; she'd been up all night with three deliveries in seven hours.

'Would you like me to cover you tonight?'

'Thanks, Julia, but it should be fine. Tonight should be quiet.' Sylvie held up her crossed fingers as she prepared to drag her weary body out of the chair.

Julia stood up with her. 'If you won't let me cover, at least let me see a couple of Leo's patients for you now.'

Sylvie blinked at her gratefully. 'Would you?'

'I can't think of anything I'd like better.'

Julia walked into her house and down the hall. In the chaos on the floor in the front room, she thought she spotted Emma's ancient history notes fighting for air amid the musical score for the new song. She could guess which had received the greater attention during the day. She found Emma in the kitchen, rhythmically stirring a curry to the accompaniment of Macy Gray.

'Mmm. That smells great.'

Emma turned down the music and kissed Julia on the cheek. 'I thought something spicy would go with the heat.'

'How was your day?'

Her daughter smiled. She had the Greeks and Romans sorted, and the Phoenicians nearly sorted.

'And the last four lines of the chorus?'

The teenager beamed. 'I think I've got them sorted too.' It had taken her hours but she was finally satisfied with the song. Shifting from her own happy news, she scrutinised her mother's face. 'How's Mrs Vella today?'

It was Julia's turn to smile. 'Even better than last night. And so's the baby.'

'See, I told you she would be all right. Must have made your day.'

Suppressing darker memories, Julia agreed it had. Even so, she confided her relief that the day was finally over.

'Over?' exclaimed Emma as she dished up their meal. 'Come on, Mum. Your days are *never* over, except in retrospect. Everyone else's day might be finished but yours could rev up at any minute and go on all night. It usually does. I've got years of Cabcharge statements to prove it.'

After two helpings each of the curry, followed by a large serve of ice cream to numb the chilli, Julia dropped Emma at Jade's for rehearsal. She then restored some order to the kitchen, made a handful of outstanding phone calls, put on a load of washing, ironed a few shirts and cleaned a dirty spot on the wall that had been bothering her for days. She even contemplated vacuuming the living room. *Anything* was preferable to reading the documents from Tracey Edwards' solicitor, which currently slumbered in her briefcase, flung deep in the boot of her car and buried beneath an old grey blanket for good measure. Finally steeling herself, she made her way down to the carport. Opening the boot, she stared at the blanket for several minutes before gingerly rolling it back and eyeing the battered black leather of her briefcase. A bag of funnel-webs would have been less intimidating.

Half an hour later, both her own medical notes and the Statement of Claim were on her dining table.

And Julia found herself once more in the laundry, being soothed by the hum and splash of the washing machine. She threw in a pile of new towels just to keep it going. When the load finished, she did another. Eventually, she slunk back towards the dining table and finally sat and looked unblinking at the documents.

Brendan Edwards had been delivered with forceps five years before. He had been born with significant brain damage. Tracey's solicitor had sent Julia a preliminary letter when Brendan was two, announcing that legal proceedings were being initiated. But there had been nothing since, nothing for three years. But now, the case Julia had hoped had gone away was back.

It had been her patient's first pregnancy, unplanned but seemingly welcome. Tracey was twenty-six at the time. Her partner, Brett, was two years older and in the army. Tracey could not usually have afforded a private obstetrician, but Brett's army health benefits paid for her care.

The pregnancy had initially gone well and, as planned, Tracey stopped working as a hairdresser at thirty-four weeks. At about that time, Julia thought that the baby was smaller than average, and had arranged some tests. These confirmed that the baby was small but were otherwise reassuring. Tracey herself was a small person and had been a small baby. As well, she was a smoker. This was surprising, since Brett was apparently very health conscious.

Julia tactfully reminded Tracey about the deleterious effects of smoking on her baby. She kept a close eye on the pregnancy, with regular foetal welfare assessments. The baby remained small but otherwise healthy. Labour started a day before term.

When Tracey presented to the hospital at midnight, she had been four centimetres dilated and coping well. Julia's own notes showed that the CTG tracing of the baby's heart rate at this stage had been normal. This was one of the things she would need to check in the records held by the hospital, but certainly the midwife, a competent and experienced nurse, had phoned her and said it was normal.

Thereafter the baby had not been continuously electronically monitored as it was not deemed necessary. Instead, the foetal heartbeat was listened to during and after contractions using a small hand-held ultrasound machine called a Doppler. The midwife had done this through two contractions every half an hour, as she was supposed to. Tracey had wanted as natural a delivery as possible, and had chosen to spend much of the labour in the shower, the hot water giving her great pain relief.

As she approached full dilatation, still in the shower, Tracey's membranes ruptured, revealing meconium-stained liquor. This meant that the baby had opened his bowels. While a reasonably common occurrence, it sometimes indicated that the baby was becoming distressed. Indeed, at about the same time, the Doppler detected the baby's heart dropping at the end of a contraction. The midwife asked Tracey to return to the bed so that an electronic monitor could be attached to give a print-out of the baby's heart rate. Decelerations were confirmed. Julia was rung at that point, and arrived at the hospital within fifteen minutes, by which time there was a prolonged drop in the baby's heart rate known as bradycardia. After examining Tracey, Julia had recommended a forceps delivery, and had duly carried this out. The delivery had been easy since the baby was small and his head was low.

Brendan Edwards at birth was much sicker than anyone had anticipated and was taken to the neonatal intensive care unit, where he spent the next few weeks. He had obvious neurological problems, and there was much debate amongst the doctors as to the cause.

Complicating the search for a diagnosis was the fact that no analysis of the blood in the baby's umbilical cord had been carried out. Julia had handed over a thirty centimetre piece of cord so that the oxygen and acid levels as they were at the moment of birth could be tested. However, in the drama surrounding the resuscitation of the sickly child, the piece of cord had been accidentally thrown out. The first blood analysis on Brendan had occurred when he was forty minutes old and was essentially normal.

The child had gone on to be significantly neurologically disabled. He needed around-the-clock nursing care well beyond what his mother could manage. As a result, he lived in the Malabar Home for Disabled Children.

The Statement of Claim contained reports from the doctors who now treated the child. At five years of age, Brendan had the mental age of a twelve-month-old baby, and there was little likelihood of improvement. He also had cerebral palsy and was unable to walk, crawl, sit, feed himself, or talk. His neck tone was poor and his head required support in a brace when he sat in his wheelchair. His spastic limbs were weak and stiff.

He had some responsiveness, however, as a baby does, and recognised a number of the people who cared for him. He was apparently very fond of his mother and would smile with delight when she visited.

Brendan also suffered from epilepsy. While seizures were not uncommonly associated with problems such as his, they were a terrible extra burden for the child and his carers. He had been known to have up to twenty fits a day, although recent changes to his medication had apparently seen an improvement.

His mother Tracey, who had long since separated from his father, lived with her own mother in a public housing flat. She'd had another child, a normal two-year-old girl, to a subsequent partner, who was also no longer around. Both Tracey and her mother were on pensions, which Tracey supplemented with two days' hairdressing a week. According to the report from the matron of the home, Tracey was a good mother to Brendan, seeing him every second day, reading to him and singing and trying to make him laugh. On clear days she would wheel him around the gardens at the home, showing him the flowers and birds and lizards.

According to Tracey's own statement, she cried every time she had to leave him. The staff at the home were kind but overworked. Much as they might wish to, they did not have the time to give Brendan the stimulation Tracey believed he needed. She felt that her son would be much better off living with her but, even with her mother's help, she could not manage his care without professional assistance. Especially as he grew bigger. She'd calculated that she would need a special house, a special car, and at least two shifts of nurses every day for the rest of her son's life if she were to look after him herself. And she had made up her mind to do it. To get the money. To bring Brendan home.

In a state of growing consternation, Julia read the entire Statement of Claim three times. Tracey's solicitors argued that there was only one reason Brendan Edwards was disabled: the actions and omissions of Dr Julia Kent. It was she who was responsible for the disastrous life the poor child was condemned to live. Her negligence was responsible for his damage.

She should have more fully investigated the child after ascertaining that he was abnormally small. She should have induced labour at thirty-eight weeks to remove him from an environment where he was not thriving. She should have insisted on continuous electronic monitoring during labour to detect foetal distress early. And, at the first sign of distress, she should have performed a timely caesarean.

Tears came to Julia unbidden, almost unacknowledged. Were they right? Was she responsible for Brendan's terrible disability? Had she made a serious error in judgement? It was a terrifying thought. She looked at her own records again and felt mildly reassured. There was nothing in her management that was obviously incompetent, but what if she was missing something? Had missed something?

She went to the kitchen and emptied the dishwasher, then poured herself a cold drink. Returning to the table, she slumped into her chair, then stood up again. This time she traipsed to the laundry but found herself beyond the solace of washing. She touched her lip where it was again bleeding. At this rate, it would never heal.

She desperately needed someone to talk to.

She thought of Patrick. He had called from the camp, leaving a message on her answering machine. They'd arrived safely, the heat was stifling and his tent wasn't quite as well-ventilated as he'd thought. But they were having a great time. Julia was somewhat surprised that he'd called so soon but, even as she thought of Patrick, she knew she could not discuss the lawsuit with him. Their friendship was still undefined, and she'd be embarrassed. For all sorts of reasons. She couldn't speak of it with Emma either; it would not be fair to burden her seventeen-year-old daughter. There was only one person she could easily talk to.

'Angie, it's Julia. I'm sorry to ring so late. I did try earlier, but your phone was engaged. Don't you have "call waiting"?'

Angie was amused. 'We've already got two lines and two mobiles. Can you imagine how many calls we could be on if we had "call waiting" as well?'

Julia had to smile as well. It sounded like one of Emma's maths questions. More soberly, she inquired after Angie's agonising time the night before. 'You seemed so upset when we met at the lifts at lunchtime.'

Angie was still not good. As she chronicled the previous day's events, it was clear to Julia that not only was her friend distraught, she felt like an idiot as well. It was belatedly obvious that her colleagues knew what de Bruin was like and hadn't been prepared to work with him. Which was why Angie had been appointed to the position so easily. Julia was shocked. Surely the surgeon couldn't be late and rude and have complications and be unavailable on a regular basis? But apparently he was. Many of the patients had multiple problems, of course, and the surgery itself was difficult. Even so, the nurses felt that he was slow and sloppy. His operating times were double the norm.

'And his complication rate is very high, Julia.'

'Doesn't this come out in peer review meetings?'

Angie exhaled. That was one of the problems. The cardiac

unit was very small, only three surgeons. Currently only two, of course, de Bruin and Littlewood. And the statistics were not presented for the individual doctor, but for the unit as a whole. Julia thought this old-fashioned and said so. In the obstetrics department, the mortality and morbidity statistics were recorded for each individual doctor, as well as the unit as a whole. It was a quality assurance measure. Surely the Children's Hospital could do that too?

It was already starting to happen, Angie explained. Just today she'd learned that Professor Macfarlane had recently instituted a six-month prospective assessment of every surgeon's performance, including the cardiac surgeons. He apparently expected this to confirm the rumours that de Bruin's operating standard was poor. But, until he had supporting evidence, he didn't think it prudent to remove him from the unit.

'Does de Bruin know he is likely to be sacked at the end of this review?'

Angie gave a short laugh. 'Why? Do you think Mac's heart attack was something else?'

They spoke about other matters for a few moments until Julia could no longer keep it to herself. 'Angie, I've got a bit of a work problem of my own.'

'What is it, Julia?'

For a moment, Julia couldn't speak. Saying it out loud would make it real. A living nightmare.

'Oh, Angie,' she gasped. 'It's awful.'

Angie waited patiently. 'Is it Stephen?' she finally asked.

'No,' sniffled Julia. 'It's a patient.'

'Oh,' said Angie, no clearer.

'It's a patient I delivered five years ago whose baby has brain damage. She is suing me for negligence.'

Angie was astounded. There was no one in her acquaintance less negligent than Julia. She'd barely seen her make a mistake with someone's name, let alone a medical error. It couldn't be right. Julia insisted it was. But she didn't want to keep Angie on the phone about it now. She knew how tired she must be. She'd just needed to share the news with someone.

Angie didn't want to let her go so easily, but Julia wouldn't be drawn on the details. Angie'd had a hard enough time in the past twenty-four hours without her burdens as well.

'I don't need you to give an opinion about the obstetric side of things. That's not why I rang,' Julia sobbed into the phone. 'It's because you will understand why I feel so threatened.'

'Tony,' said Angie very quietly. 'And Madeleine Morgan.'

'Who else?'

Chapter 7

Looking back, Julia thought that if even one of the events of those two years had not occurred, her marriage to Tony might have survived. As it was, the cumulative toll had been irresistible.

They had been trying without success for another child for several years and had even been for tests. There was no explanation. After the ridiculous ease of Emma's conception, it was doubly frustrating, and made even harder by their daughter's regular requests for a sibling. Tony reassured Julia, reminding her that even without another child, they were among the most fortunate people in the world.

'I'm certainly the luckiest man alive,' he would say, kissing her ear.

'There's no doubt about that,' she'd agree.

But the longing did not abate. And for Julia, daily surrounded by other women's babies, it was even worse.

And then it happened. After first thinking she was getting a virus, Julia recognised her nausea for what it was. As with her first pregnancy, she did not immediately tell Tony; she was fearful of inviting bad luck. And like before, he saw her breasts increase in size, and waited. Once the risky early months had passed, their joy was boundless. They painted the third bedroom yellow, tactfully overriding Emma's suggestion of purple, spent hours discussing names, saved up their leave, and planned their lives for when the baby would come. Emma, now eight, told them not to worry too much if they had to go to work. She would happily stay home from school and mind the baby.

In the last month of the pregnancy, Julia was frantically busy getting the more critical of her patients' operations and appointments out of the way before she stopped work for three months. As well as her responsibility towards her patients, she felt she owed it to Stephen.

It was while driving home from the hospital in the middle of the night, enjoying her first quiet moment of the day, that she suddenly realised she had not felt the baby move for a while. Maybe not since yesterday. That couldn't be so. It probably had moved, she'd just been too busy to notice. But she was wrong.

Baby Joseph Cabrini was well-grown for eight months of pregnancy and looked perfectly normal. No cause for his death was found, a common enough outcome.

'Probably an umbilical cord accident,' volunteered Julia's obstetrician, Leo Steiner, for want of anything else. 'It might have become compressed and cut off his oxygen.'

It didn't matter to Julia what the underlying cause was. She had let her son die. Every day, over and over, she exhorted her patients to monitor their baby's movements and to act immediately if there was less activity than usual. There was often a window of hours when the baby could be saved. But she'd been so busy with everyone else's babies, she hadn't thought about her own. He had slowed down, warning her that he was in trouble, and she hadn't noticed. He had tried to let her know that he needed to be delivered, that he wasn't getting enough oxygen, but in her preoccupation, she'd failed to register that her little son needed her.

Julia refused to take any time off work, saying it was unnecessary, but the truth was she couldn't bear time on her hands.

Even so, she struggled. Marcia vigilantly hovered about, ensuring she was coping, and dealing with the patients when she wasn't. At home she could barely make an effort for Tony and Emma, instead sitting for hour after hour staring into space, silently blaming herself all over again.

The nights were the worst. She would dream that she was still pregnant and the baby still alive. She would notice his reduced movements and he would be saved just in time. Then she would wake up.

For six months it was like this. Every day. Tony reduced his hours as much as possible, taking time off to care for Emma, who had accepted the baby's death quite well but was bewildered by the change in her mother. Tony attended to the housekeeping and the washing, keeping the three of them fed and clothed. It took a terrible toll on him, especially when nothing he said could console Julia. Bereaved himself, he was almost demented with worry.

Around this time, Tony had to go to Perth for a week to present a research paper at a major international psychiatric conference. He had submitted a summary of the paper before Joseph's death, and could not easily get out of his commitment. He had misgivings about leaving, but Julia's father said he'd come and stay, while Angie volunteered to take care of the shopping and cooking. 'Go, Tony,' Angie insisted, knowing he badly needed a break. 'I'll make sure Julia's fine. And enjoy yourself.'

The next few months saw an improvement in Julia. She still grieved but less constantly, still blamed herself but less destructively. Slowly, she moved on to a phase of partial acceptance, both of her son's death, and her own culpability. She even began to contemplate the possibility of trying again, and for the first time since the loss of her baby, made love to Tony. 'I'm sorry, Tone. I know it's been awful for you too,' she cried quietly into his chest.

'Shh,' he said, touching her lips. 'It's been nothing like as bad for me as it's been for you, darling. And you've been very brave. I love you.'

Some weeks later they attended the birthday party of a psychiatrist from Royal Eastside. Emma was mildly unwell and they nearly didn't go, but the babysitter was a regular and the party close to home. It was the first social occasion Julia had attended all year, and she was apprehensive. It was a large crowd, but mostly people she knew, and Tony stayed beside her, holding her hand and helping her with the condolences which still came from those she hadn't seen since the baby's death. She was managing well and, when Angie arrived, urged Tony to seek out his friends for a while.

He rejoined Julia when Angie left for an emergency and noticed quickly how tired she looked. She said little on the way home and he was fearful that her grief had been rekindled by seeing a friend who'd given birth to a healthy son in the week they'd lost Joseph. He remained concerned over the next few days as she withdrew once again.

'Are you all right, darling?' he asked one night in bed, putting his arm around her waist and snuggling into her.

'Shouldn't I be, Tony?' she responded coolly, moving away from him slightly.

'You seemed to be better lately, that's all.'

Julia said nothing for a few moments. 'I spoke to your old girlfriend, Sybilla Ramsey, at the party last weekend.'

'Did you? I didn't get a chance to speak to her myself.'

Julia's body stiffened. 'You didn't tell me you'd seen her at the conference in Perth.'

'I didn't think it was important, sorry. She's been living in the States for a few years, but is back in Australia looking for a job.'

Julia was very quiet. 'Sybilla seemed to think that seeing you was important. Do you have something to tell me, Tony?'

He did.

He hadn't seen Sybilla in ten years. He'd heard on the grapevine that she had recently divorced her American husband, but had not expected her to be in Perth. After congratulating him on his presentation at the conference dinner, Sybilla had suggested they catch up over a few drinks at the bar. She had always been great company and soon had Tony laughing at her wicked tales of their mutual colleagues.

It happened almost before he knew it. Sybilla made the first move, but he was hungrily receptive, not just to her body, but to the laughter and talk that went with it. That they'd been lovers before made it immeasurably easier, of course, that and the wine they had drunk. But Tony was also deliberately seeking a few hours respite from the months of unyielding wretchedness.

He'd regretted it immediately, remorse and guilt now added to his other misery, and had left the conference the next day without even saying goodbye to Sybilla. He hadn't known she would be at the recent party, and had assiduously avoided her.

'I have no excuse, Julia. It was just my stupid drunken reaction to the stress I was under. It meant nothing, it still means nothing, and it will never happen again. Ever. The guilt has nearly killed me. ' He cried into her unresponsive form.

Tony's infidelity pierced Julia's soul. The picture of his gentle hands cradling someone else's face, stroking her hair, bringing her pleasure, of his eyes gazing down at her with desire, sent Julia reeling. It was almost more than she could bear. She'd already been sinking in grief, and he had done this. White hot anger seared her, then a whirlpool of black sorrow dragged her under. Again and again. She barely spoke to Tony for the first month and when she did, she raged against him.

Over time, her doubts about him threatened to consume her. He hadn't told her about Sybilla, indeed had deliberately kept it from her. Were there others he was keeping from her? Had he been doing it for years? She knew how appealing he was, how everyone always loved Tony, and she'd given thanks every day of her marriage that fortune had bestowed him on her. Now, for the first time, she saw how easily he might have someone else.

In all the years of their marriage, she'd never once questioned his whereabouts. Now she tracked his every movement. Panic seized her when he was late home. A knife turned when he laughed into the phone. A frenzied jealousy rose up at his most innocent observations. What did he mean when he said that the newsreader had a nice voice for radio? And when he remarked that their neighbour was looking rested after her holiday, what had he noticed? Her soft tanned arms? Her sun-lightened hair? Her shapely legs?

She found herself flicking through his mail, ordering duplicate copies of his credit card bill, hovering when he took a phone call, driving needlessly by his office. A sense of worthlessness racked her being, amplified by disgust at her own behaviour.

Tony understood what she was going through, and submitted to her grillings without a murmur. He'd have cut off his right arm to have restored her equanimity. He rang her regularly during the day, came home early from work, always left a number where she could contact him, asked his friends and colleagues – even his secretaries – not to call him at home. He was penitent and patient and nurturing. Recognising her paranoia, he strove to make conversation about neutral subjects and, while every harmless comment was speared back at him, he kept talking to her, determined to reach her.

The extraordinary trouble he took to assure her of his love slowly seeped into Julia's consciousness. Since she now believed he could have whoever he wanted, why was he still with her? Unless, as he said, he loved her. And only her. It would be a long time before she felt about him the way she had before but, eighteen months after Joseph's death, things were just turning the corner for them when Madeleine Morgan died.

Madeleine Morgan began therapy with Tony Cabrini when she was twenty-one. She was initially brought by her husband, Greg Islington, who was twice her age. Greg was desperately worried about her; she took pills to perk up, then pills to calm down, drank immoderate quantities of alcohol, and drove like a maniac.

And she kept asking him to hurt her.

She was a beautiful young woman, and Tony initially thought that Greg must have been very rich to have attracted such a glamorous young wife. But although Greg was a successful stockbroker, it was Madeleine who had the real money.

She was the stepdaughter of Bernie Morgan, one of Australia's richest men. Bernie had started out with a fleet of buses in the sixties and presciently moved into air travel just as it was becoming affordable for the average person. Business had boomed, and he'd expanded into leisure resorts, freight and a string of hotels. He was a business icon, a self-made man.

His family life was not so successful. The characteristics that won him accolades in business saw him a failure as a husband and father. His first wife, Adelaide, had left him in their tenth year of marriage claiming, amongst other things, that he had dislocated her shoulder while dragging her up some stairs. His lawyers won him custody of his son Jeremy, quietly and expensively silencing Adelaide's claims that he had beaten the small boy also.

Soon after, Bernie became involved with one of his secretaries, the comely and kind Estelle Harrigan. A widow in her late twenties, she was struggling with two young children and a pile of bills. Never a good judge of character, and desperate to provide her family with a better life, she was receptive to the attentions of her boss. Before long, she was Bernie's wife, settling into his waterfront mansion with seven-year-old Damien and five-year-old Madeleine.

It was to be a fatal mistake for the three of them.

Damien suffered immediately. Bernie provoked and tormented the child, then beat him when he reacted. Nine-year-old Jeremy, relieved to be a perpetrator rather than a victim, felt encouraged to do the same. Over the years Damien suffered many injuries, including a broken nose and three lost teeth when Bernie punched him for answering back. The cause of the injuries was always concealed.

From the age of thirteen, things were especially grim for Madeleine. Bernie often hit her as well, but one day, while slapping and kicking her for covering her ears when he yelled, he took her torment further and raped her. Madeleine remembered the first time quite clearly and thought that Bernie had been as shocked at what he had done as she was. But from then on, he developed a taste for punishing her in that way.

She told no one. She could not tell her stepbrother, Jeremy, who was brutish like his father, and she would not tell Damien, whom she loved. She knew what he would do and what Bernie would do to him in return. Her mother, Estelle, might have guessed, were she not rapidly sliding into alcoholic incoherence.

Madeleine coped with her unhappiness by writing fantasy stories based on children's fairytales. In each, a young woman who was being mistreated by a cruel male villain ultimately vanquished her oppressor.

Her brother, Damien, didn't cope at all. He suicided at the age of eighteen, using an unknown number of tablets together with a bottle of brandy. He had written a note, but the death certificate signed by the family's doctor attributed his death to accidental alcoholic poisoning.

Madeleine's sexual relationship with Bernie continued but its nature, still immensely damaging, changed as she grew older. While she could do nothing about his assaults when she was younger, Madeleine at sixteen could have brought them to a halt. But by then she'd realised they gave her some power over her stepfather. That and the money he showered on her in his moments of remorse were why she let it continue.

About a year later, Estelle also died. The loss of her mother so soon after her brother's death triggered a profound anger and depression in Madeleine which saw its expression in self-injury. She began to drink heavily and take pills, along the way embroiling herself in a string of brief, destructive relationships, mostly with much older men. Then, at twenty, she impetuously married Greg Islington, whose first wife had divorced him because he was infertile and who, perversely, reminded her physically of Bernie. The similarity ended there; Greg was a good man who treated her with kindness and respect.

While Madeleine soon regretted the marriage, her husband was becoming increasingly distressed by what he recognised as his new wife's deep self-loathing.

Greg accompanied Madeleine to the first session with Tony, but thereafter she went on her own. In the beginning she often missed appointments and, when she bothered to come, was dishevelled, inebriated and trailing ash. It had not been her idea to seek therapy, her actions seemed to say, and she was making her pathetic protest. It took Tony a long time to gain her trust, only slowly appreciating the extent of her damage and the depths of her insecurities. After her experience with men, Madeleine clearly expected him to hurt her too. At the same time, she could not keep her grief and guilt to herself much longer. She was desperate to share her heartache with someone, but only if what she said was never passed on to anyone else. Tony explained that their sessions were absolutely confidential. He would never reveal anything that she told him.

From that time Madeleine made progress. As she shared with Tony the demons that haunted her, she began to shed her self-destructive behaviour. As her confidence grew, she showed Tony some of the fantasy stories she had written in her darkest hours. He was troubled by their grim content, but impressed by the power of her writing and suggested she consider a career as a journalist or novelist. He encouraged her to begin writing again. Bashfully, Madeleine admitted she'd already started.

During the first year Tony saw her every week, sometimes twice a week. Over that time, as she learnt to deal with the sorrow and shame and loneliness in her life, Madeleine became more assured. She got a job in a small shop, was rarely intoxicated and even managed to stop smoking for a few days at a time. She radiated good health, was almost perky during their consultations and talked with optimism about her future. Tony, by now very fond of her, was delighted to see her become whole again.

Things continued to go so well that, a year and a half into her therapy, Tony proposed cutting back the frequency of Madeleine's sessions. She took the suggestion badly.

'Are you tired of me, Tony? Are my problems no longer interesting?' she asked in a small voice.

'Of course not, Madeleine,' he replied, bewildered at her reaction. 'I'm reducing your sessions because you've made such wonderful progress. You don't need to come so often any more.' But, as her lip trembled and her eyes filled, Tony relented.

From that day, Madeleine regressed, and now slid into the

71

chair in his office drug-affected and incoherent and wearing clothes it appeared she'd slept in. She was sometimes hostile towards him, sometimes cavalier. But mostly she was like a small lost kitten. His heart went out to her. At the same time, he noted that she never missed an appointment. In fact, he had to see her more often.

He understood what she was doing but was surprised how important their sessions had become to her. He had thought she'd moved beyond the need for such intensive therapy. At the same time he acknowledged that this was her first setback, and he had other patients who felt nervous at the thought of less frequent counselling.

It was not until a few weeks later that it became clear to Tony that Madeleine was infatuated with him. She was making oblique sexual references and twice deliberately brushed her body against his as she walked out the door. Concerned, he began to consider transferring her care. He consulted with his colleagues who agreed that he needed to be careful but reminded him that it was not uncommon for patients to become infatuated with their therapist. As long as he was strictly professional in his dealings, they didn't see why he couldn't continue to look after her.

Tony was not altogether comfortable with their advice. He didn't want anything to retard Madeleine's healing, certainly not something he himself was contributing to. Until recently he'd expected she would be off his patient list altogether in another twelve months.

He desperately wished he could talk to Julia about his dilemma. At any other time, she would have been the only person whose advice he sought, her sensible, kind-hearted wisdom leading him quickly to the right decision. But while things were slowly improving between them, an awkwardness still lingered. Tony knew that the last thing Julia needed to hear at the moment was that he thought one of his patients was in love with him.

For a couple of months Madeleine was sober again, and bright, taking particular care with her appearance. Tony was heartened by the transformation, unaware that her joy sprang from her finally recognising how she felt about him. And her belief that he loved her as well. She was going to leave Greg, and then she and Tony would move in together.

Soon after, Madeleine made her feelings known to Tony. The session that followed was not pleasant for either of them. Tony was distressed by her open declaration of love and alarmed that she believed it was reciprocated. He calmly explained that he was married, and that even if he wasn't, it was against the law for therapists to have sexual relationships with patients. He was extremely fond of her, as she well knew, and proud of her progress and potential, but that was the extent of his affection. There was no possibility of any relationship for them beyond that.

Madeleine was hurt at his rebuff and frustrated at his refusal to admit his desire for her, but she would not give him up. They wouldn't have to worry about the law once everyone saw how much they loved each other but, if there were still problems, they could flee to any place in the world. She had money enough to keep them in luxury for the rest of their lives. As long as they had each other, nothing else would matter.

They covered the same path for a long time. Finally Tony stood up and called in his secretary. He asked her to make an appointment for Madeleine to see Dr Barrington, a female psychiatrist with whom he had already discussed her case. He was handing over her care immediately. He turned back to Madeleine to explain his decision, but she darted from the room in tears.

She did not attend the appointment with Tony's colleague and she did not return his phone calls. For several weeks no one even knew where she was. Tony spoke to her husband Greg, who was in a state of extreme agitation about her. She was back to her old ways, but worse, he said. And she was refusing to talk to him.

Tony was frantic also, daily dreading that harm would befall her. Guilt sat like a cloud above his head; he should have handed over her care months ago, when she first started to regress, and before it had got to this. But the miseries in his own life and his preoccupation with Julia had blinded him to the extent of Madeleine's attachment.

Julia immediately noticed the change in Tony, the air of tension that cloaked him, the haunted stare that had taken over his eyes. She waited for him to tell her what the problem was. But he was as secretive as he was preoccupied. Soon after, Madeleine started to ring the house. Tony never gave his private number to patients, but for someone of Madeleine's determination and resources, obtaining it would have been easy. If she reached Julia when she called, she would hang on for a long minute saying nothing and then disconnect, while if Tony answered she sobbed quietly down the line. Julia watched Tony's face during these calls, noting his mixture of alarm and relief, listening while he asked, 'Madeleine, is that you? Are you all right?' and hearing him command the caller not to ring him at home. She waited for his explanation, but none came. And, after months of relative calm, she felt the familiar churn of jealousy once more.

More than ever, Tony wanted to discuss the problem with Julia but, taking in her anguished glance, he understood how badly it would upset her; she was only now becoming secure again, only now starting to feel confident of his affection. It would not be helpful for her to learn that a beautiful young woman believed she had his love. He would go to any length to save her from that.

At around the same time, Madeleine's husband, Greg, found her diary and read that his wife and her psychiatrist were engaged in a passionate love affair. A love affair she had graphically recorded in all its tenderness and illicitness over dozens of pages. Greg rang Tony and laid the accusations before him. Tony quietly denied the impropriety. Learning what Madeleine had written, however, dragged him to new lows of failure and regret.

One evening several weeks later, Madeleine visited Tony at home. He was alone, which she must have known, Julia and Emma having gone to the shops. When he opened the front door, she fell drunkenly into his arms. And Greg's private detective, in a car across the street, took a dozen photos.

Her skin was sallow, her clothing soiled, her speech confused, but Tony was overjoyed she was at least safe. He showed her into the kitchen where she sat, crying desolately of her love for him. No one had ever understood her like he did. Surely he loved her a little bit? He didn't have to live with her, she now realised that wouldn't be possible, but couldn't she have him some of the time?

Again, there was no way to happily resolve the situation. Tony told her that he would always be her friend, but could never be anything more. Gently he reminded her how well she'd been doing; it would be a pity to let something like this set her back. She was talented and intelligent and had her whole life in front of her. She should reconsider what a good man she had in Greg; he could probably make her happy. But if she was determined to leave him, then Tony was sure there were a hundred others who would be delighted to share her life, honourable men who would look after her and be worthy of her love.

In the meantime, now that he had finally located her and mindful of what she had written in her diary, Tony was desperate for her to come under the immediate care of someone else. He would ask Dr Barrington to see her tonight. Madeleine nodded slowly in seeming agreement but, the hopelessness of her situation dawning, fled while Tony was phoning his colleague. He ran to the front door just in time to see her sports car screech out of his drive. And Julia come in.

Julia said nothing for two days but by the third had had enough. She asked Tony outright if he was having an affair. He denied it. She asked who Madeleine was. He explained that she was a very disturbed patient whose therapy he was having problems with. And whose care he was transferring to Jacqueline Barrington.

'Why are you transferring her care?' asked Julia carefully.

'Because I'm failing in the management of her problems,' he confessed, aware of his understatement.

Julia then asked why he'd given a patient their home phone number and address. He explained that he hadn't but that somehow she'd tracked him down.

'So she's stalking you?'

'She thinks she's in love with me,' he admitted reluctantly.

'And are you in love with her, Tony?'

'Of course not,' he snapped, the strain finally telling. 'For God's sake, Julia, do you have to harp on and on about this? I've told you a million times, there's no one else. You're the only one I'm in love with. What do you want me to do? I made one mistake, once. And you keep throwing it back in my face. For nearly a year I've had to live with your prowling paranoia. Haven't you got your pound of flesh yet?'

It was himself he was angry with, of course, not Julia. It was he who was the architect of their marital disharmony. And it was his poor judgement that had harmed Madeleine. His patient was missing again and the weeks of guilty anxiety were tearing him to shreds.

The last time he heard from Madeleine was one evening when, as before, he was at home alone. Her voice on the phone was unmistakably drug-affected, slurred and halting. She told him that she had decided to do it, to follow Damien and end it all. She had the pills and the brandy and was going to join her brother tonight. Greg was away and she was at home on her own. Tony slammed down the phone and raced to the address she had given him.

She opened the front door even before he was out of his car, and ran towards him. Wearing the briefest of negligees, she was clearly much less inebriated than she'd pretended to be on the phone.

The private detective took a roll of photographs.

'Tony, you came.' She hugged him and took his hand, leading him into the house. She planned to seduce him, to prove that he did indeed love her.

Tony's first emotion was relief. But his dominant feeling was anger that she had tricked him. 'Put some clothes on, Madeleine.'

'Oh, darling,' she persisted, clinging to him.

He gently pushed her away and refused to talk until she was dressed. He then made her sit across the dining table from him.

'You didn't keep your appointment with Dr Barrington.' Tony was steely.

'I wanted to see you, not her.'

'You can't see me any more, Madeleine.'

'But I love you, Tony.'

They had the same exchange in various forms for an hour. Madeleine would not give up the idea that he loved her in return. Since reasoning with her was clearly failing, Tony decided to be forceful. Perhaps too forceful.

He told her that he was not going to see her again. She was not to phone him. If she did, he would hang up. She was not to come to the practice. If she did, he would walk away. For now, he would like to admit her to hospital immediately under Dr Barrington's care. She needed close observation and he wanted to be sure that she was safe.

Madeleine was quiet then, acknowledging his right to be angry. She was being silly. But she didn't need to go into hospital. She would visit Dr Barrington in the morning. She was joking about the suicide threat, and hadn't gone through two years of hard work to throw it all away now. She thanked him for being so patient with her and apologised for embarrassing him.

This was more like the Madeleine he used to know and Tony felt himself relax. 'You will thank me for this decision,' he said as he left. 'You are a wonderful person with a wonderful future. Dr Barrington will be able to help you realise it.'

'Thanks, Tony. I'll see her in the morning.'

But by morning, Madeleine Morgan was dead.

Chapter 8

Marcia and Patricia were gleefully exchanging details of the morning's phone calls from Stacey, Stephen's wife. Julia could hear them giggling as she came through the empty reception area to the desk, en route to her operating list at Royal Eastside, and their happy mood lifted her more sombre one. The Mitchells were in the midst of extensive renovations to their mansion and Stacey rang at least three times a day to speak to Stephen about them, mostly to suggest costly additional work. That there was amusement but little malice in the clerical staff's attitude towards Stacey was testimony to their generous natures.

A few years before, Stacey had briefly worked at the surgery as acting practice manager. Never letting anyone forget she was also Stephen's wife, she had managed to upset the entire office within a month, interfering in everyone else's work but unable to do her own. Luckily, the job was more demanding than she'd anticipated, and she had quit just as the other employees were considering their own resignations. She still dropped by the practice regularly, however, and never passed up the opportunity to suggest how things could be better run.

Too circumspect to discuss one boss in front of another, however mildly, the secretaries terminated their discussion as Julia joined them. 'I've just boiled the kettle,' said Marcia. 'Would you like me to get you a cup of tea? Or would you rather something cool to drink?' The heatwave was in its fourth day, with a change promised this evening.

'Thanks, something cool would be lovely.'

'Did you see Leo's latest postcard?' asked Patricia.

'The one from Prague? Yes, I saw it yesterday. Who's going to send us funny cards when he comes back?'

'I'll go to Europe and do it,' volunteered the practice manager. 'If you pay my fare.'

'I'm sorry I'm late.' Julia hurried into the operating theatre just after one o'clock and came to where Angie stood at the head of the operating table. The first patient was nearly asleep.

'Thanks for starting,' continued Julia. 'I've got someone in labour.'

'Here or at St Agatha's?'

'Here, thank God. I'm hoping she'll do the right thing and deliver just as we're finishing.' She could tell Angie hoped so too. It did nothing for the smooth running of an operating list for the surgeon to disappear for an hour in the middle.

The last case, a hysterectomy, took longer than expected as Julia peered deep into the pelvis, her frown sliding her cap towards her mask. She muttered something about the blood loss and called for yet another suture. The scrub nurse eyed the clock as she handed it over. The bleeding was minimal and the operation should have been finished thirty minutes ago, but still Julia fretted and stitched. Finally the scrub challenged her. 'Are you making a blanket in there, Dr Kent?'

Julia looked up sharply. 'Are you offering to take over responsibility for Mrs Alameddine, Verity? Would you like to be the one who reopens her in two hours because her operation wasn't done properly?'

While the scrub shrugged, the rest of the staff avoided each other's eyes. It was not like Dr Kent to snap at anyone. It wasn't like her to take so long with such a simple operation either. But only Angie understood.

Shortly after midnight, the weather bureau's prediction of an end to the sweltering heat came to pass, and a powerful storm worked out its swollen anger on the eastern suburbs of the city. The sky was illuminated by brilliant lightning, while the rain hit like stones even before it became hail, and the wind lifted trees onto roofs and roofs onto the ground.

It was the noise rather than the light which woke Julia, but it was the electricity of the sky which mesmerised her thereafter. She got up to check the security of her windows, and then climbed back into bed, but not into slumber. While the lightning flashed from negative to positive, Julia's thoughts went in reverse and she arrived, inevitably, at her lawsuit.

After finishing her operating list and attending a mercifully straightforward delivery, she had trekked down to medical records to look at Tracey Edwards' hospital file, hoping that it would corroborate her own private notes and relieve her anxiety. But the records' team had been too busy to pull a non-urgent file. Instead, they'd filled in a requisition form for the night staff. The file would be ready for Julia tomorrow. Probably.

Despondent, she'd made her way home to a silent house, her only comfort Emma's scribbled message that she'd 'killed' the ancient history exam. She'd eaten last night's curry in front of the news, indulged in a long shower and changed into her pyjamas. Briefly cheered while devouring a block of fruit and nut chocolate in front of a sitcom, she had plunged back into self-pity soon after.

Before she even knew what she was doing, she'd climbed to the top shelf of the linen press. And retrieved the Statement of Claim from where she'd tossed it the previous night, out of sight among the second-ranking bath towels. Taking it down, she'd shivered again at the touch of its fine, embossed pages. Then, for a second night, she'd pored over the expert opinions that laid the blame for Brendan Edwards' disabilities at her feet, and rocketed between anger and despair.

Anger that such reports could be written by people who hadn't been there when Brendan was born. Who didn't know how careful she was, didn't realise she would never take a chance with a baby's wellbeing.

And despair that perhaps they were right.

In the thrall of both nature's fireworks and her own terrifying thoughts, Julia was not sure how long her pager had been beeping. From its small screen screamed the command to 'Call St Agatha's delivery suite urgently, Judith Robinson in labour, CTG abnormal'.

Her pillow accepted her groan. Going out on a night like this must surely qualify her for a bravery award. She dialled. 'Nancy, it's Julia Kent. Someone paged me.'

'I did, Dr Kent. Mrs Robinson came in twenty minutes ago in good labour. She had thick meconium on her pad, so I put on a trace. It shows quite pronounced late decelerations.'

'How far dilated is she?'

'Five centimetres.'

No difficult decisions here, thought Julia comfortably. Judith Robinson needed a caesarean. Had she been closer to full dilatation, Julia might have had to consider pushing on a bit longer in order to apply forceps.

'Is a theatre available?'

'They're just finishing a bowel obstruction and will be free by the time you get here. And the anaesthetist knows to stay.'

'Thanks, Nancy, I'll be right there.'

Julia gathered her things, contemplating what she was about to do. A timely caesarean. As she went out, she turned to glance at the Brendan Edwards' documents where she had left them on the hall-stand near the front door. Documents which accused her, among other things, of failure to do a 'timely caesarean'. They just didn't know how difficult it sometimes was.

With curtains of rain reducing visibility to a few metres and much of the storm damage still uncleared, all but the young cancelled Friday evening plans and sought the safety of home. Slowing down after her broken night and long day, Julia resisted the lure of her own snug, dry cottage, and forced herself to turn right at the lights and head back to the surgery instead. Her in-tray had still not learned to clear itself.

She was surprised to find Stephen at Waratah House. Friday was the one day he tried to get home early.

'Do you have someone in labour?'

'No, thank heavens. I'm still catching up after the last delivery. Alicia Keenan-Smith.' He grinned, seeing the funny side for the first time. 'It was a bit of a disaster, I'm afraid.'

The retail heiress had completely intimidated the midwives within a couple of hours of arriving. She'd asked to be moved to a room with a nicer colour scheme and had insisted on an epidural when she was barely in labour. She'd then demanded to know why things were going so slowly and what was going to be done about it. In particular, what Stephen was going to do about it.

Julia laughed. The heiress had spent her life delegating to other people the jobs she didn't like. She had probably never really believed that she was going to have to deliver the baby herself, subconsciously thinking that in the end someone else would do it for her. 'You gave in and did a caesarean, didn't you?'

'Of course,' he chuckled. There was no doubt in his mind that Alicia could easily have delivered vaginally, given a bit more time, but she was having none of it. His decision to operate was made easier by the midwives' refusal to look after her any longer unless she stopped abusing them.

'To which she promptly said, "Piss off!"' anticipated Julia.

Stephen looked surprised. 'You've heard all about it then, I take it.'

Julia had heard nothing, but could have written the script months earlier. What she did not tell Stephen was that she herself had knocked back Alicia as a patient when she'd rung to book in for her pregnancy. Or rather, Marcia had, instinctively discerning that the heiress was one of the handful of people who simply weren't worth the trouble. Alicia had booked instead with Stephen, who enjoyed being the obstetrician to the eastern suburbs glitterati.

'You will take on these VIP patients,' Julia chided.

Stephen smiled in acknowledgement. 'Now you know the sad, sorry tale of my ruined afternoon, may I ask why you are here at seven o'clock on a Friday evening?'

Julia gestured to the rain; it was good weather for work, although there were places she'd rather be. Especially after the disappointment of her second abortive attempt to obtain Tracey Edwards' hospital file. Her requisition form had been misplaced, and she'd had to fill out another one. And go back again on Monday. 'I lost a bit of time this afternoon,' she said noncommittally. 'Attending to a few personal things.'

'When Stacey says that, it means the beauty therapist. Or the hairdresser.' Stephen looked at her for the telltale signs.

'Something like that,' Julia agreed. 'And then I nearly went home, but realised that I could never relax if I didn't deal with the phone calls at least.'

'Of course when you call them, you'll find that they've gone out to dinner with friends or to the movies, the sort of things you'd like to be doing,' Stephen said sharply. 'And then they call again the next day when you are operating or delivering and simply don't have time to talk, and leave another message asking you to call. It drives me mad.'

He was quite worked up by now. The phone calls were the worst part of the job for Stephen, even worse than delivering in the middle of the night. 'And it's all unpaid work as well,' he added, arriving at what really irked him about it. 'Can you imagine your accountant or solicitor talking to you on the phone for fifteen minutes about your affairs, at your request, and not billing you?'

Julia murmured neutrally. Stephen always thought that he was overworked and underpaid. It was not a conversation she wanted to have and she deflected him by asking how much longer he planned to be in the surgery.

'I've given myself an hour.'

'I'll race you.'

'You're on.'

Two hours later, Stephen appeared at Julia's door. She was on the phone, but gestured for him to take a seat.

'Yes, I'm absolutely certain you don't have cancer. It's only very mildly abnormal. You simply need to have it repeated in six months.' For the third time Julia explained that dozens of mildly abnormal pap smears crossed her desk each month, and that many of them were back to normal at the next check. But her patient had seen stories on television about people being falsely reassured by their doctors, and then succumbing to a preventable disease. Julia felt for the woman. Her concern was understandable. If she'd prefer, Julia would be happy to repeat the pap smear in two months. She did prefer.

Julia put down the phone and made a brief entry in the file before tossing it onto her 'completed' pile on the floor. Unfortunately, the 'to do' pile on her desk remained the bigger one. She turned to Stephen.

'On your way out?' It was nearly nine.

'Yes. I'm not finished, but I've had enough. I've stayed much longer than I intended. We both have.' He pointed to her clock. 'Stacey says my dinner's hardly worth eating, but I might catch the last of the cricket on the telly. What about you?'

'I've had it too. I'll pack these up and walk out with you.'

They locked the surgery door and dashed through the heavy rain to the shelter of the carport. Hearing Stephen puff after such slight exertion, Julia gazed at her colleague with concern. He'd recently been gaining weight, losing hair, and wearing himself out faster than he normally did. And she knew he was booking more than his usual heavy load of thirty confinements a month.

'I realise you're in great demand, Stephen, but surely it's not necessary to book so many?' she said after gently broaching the subject with him.

'It is actually. But it's just a short-term thing, for the next year or so. I couldn't keep it up for any longer, to tell the truth, but I need to do it for a while.'

'But why?'

'For the money.'

'What?' Julia was incredulous. 'You are joking? I make a very good living, and you must make double what I do. How can you possibly be short of money?'

'There's a one-word answer to that.'

'Gambling?'

'Stacey.' He paused briefly, torn between disloyalty to his wife and a desperate need to talk to someone about the pressure he was under to finance a lifestyle that was more expensive by the day.

'We're doing substantial renovations at home, as you know, and unfortunately the cost keeps blowing out.'

'But I thought you had a fixed-price contract with the builder.'

'I do. But unfortunately, I don't have a fixed-price contract with Stacey.'

'Oh.' Julia knew when to hold her tongue.

Stacey kept adding bits to the renovation, apparently, and the price was skyrocketing. Stephen joked that his wife might even run off with the builder when the job was finished, since he'd have all their money by then. Julia didn't smile. 'And so you've increased your workload to impossible levels to pay for it all?'

'I have.'

'And to pay for this as well?' She gestured to his brand-new baby blue BMW convertible with the softest of white leather upholstery, probably taken from the hide of a week-old calf.

'It was time for a new car. The Saab was over two years old.'

'My car is five years old.'

'You obviously need a new lease agreement.'

'It's not leased.'

'You obviously need a new accountant.'

Chapter 9

Luxuriating on the couch surrounded by the Saturday papers, Julia watched the water spill over the gutter and rollick down the windowpane. Since Thursday night it had been relentless, and she snuggled further under her light rug, grateful that she wasn't one of the thousands without a roof and power. Her mind turned to poor Patrick and Ryan in their tents; she hoped they were dry.

Certainly Patrick had sounded cheerful enough when he'd called last night. The camping area was outside mobile range but he had braved the rain to join the long queue at the pay phone for his three minutes. He was enjoying himself despite the weather, but was looking forward to coming home on Monday. Julia laughed out loud at the tale he'd recounted of the school principal's tent being washed into the river. While he was sleeping in it. Her laughter softened to a smile. Patrick had phoned twice in three days, despite the obvious inconvenience. This wasn't usual for them and a tingle shot through her at what it might mean.

She was also thrilled to finally have a weekend free. It would have been nicer if Patrick had been around, but it was still a rare joy. She had worked so many weekends recently, including the last two – her own and Leo's – but now, after nineteen days straight, she had a day off. A small whoop of indulgence escaped her.

Her leisure was especially sweet since it was unexpected; she was supposed to have been on call this weekend as well, covering for Sylvie whose turn it was. But at the last minute Sylvie had decided not to go to Melbourne to visit her sick mother. She had a patient she couldn't leave, Vicky Poulos, whose last baby had died a day after birth from a major problem with his heart. Vicky was pregnant again, due next week. Although every test showed the baby to be fine, Vicky and her family had started to panic, fearing that this time as well, something would snatch their precious child away. They were desperate to have the baby safely delivered before anything could go wrong. There being no other time available, Sylvie had agreed to a Saturday induction.

For the past three months, Sylvie had done little weekend cover for the practice. She was supposed to do one in four, more with Leo away, but since her mother had become ill, she'd had no option but to spend nearly every weekend in Melbourne looking after her. Gerda Berger, now widowed, was deteriorating from a rare neurological disorder, but still wished to remain in her own home. The nursing service came weekdays, but on weekends, with her brother based in Hong Kong, there was only Sylvie. But she wasn't going this weekend and had hurriedly arranged a private nurse. Her mother was not pleased. Sylvie, on the other hand, was grateful for the excuse to stay away.

As a result, she was covering her colleagues for the weekend, and would even do their Saturday morning rounds. Rounds were so time-consuming they weren't normally considered part of weekend cover, each doctor usually coming in to do his or her own. Indeed, Julia still planned to go to the hospitals later to check on a few of her more worrying patients, but Sylvie would see them in the meantime. It was the least she could do, she'd said, after the cheerful and generous way Julia had helped her during this difficult time.

Julia's head turned towards the hall. Emma was up. Following the sound of her daughter's tinkling, she slid out from under her newspapers and walked apprehensively towards the music room. 'How's it going, darling?'

Emma turned on her stool and growled. 'It's awful. We're going to be terrible. They're going to boo us off the stage tonight.'

Julia came over and hugged her. 'You have nothing to worry about, darling. I've listened to you for months and I know you'll be wonderful. Even international stars feel nervous before a show.'

Emma looked unconvinced.

'Why don't I make you some breakfast?' Julia suggested.

Emma was not hungry. In fact, she thought she was going to be sick.

It was just nerves, Julia assured her. She should eat something substantial now as she'd be too excited and busy to have anything later. And they couldn't have her fainting in the middle of her debut, could they? 'I'll just go and whip up some of my famous scrambled eggs.'

Emma smiled weakly.

Sylvie was just leaving Royal Eastside Hospital when Julia drove in and pulled up beside her. It was after eleven.

Julia got out of her car. 'Hi, how's it going?'

Sylvie beamed. 'As of forty minutes ago, it's wonderful.'

'Vicky Poulos's baby?'

'Three and a half kilos of healthy, screaming boy.'

Julia could well imagine how the mother of the baby must feel. 'That's fantastic, Sylvie.'

Sylvie's face clouded. 'What are you doing here anyway, Julia? Don't you trust me with your patients?'

Julia baulked. She kept forgetting how insecure Sylvie was. She confided that she'd come for a mopping-up operation after her disasters of the previous week. There were a couple of patients she really needed to check on herself. One was Gina Vella. Had Sylvie seen her yet?

'I've seen everyone, Julia. Just remind me which one she is.'

Sylvie related her night. She'd been up since midnight, and done two deliveries before six. Then she'd done rounds at St Agatha's before returning to Royal Eastside to start Vicky Poulos's induction at seven-thirty. While Vicky was labouring, she'd done the Eastside rounds. Altogether, she had seen twenty-seven patients, not including babies. Not surprisingly, she was unable to remember the details of most of them, but she did know that everyone was well except for one of Stephen's hysterectomies, who was anaemic.

Julia looked at her younger colleague in amazement. 'That's quite a night, Sylvie. I'm glad it wasn't mine.'

She inquired how Sylvie's mum was coping on her own for the weekend. Sylvie frowned. She had remote-accessed her answering machine an hour ago. There were already three messages from her mother. The first was a call at six to remind her daughter how weak she was. The second was just after eight to inform her that the nurse was already five minutes late. And the third was at ten, to complain that the nurse was Filipina and Gerda could hardly understand her.

'She's just missing you, Sylvie.'

'What she's missing is the fact that I'm not there to be bullied,' Sylvie retorted sadly, not really wanting to discuss her mother. She felt miserable when she was with her, and guilty when she was not.

Sylvie was then paged to the emergency department and Julia went to do her rounds. Before departing the hospital, she sought out her younger colleague and found Sylvie busily organising a theatre for a patient of Leo's who was miscarrying.

'Would you like me to do the rest of the weekend?' she asked when Sylvie put down the phone. 'You could still go to Melbourne if you wanted.'

Sylvie was momentarily overwhelmed at Julia's kindness. Joining the practice had been one of the luckiest opportunities of her life. But she declined the offer. Julia deserved a weekend off.

As did she.

'Don't think I'm trying to be nice, Sylvie,' Julia said as she left.

'I'm simply protecting my turf. The eight patients I've just visited all told me that they didn't need to see me today. The wonderful Dr Berger had already fixed them up.'

On the way to Angie's, Julia's mind was drawn to Vicky Poulos and her two sons. One that had died, and now a perfect, healthy boy to push aside the heartbreak. And the guilt. Her car swerved into the next lane as the intense, familiar ache hit. Joseph would have been nine.

Julia eased her car up the steep battleaxe drive. Angie's was a modern house, beautifully positioned at the top of the last hill before the water and designed to take advantage not only of the commanding Pacific views, but also the weather. Mostly glass and timber, it bathed in sunlight all winter and served as a corridor for sea breezes in summer. Even in today's rain, it was cloaked in a quiet, ethereal beauty. Julia pulled up behind Angie's car, realised she'd left her umbrella somewhere at Eastside, and scurried in the pelting rain to the front door.

It was opened by Angie's fifteen-year-old son Ben, whose expectant countenance faltered when he saw it was Julia. He gazed beyond her to make sure there was no one else and then invited her in. 'Mum's in the kitchen.' The information was unnecessary. The aromas that filled the house led the way.

'Is she having a party?' Julia asked. Angie hadn't said anything.

'Nuh. It's just pastries for Richie's school cocktail party tonight.'

It was that and much more, of course. Angie was a joyous cook who never lit just one side of her double oven. As well as a hundred curry puffs and fish cakes for the school, there were three trays of lamingtons for the cricket team's fundraiser and two dozen lemon tartlets for a friend's christening.

'I see I should have picked up a cake on the way over,' said Julia as she kissed Angie and shed her wet coat.

'I did get rather carried away,' Angie conceded with a giggle. 'But it's such perfect cooking weather.'

Angie spent most Saturdays ferrying the boys to cricket and

tennis and surf-club carnivals. But forty hours of deluging rain had put paid to outdoor sport this weekend and freed her to play in her kitchen all day. Twelve-year-old Richie was chatting online, while Ben was once more searching the driveway for the pert but tardy Rachel, who'd said she would bring over what she'd done of her history essay to compare with the few paragraphs he'd managed.

'He's a bit lovelorn,' said Angie humorously. 'But I've told him he can't go to the dance tonight if his history's not finished.'

'Emma's dance?'

'Yes,' admitted Angie, scowling at her mistake; she knew how upset Julia was at not going. 'Is she nervous?'

'Very. But probably no more than I am.' Julia wondered how she would get through the next few hours. It was like her daughter's first day of school all over again. Waving goodbye and leaving her there, hoping she'd be all right.

Angie made coffee and offered Julia a selection of the day's delicacies. The boys had already stuffed themselves silly, she explained, and Geoff was at the university.

'On a Saturday?' asked Julia.

'He had to look something up in the library. A reference book that can't be borrowed or something. He's writing a chapter in someone's textbook. Anyway, hurry up and get the cups or the coffee will go cold,' Angie bossed.

Julia obliged, fetching two old mugs from the top cupboard. It was a ritual they followed every time Julia came. Never good quality, the mugs were now faded, chipped and dated. But the writing on them could still be discerned – 'When we're rich and famous, we'll look back on this and laugh'.

Julia had bought them for Angie during their terrifying first year as residents at the country hospital. 'Well, are we rich and famous yet?' asked Angie as they toasted each other.

'Not so rich that I'm going to buy you new coffee mugs.'

Swallowing her second curry puff and reaching for a lemon tart, Julia quizzed Angie about Adrian de Bruin. She was curious to know how he'd reacted on learning the awful news about little Jacob Newton. Angie hadn't actually seen him, but hospital

91

gossip had it that he was indignant at not having been contacted. He'd been home all night, he insisted; if anyone had bothered to ring, he'd have come immediately.

'Maybe that's right,' defended Julia, thinking how terrible it would be if the hospital claimed they'd tried to get her in an emergency and yet her phone had never rung.

Angie was not so trusting. She'd frantically tried all de Bruin's phones and his paging service herself. As had the switchboard. And this was not an isolated incident. What was just as telling in Angie's eyes was that de Bruin hadn't even bothered to look in on the child before he'd left the hospital for the day. 'He knew the operation hadn't gone well, Julia. And he didn't care.'

Julia nodded grimly and wondered whether Angie had heard any more about Professor Macfarlane's likely return. It looked like it would be late January. The professor was adding some long service leave to his sick leave to give himself a reasonable break.

Angie was suddenly uncertain. 'That's *if* he comes back, of course.'

'Mightn't he?'

'He says he will, but a heart attack followed by three months contemplation could prompt thoughts of retirement in a man of sixty-seven.'

Julia was surprised. 'Did you know he was that old?'

He had to be, of course, but to Angie he had always been ageless. And immortal. She'd expected that he would keep operating for another ten years. At least. Lots of famous surgeons did, especially since they could pick the eyes out of what was available, and keep their energies for the more interesting cases.

Angie wasn't sure what she would do if Professor Macfarlane didn't return to work. It would be difficult to quit; she'd be leaving the hospital and its sick children in the lurch. But if staying meant working with Adrian de Bruin, she might have no choice. The department of surgery performance review was continuing, thank God, but the audit wouldn't be finished until February, and the data not reported until April. Still six months away.

'Unless,' said Angie, the idea occurring to her for the first time. 'Unless someone pushes for the release of interim figures after the first three months.'

'I'm sure we could find someone to do that,' Julia said conspiratorially. 'What about the acting head of surgery while Macfarlane's away? Who's that?'

'Old Daryl Forsyth,' replied Angie. 'Not much help there.'

'Forsyth? Isn't he retired?'

'He should be. He's always been a hopeless surgeon and not getting any better with age. There was talk of not reappointing him at the last triennial accreditation, but he made it known that he wouldn't go without a fight. The hospital administration just caved in.'

Julia glared. 'That's what makes me so mad, Angie. You have known incompetents like Forsyth and de Bruin running amok with patients' lives and *I'm* the one who gets sued.'

Angie gently asked about the lawsuit. Julia glumly gave an outline. Angie was reassuring; she was not an obstetrician, but it seemed to her that Julia's management had been appropriate. Angie anaesthetised children like Brendan regularly, and a lot of the time no one knew why they had the problems they did. It was just a mistake of nature.

Julia was not consoled. Tracey's lawyers had a squad of experts who said they could prove it was *she* who was to blame for poor Brendan's suffering.

Angie didn't know what else to say. What Julia needed was professional medico-legal advice. 'Have you spoken to the Doctors' Defence Organisation yet?'

Julia nodded. She'd had several phone conversations with the malpractice insurer and was going in to see them on Monday. Suddenly her jaw trembled and the tears came quickly. 'I'll die if I have to go to court, Angie.'

Angie reached out and took Julia's hand as they both remembered what it had been like for Tony.

Chapter 10

Madeleine Morgan killed herself with brandy and pills as she'd said she would, and as Damien had. Taking the time during her last hours to make a final entry in her diary, she recorded the story of her crushed dreams; of how her lover had taken her to new heights of ecstasy, touched parts of her she hadn't known existed, made her believe in herself and her future. But then, having drunk of her love and trust, he had lost the taste for her and spat her out, destroying her forever.

While she had written the words for Tony, it was her shattered husband, Greg, who read them, sitting in his bedroom, their bedroom, reading and rereading every note she had made, until the hours became days. At times he would flick his eyes from her small, neat script to the detective's photos of her youthful beauty, before returning once more to the diary, all the while crying for her with tears that seemed unstoppable.

When the final post-mortem report, issued a month after her death, revealed – amid the details of the size of the liver and the weight of the brain – that Madeleine was two months pregnant at the time of her death, Greg Islington could no longer suppress his hatred of Tony Cabrini.

Betrayed by the doctor he himself had chosen, Greg handed the diary and photos to his lawyer, who passed them on to the Health Care Complaints Commission. Tony was subpoenaed to give an account of his role in the death of Madeleine Morgan Islington before the New South Wales Medical Tribunal.

Tony barely gave the Tribunal letter a glance. Nothing could make him feel any worse than he already did. His devastation at Madeleine's death was enormous and he was unable to escape the truth which tormented him night and day. That she had told him she would kill herself, and he had let her do it. Relentlessly, he went over her behaviour that night, replaying her every word and blaming himself for his blindness. The anger that had welled up in him at her subterfuge had distracted him from how desperate she was.

It didn't bother him that the Medical Tribunal wanted to ask him why he had let his patient die. Guilt-stricken and remorseful, he asked himself the same terrible question every day.

Julia had never seen Tony like this before. He'd been preoccupied and distant for months, but now he was unreachable. She heard him muttering to himself in the bathroom when he thought he was alone. She saw him suddenly drop his head into his hands at the dinner table as if something had hit him from behind. She felt him toss restlessly in the early hours of the morning, then give up and go downstairs. And stay there for the rest of the night, sitting in the kitchen in the dark, noiselessly still.

She tried to talk to him but he shut her out. She knew that his patient, Madeleine, the young woman who used to phone, the one he'd said thought she was in love with him, had killed herself a few months before. But that was all she knew. Except what she saw with her eyes.

Over time, Tony let slip about the Tribunal hearing.

'When were you planning to mention it, Tony?' Julia asked, aghast.

'I didn't want to worry you,' he said honestly.

'Your not telling me anything is worrying me more. You don't sleep, you barely eat, you talk to yourself but not to me. Whatever is going on, Tony?'

He turned away from her pleading eyes. 'I'm sorry, Julia, but I just can't discuss it at the moment.'

'Why, Tony?' she called after him. 'What are you hiding?'

He spun around, suddenly angry. 'What sort of question is that?'

'The sort a wife asks a husband when everything about him has changed and he won't tell her why.'

'Maybe if a husband had a wife who trusted him, he'd feel more comfortable telling her what she wanted to know.'

Worn down by everything that had gone wrong in the past two years, Tony was beyond caring. He didn't even bother to contact his malpractice insurer, the Doctors' Defence Organisation, about his impending hearing before the Medical Tribunal. When Julia learned this, she was again shocked at his behaviour. She dialled the phone for him, insisting he talk to them. Just as she insisted on going with him to the initial appointment with the solicitor.

'Dr Cabrini, have you brought the documents the Complaints Commission sent you?' asked the grave, no-nonsense DDO solicitor, Carol Johnston, who had been allocated to the case. Tony had. He retrieved a rather large but still unopened envelope from his briefcase, and handed it to her. Ms Johnston's eyes were wide, but not nearly as wide as Julia's.

'You haven't read them, Tony?' she asked, pre-empting the solicitor. She hadn't known there were documents.

'I couldn't face them,' he replied truthfully.

Ms Johnston opened the envelope and spilt a copy of Madeleine's diary together with the detective's photos onto the desk. In every picture, Madeleine was in Tony's arms, and in one set, she had virtually no clothes on. Over the next few minutes, Julia lost all colour from her face. She'd had no idea that this was what the Tribunal was about. Little wonder Tony hadn't wanted to tell her.

The solicitor took them through the diary first. Tony sat

96

dejectedly, winded at the sight of Madeleine's familiar hand-writing, at words that looked so fresh she might have written them yesterday. Except she'd been dead three months.

The photos struck him badly also. Not their content – he knew the innocence of the encounters. It was the sight of her still alive, her youthfulness and vulnerability captured forever by the photographer's prying lens, that sent a knife into his bowels.

Julia was reeling in her own version of Tony's hell. Only vertigo kept her from running away, the certain knowledge that if she stood, giddiness would propel her to the floor. Suddenly unable to breathe, she asked for a window to be opened. But it didn't help. While she couldn't bear to look at the diary and photos, she noticed that Tony couldn't look away.

Finally the solicitor turned their attention to the pathologist's finding that Madeleine Morgan was pregnant when she died. Tony thought nothing of the information; promiscuity was just another way Madeleine hurt herself. But Julia choked at the news. A baby. The girl was going to have a baby. Had she known this when she killed herself? Had Tony known it too? Oh my God, Julia asked herself in horror, whatever had Tony done?

The information part of the meeting now over, Ms Johnston leaned back in her chair and sighed. Gauging by the body language of Dr Cabrini and his poor, shocked wife, the high-profile case she had been given was starting to look a lot more complicated. 'Well, Dr Cabrini, how much of this is true?' she asked, her voice suggesting she thought most of it was.

Julia studied her hands in voiceless misery, waiting to hear her husband's explanation. But Tony choked on his words of denial.

He *was* guilty, after all. Not of the charges laid against him. But guilty of everything else. Of betraying Madeleine and Greg's faith in him. Of being so distracted by his personal problems with Julia that he hadn't appreciated the extent of Madeleine's attachment to him. Of taking too long to transfer her care, at least partly because she was one of his favourite patients. Of making decisions based on emotion rather than clinical judgement, hoping she'd soon come good. Of not putting her into hospital when it was obvious she was out of control. And most terrible of all, he was guilty of walking away after she'd warned him she was going to kill herself.

Julia and Tony did not speak for days after the DDO meeting. Tony was largely oblivious to his wife's feelings, cast adrift as he was on his own tortured raft. After three months of trying to cope with Madeleine's death, having his face now slammed up against words and pictures from a time when she was still alive crushed what tiny shred of peace he'd been starting to find. And sucked him back into his vortex of guilt.

He couldn't believe he hadn't seen it all coming. The clues now leapt out to jeer at him. But, at the time, they had passed him right by.

Julia slid into her own deep pool of misery. Crushed by what she'd witnessed, she also felt such a fool. Before the meeting with the DDO solicitor, she'd naively believed the Medical Tribunal hearing to be an almost routine matter of reviewing the responsibility Tony owed a patient to minimise the risk of suicide. Especially such a prominent patient. Now she laughed bitterly. How could she have been so stupid? The Tribunal hearing was not about Tony *missing* the fact that his patient was likely to kill herself. It was that he'd *driven* her to it.

Julia collapsed under the weight of such thoughts, torn between what her eyes saw and her ears heard. Her mind was filled with a husband who was the walking personification of guilt, an image now corroborated by the diary and photos, which screamed that he had indeed done this terrible thing. And against all this visual evidence, she only heard Tony's faint denial.

Unable to remain silent any longer, she confronted him. 'Where is the truth in all this, Tony?' she entreated, desperate for words that would lift the leaden weight from her heart.

He was very cold. 'I've told you the truth, Julia. I did not have a sexual relationship with Madeleine Morgan. Her diary is an invention and the photos I've already explained. A number of times.'

'If none of it's true, why are you so upset? I've never seen you

98

like this before, not even when . . .' Julia's painful memories trailed off. She tried again. 'A girl with a psychiatric history kills herself. It's not that unusual, is it? Why can't you get over it?'

His anger ripped her open. 'You try getting over it, Julia. You try getting over that someone warned you that she was going to kill herself, and you didn't take it seriously and then she did it. And you weren't someone peripheral to her wellbeing. You were the one responsible for it, for God's sake. If you can get over that, Julia, then you're more together than you've pretended to be for the past two years.'

Julia flinched at his hard words. This whole business was changing Tony so quickly, he would soon be someone she no longer recognised. But she would not leave it be. Too much was at stake. 'So why did you go alone to her house that last evening, Tony?' It was a stumbling block Julia kept coming back to. The Tony she knew would never have made such a fundamental error. Not if his explanation was as innocent as he claimed.

Tony was exasperated. 'I told you, Julia. She said she was going to kill herself.'

'All the more reason not to go alone,' she persisted, a sense of hopelessness flooding over her. 'Why didn't you call an ambulance on the way? Or after you got there? Or one of your colleagues to come and join you?'

'I didn't think,' was all he could offer.

It wasn't enough for Julia.

They saw Carol Johnston twice more. On neither occasion had Tony written the report she needed to prepare his defence – the report about his patient, her therapy, her death, and his relationship with her.

The solicitor was becoming angry. 'I think that you fail to realise the seriousness of the allegations against you, Dr Cabrini. I want you to know that in the past twelve months, the Medical Board has struck off ten doctors in New South Wales as a result of adverse Tribunal findings. Many of them for life. Think about that. You're only forty. Think what it will be like not being able to practise as a psychiatrist – indeed, as any sort of doctor – ever again. Because that's what looks like happening.'

Once at home, Julia couldn't keep her frustration to herself any longer. If he was innocent, as he claimed, why hadn't he written the report? 'Do you want to be deregistered?'

Tony shook his head pathetically. He simply couldn't bring himself to do it, to look at Madeleine's file, to write her name, to hear her voice as he went over his notes. He couldn't bear to see where he might have dealt with her differently and she might still be alive.

Alerted by the portent in his words, Julia carefully asked in what way he might have dealt with her differently. But Tony gave the same explanation he always gave. He should never have left her alone that night. And he should have handed over her care months before.

'But you said you tried to hand her over, Tony,' insisted Julia, repeating what he'd told her. 'And all she did was disappear. She didn't have any intention of seeing someone else. You did what you could. Didn't you?'

Julia's eyes pleaded for confirmation, but Tony no longer saw her. His own anguish curtained his vision, blinding him to hers. He simply shook his head in defeat. 'It was . . . too late.'

The pressure mounted on Tony to provide a written response, but still he couldn't do it. Julia watched with growing pessimism; these were not the actions of an innocent man. Desperate, she finally wrote the report for him, using snippets of information he'd grudgingly shared with her. He rejected nearly all of it.

'I can't say these things about Bernie Morgan, Julia.' He pointed to the first five pages she had written. 'The Medical Tribunal is a public court. Not that he doesn't deserve it, the bastard, but Madeleine doesn't. I can't do it to her.'

'But why not, Tony?' Julia asked, drenched with doubt about the stranger before her. 'It's the truth, isn't it?'

'It's because it's the truth that I can't. Don't you see? She told me all those things in confidence. She made me promise that I would never tell anyone.'

Tony had felt a failure as a husband almost since Joseph had died. And he'd felt a failure as a psychiatrist for the last three months at least. Well, he wasn't going to fail in this too. He'd made Madeleine a promise he would never tell anyone what she'd told him in private. And he wasn't going to let her down a second time.

'She's dead, Tony.' Julia couldn't fathom his misguided loyalties.

'It doesn't matter. I promised her.'

'She's dead,' Julia repeated.

'So? Don't you have some private things you'd rather were still private after your death?'

Julia couldn't take it much longer, watching Tony do nothing to defend himself against the Tribunal charges, tearing up the report she'd written, sitting around wasting and pining for that poor girl. In her eyes, there could be only one explanation: he had done what they claimed.

They had a final confrontation. She begged him to tell her the truth, the missing bits of the story that would account for his behaviour. Because whatever it was, she had made a decision to support him.

'Ha!' Tony laughed in her face. 'What a joke that is. You bleed me to death over one tiny mistake with Sybilla. And now you turn around and talk about supporting me in something infinitely worse. Just listen to yourself, Julia.'

She winced at the truth in his allegation and apologised. She was sorry about her behaviour after Sybilla, but she'd been so shattered she couldn't help it. She was stronger now. 'And I want to believe in you, Tony.'

'Then why not just do it? Make a decision to believe in me, Julia.'

She was solemn; he'd made it very hard. There were only two choices available to her, she explained, looking into the eyes she'd always loved. 'Either I believe you had an affair with Madeleine Morgan as the Tribunal claims. Or I believe that you, a trained professional, one of the most intelligent, insightful people I know, made every mistake in the psychiatrists' handbook.'

'And which do you choose?'

'I find it hard to believe you'd make all those mistakes.' Her voice was small as she verbalised it for the first time.

He found it difficult too. That was what was killing him. 'I'm afraid my eye wasn't on the ball.'

'Where was it, Tony?' Her tone was provocative.

'For God's sake, Julia,' he shouted. 'Where do you think it was? On you! My every waking moment has been focused on you for two years. First when Joseph died. Then when you fell apart. Then, after Sybilla, when you became obsessed with my every movement. All day at work I tried to think how to make you feel better. I busted my gut to get home on time and when I got here I couldn't even use the phone to sort a few things out because you were paranoid about that too. Nothing I did was free of threat to you, nothing I said free from double meaning in your eyes. It's been harrowing, Julia, absolutely harrowing. And into the most distracted, distressing time of my life walked Madeleine Morgan.'

'So now you want me to take the blame for your professional as well as your personal mistakes, do you, Tony?' Julia was livid. 'Well, I won't.'

'Don't worry, Julia. I don't expect you to take responsibility for anything at all.'

The Medical Tribunal inquiry into the professional misconduct of Dr Tony Cabrini with respect to the death of 'travel empire heiress' Madeleine Morgan ran for over a week. It was a public hearing, the Tribunal made up of a district court judge, a psychiatrist, a general practitioner, and a lay person. The Health Care Complaints Commission, prosecuting the charges before the Tribunal, was represented by a solicitor and a barrister. Tony likewise had Carol Johnston and a barrister retained by the DDO.

The charges against Dr Cabrini were listed for everyone to

see. It was one of the biggest news stories of the year, and the allocated courtroom was so crowded with media from around the country and hundreds of curious members of the public that, on the first day, the hearing was moved to a vastly bigger court. The story sold newspapers like nothing had since Fergie's toe-sucking, the sub-editors outdoing each other with their headlines. It really didn't matter what Dr Cabrini was going to say. The journalists knew about the diary and had seen the photos. The doctor was guilty.

Even before the trial started, interest was phenomenal. There was an eight-page newspaper supplement the weekend before which brought together all of the famous medical sex scandals of the century, lending credibility to the public's growing belief that some psychiatrists saw sex with their patients as an integral part of the overall course of therapy. On the first day of the hearing, the *Sydney Morning Herald* led with 'The Heiress and The Psychiatrist. I Did Nothing Wrong', while the *Daily Telegraph* went with 'Shrink to Sink in Stink?'

The trial opened with the prosecution case. Their first witnesses were Greg Islington and his private detective. Madeleine's diary and the detective's photographs were tendered in evidence. Tony's appointment schedule was used to show how often he had seen the deceased woman. 'She Was Always Here – Psychiatrist's Secretary', reported the *Telegraph*.

The prosecution then called two well-known psychiatrists as expert witnesses. Both were asked whether it was common for a psychiatrist to be attracted to a patient. Both admitted that it was. Acting on that attraction was, however, grounds for immediate disqualification from practice. This was so even if the attraction was reciprocated, or indeed initiated, by the patient. The relationship between psychiatrist and patient was deemed to be too profoundly unequal, and the potential harm to the patient too significant, to allow it. All psychiatrists knew this.

The experts were asked if any aspects of Dr Cabrini's management of the dead woman were suboptimal. Both said that the frequency of Madeleine's visits should have been reduced in the second year. If she was making such poor progress that they couldn't be, then she should have been transferred to another therapist.

Both psychiatrists had looked at Tony's notes, made after each visit, and thought that they were brief and inadequate, often only a couple of words. His records fell below acceptable standards.

The experts also said that it was highly unusual for a psychiatrist to visit a patient alone at home, especially at night. In doing this Dr Cabrini demonstrated very poor clinical judgement. Or worse.

By the time Tony's defence began there was no doubt in anyone's mind that he was guilty of all charges. His barrister took him through his testimony, what there was of it. Tony stonily maintained that all of the charges were false. He had never behaved improperly towards Madeleine Morgan. In particular, he had never had a sexual relationship with her. But he offered nothing to support his claims.

The newspapers had a field day, turning his every explanation about the diary and the photographs and the pregnancy into a lurid headline.

'She Fell into My Arms – Psychiatrist. More Photos Inside'.

'The Baby Wasn't Mine – Psychiatrist'.

'When I Left Her, She Was Fine – Psychiatrist'.

'She Was Prone to Flights of Fantasy – Psychiatrist'.

Still Tony offered nothing about Madeleine's background, her fixation with older men, her infatuation with him, her attempt to lure him to her house for the purposes of seduction, her fantasy stories, her refusal to see another therapist.

The onus was on them, he said obdurately. Let them *prove* he had done something wrong; they wouldn't be able to. And he wasn't going to compound further his pitiful failure to protect Madeleine by exposing the sordid details of her brief, sorry life. He saw what the newspapers were doing to him; he knew what they would do to her. And he wasn't going to let it happen.

Although a sizeable crowd of journalists and voyeurs waited outside, the house itself was empty when Tony went home in the second week of his trial. Emma had been sent to her grandfather in Wollongong with instructions for her to hear as little as possible, while Julia was staying in a small local hotel.

She had accompanied Tony on the first day of the hearing to lend him support, but found she couldn't stay. It was like a needle forced under her fingernail, watching him insist on protecting his dead patient's secrets, seemingly at all costs. She'd moved out of their home that evening.

Despite her subsequent absence, the footage from the first day had put her on the television and in the newspapers daily since, and not as Mrs Cabrini – rather as the far more exciting 'prominent eastern suburbs gynaecologist, Dr Julia Kent'. More than a few patients cancelled their appointments. Much worse, some of the hospital staff turned away from her as well. Julia knew what they were saying. That it was unsurprising her husband sought solace elsewhere given the hours she worked. If she had taken care of his needs, he mightn't have strayed. Although, at thirty-five, she probably couldn't compete with a looker like Madeleine Morgan anyway.

Not that any of this would have mattered to her in the slightest if only she could have believed her husband's denials.

Tony sat amid the detritus of his half-eaten take-away in his silent, dark kitchen. He had fleetingly considered driving somewhere else to eat it, but knew that he might as well come home; the small, intrusive entourage of press photographers would follow him wherever he went. At least here in his kitchen they couldn't see him. Not with the lights out.

Some time during the hellish evening, there was a soft tap on the back door. He looked up, hoping it was Julia. She'd been gone just a week but he was missing her badly. And he needed to apologise for the horrible things he'd said to her recently. And for what he was putting her through. But it wasn't Julia at the door, it was Angie, carrying a container of her famous lamb curry. She had parked in the next street and ducked in through his neighbour's yard and over the back fence. He put his finger to his lips as she entered, went into the lounge room which faced the street, closed the curtains, and turned the television on rather loudly. He then shut the door and returned to the kitchen.

'Thanks for coming over, Angie.' He gave her a grateful hug. 'And for the curry. I need some decent food.' He indicated his unsatisfactory repast.

'I thought you could probably do with something nice. And some company. Geoff said to say hello.' Angie opened the bottle of wine she had brought, filled two glasses and took one over to him. 'How are you going?'

'Not good,' he answered grimly.

Angie had not been able to get to court because of work, but had read about it all in the papers and had come to the conclusion that things looked very bad. Certainly that was what everyone was saying.

'Have you seen Julia?' he asked hopefully.

Angie had seen her a couple of times briefly, but Julia had cancelled most of the week. And she was having next week off as well. 'She's having a hard time too, Tony.'

He nodded, aching for her.

Angie sat beside him. 'What are you going to do?'

'What do you mean?'

'You can't leave things like this.' She knew about the information he was concealing. 'Don't you think your judgement's slipped a bit? After the baby, and Julia's depression?'

Reluctantly, he agreed. He had completely underestimated the damage the trial could inflict, foolishly holding to the belief that, since he hadn't done anything wrong, he couldn't go down. But he was being crucified, inside the courtroom and out. He looked at Angie sadly. 'I don't know how to do it, to defend my reputation without damaging Madeleine's.'

'Perhaps there's a way, Tony.'

The following morning Angie accompanied Tony to the offices of the DDO for an urgently scheduled meeting with Carol Johnston and the barrister. The lawyers were not surprised to see the defendant; things were going badly for him. They were, however, surprised at what he had to say.

The Medical Tribunal inquiry into Dr Tony Cabrini's role in

the death of Madeleine Morgan was closed permanently to the public from that morning. The Tribunal members, having been apprised of the highly sensitive nature of the material to be produced, readily agreed to this unusual request. Indeed, Tony insisted that he would only provide the evidence if the session was in camera. And everyone present was sworn never to reveal the information disclosed. Greg Islington and Jeremy Morgan were present. Bernie chose not to be.

Tony then produced the hours of tapes which had been made during his consultations with Madeleine Morgan, together with the transcripts which he had typed from them as his true records of her care. These clearly revealed what she and her brother had suffered at the hands of Bernie Morgan, how damaged and insecure and hungry for love she was, how she gravitated to unsatisfactory relationships with older men, and how she used the writing of fantasy stories as an escape from her pain. Tony supplied one of her stories, admitting he had others but wanted to protect her privacy as far as possible. Finally, the tapes showed how she'd vigorously repudiated any attempt on Tony's part to reduce her visits and that, when she'd repeatedly declared her love for him, he had deflected her. Tony acknowledged that she was attempting to seduce him on her last night, and that he'd been so angry with her he had failed to recognise her desperation.

'So why didn't you give us these tapes before, Dr Cabrini?' asked the floridly indignant Tribunal judge. 'All relevant material was subpoenaed. Do you think we like wasting our time?'

'I'm sorry, Your Honour,' was all Tony managed, overtaken by distress at the thought of betraying Madeleine's confidences even in this limited forum.

It took weeks, of course, for the tapes to be verified, but the final result was that all of the original charges against Tony Cabrini were dropped. A new charge was laid. That of deliberately withholding evidence from a Medical Tribunal. For that he was disqualified from practice for twelve months. The case was closed and all parties bound by confidentiality agreements.

From being on the front page of the papers every day, on the news every night, and the major topic of every Sydney conversation for a fortnight, suddenly the story was gone. The assembled media were furious about confidentiality being requested by Dr Cabrini at this late stage in the proceedings, and they filled the space with speculation from commentators about what the closed Tribunal might be hearing.

Julia came to see Tony. He looked at her eagerly, expecting her approval of his decision and her relief at his vindication by the Tribunal. Instead, she was ropeable.

'You can't honestly believe that allegations in public and defence in private is a *good* outcome?' It was the worst possible scenario: besmirched but not redeemed. As if he'd felt he deserved to be punished. 'Why didn't you tell me about those tapes, Tony?' Her anger flashed wildly. 'How could you put me through this so needlessly? Not just the trial, but the months of misery before it? How could you do it to Emma?'

Tony stammered inadequately, only now realising the extent of the damage.

Julia was bitter. 'I suppose it was payback for what I've put you through over the past two years.'

'Don't be ridiculous.'

'Ridiculous? You've made the point often enough.' She'd dwelt at length on his recent words.

Her accusation stung him; she had every right to be upset. He hadn't meant the things he'd said; they were unfair, spoken at a time of extreme stress, and he regretted them. 'I'm so sorry.'

Her rage was not appeased. She was sorry too, but she no longer knew who he was. Who they were. The trust needed to continue their marriage was gone.

Chapter 11

More tears than she thought she possessed rolled down Julia's cheeks as she drove home after her lunch with Angie, rivulets of anguish about her future swelling the torrent of sorrow for her past. How would she ever survive another court case?

It was seven years since the cluster bomb of Tony's trial had blown a thousand holes in her life, but pieces of shrapnel still worked their way to the surface, festering and breaking through her skin. It was only very recently, the last twelve months or so, that people had actually stopped asking about her ex-husband and his famous patient, quizzing her about what *really* happened, inquiring what Tony was up to now. And offering her the benefit of their unsolicited opinions. As if she was a disinterested party.

Dating had been even worse.

Venturing fearfully out of her bunker a few years after her divorce, it had taken only a handful of miserable evenings for her to realise that her prospective partners were far more interested in Tony and Madeleine than they were in her. She'd been particularly crushed by Mark Reynolds, an accountant she'd gone out with for several months. He seemed attentive and thoughtful and Julia, wary at first, was slowly warming to him. Until the evening she'd overheard him talking about her on the phone to his mate, laughing uproariously at how frigid she was, and offering his insights into why her husband had cheated on her in such a spectacular fashion.

Julia sniffled loudly into her tissue at the mortifying recollection which, while the worst, had been one of many. Only in the past year had she noticed the collective interest in the case diminishing, finally displaced by new dramas about other poor sods. Slowly, she was being allowed to go back to being just Julia Kent again. And what had happened? Tracey Bloody Edwards had decided to sue her. And she faced the prospect of being blown apart once more.

While the heavens continued to weep, her private downpour had spent itself by the time she arrived home. There was a note on the hall-stand from Emma; she'd gone to Jade's for the final practice before tonight. Julia looked at her watch and felt the goose-pimples rise. When she phoned, Emma was nervous and discouraged. Things were not going well. They couldn't agree on the order of songs, Lisa had a headache, Petra's finger was sore, and Jade seemed to be spending a lot of time in the bathroom.

'But you're all right, darling?'

'I thought I'd wait until they pulled themselves together before I had my collapse.'

'Everything's going to be fine, I'm sure of it. Would you like me to pick you up afterwards?'

Emma hesitated. 'Actually, Mum, I've decided to stay the night at Jade's. By the time the dance finishes and we pack up our gear, it'll be after midnight.'

'And by the time you stop talking about it, the sun will be coming up,' Julia predicted. 'Well, good luck, darling. I'll be thinking of you.'

As she waited for the kettle to boil, Julia remembered her own mother. Helen Kent had died a decade ago when Emma was nearly eight. A kind, exuberant woman, Julia missed her enormously, especially now, as her own daughter reached adulthood. An only child, Julia had spent hours in her mother's good-humoured company, visiting the sick in the neighbourhood, laughing over card games at Mrs Graham's, scouring the nurseries for new plants for the garden. It had come to an abrupt end when, at the age Emma was now, Julia moved to Sydney to study and later to work. She'd always intended returning to Wollongong permanently when she qualified. With shame and sadness she recalled making such a promise to her mother.

But by the time she became a consultant, there were no jobs readily available in Wollongong. Not that she'd tried hard to find one. Tony's preference was for Sydney, although he would have gone anywhere she'd asked. It was she, caught up in the thrill of her career and wanting to work with Stephen and Angie, who hadn't thought it mattered. Who'd said that Wollongong was just an hour down the coast. Who'd assumed that there was all the time in the world, that Mum and Dad would be there for ages. And yet, a year later, her mother had died suddenly, suffering a stroke a few months short of sixty.

As Julia poured the boiling water over her teabag, out of nowhere conscious one word sprang unbidden into her mind. Dad. She was doing the same with him as she'd done with her mother, taking him for granted, assuming he would always be there. Feverishly, she tried to work out the last time she'd seen him. It must have been the June long weekend when he'd come up for the Queen's Birthday Racing Carnival. She counted the months on her fingers. Four, nearly five months. It couldn't be. But it was.

She reached for the phone almost frantically and dialled. 'Dad, it's me.'

'Princess, how are you?' She could hear the Saturday afternoon sports on the TV in the background.

'Fine. I wondered what you were up to this evening.'

'Irene and I have tickets for the dance at the club,' he replied, referring to a local woman he'd occasionally gone out with since the death of Julia's mother. 'Why, do you need me for something?'

'Nothing, Dad, just checking that you're still kicking up your heels.'

'Only on Saturdays, Julia. I'd have to be reshod if it was more than that.'

There followed a conversation about his flame trees which were just coming into bloom, Emma's exams and her band, Julia's work, and Tony. For some inexplicable and irritating reason, her father always asked about Tony. It was as if they had never been divorced.

'I'm sure he's fine, Dad, but I don't see him. He's in Brisbane.'

'Well, if you do see him, say hello from old George.'

'I will, Dad. Anyway, I won't keep you. You've got things to do.'

'I'm glad you rang, princess.' He had turned the TV down, and was serious now. 'If you'd like to come down sometime, Julia, it would be good to see you.'

'I've had to work a lot of weekends recently, Dad, but I might have one off soon. We could catch up then.'

'I would like that, Julia.'

'I'll see what I can do.'

''Bye, princess. Thanks for calling.'

Julia drank her tea, looking again at the note Emma had left her. They were more pen-pals than family at the moment, really, two busy adults sharing a house. It wasn't much fun when your only child hardly needed you any more. Did Dad feel like that too? She was back on the phone in minutes. 'Dad, it's me again. Could I come and stay tonight?'

'Of course, princess. It would be nice to see you.' He paused. 'Is there a problem?'

'I'm just missing you, Dad. I've got the rest of the weekend off and Emma's busy, so it seems a good time to come down and visit. I want you and Irene to still go to the dance, but if I leave now, I'll be there long before you go out, and then we can catch up a bit more in the morning. We could all go out for breakfast.'

'Irene won't be here for breakfast, Julia.'

'No?'

'It's not that sort of relationship. We just go to the dances.'

112

'Okay, you and I can go out for breakfast then. How about that?'

'I cook a pretty mean breakfast myself, Julia.'

Julia turned the bend coming down the highway into Wollongong and absorbed the breathtaking vista of the ocean as it suddenly filled her vision. It still always took her by surprise. Coming home. The area where she'd grown up was changing only slowly. There were a few larger modern brick dwellings but mostly the small old fibro cottages remained. A handful of the original neighbours were still there as well. She thought she recognised old Mr Stubbs walking to the corner shop, while Gracie Marsden was calling for her cat as she always did in the afternoon. She pulled up outside her father's house, the home of her childhood, a pale green two-bedroom fibro original. He had built a sunroom out the back when Julia was a teenager, so that she'd have somewhere to entertain her friends, and so that her mother could look out on her garden as she drank her tea.

The garden was the most remarkable thing about the place. Julia's mother had always been green-thumbed, and the profusion of colours and fragrances she cultivated formed an inextricable part of Julia's childhood memories. Her father, George, had taken little active interest, although he clearly delighted in the effect. After Helen died, however, he couldn't bear to see her decades of joyful work laid to waste, nor her membership of the garden club lapse. She'd been secretary of the club for many years, its circulars always piled high on the kitchen table, competing for space with Julia's homework. And so he became a gardener himself and found that he loved it. The planning, the planting, the nurturing, the pruning, the seasons of his flowers now mapped out his life. Just as much as the racing and football calendars. It had been an unexpected source of pleasure and friendship for one who was slightly withdrawn.

George had obviously been looking out for Julia and was at her car immediately she pulled up, his umbrella open in the light rain. 'Hello, princess. How are you?' he asked as he kissed her, his Yorkshire accent still thick after all these years.

'I'm fine, Dad. It's great to see you.'

'And I'm glad you could come.' He carried her bag as they took the path that led around to the back of the house.

'Dad, the garden's wonderful,' Julia exclaimed in delight. 'Mum would be so pleased.'

If her father hadn't been up to Sydney since June, she realised with a shock that it must be at least two years since she'd been here. She thought that couldn't be right. But her father confirmed it when she praised the climber which luxuriated over the lattice behind which he hid his garbage bin. 'I planted the star jasmine shortly after you were here last time. Two years ago.'

'It's grown well, hasn't it? It looks fabulous, and it really tidies up that corner of the yard.' Julia felt ashamed.

She was momentarily stunned to see that the swings which her father had built for her as a child, and which Emma also had loved, were gone, replaced by a bed of gardenias. She didn't comment. He was nothing if not practical, and fragrant white flowers were surely more pleasant than unused rusty children's toys. Removing the swings would have pained him nevertheless.

The rain became heavier and he shepherded her into the kitchen through the back door. The warmth from the oven and the smell of baking greeted her. 'Cooking, Dad?'

'I've just finished a batch of scones, and now the roast is on for dinner.'

'Who's coming?'

'You.'

Julia looked to see if he was joking. He wasn't.

'Oh, Dad, you didn't have to go to all this trouble. I could have taken us out to dinner.'

'That's the thing with you young people, wanting to go out to dinner all the time, spending five times what it costs to eat at home. For what? To be robbed, that's what.'

Julia laughed. He hadn't been born in 1929 for nothing. 'You're right of course, and it smells great. I haven't had a baked dinner since I don't know when.'

'Since the last time you were here probably.'

114

Julia looked around the house, comforted that inside, at least, there were no noticeable changes, nothing to further emphasise the years since she'd visited.

As the dinner neared readiness, her father asked her to set the table for the two of them.

'Is Irene coming over after dinner, or will you be picking her up?'

'Neither. I'm not going to the dance.'

'What?'

'I didn't really want to go in the first place, but couldn't easily get out of it. But when you were coming I had the perfect excuse.'

'You can't tell a woman just hours before a dance that she doesn't have a partner, Dad. She probably bought a new dress.'

'The club has these dances once a month, Julia. She can wear it to the next one. She understands.'

The leg of lamb was served with mint sauce, gravy, and five vegetables – four more than Julia would eat some weeks. She hugged him in delight. 'Thanks, Dad. It smells wonderful.'

Neither of them had finished eating, but at seven-fifteen her father briefly excused himself to duck into the sitting room off the kitchen. He wanted to catch the interstate horse racing results, the high tide information and the weather forecast at the end of the television news. Julia smiled to herself. They were the important determinants of his existence.

They cleaned up the kitchen together which, given the number of baking dishes and pots he had used, took some time. Afterwards they settled in the sitting room with their cups of tea. Her father brought out a fruit cake, and proceeded to cut some large slices.

'Do you mind if I skip the cake for now?' Julia groaned slightly. She'd had three scones soon after arriving, and then the roast.

He stopped slicing. 'On another one of those diets, are you, princess?'

'No, Dad, I'm just full. Most people would be after what I've eaten.'

'Do you mind if I have some?' Her father had always eaten what he liked with none of it showing on his spare frame.

'Why would I?' she laughed.

They spoke about Emma for a while. Her father knew all about his granddaughter's band and its inaugural performance tonight. Playing down her disappointment, Julia explained that parents were not invited.

'Nor grandparents, I suppose?' he asked cheekily.

'You might actually be acceptable, Dad. They'd probably think you were cool.' She shot an anxious glance at the clock. It was eight-thirty, nearly time. As the butterflies made a circuit of her stomach, Julia silently wished the girls good luck.

In the struggling dawn of the drizzly new day, Julia and her father climbed the low rocks to his favourite fishing spot just south of the city. Settling down for the inevitable wait, George asked about her job. He thought she worked too hard, but realised she loved it, and had long given up suggesting she try to cut down her hours.

Julia fleetingly considered telling him about her lawsuit but decided against it; he was in no position to give useful advice, and it would just upset him. He'd seen how she suffered last time. Instead, she entertained him with the latest tales of Stacey and Stephen's renovations. An hour or so later it started to rain in earnest and they packed up. Her father had caught three size-able bream, and Julia some seaweed. They ate his offerings for a late breakfast.

By early afternoon Julia had to leave.

'I'm really glad you came, princess.'

'I'm glad too, Dad. Thanks for a fantastic dinner and a sensational breakfast.'

'What? You didn't like the scones?'

'Them too,' she giggled, wondering if she'd ever be able to do up the top button on her jeans again.

She pulled out of his street, tooting and waving. Less than twenty-four hours in her father's house had put her life in

116

perspective. She felt so happy winding her way up the highway to Sydney that when the sun put in an appearance in the mid-afternoon, she felt it had come out just for her.

'How was last night?' Julia asked Emma very casually. She had been dying to know all day, but Emma was still not home when she got back from Wollongong, and she'd not wanted to ring her at Jade's. By the time her daughter arrived to shower and change a little later, Julia had ducked to the shops to get the week's provisions, collect her dry-cleaning and pick up something nice for dinner. Then, by the time she returned, Emma had once again gone out. She would be back at seven, according to her note, which also said 'It was fantastic, Mum', which was promising.

The two of them were now sitting comfortably on the back verandah looking down to the beach as the sun cast lengthening shadows across the backyard. Their vision took in happy bathers packing up at the end of an unexpectedly sunny Sunday afternoon, and hopeful board riders, still in the water, trusting another great wave would come their way before they too called it a day.

Julia opened a bottle of wine while Emma flipped through the pages of the new *Rolling Stone* magazine. They were to have a stir-fry of beef and noodles shortly, but for now were content just to sit and relax. Julia waited for the answer to her question.

'They seemed to like our new song,' replied Emma, not looking up, tentative even with her own mother about an event so important. 'We played it three times.' She smiled, finally turning to face Julia. 'It was great,' she concluded.

'Were you nervous?' asked Julia.

She'd had diarrhoea all afternoon, Emma confessed, but once they'd started playing, she relaxed and enjoyed herself. They had forty-five minutes at the start of the night and played a few covers first to warm up. Then they played their song, introducing it as their first completed composition. The response had been great, so they played it again right away and it had been even better the second time. They followed it with another couple of

117

covers, before finishing with 'He Didn't Call' again. And then it was over, and the other bands had their go. Emma was aglow with the memory of it all.

'One of the other bands was Jason McKenzie's.'

'Jason McKenzie?'

'One of the McKenzie boys from down the road, next to Mrs Miller.'

Julia nodded with vague recollection.

'His band. They were pretty good too, but they only do covers so far, although he says he's writing a new song. He might come over later this week to show me,' Emma added noncommittally, but with a touch of colour in her cheeks.

There was further good news. Danny, who'd organised the gig, thought that he might have a spot for them at another dance next weekend, a local school's Year Ten formal. One of the bands had pulled out and they were looking for someone who'd play for free. 'And because it's a boys' school, he thinks they'll go for an all-girl band.' Emma pulled a comical face.

Julia was tickled pink. 'It sounds like everyone thought you were terrific, darling. I just wish I could have been there.'

Emma looked uncomfortable. 'Sorry.'

Her mother understood; it had been the same when she was seventeen. But it would have been great to have been present for the first real gig, seeing them up on a stage, taking in the cheering crowd, hearing the applause. It was always going to be different from watching them in Jade's garage. 'I think I was nearly as excited as you, Em. And I'm sure the other parents felt the same.'

Julia didn't know, and her daughter wasn't about to tell her, that the other parents had in the end refused to stay away. Jade's dad said that he'd put up with the noise in his garage and parked his car on the lawn for so many months that he'd earned the right to be there, whilst Petra's parents said that they were going along to protect their capital investment. Petra thought that they meant the guitar they'd helped her buy, but her brother told her that they really meant Petra herself. And Lisa's mother was a teacher at one of the local schools and went as a supervisor. Only Julia hadn't been there.

'So, how was Grandpa?' asked Emma, desperate for a change of subject as they went inside to prepare their meal.

'He was great. Why don't you call him and tell him all about the dance before we eat?'

As Emma went to pick up the handset, the phone rang, and she squealed. She then handed it over to her mother; it was Patrick.

'How's it all going?' Julia asked, blushing.

'You can imagine,' Patrick laughed. 'The two hottest days of the year, followed by the three wettest. Not ideal camping weather. What about you?'

She thought about Gina Vella and Tracey Edwards. 'I've had it easy in comparison.'

They chatted for a few minutes before he had to go. The queue for the phone was long. 'I'll call you tomorrow when we get back. Maybe we could catch up in the evening?'

'That would be lovely. Bye.'

Emma looked at her meaningfully. 'He's rung a lot this week, hasn't he?'

'I can't really recall,' replied Julia lightly.

She could have recited every word he'd said.

Chapter 12

Before heading into the city for her meeting with the DDO, Julia nicked into the surgery to see Leo, back this morning from his holiday. Following the laughter to his office, she found her cheery colleague regaling the staff with his travel tales. He hugged her warmly. 'How are you, Julia?'

Julia nearly cried, she was so pleased to see him. 'I was fine anyway, Leo, but I'm definitely much better now that you're back.'

The secretaries reluctantly dispersed to their work and Leo asked about Emma. Julia filled him in on the big gig. She then glanced at her watch. 'And right now she's picking up her pen for her last ever school examination.'

'Little Emma all grown up,' Leo chuckled fondly. His own three children were now in their early thirties. 'I can still remember when you first came back from London and you used to bring her on Saturday rounds.'

'And she would go from patient to patient asking for a chocolate,' Julia recalled with a giggle.

'Saying that Mummy wouldn't make them better if they didn't give her one.'

Still laughing, Julia asked how Sandra had enjoyed the trip.

'She had a fantastic time, quite wore herself out. Says she needs another holiday to recover from it all and wants to know where I'm taking her.'

Julia could hear her friend's cheeky gibe and was pleased; no one deserved a treat more than they did. Glancing at Leo's clock, she gathered her handbag and made ready to leave for the DDO.

Leo watched her move towards the door. 'You're not in the surgery this morning, Julia?'

'I've got a few little errands to run,' she said obliquely. She'd told only Marcia and Angie about her lawsuit; now was not the time to bother Leo with her sorry predicament. Although she could have done with the good wishes she knew he'd offer. She assured him she'd be back after lunch to hear all about his holiday.

'If that's what you really want,' he cautioned, eyes glinting, 'I'll make sure Sandra brings in the first five hundred photos.'

On her way to the DDO meeting Julia's mind turned to Patrick as it had countless times in the last few days. Emma was right, he had rung a lot. It was enough to get a girl's hopes up. But she was not a girl, and she was not going to read anything into it. Her mature self-control, however, didn't extend to not counting the hours until she saw him again. She was down to ten and a half.

She stole a surreptitious peek around the reception area of the DDO office. She had been here before, of course. With Tony. The colour scheme was perhaps different, and she was aware they'd expanded to take over the floor above as well, but otherwise it was much the same as it had been seven years ago. She knew from when she'd rung last week that Carol Johnston, the solicitor allocated to Tony, no longer worked here. Even so, as the bustle of people came and went, she kept her head down, her face buried in a magazine, dreading that someone would recognise her.

She wasn't seeing a solicitor today, wouldn't for a few weeks yet. Her initial appointment was with Dr Jennifer Pereira, a medical doctor who, for the past two years, had been the insurer's major claims manager, handling cases worth over a million dollars. The DDO had a policy of seeing its members within days of a lawsuit being filed. It was important to take control of the proceedings early. It was also important to provide emotional support. There were few things more stressful for a doctor than malpractice litigation.

Despite that, apart from her fear of being recognised, Julia was surprised at how quietly assured she was feeling. For the first few days after receiving the Statement of Claim she had been too shocked and upset to think clearly. But visiting her father had distanced her from the problem and allowed her to consider it with more detachment. Last night she had gone over her own notes again and completed the detailed account of the events that the DDO had requested. The exercise had given her confidence. Even with the perspective of time and in the bright glare of litigation, she could not readily fault her management of Tracey Edwards.

She had detected the baby was small. She had performed a selection of tests to reassure herself that he was receiving enough oxygen via the placenta. She had watched him closely over the last month of pregnancy. And when he became distressed at the end of labour, she had quickly delivered him. Even now, five years on, she would do everything in exactly the same way. Once the DDO and Tracey Edwards' lawyers understood this, the lawsuit would be withdrawn.

'Dr Kent?' A woman in her late twenties emerged from behind the frosted glass door. She smiled, extending her hand as Julia stood up. 'I'm Jennifer Pereira. Thanks for coming.'

The major claims doctor was a small but voluptuous brunette, smartly dressed in a navy suit with a longish jacket which flattered her stocky form. Her long hair fell down her back, and was curled into a most impressive fringe across her forehead. She had pale skin with a scattering of prominent freckles and a pair of inquisitive brown eyes. Julia warmed to her immediately.

122

Seated at her desk, Jennifer Pereira looked down at a copy of Tracey Edwards' Statement of Claim. Despite her new-found confidence, Julia shuddered involuntarily at the sight of it. Had it really only been in her life for six days? The claims manager asked whether she had brought the hospital record of Tracey Edwards' labour.

Without going into any of the sorry detail, Julia explained that, while she didn't have the records yet, they had been ordered. She hoped. Jennifer was not concerned. The DDO would be requisitioning the entire hospital record anyway, but it would take a couple of weeks to arrive.

'Did you find time to write an account of the events as you saw them?'

Julia opened the folder on her lap and lifted out the report which had renewed her faith in her clinical judgement. They went over it for the next hour. By the end of her explanation, Julia felt even more certain of the medical decisions she had made; she had done everything an obstetrician reasonably should.

She looked at the claims manager hopefully, but the other doctor was more measured. While Julia's report was excellent, the experts' reports for the plaintiff's side were just as persuasive. It could be argued that Julia might have managed both the pregnancy and the labour more proactively. That such a small baby should perhaps have been delivered by caesarean section. That, at the very least, his heart rate should have been continuously monitored in labour. On the other hand, Jennifer conceded, Julia's counter-arguments for a less interventionist approach sounded reasonable as well.

The claims manager shrugged her shoulders. 'That's why we'll end up in court rather than settling, I'm afraid.'

Julia didn't understand the distinction. Realising this, Jennifer elaborated. When a patient had suffered undeniable harm at the hands of a doctor, the case didn't go to court. There was no need. There was nothing to be argued or challenged. The patient was simply compensated for the doctor's negligence. Quietly. No one else even heard there'd been a claim. It was when it appeared that the doctor had done everything properly, or nearly so, that the matter had to go to court. For the case to be argued, the claims defended, and a judge to decide. Paradoxically, it meant that the good doctors got the bad publicity, while the bad doctors got none.

Julia's gaze travelled from the solemn face of the claims manager to the detailed report she'd spent hours writing, the one she had innocently trusted would terminate the lawsuit. It had turned around and bitten her. 'Do you mean that if I had clearly mismanaged Tracey's pregnancy and labour, I wouldn't have to go to court?'

'That's right. We'd just settle. Hand over some money and close the case.'

Hours later, Julia was still so dumbfounded by the DDO doctor's remarks that she nearly missed her turn-off on the way home. Changing lanes suddenly, she invoked an impassioned fuss of horn-blowing from a neighbouring car she barely registered. Thank heavens she was seeing Patrick shortly; she desperately needed some cheering up.

Julia heard her daughter's laughter as she walked in the door. She put her head into the music room to say hello.

'Hi, Mum, this is Jason McKenzie. I told you about him. He was at the dance on Saturday night. He lives just down the road, next to Mrs Miller.'

'Oh yes, I remember. How are you, Jason?'

'Fine thanks, Mrs Cabrini.' He seemed pleased to have been discussed.

He was an agreeable young man, Julia thought approvingly as she spoke to him, solid and sunny, a change from the rather intense boyfriends Emma had brought home over the past year. He and Emma were planning a meal at a noodle bar, followed by a trip around the local band scene for a bit of reconnaissance.

Julia excused herself to answer the phone. It was Patrick. He was not in Sydney as planned, but stranded at the camp. They were flooded in. While the rain had stopped yesterday, the river had continued to rise, and the bridge over the only road out was now under water. The level had peaked and it was hoped that they would manage their escape tomorrow.

124

'Are you all right?'

'We're fine. I am disappointed, though. I was looking forward to seeing you. And I've had enough of camping for a while. The boys think it's very exciting, of course.'

Julia was disappointed too, even more so since the meeting with Jennifer Pereira had taken the wind out of her sails.

'Will tomorrow night suit you as well, Julia?' Patrick sounded uncharacteristically tentative.

'Yes, of course. It would be lovely. I'll look forward to it.'

'Good. I'll ring you as soon as I'm back in town.'

Emma and Jason came into the kitchen to say goodbye. Her daughter had the excited air of new love. Julia recognised it and smiled. 'By the way, Em, how did the art exam go?'

Her daughter paused, the final school examination now consigned to the past. 'Oh yeah, it was fine, Mum.'

'So that's it with school then? All over?'

Emma laughed, taunting. 'You never know. I might go back and do it again. It wasn't as bad as I thought.'

She kissed her mother, followed Jason to the front door, and then came back alone. There was something she'd forgotten.

'By the way, Mum, Dad rang.'

'About the exam?'

'Yes. The exam and the band. And something else.'

'Oh?'

'He's getting divorced again.'

Chapter 13

Waiting at her fifth consecutive red light in the morning traffic, Julia thought about Tony and wondered what had gone wrong for him this time. Not that she'd expect to know; she hadn't seen him since their own divorce. In the early years, she couldn't bear even a glimpse of his face when he came to collect Emma; George and Angie had dealt with such things for her. Now, of course, Emma and her father made their own arrangements, and there was no need for them to meet. She knew he'd remarried only four years ago and, while she didn't know Cecilia, Emma stayed with them several times a year. Not that Emma had warmed to her stepmother much, but she adored her three-year-old stepbrother, Antonio, proudly relating his latest milestone and every new phrase after each visit. Julia's grip tightened on the steering wheel. Emma had always wanted a little brother.

Julia frowned and looked closely at the first patient of the day, a rather sophisticated but distinctly nervous thirty-eight-year-old who sat torturing the strap of her handbag. She'd heard what the woman had said, but it couldn't be right. She asked again. 'How long did you say you've been trying to fall pregnant?'

'Twelve years.'

There was no doubt this time. 'Have you seen other doctors about this problem?'

The woman had, of course, dozens of them, but no matter how many times she'd been through this previously, it remained acutely embarrassing for Amanda Hewson to recount the cause of her infertility.

'You've never had sexual intercourse?'

'That's right,' the patient whispered. 'I haven't. Ever. It just hurts me so much when we try that we gave up. Years ago.'

'How long have you and your husband been married?'

'Fifteen years in January.'

'Oh.'

Difficulty with sexual intercourse was an uncommon, though recognised, cause of infertility, but in gynaecological practice it was not an uncommon problem in itself. At least once a month Julia saw a patient for whom penetration was so uncomfortable that intercourse was impossible. Only rarely was there an anatomical cause, apart from tight muscles at the entrance to the vagina, made tighter by fear. The vast majority of patients sought help soon after recognising the problem, were highly motivated and, with the use of vaginal dilators of increasing size to stretch the muscles, overcame the discomfort within weeks.

A much smaller number failed to achieve any benefit from the dilators. A handful failed to insert even the tiniest one. In these, a large part of the problem was psychological.

While many partners were supportive in the beginning, unless progress was made quickly, the rate of relationship breakdown was significant. Nevertheless, every few years Julia would see a situation like this, where the husband had stayed. Whatever the reason, the lack of marital sex obviously suited him too. Julia moved to deal with the issue at hand. Conception. 'Why don't you tell me about your menstrual cycle?'

'It's still regular, twenty-eight days. Every month. Like clockwork.'

'Do you get much pain?'

'Hardly any.'

'Can you tell me whether your husband has ever had a sperm count?'

'Dr Kent, Bill has had so many sperm tests that we could have cleared our mortgage if he'd been paid to donate them as the medical students are. He's a very experienced masturbator.'

'I see.' Julia stole a look at her patient to ascertain if this comment indicated a sense of humour. It didn't. 'And tell me, Mrs Hewson, what methods of getting pregnant have you tried?'

'What we've tried, Dr Kent, is artificial insemination.' She opened her handbag to reveal a screed of ancient-looking temperature charts. 'This is what we do.'

In meticulous detail she explained how, using temperature charts and changes in her mucus, she had tracked her fertile time each month, for twelve years. Then, when the time was right, Bill had masturbated. Amanda had collected the semen into a fine plastic syringe purchased from the chemist, which she then tried to introduce into her vagina. Without much success. Nearly every month. For twelve years.

'Have you seen a sex therapist about this problem?'

'A few, but they weren't much help. They kept trying to imply that the problem was psychological, when it's not. It's physical.'

'I see.' Now was not the time to suggest further therapy even though this was principally a sexual rather than an infertility matter. 'Have you considered an IVF program, Mrs Hewson? That way you could be sure that the sperm, which you say are excellent, are getting where they need to go.'

'We did consider it for a while, Dr Kent, but we didn't like the idea.'

Julia paused, uncertain what to say next. 'What didn't you like about it?'

'We thought it sounded unnatural.'

In the break between patients, Marcia popped her head in the door. Someone called Patrick had rung and was now back in

Sydney. An electric current seemed to lift Julia's skin from her skeleton as she reached for the phone. She forced a tone of restraint. 'Hi, Patrick. Did you come back by boat or car?'

'Submarine. At least that's what it felt like when we crossed the river. And now that I'm finally home, I'm looking for company other than ten-year-old boys. Are you still coming over tonight?'

'Yes, of course,' she said, more quickly than she intended. She slowed herself down again. 'Would you like me to bring something?'

'I thought I'd just cook some pasta. Probably with prawns and tomatoes and just a little chilli.'

Julia bathed in the sexy murmur of his voice. 'Sounds wonderful, Patrick.'

'I wouldn't go that far, Julia, but at least it's not out of a tin.'

'I'll bring some wine,' she offered, with a surge of expectant happiness.

Finished with her make-up, Julia was just selecting some earrings when the phone rang. She froze, knowing instinctively it was the hospital. Her fear was confirmed. Felicity Kable had presented in labour at Eastside. It was her second baby. Her first had been a breech vaginal delivery in which everything had gone well. This baby was also breech and Felicity wanted to deliver vaginally again. Her pelvis was a good size and the baby no bigger than the last. They had discussed it all in detail several times and Julia hadn't seen any reason to do things differently. Until now.

Suddenly she was seized with panic. What if she couldn't deliver the baby as easily as the previous one? What if it turned out to be bigger than she thought? What if she broke the baby's leg while delivering it? Or its arm? What if she overtwisted its neck? What if she couldn't get the shoulders out? Or the head got stuck? Breech deliveries could be very tricky.

'Sorry, Dr Kent. I missed what you said.' The noise sounded like a primeval groan, but the midwife needed to be sure the obstetrician hadn't given her an order regarding the patient.

Breathless, Julia asked how far dilated Felicity was. Three centimetres.

'But the contractions are picking up. When she gets going, I don't think she'll take very long.' The midwife was looking forward to the delivery. Most breeches were delivered by caesarean these days.

'I'll come now, Liz.'

'I didn't mean that you needed to come yet, Dr Kent.' The midwife was embarrassed. 'Just that I thought she'd do well.'

'I'll come now anyway, Liz. So I can keep an eye on her.'

Julia rang Patrick to explain that she would be late for dinner. After the previous night, he was doubly dismayed. 'Can't someone cover for you?'

'Not at such short notice, I'm afraid. Anyway, hopefully the delivery won't take long and I'll be there in a little while. I'll let you know as soon as I can.'

When Julia arrived at the labour ward, Felicity's contractions were becoming stronger and she had commenced using the nitrous oxide gas for her pain. Over the next hour, the baby's buttocks moved down into the pelvis. The CTG heart tracing, normal until this point, began to show decelerations. The midwife was not concerned. They were only the brief and benign Type 1 decelerations which were common at this stage of labour. Julia, on the other hand, was alarmed and pored over the trace very closely.

Felicity's husband, Neville, noticed her disquiet. 'Is there something wrong, Dr Kent?'

Julia's agitation was growing. An intense pressure lodged in her chest; it was accompanied by a sharp pain behind her eyes as the headache built. She forced herself to speak calmly. 'There could be. The baby's heart rate is slowing more than I'd like.'

Felicity and Neville looked at her for guidance.

'It might be safer to do a caesarean. A wrong decision now could mean a life of disability.'

The midwife glanced at her sharply. There was nothing out of the ordinary with the trace, the labour was going well and the baby would be born within the hour. Julia knew what she was thinking, but Liz wasn't the one ultimately responsible.

Felicity signed the consent and at ten o'clock young Andrew Kable was born in fine condition by caesarean section. Liz didn't look at Julia as she handed the baby over, but the parents smiled broadly. She had saved their son.

Just before the operation Julia had phoned to let Patrick know that she wouldn't be getting there tonight. She was very disappointed; his unusually frequent contact over the past week had set her expectations aflutter and she'd been dying to see him. 'I'm sorry, Patrick, but I won't be finished much before eleven.'

He was resigned by now. 'Maybe tomorrow night?'

'Maybe,' she replied, knowing better than to tempt fate again.

Before she left the surgery the following evening, Julia rang the labour wards at both hospitals. She rang again when she got out of the shower. The coast was clear.

As she replaced the receiver at Royal Eastside, Liz Ellison turned to the other midwives. 'I don't know what it is about Dr Kent this week. She scrutinises the CTG for any little dip, does a caesarean at the drop of a hat, and now she's ringing up every thirty minutes to make sure she has no patients.'

'Menopause, I'll bet,' replied an older midwife knowingly as she patted her flushed forehead with her hanky.

'Maybe she's pregnant,' suggested a much younger nurse.

'Whatever it is,' concluded Liz, 'you'd think she'd know what to do about it.'

Patrick hugged her happily. 'You're finally here! And we're only forty-eight hours late for our dinner together. Come in, come in. I'm helping Ryan with his homework. Come and see what we're doing.'

The ten-year-old was bent intently over the table affixing glue to pieces of timber as Julia entered. It looked impressive.

'What are you building, Ryan?'

'The Warragamba Dam,' he said proudly. 'My school project.'

'It's wonderful,' she enthused.

Privately, Julia wondered why primary school teachers persisted with projects. Everyone, even the youngest child, knew that if the student did the project largely unaided, as intended, the mark awarded by the teacher was rarely better than fair. On the other hand, if the parent did nearly all of it, the mark was always excellent. It was an ongoing dilemma for parents. Did you encourage your child to be resourceful or did you do it for them? Luckily for Ryan, the projects handed in by the children of architects, designers and carpenters were universally of a high standard.

'It's great to finally see you, Julia,' said Patrick, his eyes smiling as he recapped the superglue and pushed Ryan off to wash his hands before dinner. He gazed at her appraisingly. 'You look terrific.'

'Thanks,' she said, gratified he'd noticed the trouble she'd gone to. 'You look a little sunburned yourself.'

He touched his nose selfconsciously. 'I was careful on the really hot days, but when the sun finally came out late Sunday after three days of rain, it caught me unawares.'

He led her into the kitchen where he gave the large casserole pot on the stove a stir.

'Mmm, it smells fantastic, Patrick.'

'An old recipe of my mother's,' he said, pleased. 'By the way, you missed a great meal last night.' The prawns had been really fresh and the pasta handmade. He and Ryan had happily shared her portion.

'Would you like to know what I had for dinner last night?'

'Lobster Thermidor?'

'Close. Two gobbled pieces of Vegemite on toast in the labour ward tea room while waiting for theatre to be ready for my caesarean.'

'Poor Julia.'

Julia stayed for hours, long after Ryan was asleep. Patrick told her about his time at the camp, including his hapless attempt at abseiling and his inability to tie a knot that didn't slip. It had taken only a day of inedible meals for him to realise where he should direct his camping skills. Assertively relieving the chef, he'd then combined the available provisions to whip up a more palatable camp cuisine.

Julia told him about her early-morning fishing expedition with her father and her catch of the day. Patrick laughed. Fishing was another of his wilderness survival failures as well. He didn't come close to catching anything, didn't even lose his bait.

'I don't think you need to see it as a failure. You've simply evolved beyond the hunting and gathering stage.'

'You're right there. Genus "Electricity Man", that's me. Hook me up to a power supply and I can do anything.'

It was nearly midnight when Julia noticed the time. 'I really must go. We've both got to work tomorrow.'

He put his hand on her arm to stay her. 'Before you leave, I wanted to talk to you about something.'

As he started to speak, his voice was unsteady. Over the past few weeks, he explained, he'd thought a lot about their friendship and where it was leading. He could have left things to drift for a while longer, but believed she should know how he felt. Firstly, he wanted to say that he was, and always would be, very grateful to her for helping him get through these past months. Her compassionate and sensitive support during his time of sorrow had been overwhelming.

His words sounded rehearsed, and they were. Julia froze. He wanted to be 'just friends'.

Patrick went on. Not that he was over his grief, of course, but he was much better than he would have been without her. She had been really wonderful. Listening to him for hours, never making him feel that his sorrow was a burden to her. Everyone else had expected him to be cheerful after a couple of months, to laugh and have the world laugh with him. But she had allowed him to repeat himself over and over, to bawl and howl, to impose endlessly upon her time and kindness.

Julia's heart had stopped. She waited for his tone to change, listened for his disclaimer. For the words that said he now needed to move on.

'Julia, I have spent the last week trying to imagine what my life would be like if you were no longer around. And what I've realised is that I love you.'

Chapter 14

Simmering with uncharacteristic bitterness, Julia slumped, resentful and nervous, onto the couch in the waiting area of the DDO offices. Why did this bloody lawsuit have to happen? Hadn't she endured enough judicial proceedings for one lifetime? And if it *had* to happen, why did the timing have to be so terrible? Why not last year? Or even next year, when her relationship with Patrick was not so fresh? Why *now*, when everything was suddenly so wonderful?

On the night three weeks before, when Patrick had revealed the depth of his devotion, he had pushed Julia into a crevasse of stunned, speechless confusion. It couldn't be true, what he said. He couldn't possibly feel that way about her; no one had for so long. He was making fun of her. But then he had taken her face in his hands, touched her lips with his and repeated his words. In a giddy spin, she'd seen it was *she* who was doing the mocking; she, so damaged from rejection and betrayal, who had come to see herself as unlovable.

For hours Patrick had stroked her hair and said her name and made little punctures in her shell of protection. And she'd let herself believe that it might be true; he might love her. A slow wash of vertiginous happiness had bathed her. And then he'd made love to her for the first time, and the second, and then again, and she'd found the unsurpassable surpassed. Recalling those first few days still brought a bump to every pore. She'd been riding a magic carpet ever since, a smile perpetually on her face, an aura of joy radiating from her like a small sun. She initiated sparky conversations in lifts and shops with people she didn't know, hummed snatches of love songs she thought she'd forgotten, bounced through her days – and nights – needing almost no sleep, energised by Patrick's love and electrified by his touch.

Her near-perfect joy was marred only by this other development in her life.

Jennifer Pereira smiled as she approached Julia. 'Thank you for coming in again. It's nice to see you.'

Shrouded in silent self-pity, Julia felt herself brighten marginally at the presence of the agreeable young DDO doctor. Since their first meeting last month they'd had several telephone conversations, and Julia found she liked and respected Jennifer. The claims manager was not only genial, she was also intelligent and had grasped the essentials of Julia's case very quickly.

Jennifer led Julia through the frosted glass door into the main thoroughfare. From there they went down a narrower corridor on the left and into an office where a young man sat behind a desk, folder open, yellow highlighter in hand. He stood to greet them, smiling with fresh-faced enthusiasm.

'Julia, this is Richard Tripp, one of the solicitors here at DDO. He's the person who will be principally responsible for handling the legal side of your case.' They shook hands. Richard then invited Julia to take a seat, gesturing to the comfortable chair across from his desk. Jennifer took a seat beside Richard so that she also faced Julia.

Taking in the youthful pair, Julia wondered, not for the first time, why her malpractice organisation seemed unable to employ staff over the age of thirty. The place was full of kids. While not denying their keenness or even their ability, she would have felt more confident of her defence if it had been in the hands of someone older. Ideally older than herself. What could someone of thirty know?

Richard Tripp sorted through the sizeable bundle of papers which sprawled over the desk in front of him. Watching him, Julia caught herself wondering how many more desks would be carpeted in such documents before they were finished with Tracey and Brendan Edwards.

The lawyer looked up and fixed her with his courteous gaze. 'How are you coping so far?'

'I'm fine,' she replied quickly, making sure her smile was in place, and ignoring the heaviness in the back of her head that foreshadowed a throbbing migraine by lunchtime.

'Good. What we are going to do today is go over the case with you from beginning to end.'

They started with Julia's own notes on Tracey Edwards' pregnancy and worked their way methodically from the very first antenatal visit through to Julia's detection that the baby was small, and finally on to the labour. They examined in particular the development of foetal distress at the end of labour, the forceps delivery of the profoundly unwell baby, the difficulty with resuscitation, and the transfer to the neonatal intensive care unit. Julia found it all reassuringly straightforward.

Richard Tripp then opened the folder containing Tracey Edwards' Royal Eastside Hospital medical record. Over the next few hours, they read and reread every word the midwives had written, noting in particular the point at which a problem had been identified, and the times when Julia was contacted and had arrived at the hospital. The solicitor was particularly interested in the decision to listen to the baby's heartbeat intermittently with the small Doppler machine rather than choosing to continuously electronically monitor the baby in labour.

'Continuous electronic monitoring was never even suggested,' Julia replied.

'But you would have been the one to suggest it, wouldn't you?'

'I didn't think it was necessary.'

'But it obviously was, wasn't it?' he challenged.

'How can you say that?' Julia retorted, perplexed.

'Brendan Edwards.'

They passed many hours in similar exchanges, stopping only briefly for lunch. Giving the lie to his polite manner, Richard was sharp and unrelenting in his probing; over time, Julia felt she was being flailed with a whip.

'Whose side are you on, Richard?' she demanded after a particularly brusque difference of opinion about whether or nor she should have chosen caesarean section over forceps.

'The DDO's, Julia.'

'Oh.' Suddenly she felt deflated; until now she'd thought her side and her insurer's were the same.

'And we're on your side as well,' he said, his voice softening. 'It's my job to ask the hard questions, the ones that Tracey Edwards' lawyers will ask if the matter goes to court.'

Julia felt mollified for a minute but when they moved on to Brendan's latest medical reports, Richard was severe again. 'He's certainly got a lot of problems, hasn't he, Julia? If his lawyers can show that his disabilities are due to mistakes on your part, this will be a very expensive claim. About ten million dollars.'

Julia gasped. 'That much?'

'Possibly more.'

Julia felt her back slide down the chair. No wonder he was giving her such a hard time.

Jennifer Pereira handed Richard the file containing the medical experts' reports commissioned by Tracey's lawyers. The strongest were statements from two prominent obstetricians claiming that Julia's management was negligent, and that this negligence was the cause of Brendan's disabilities.

Realising what was coming, Julia slumped further in the chair. Any lower and she'd be on her knees; which might not be inappropriate at this point.

'You could find this part rather upsetting,' Richard warned.

'I've already read them,' she said flatly. Several times in fact. And on each occasion had thought she might be sick.

The importance of these reports, Richard explained, was that they highlighted what the plaintiffs' team felt were the main areas of negligence. Julia's responses to the claims were equally important. With both, the DDO could start to build her defence. He pointed to the two reports. 'Which would you like to tackle first?'

She suppressed a hysterical giggle. It was a choice between arsenic and strychnine, after all. Dr Willard was highly critical of her management, but Professor Jones' analysis was probably worse. They may as well start with him.

But before they did, she wanted to say something about Chris Jones. He had almost no credibility amongst his fellow obstetricians. Not only did he make a lot of money appearing for plaintiffs against his colleagues, but his own involvement in clinical obstetrics was minimal these days. His private practice was only small, while his public practice was limited to one antenatal clinic a week. He didn't even do a day in the labour ward any more, Julia exclaimed, as if that summed up the professor's hypocrisy perfectly.

Richard shrugged indifferently. All that might be of significance to Julia and her colleagues, but to the judge, and the jury if there was one, Chris Jones was a very important man. He was a full professor at a prestigious hospital and the author of a number of eminent medical textbooks.

'All written by his assistants,' Julia interrupted.

'Possibly,' Richard conceded patiently. But that information was not generally known. And yes, it was true that the professor's credibility was diminished among his obstetric colleagues, but the judge would probably be unaware of that as well. 'He'll most likely find Professor Jones extremely persuasive. We have to run the case on its merits.'

'But what hope do we have?' Julia moaned, stung by Richard's dismissal. 'Given the ferocity of Professor Jones' report, we may as well give up now.'

Richard understood her concern. But not every case Professor Jones appeared in was won by the plaintiff. The DDO had won a few too. Quite a few, in fact. Richard beamed, relating a particularly good result.

'And will they pay me ten million dollars if we do win?' Julia was petulant now, the weeks of worry finally showing.

Richard looked surprised. 'Of course not. But we won't have to pay her either.'

Julia persisted. 'That's hardly a win, is it? She gets ten million if she wins, but I don't get anything if I do.'

'But you're not suing her, Julia, she's suing you,' he returned reasonably.

'Well in that case, I think I'll sue her too.' Julia was stubborn. 'For all the anxiety, sleeplessness, distress, and loss of concentration that I've suffered since she started this case.'

Richard Tripp heard her out. He took off his glasses and rubbed his eyes. The action made him look older. Julia warmed to him slightly.

'I understand how upset you are, Julia, and you're right to feel she's causing you a lot of trouble. She is. But she's got some impressive reports and a plausible case and your anger won't get you anywhere unless you can refute her claims.' He paused, waiting for her reply, but Julia had nothing more to say. 'Shall we start?'

Working their way doggedly through the obstetric experts' analyses took the three of them well into the evening. Nearing the end, Richard Tripp asked if Julia would like some coffee. He was definitely looking older than thirty now. She accepted gratefully and, while he and Jennifer stepped out for a few moments, took advantage of their absence to swallow the aspirin she had deferred taking all day. She was living on them at the moment.

Eventually they finished and made plans for the next meeting; it would be held over until mid-January because of the Christmas break. As Richard methodically packed away the papers, Julia asked, 'When will you decide if, um . . . if . . . you're going to settle or fight it in court?'

'When we get our own experts' reports.'

'And when will that be?'

Richard's eyes crinkled slightly. 'Well, they are doctors, Julia.' Seeing the expression on her face, he became more serious. 'A couple of months.'

She dredged up her last shred of energy. 'Do you think we could try and have them by the time of the January meeting?' She had to know; being in limbo was killing her.

Richard looked at Jennifer, who nodded. 'We'll have them by then.'

Jennifer took Julia out to the foyer, confiding with her encouraging smile, 'I thought you handled all that very well. Most doctors fall asleep or fall apart after the first few hours.'

Julia murmured neutrally, on the verge of both. As she stepped into the lift, Jennifer told her that if the DDO did decide to fight this claim in court, there were two things she could do to help her case.

Julia stepped back out of the lift and let it go.

The first, said Jennifer, was to go through the obstetric literature for the period around the time of Brendan's birth, and establish what the consensus was regarding the place of electronic monitoring of labour. This was crucial, of course, since she had chosen not to electronically monitor Tracey's labour. They needed to be able to defend that decision.

Secondly, she should go back through all the medical records, both her own and the hospital's, and dissect them fanatically, picking over every little detail regarding Tracey's pregnancy and labour, avidly searching for anything that might be relevant.

Julia gave an exasperated sigh. 'I've been over the records a dozen times already. They'll fall apart if I handle them any more. Everything I can remember is in my written statement.'

'That's probably right,' soothed Jennifer. 'But you've been doing it defensively. I want you now to do it proactively, to relive those months, antenatal visit by antenatal visit. There might be things you've forgotten, little things that didn't seem important at the time, but might now suggest that Brendan Edwards was never going to be quite right.' Jennifer regarded Julia very seriously. 'And I want you to search for clues that might suggest Tracey contributed to the problems her son now has.'

Chapter 15

Julia and Patrick walked along the beach in the lemony glow of the late afternoon sun, and it seemed the whole world walked with them. Couples, families, kids and dogs all refused to be indoors now that summer had come. The cold windy weather of the past few weeks was gone, yielding to a high-pressure system and a succession of days bathed in brilliant sunshine. Sydney in mid-December had come alive with alfresco living. Restaurants with pavement licences, and many without, spilt their customers into the welcome warmth. The coincidence of the festive season, the end of the work year and the balmy evenings induced a mood few could resist.

Julia and Patrick made their own joyful eddy in the tide of passion washing along the coastline, whirling and splashing with the thrill of their new love. Julia, in particular, was affected; it was so long since she'd been captured by romance, seduced by the joy of being chosen, and she radiated with the happiness of it.

Playfully synchronising their steps and drawing each other a little closer, they meandered along the water's edge. A dinner booking had been made for eight o'clock; in the meantime they sought the warm low rocks and shallow pools at the northern end of the beach. Massaged by the waning sun, they found a comfortable spot and perched side by side, talking about everything and nothing and languorously paddling their feet. Their perfect bliss was interrupted by the musical tone of Julia's mobile.

Patrick groaned. 'I'll die if you have to go.'

'Me too.' Julia felt the intrusion even more keenly. It had taken thirty minutes of Marcia's phone calls to enable her to get away from work early and snatch this time with Patrick. Driving to the beach she'd rung both hospitals to make sure she was in the clear; and had counted her chickens. Resentful frustration surged as she warily spoke into the phone. Then the muscles in her face relaxed. It was simply a patient wanting to go home with her baby tonight rather than have her husband come back in the morning.

'Are we going to have to live with these interruptions for the rest of our lives?' Patrick asked as Julia put her phone back in her bag.

'Phone calls?'

'And call-backs to the hospital at any hour of the day and night.'

'Do they bother you?'

He tried not to laugh. 'Some times more than others, of course.' Having intimate moments interrupted by the sudden departure of a lover was a new experience for him. But, yes, in general it did bother him that her job was so all-consuming. And so bloody unpredictable. 'I want to have you all to myself,' he purred, softening the complaint and snuggling closer to her. Only recently had he gained any insight into what her life was like.

Julia understood how he felt but, in truth, her job was much easier now, with Leo and Sylvie in the practice. 'One in four is not that bad, Patrick. Really.'

'But that's just the weekends. You're still on call every night during the week. And even when it is your weekend off, you do hours of rounds on Saturday. It makes it hard to plan a weekend away, doesn't it?'

'I suppose it does,' she conceded. Weekends away had never been a big part of her adult life.

He caressed her. 'I'm sorry, darling. It's just that I'm finding it hard living around your work. Even tonight, we might start to eat only to find you suddenly have to go. I could be left on my own in the restaurant.'

Her eyes glimmered. 'I'll make sure I order something you like.'

He pouted slightly. 'It's all right for you. I'm the one who'll be left like a shag on a rock.'

She was bemused at his tirade. She'd much prefer to be the one left behind with the fresh seafood and more than her share of a nice bottle of wine. But the last thing in the world she wanted was to see him upset; he'd been so wonderful to her. And he was new to obstetricians' hours; it would take him a while to get used to them. She nestled in closer. Perhaps it might be better if they ate in during the week, and saved their nights out for her weekends off.

That would solve part of the problem, he agreed. But he'd still be left alone when he expected to be with her. He slowly stroked her neck. He didn't mean to whinge. It was just that he seemed less important than her job. 'You are so very special to me, Julia. I want to be the same to you. '

'But you are,' she replied honestly.

It was after eleven when they strolled back along a moonlit and much emptier beach, their bare feet sinking pleasantly in the still-warm sand. Julia's phone had been blessedly silent all evening, although she'd made several unnecessary trips to the bathroom to ring the hospitals and establish she was still in the clear; Patrick's comments had unsettled her. They'd been talking since they met and were talking still as they drifted back to their cars. With a smile, Julia noticed there was nothing Patrick couldn't discuss with robust enthusiasm; even now he held forth on the current overprescription of antidepressant medication before moving on to the government's plans to change family trust laws. Being only partly informed on a subject did not impede his cheerful opinion; his exuberance for every aspect of life was one of the things she most liked about him. He was a better talker than listener, perhaps, but many men were like that. She was happy to be his audience.

They splashed in ankle-deep waves and stopped for a minute to view what must have been a convoy of tankers out where the sparkly black of the sky met the matt black of the ocean. The lights which traced the boats' silhouettes reminded them of Christmas, now less than a fortnight away. Patrick would be having Christmas lunch as usual with Genevieve's family at Campbelltown, fifty kilometres out of Sydney. His wife had been one of five girls, and they would all be there with their families. Julia insisted he still go, and alone; it was too soon for her to accompany him to something like that. As long as she had him back on Christmas night for a few hours, since that was all she'd have of him this year. On Boxing Day, Patrick was taking Ryan to his parents' farm for two weeks. His mother and father usually came to Sydney at this time, but were not coming this year. His brother, Sean, had broken his leg in a fall from a tractor and couldn't take over for them. Instead, Patrick was going to give a hand.

'I thought you might like to come with us, Julia.' The moonlight glanced off his excited smile. He'd been keeping the invitation a surprise until now. 'Mum and Dad and Sean have heard all about you. They can't wait to meet you.'

'Oh, Patrick,' she stammered, suddenly overcome. He'd told his family. She hadn't told anyone except Angie and Emma; it was only seven weeks, after all. Not that that was the reason. The truth was that daily she expected him to take her hand and regretfully say he'd made a mistake, she wasn't what he wanted after all. And now he was asking her to visit his parents' farm. She hoped he couldn't see that her eyes were fast becoming as wet as her feet. There couldn't have been a nicer Christmas present.

And then she recalled that she wouldn't be able to go.

Though it was Leo's turn to cover for the practice, she had accepted a number of bookings of special patients due at this time, about a dozen of them. They were mostly fellow doctors and midwives she knew, and patients with medical problems, and she'd promised each one that she would personally look after them in labour. Back in May, when they'd booked, it had not been a problem. It was Emma's year to have Christmas with her father in Brisbane and Julia had expected to be on her own doing nothing much, so she may as well be working. It was too late to say now, a week before their babies were due, that she had found something better to do.

Although crushed with disappointment, she didn't want to rekindle Patrick's earlier irritation about the primacy of her work; he wouldn't understand why Leo couldn't simply cover for her. So she hid behind her daughter. 'I'd love to come, darling. It would be fantastic to go to the farm with you, but I wouldn't want to leave Emma for a week. Perhaps I could come for one or two days.' Even that would be difficult.

It was clear Patrick couldn't believe what he was hearing. Emma was never home, he said. She was working or rehearsing or with her new boyfriend. She wouldn't even know her mother was gone. He looked imploringly at her. 'Come away with me after Christmas. Let me show you off.'

Riven by the hopelessness of her competing obligations, Julia temporised. 'I'll see what I can manage, darling,' she said brightly, knowing she'd never pull it off.

As Julia made her way back to the surgery after her Thursday afternoon operating list, she worried about Angie. Normally unflappable, her friend had been offhand and snappish with little provocation all afternoon. Now that Julia thought about it, she'd been like it for a while. There was something wrong but Julia didn't know what it was. By rights, Angie should have been happy this week. Her operating sessions with Adrian de Bruin would end next Tuesday and, after Christmas, Professor Macfarlane would be back. The famous surgeon had scoffed at the idea of retirement. Young Angie would probably retire before he did, he'd said. Even this had not seemed to lift her friend's spirits.

Julia had hoped to catch up with Angie this evening, but she'd dashed off at short notice to take Richie to his school concert in time for costuming and make-up. Geoff was supposed to do it, but he'd rung while they were operating to say that something had come up at work and he would be delayed. Angie made no comment, but to Julia it seemed very late in the year for a university professor to be having problems at work that couldn't wait.

Arriving at the surgery, Julia passed the last of Leo's departing antenatal patients. Of the secretaries, only Marcia remained and she was preparing to depart also. 'There's good news in your in-tray,' she alerted as she left.

'Oh?' Julia went to the back of the reception desk to look; a smile crept into her eyes. Cristina Santos was pregnant. The twenty-eight-year-old had nearly died from Hodgkin's lymphoma a few years ago and had spent months on chemotherapy before going into remission. The treatment had saved her life but damaged her ovaries. Her periods had stopped and she had become infertile. While the damage was often permanent, luckily for Cristina her periods had resumed recently. And now she was pregnant. It was the high point of Julia's day.

Seated at her desk, surrounded by her paperwork, she made good time. Most were normal results or correspondence that needed only her tick. But then, a brace tightened around her heart as she picked up the parchment-quality pages. A solicitor's letter.

Scanning the words, she exhaled slowly, loath to relax prematurely, and read the letter again. The patient was suing a motor vehicle insurance company. *Not her*. The woman blamed her period problems on a motorbike accident and was seeking support for her claim from her gynaecologist. Still trembling, Julia moved the papers to the 'too hard for now' pile.

Some time later, she looked up to see Leo in her doorway. He was on his way out. 'The surgery's not the place to spend such a lovely evening, Julia.'

'I couldn't agree more. But I can't leave it all till winter, can I?'

146

She gestured to the not inconsiderable pile of papers on the floor beside her desk. 'It would fill the whole room if I did.' Even so, she stood up, finished for now. The solicitor's letter had frightened her. 'I'll walk out with you.'

Leo was aflame with paternal joy. 'Alex has just discovered she's pregnant,' he said, referring to his older daughter.

Julia gave a small whoop, thrilled at the news. Alex was a lovely girl who'd been married six months and made no secret of wanting half a dozen children.

Leo moved on to the other part of his disclosure. 'I was wondering whether you'd agree to care for Alex in her pregnancy?'

Julia was caught off-guard. Alex lived in St Ives; it would be a long way to the eastern suburbs for each visit. 'Surely there's someone closer?'

Of course there was. In fact Leo's other daughter, Leonie, had seen someone on the north shore when she'd had Louis, and been very happy. 'But you know what Alex is like, Julia. Things never go smoothly for her. Sandra and I would just feel happier knowing that she was in your very capable hands.'

Julia gave a weak smile. 'Actually, Leo, they might not be as capable as you think.'

Before she knew it, she had told him the whole sorry tale of her pending litigation. Tears came with the words, the pent-up anxiety finally free to spill. 'It's not just *this* case I can't face, Leo. It's the *last* one. I'm terrified that someone will recognise my name, and drag the Madeleine Morgan stuff out all over again. And I'm so determined that no one will ever, *ever* sue me again, it's affecting the way I practise. I've completely lost my confidence. My caesarean rate will be one hundred percent by the time Alex has her baby.'

Leo nodded slowly. Since his return from leave he'd several times overheard the midwives complaining about the change in Julia. Now he understood what was happening. Even so, he had not expected anything like the distress she'd just revealed. He knew all about Tony and Madeleine, of course, better than almost anyone. But it was years ago now, and she always seemed so competent and self-assured. Even working with her every day, he would never have guessed that the misery and shame of that time still affected her so badly.

He put his arm around her and commiserated. He could understand how awful it must be, but she mustn't let it get her down. She was one of the best doctors he'd ever worked with. 'In fact, I was just saying to Sandra the other night that I've enjoyed these last few years better than all the others of my career. And that's largely because of you, Julia.'

As she sobbed at his kindness, he asked if there was anything he could do to help.

She pulled a ridiculous face. 'Yes there is, in fact. You can march down to the DDO and order them to settle. So I don't have to go to court.'

'They might settle?' he asked expectantly.

She shook her head, miserable once more. The final decision wouldn't be made until next month. But it didn't seem likely.

'Have you asked them to?'

'Not exactly,' she admitted. 'The case is worth millions, Leo, possibly ten million. It's not the sort of money you just hand over.'

'They can often settle for less,' he encouraged. 'All parties want to avoid litigation.'

'It'd still be millions.'

He asked whether she'd told the DDO about her history and her fears of a public court battle. She hadn't. She figured that the fewer people who knew about both cases, the less chance of someone linking them together to maximise publicity. She hadn't even told Emma about the current matter. Just Marcia, Angie and now him.

'Anyway, hopefully there won't be any publicity,' she said more cheerfully, remembering what Jennifer Pereira had told her. 'Apparently these medical negligence actions are heard every day of the year, and almost none are reported.'

'You should keep telling yourself that fact,' he encouraged.

Her cheer slipped. 'Telling myself is not the problem, Leo. Listening to myself is.'

'Mum, could I ask you something?' Emma was in her pyjamas, sitting on the end of Julia's bed. She seemed a bit hesitant and Julia put down her magazine, intrigued. It must be something to do with Jason.

'It's about Dad.'

'What about Dad?'

'You know how I was supposed to have Christmas with him this year?' It was Tony's turn to have his daughter, but with her job, and the band, and Jason, Emma had recently decided to stay in Sydney. She continued: 'Well, of course, he was supposed to have both me and Antonio. And now he's got no one.'

'No one?' Julia asked, amused. 'Just a mother and six brothers and sisters and a squillion nieces and nephews.'

'It's a lot less than he thought he'd be having,' Emma persisted. 'He hasn't got either of his own children for Christmas.'

Julia looked at her daughter kindly. 'I know it's disappointing, darling, but he's going to see you both after Christmas.'

'So the answer is no?'

Julia frowned. 'I didn't realise that you'd made a request, Em.'

'You know what I'm going to ask, Mum.'

'Honestly, darling, I have no idea.'

In the early hours of Friday, Julia groaned at her stupidity. Leo was generously covering her tonight, so that she could have eight hours of unbroken sleep in preparation for her busy weekend covering the whole practice. And what had she gone and done? She'd told Emma she'd have an answer in the morning. Now she'd have to stay awake until she worked out what it was.

Her daughter's request had been totally unexpected, although Julia now wondered why. From the teenager's point of view, it was a perfect solution. Her father wanted to spend Christmas with her. She couldn't go to him in Brisbane but there was nothing to stop him from coming to her in Sydney.

As she lay in the dark, Julia realised that she wasn't sure of the extent of Emma's request. Was it that she wanted her father to come for lunch on Christmas Day, or was it that she wanted him to stay with them, rather than at his usual hotel, over the four days that he would be in Sydney?

She thought about her ex-husband and decided that the answer had to be no. It was not realistic to expect that she would be able to cope with his presence at the moment. If not for Tracey Edwards, she might have managed, but not now. The new case had refreshed the memories of the old one, immersing her in the layers of heartbreak and anger all over again. Seeing Tony would just make it worse. While Emma was in close contact with him, phoning weekly and visiting every couple of months, she herself had deliberately not laid eyes on him since he'd betrayed her and humiliated her and very nearly destroyed her. Now was not a good time to start. Comfortable with her decision, she fell asleep.

In the morning she awoke more refreshed than expected after her short night and enjoyed a few peaceful moments before she suddenly remembered what she had to tell Emma.

She thought about her extraordinary, marvellous daughter. Although Emma herself had been confused and badly shaken by her parents' sudden separation and her father's departure from Sydney, she'd immediately turned her attention to the care of her mother, whom she'd quickly realised was in a state very similar to when the baby had died. As Julia had struggled, very unsteadily at first, to negotiate that time and build a life as a sole parent, Emma had been sensitive and intuitive beyond her years, loving and funny and kind. Without her, Julia would have completely collapsed.

She stopped short. Tony had missed those years. He hadn't given her any trouble over Emma, never once questioning that she should live with her in Sydney even though his own home was now in Brisbane. And, despite the constraints of distance and work and a new family, he had always been loving and accessible, generous with both his money and his time, to the daughter who was growing up without him.

However Julia might feel about Tony, Emma loved him. And this was her home too. And it was technically her last Christmas

150

as a child. Possibly her last in Australia for a while. She only planned to be away for six months, but who knew what life held? She should have what she asked for. Her parents together for Christmas for the first time since she was ten.

Julia got out of bed and went to find her daughter.

Chapter 16

Lounging in the two comfy chairs which overlooked the
ocean, Julia and Sylvie were deep in lunchtime conversation about Emma's exam results which had come out that
morning. Julia was relieved that the score would secure her
entry into the fine arts degree she wanted to do. Sylvie wondered how Stephen's son, Justin, had done, but would not dare
ask. Stephen had expressed frustration more than once at his
son's casual approach to his studies. A high-achiever himself, he
couldn't understand someone less driven.

'I think the money irritates him as well,' Julia confided.

'The money?' asked Sylvie.

'The school fees.'

'Really?'

'Yes. Stephen once told me that for the three of them, with all
the extras, it came to over fifty thousand dollars a year. Every
year.'

'You're kidding?' Sylvie couldn't contemplate such a sum on
school fees.

As if he had heard them, Stephen breezed into the room. 'Is

everyone having a slow day?' he chirped. He rarely had time for a break, but his first two afternoon appointments had beaten the Christmas rush and delivered already.

'Yes. Julia and I have cancelled all our patients for the rest of the week. We intend to relax instead.'

Stephen grinned. 'I suppose you're off to Noosa?'

'The Bahamas,' corrected Julia, crumpling up her empty lunch wrapper as tightly as possible and making a successful shot at the rubbish bin in the corner. 'So what are your plans?' While it was Leo's turn to be on for the practice over the ten days of the Christmas holiday break, Julia knew Stephen would be available for his patients most of the time.

'We're going to Whale Beach.'

'Of course,' she exclaimed. 'How could I have forgotten?'

Stephen and Stacey's five-bedroom holiday house had an almost uninterrupted view of the stunning expanse of sand and sea that was one of Sydney's most exclusive beaches.

'We'll probably go on Friday after lunch,' Stephen said between mouthfuls of sandwich. 'Stacey and the kids will stay until the end of January, while I'll be off for the ten days. Although I'll be coming back for confinements, of course.'

'And do you have many due at this time?' Julia was being mischievous; she knew how heavily booked he was.

'Afraid so. I tried to limit them, but not very successfully.'

'Didn't try very hard, maybe?' she challenged gently.

'As hard as I could.'

'Well, I'm sure you'll be much happier spending the holiday break in the labour ward. You must really be looking forward to eating toast with the nurses rather than feasting on mud-crab and Moet on the deck at Whale Beach. I know I would be.'

Stephen poked out his tongue at her, took the final bite of his lunch and scrunched up his wrapper, ready for his shot at the bin. 'Well, smarty-pants, what are you doing for Christmas?' he asked.

Julia paused. 'Tony's coming to stay.'

'What?' Stephen was shocked, so shocked that he missed the bin with his balled wrapper, even though it was less than two metres away and he was the reigning champ.

'To see Emma,' she clarified.

'Oh.' Stephen still looked surprised. 'Do you see a bit of him now?'

'No, never. It's just that this year was his turn to have Emma but she can't go. So she asked if he could come here instead.'

Stephen was wary. 'How do you feel about it?'

'It should be okay,' Julia replied, deliberately nonchalant. In reality, she was only coping with the storm of emotions Tony's imminent arrival aroused by refusing to think about it.

Knowing she too was quite heavily committed over the break, Stephen teased her back. 'That explains your lightly booked schedule.'

Julia acknowledged the problem. Indeed, several of her patients were already overdue and could be counted on to deliver on Christmas Day itself.

'Surely you can get the overdue ones delivered before then. Induce them all tomorrow.'

'Unfortunately, none of them wants to be induced. They want to go naturally.'

'Having a baby on a public holiday is not natural. Not for the doctor, anyway.'

Sylvie, who had been busy with a large mango during all of this, washed her hands and face at the sink and rejoined the conversation, observing that women just didn't realise the implications of conceiving on April Fool's Day – that their baby would be due on Christmas Day. Stephen chuckled, declaring it to be the likely origin of the name, before returning to his office to take a phone call.

Alone with Julia as they repaired their lipstick in the tea-room mirror, it was Sylvie's turn to moan about her Christmas. She was spending a week in Melbourne with her mother and wasn't looking forward to it.

'Is your brother coming back from Hong Kong?'

Sylvie suspended the lipstick as the O of her mouth reshaped itself into a scowl. 'You've got to be kidding. Come and see Mum? Never. He's going to New York on business this week, and has decided to stay there for Christmas with friends.' Her mouth softened slightly. 'Not that I blame him. Poor Freddy, she does bully him.'

'So it'll be just you and your mum?'

Sylvie nodded gloomily. There was no other family and her mother had never made many friends. Even the neighbours she occasionally chatted with were in nursing homes now. Everyone in the street seemed to have moved on. Sylvie stared mournfully at Julia in the mirror. It wasn't much fun being sick and old on your own, she could see that. But her mother made it so much worse than it needed to be.

Two days before Christmas at 4.45 pm, Angie picked up the phone to ring pre-op and send for the final patient on Julia's list. Julia herself was miles away, still stunned by what Leo had told her just before she'd come to the operating theatre.

Dr Ruth Levy, his wife's GP and an old family friend, had rung him this morning on behalf of Sandra, who hadn't wanted to be the one to tell him. She'd apparently been feeling very tired for a while and had gone to Dr Levy for a check-up. The doctor had found swollen lymph glands in her left groin. Full of tumour from a tiny melanoma on her leg. A biopsy had confirmed the diagnosis.

Leo was furious with himself. 'She's been exhausted for months and I didn't think anything of it.'

Not that it would have made any difference, Julia thought sadly. The prognosis would still have been terrible.

Leo had immediately rung Sandra, who'd been surprisingly calm. She, who always fretted over everyone else, was quite sanguine about the fact that she was probably dying. She'd had her suspicions for a while, she explained, giving her time to come to terms with the notion of cancer. She had one request of Leo: she wanted no one except him to know of her illness until February. She was not having it overshadow her children and grandchildren's summer holidays. Putting down the phone, Leo had frantically sought Julia, his burden too big to bear alone.

Julia's sad thoughts were interrupted by the assistant director of nursing for operating theatres, ADN Dilys Aboud, who strode into theatre four, clipboard in hand. A large woman in her mid-fifties, she had always, even as a young trainee nurse, looked like the matron she was destined to become.

'Well, Dr Kent,' she said in her typical peremptory way, dispensing with a greeting as usual. 'It doesn't look like you'll be finishing by five o'clock. Does it?'

'Good afternoon, Sister Aboud, and a happy Christmas to you.'

'I won't be seeing Christmas at this rate, Dr Kent. I'll still be here, hurrying thoughtless surgeons out of the theatre suite.'

'Then you'll be doing what you love best.' Above her mask, Julia's eyes sent an impish smile.

'What I would love best, Dr Kent, is to be finishing my shopping, cooking my plum pudding, and wrapping my presents. Now, would you care to answer my question. When do you anticipate that you will be finishing this list?'

'We're just concluding this case and then there's only one more to go.'

'So you'll start the next one by five o'clock?'

'Yes. We've just sent for her.' Julia looked at Angie.

'And when do you think that you will finish that one?'

'It should be quite straightforward.'

'That's not exactly answering the question, Dr Kent. A straightforward oesophagectomy can take six hours.'

'We'll be finished by five-thirty or just after.' Julia hoped.

'You had better be. At the present time I've got seven operating theatres running over. That's overtime for a lot of nursing staff, Dr Kent. And it's a big hole in my budget, which has to be made up from somewhere.'

Dilly was a good manager and Julia appreciated her problem, but she and Angie didn't want to run late either. 'We've got shopping and plum pudding and presents too, Sister Aboud, but we're under pressure from our patients to get them fixed up before Christmas.'

'I understand, Dr Kent, and I do sympathise. None of us is at fault. But, as it stands now, your job is to try to squeeze as many patients as possible onto your lists. And my job is to stop you.'

Julia and Angie dawdled beside their cars in the doctors' car park. Angie needed to do some last-minute food shopping, while Julia was meeting Patrick at his work Christmas party, but, since the shops would be open until ten and Patrick would need time to mingle with his clients, they had a few minutes to spare. It was the last time they'd see each other until after Christmas.

Julia was still wiped out by Leo's news about Sandra. Not that she could tell Angie. As much guilty as comforted at having shared his sorrow, Leo had insisted it go no further, not until Sandra said. As it was, Angie noticed nothing special. Julia had been moody and distracted ever since that wretched lawsuit had landed on her desk. And even worse since Emma had invited her father to stay.

'What time are you picking Tony up tomorrow?' Angie asked cautiously.

Julia switched from one horror to another. 'His plane gets in at six. I told him not to come any earlier because I've got the practice's lunch. The traffic to and from the airport will be impossible, of course. But we've got ten days to recover.'

'Ten days?' exclaimed Angie. She'd thought Tony was only coming for the long weekend.

'So did I,' Julia confessed bleakly. And so had Tony initially. But the separation from Cecilia and Christmas without little Antonio were getting him down. He was off work until the fourth of January. And so he'd rung yesterday and asked if he could stay a bit longer.

'And I said yes.' Julia shrugged with defeat. Then, seeing Angie's expression, she challenged: 'What else could I do?'

Angie agreed she had little choice but, aware of Julia's apprehension about Tony's intrusion into her life at this time, was anxious for her all the same. She quickly shifted the focus from the ex-husband to the new boyfriend.

'How's Patrick taken the news of the visit?'

Julia immediately flushed crimson with guilt. 'I, um, I haven't filled him in on all the details yet. Any of the details, actually.'

Angie's look betrayed her disbelief.

'I know, I know,' Julia moaned hopelessly. With Patrick so unhappy about her not going to the farm, she hadn't marshalled the fortitude to tell him about Tony's visit. Although she'd have to soon, of course. After all, he and Ryan were coming for dinner on Christmas night and Tony would be there. 'Oh, Angie, I don't want him to think I'm not going to the farm because Tony's coming.'

'But Tony's coming to see Emma,' Angie reminded her.

'You and I know that. But Patrick might see it differently. He might think there's still something between Tony and me.'

Angie didn't see how Patrick could. They hadn't seen each other for seven years, for heaven's sake. Tony was coming to visit his daughter because she couldn't go to him. And Julia was staying in Sydney because of a long-standing commitment to her patients. And as for there being something between her and Tony, well there was, wasn't there? A whole bucket of things. Angie ticked them off on her fingers: betrayal, heartbreak, anger, resentment, possibly even hatred. Ever since the trail of destruction wreaked by Madeleine Morgan. Surely Patrick understood that.

Julia was even more shamefaced. Almost squirming, she told Angie she wasn't sure if Patrick knew about Madeleine either. She'd given him lots of opportunities to ask about her marriage and her divorce, but he hadn't. Not once. She thought perhaps he already knew, but if he didn't, she certainly wasn't going to force it on him. Not after spending the last seven years running away from people who saw her only in those terms. It was time for sleeping dogs to lie.

Angie was gentle, already guessing the answer to her next question. 'He doesn't know about the new case either, does he?'

'No, not yet. I haven't told anyone except you, Leo and Marcia.' Julia couldn't prevent a pathetic slump. 'I'm the world's biggest coward, I know, but I keep hoping the case will settle and no one else will ever need to learn about it.'

As Angie touched her shoulder, Julia knew she didn't have to explain further; better than anyone, Angie understood the moat she'd dug around herself. 'Enough about me,' she said abruptly. 'Cheer me up with your Christmas plans.'

It was her friend's turn to slump. 'I'm afraid they might not be any brighter than yours.'

'Oh?'

'I think Geoff's having an affair.'

Chapter 17

Julia was late for Patrick's Christmas party but, once Angie had started to talk about Geoff, the time had gone quickly. More upset than Julia had ever seen her, Angie confided the little and not-so-little happenings of the past few months which had given rise to her concerns until, last week, she'd taken the shocking step of hiring a private detective. There was no realistic alternative. She wouldn't ask Geoff directly, for a myriad of reasons, and she couldn't easily follow him. But she needed to know. It was tormenting her terribly.

Listening to the chronicle of Geoff's unaccounted-for absences, Julia cringed, kicking herself. Angie's suspicions, one or two at first, then a more upsetting handful, and now an oppressive avalanche, had clearly been worrying her sick for months and yet she'd said nothing. While she, preoccupied by the dramas of her own life, hadn't thought to ask.

As Angie spoke, Julia realised she'd never been that fond of Geoff. He was exceptionally attractive, she had to give him that. Even at forty-five, his tall, well-built frame, rich dark hair and unlined face fairly glowed with handsome good health. Mind you, he nurtured himself. No matter what else he had on, he always found time each day to swim a kilometre in the university pool, and follow it with a session of weight training. He wore only the finest clothes, drove an expensive European car, lived in one of the best streets in the area, and had his hair tended at the most exclusive salon.

Angie had always excused his self-indulgence as a manifestation of personal inadequacy; despite his physical and intellectual blessings, her husband was fundamentally insecure. Angie thought this probably sprang from his unsatisfactory relationship with his father, a notorious womaniser who finally left Geoff's mother to bring up the ten-year-old on her own, and never once came back to see his son. By the time Geoff was old enough to have forgiven him and want to seek him out, the older man was dead. Geoff had never been able to fill the void of his father's rejection, all his life needing reassurance that he was good-looking and talented and clever. Angie, who loved him, had been happy to give him that reassurance.

He was also a good family man, she insisted. While selfish and thoughtless on occasion, he was seldom cross or irritable, his sunny nature making him a good father to Ben and Richie, and a pleasant companion for her.

Despite Angie's defence of Geoff, Julia realised that, deep down, she'd never really trusted him. Still, she was surprised to hear her friend express doubts about her husband sixteen years into their marriage. She had seemed so content.

Angie told her about Ritzy Rainer. The private detective operated out of an anonymous modern suite in the heart of Bondi Junction. She was fiftyish, plump and businesslike, and far less glamorous than her name. If it really was her name. She'd interviewed Angie at length. Confirming infidelity was often quite easy, apparently, but determining the seriousness of an affair and the threat to a marriage required more than just surveillance. And took much longer. They'd agreed on a fee which Angie thought outrageous despite Ritzy's assurances that women with 'the goods' on their husbands invariably did much better in property and custody settlements. Angie had meekly

161

protested that she didn't want a divorce; she just wanted to know the truth. Phlegmatic until now, she suddenly began to weep.

Julia reached out to her. 'I'm sure it'll be all right, Angie. There'll be a perfectly innocent explanation for his absences.'

'And what if there's not, Julia? I love him so much. I don't know what I'll do if he leaves me.'

Vaucluse Manor was a magnificent historic house built in 1882 by one of the senior lawyers of the Sydney bar as a present to his wife on their tenth wedding anniversary. Julia had heard enough of the story to know that an equally grand but smaller house in an adjacent suburb had been built for the lawyer's mistress the following year.

Patrick's firm had supervised the recent renovation of the mansion, restoring it to its former glory. It now served as a function centre, and was a magnificent place for a Christmas celebration.

Patrick's was not the only party being held here this evening, and the car park, though large, was full. As Julia turned off the main road into the long private drive leading up to the house, she met with a line of stationary traffic. Realising she could sit for a day without moving, she made a pre-emptive strike. Seizing a brief gap in the traffic, she pulled out of the line of cars, executed a three-point turn and exited the private grounds in search of parking elsewhere. In her rear-view mirror, she saw women in various styles of elaborate evening wear disgorging themselves from vehicles and making their way to the manor. She baulked, her eyes involuntarily drawn from their finery to her own slightly crushed pantsuit.

She carefully rejoined the main road traffic, moving slowly as she looked out for a side street where she could leave her car. With her free left hand, eyes glued to the road, she rustled in her handbag for her invitation, until she realised she didn't have one. Her invitation had been verbal. She hadn't asked about the dress code – these were architects, after all, and Patrick, who knew she would be coming directly from the operating theatre, had not mentioned anything special. He had not even said 'cocktail party' just 'Christmas drinks'. She cursed.

It was already eight o'clock and she'd promised him she would be there by seven. If she went home to change, the party would be finishing as she arrived. In fact, if she didn't find a parking spot soon, there would be almost no point in going. The Vaucluse area was full of grand old blocks of units built before the time of the motor car; almost all of the street parking was restricted to residents. Julia lurched forward in hope then braked in disappointment as parking spots became driveways and bus stops and no-standing zones. Her anxiety climbed. Patrick would be watching for her, wondering where she'd got to, thinking she'd been called yet again to work. Even if she found somewhere to park now, she was well over a kilometre from the Manor. About to give up, she spied a spot being vacated and slipped in before she had time to surrender to the call of a glass of wine on the couch at home.

She ran all the way, pausing only at the vase at the bottom of the grand marble staircase to pinch a couple of orchids, which she pinned to her lapel in a feeble attempt to look dressy. The party was in full swing. Standing in the doorway she scanned the large crowd and was relieved to see that the dress standard was mostly casual, even for the women, although a small number were taking the opportunity to show what their credit cards had been doing lately. The evening gown set was thankfully at another function.

It took a minute before she saw Patrick. He was at the far end of the room regaling a group of clients with a story that was evidently very funny. Her heart leapt at the sight of his golden face alive with laughter. Just then he turned and, taking in her presence, his smile grew even larger. He made his way deliberately towards her, his eyes not leaving her face, his dilated pupils piercing her own with passion. He kissed her slowly on the lips before he said a word. The greeting he whispered into her ear generated a blush she felt would cause the lights to fuse.

'Later,' he promised softly, his hand under her chin, his eyes

163

still locked on hers. 'For now, let me introduce you to everyone. I've told them all about you.'

As Julia found her breath again, Patrick appropriated a glass of champagne for her from a passing waiter and led her proudly by the arm to meet his business partners, Nathan and Henry. Together with their wives, they were in the midst of an animated discussion with a major client.

After a while Patrick excused himself to mingle with his guests, leaving Julia in a group which included the wives of his partners and the final-year architecture student attached to the practice, a young woman named Natalie Anderson. Over time, Julia and Natalie struck up an easy conversation about the new and the old architecture of the eastern suburbs. The younger woman was intrigued to learn that Julia had met Patrick when he did the plans for her house; she'd wrongly assumed that they must have children at the same school and seemed surprised to learn that Julia's daughter was nearly eighteen. They spoke for a long while and Julia was thankful for her kindness in a room full of strangers.

They didn't make it to the bedroom; indeed, they barely made it inside the house. As Julia eased her car into his driveway, he'd prised open her door before she'd even turned off the ignition, his hands on her face, his mouth hungrily seeking hers.

He was now in the shower while Julia was propped up in his bed, reading glasses on her nose, thumbing through the advertising brochure of the famous mansion where the Christmas party had been held.

'Your firm did a wonderful job on Vaucluse Manor, Patrick,' she said as he emerged from the bathroom. 'The whole house fairly "resonates with the feel of the 1880s".'

'As if you'd know,' he laughed, throwing a pillow at her.

'I'll have you understand, Patrick Whitfield, that in my previous life I was his mistress in the other house, and I often stole to Vaucluse Manor to see how *she* was living. That's how I know.'

'I can't imagine you ever being the "other woman", Julia. You're clearly madam of the house material.'

'How unromantic,' she said, affecting a pout as she got out of bed and moved towards him, slowly undoing the satin tie at the front of her negligee. 'Let's pretend I'm the other woman tonight, shall we?'

The crowds and the parking could just about ruin Christmas if you let them, thought Julia as she joined the throng at the bakery. Only just after dawn on Christmas Eve, the place was already packed; she dreaded to think what it would be like in a few hours. She suppressed a yawn in the slow-moving queue; it had been a glorious evening, but a restless night. Even so, with the melee that was her mind, it was surprising she'd slept at all. She'd bet a million dollars Leo hadn't. Or Angie.

While the man ahead of her dithered over poppy or sesame, Julia's thoughts filled with Leo. Sandra was the light of his life, a laughter-filled bubble of a woman who sprinkled happiness wherever she went. The sort of person you couldn't imagine dying, couldn't imagine living without. Maybe Leo was mistaken, maybe the prognosis was not so dismal. But in her heart she knew it was.

And what about poor Angie, suddenly bisected by doubts about the man she had lived with for sixteen years and loved for much longer, a man who had hurt her before? Maybe she was wrong too, maybe Geoff was planning a surprise for her, a big party or a grand holiday. But again, Julia's heart doused her hope. And she knew exactly how Angie would be feeling.

Which brought her to Tony.

From her sadness, Julia rescued a grim laugh. What a predicament she'd devised here. Not only was Tony arriving in twelve hours, but Patrick knew nothing about it.

Tony. She still stumbled over the name, the memory. And still nurtured an abiding resentment of the hurt he'd dealt her, the casual way he'd humiliated her not only by his infidelity but by the needless public ridicule that had accompanied it. What *on earth* was she doing letting him stay? How could she *possibly* have agreed to it? She nearly howled at her own idiocy, but instead said, 'I'll have two baguettes, four croissants and a lamington, thanks.'

Leaving the bakery, a cold anger settled over her at the thought of Tony's arrogance. How dare he presume to saunter back into her life at the click of his fingers, just because his had fallen apart again. Which brought her to another resentment: he'd had a new life so much sooner than she had, stepping unburned from the embers of what they'd had almost straight into the arms of someone else. While she'd endured years of skin grafts.

And he'd had Antonio.

She roughly shelved her anger at Tony for later and turned her focus to Patrick. He was still asleep on her return, his gentle hands tucked under his face, the sheet slowly rising and falling with the excursions of his chest. She smiled as she remembered their night. No wonder he was exhausted; he had the staying power of a teenager.

Her face then clouded with disquiet once more. It was not that she'd wanted to conceal Tony's visit from him. It was just that, after seven years living with the fallout of that awful time, she was so grateful to be finally in a relationship with someone where her history as Mrs Tony Cabrini was irrelevant, and she didn't want to spoil it. Patrick had let her start afresh, just as Julia, and it had been enormously healing.

But now, with Tony coming to stay and Patrick set to meet him tomorrow night, her divorce and what preceded it could no longer be avoided. Indeed, what madness had let her waft along in a mist of denial, expecting she'd never have to talk about it? Shivering at her messy dilemma, she regarded Patrick's beautiful face. Despite the affection he'd wrapped her in these past two months, she was still insecure in his love. Even so, she knew he'd understand both about Tony's visit and about her past. But, as she waited for him to wake, a tiny tremor shook her.

Over breakfast, she finally summoned up the courage, leading in by asking if there was anything Ryan didn't eat.

'Oh God, Julia, I'm sorry,' Patrick cried out. 'I meant to tell you, but in the drama of organising last night I forgot. I'm so sorry.' His face was pink with embarrassment.

'Forgot what?' Julia was bewildered. Wasn't Ryan coming to Christmas dinner tomorrow night?

Neither of them was coming.

Patrick was mortified as he explained his change of plans. Not all of Genevieve's four sisters could get to Campbelltown at the same time; some would be coming for lunch, some for dinner, and Ryan had pleaded to be able to stay for both meals so that he could catch up with all his cousins. He especially needed them this year. And Patrick had said yes, of course they could. But he'd forgotten to tell Julia.

'Oh,' was all she could say, as disappointment fused with relief.

Chapter 18

The surgery bustled despite there being only a handful of patients to see; all four doctors were in at once, together with Justine, the junior secretary, who'd agreed to work Christmas Eve, and one of the typists, who was trying to get the letters out before the post office shut down for four days. It was a morning of tying up loose ends.

Patricia, as practice manager, came in to finalise the business side of things for the end of the calendar year. Julia could hear her at reception talking to Stephen, who'd buttonholed her to discuss the increase he had sustained for his share of practice costs over the past few months. He failed to see why he should pay so much more than the other three doctors.

'It's not a lot more, Stephen,' said Patricia reasonably. 'It's only an extra five hundred dollars a month.'

'Everyone is here for the same number of sessions, Patricia, so why aren't their bills the same?'

'Stephen, when you are here for a session, you always squeeze extra visits in before and after the usual hours. You see many more patients in the month than the others, you use up more secretarial and midwife time, and you consume more disposables.' She was firm. 'You should pay more.'

Julia listened to Stephen's petulant tone. It was his practice, he said. Surely there should be some allowance for that? Patricia reminded him that she was only doing what she'd been asked to do by the partnership. If he thought that his financial arrangement with his colleagues should be varied, then he should discuss it with them. 'But, as it currently stands, you are billed according to the number of patients you see.'

As he slunk back to his room, Julia thought he mumbled something about bringing Stacey back.

Julia was on the phone with her patient, Jane Steel. Again. Since her first appointment in October, Jane, now sixteen weeks, had had two scheduled monthly appointments, three extra appointments, and a consultation on the phone every second day. The secretaries tried to direct most of the calls to Erica, the practice midwife, but Jane insisted on speaking to Dr Kent at least once a week.

Not that she seemed to have any particular problems; Jane just worried. Today she was concerned about nausea, which had recurred in the past twenty-four hours. She felt quite sick and thought she might vomit. Julia reassured her that this was probably nothing to be troubled about, and would likely settle soon. There was nothing to be done until then except keep up her fluids.

'But what about the baby?'

'Are you worried about the baby, Jane?'

'Of course I am. If I'm nauseated and not eating, how will the baby get its nourishment?'

Julia reassured her that a couple of days of not eating was not a problem; babies made sure they got what they needed. Even patients who were sick for the whole nine months had babies that were fine.

'As long as you are sure, Dr Kent,' said Jane, still disquieted.

Julia hesitated. It was impossible to be absolutely sure of anything in pregnancy. It was an unpredictable time and doctors of her experience knew that patients who worried excessively had to be taken seriously. Anxious patients often did develop problems, 'self-fulfilling problems' as Stephen called them. She was therefore cautious. 'If you get worse over the holidays, Jane, just ring the practice's after-hours number and speak to Dr Steiner. He's covering me for the ten days, and I'll make sure he knows all about you.'

'I won't be able to speak to you personally?'

'I'm having a break, Jane.'

'I'm sure I heard your receptionist tell another patient that you would be around.'

'She might have meant that I would be in Sydney. But I am not back at work until after New Year.' Julia hated being less than completely truthful, but was starting to fear that Jane Steel would be popping over for breakfast on Christmas morning. Her fear was confirmed.

'Could I have your home number in case I need to talk to you?'

'I'm sorry, Jane. It's the practice policy not to give out private numbers. Dr Steiner will be available if you need to speak to someone over the break.'

It was another ten minutes before the phone call ended. Julia glanced at her patient's record as she put the file away. Jane Steel wasn't even halfway; there were another five months of this ahead. She wasn't sure who'd be happier when the pregnancy was over, her patient or herself.

'Here's to us!' Stephen proposed as he raised his glass of champagne and grinned at his colleagues around the table. Their lunch was coming to an end. For over three hours they had sat on the covered verandah of Stephen's favourite restaurant, feasting and talking and enjoying the view over Rose Bay.

'To us,' they replied.

'And to our Christmas,' he went on, rather in the mood now. 'Let the skies be blue, the days warm, the turkey moist and the wine plentiful.'

170

'And the patients be at home,' finished Leo, to whom it mattered most.

'And the patients be at home,' the others chorused.

Stephen, Julia, Leo and Sylvie were holding their second annual partners' Christmas lunch. They'd had some drinks and finger-food in the office a week ago for the staff, but the lunch was just for them. The first 'doctors only' lunch had happened last year, seemingly by accident. The office staff had begged off at the last minute. Mostly working mothers, there was too much to do, they'd said. The rare half-holiday was better put to shopping than lunching; there would be enough of lunching over the coming weeks.

And so, with the booking already made, the four had found themselves alone at lunch, having a much better time than they'd anticipated, so good that they'd decided to make it an annual event.

'How is your mum, Sylvie?' asked Stephen as he put down his champagne glass. 'Is she still at home?'

Julia was surprised and pleased to see Stephen being congenial towards Sylvie. She knew he thought highly of their youngest colleague professionally, but he found her manner aggravating. Sylvie was in the habit of bothering him for advice about her patients, often when he was flat-out, and even though she'd already resolved the problem herself. Julia understood she was just seeking his approval, but her intrusions irritated him enormously.

Perhaps if she had been pretty, thought Julia, he might have warmed to her more. Julia herself felt very differently, welcoming her young colleague as a breath of fresh air in her working life. Not only was Sylvie smart, but her mind worked in an unconventional, challenging way that Julia found refreshing.

Sylvie's relationship with Leo was similarly good. Nothing gave the older obstetrician greater pleasure than discussing the management of a medical problem and, like Julia, he met her more intense moments with some gentle teasing. She was growing in confidence from working with them.

'She's not well at all,' Sylvie replied. Her mother could now

171

do very little for herself and would soon have to move into a nursing home. At present she was just managing because she had a daily nurse to shower her, some help with basic cleaning, and Meals-on-Wheels. But she had such little mobility, she could hardly get to the bathroom or to the kitchen for a drink. And she fell and hurt herself constantly. But even with all that, she was fighting to stay in her house.

'What she really wants,' said Sylvie, 'is for her situation to become so desperate that I'll be forced to go home and look after her full-time.'

'But that's impossible,' declared Stephen, for whom it would have been. He barely saw his own mother, a charming and undemanding woman who lived only half an hour away.

'Not for some, Stephen,' Leo chimed in. Julia knew he'd been listening with singular interest; the best way to care for a terminally ill loved one was now an issue of great importance. Last night, Sandra had told him she'd decided not to have any treatment. She couldn't see that surgery, radiotherapy or chemotherapy had much to offer given how far her cancer had spread; the possible extra months of survival would be swallowed up recovering from the treatment. Julia understood the decision, but knew it increased Leo's feelings of helplessness. Sandra had also made her feelings clear on another matter. If she was going to die, she wanted it to be in her own home, in her own bed, looking out at her beloved garden and surrounded by her family.

'It is only these past two generations that have abandoned their family members to nursing homes,' Leo continued. 'In the past, and for that matter in the present in many cultures, the older members of the family were treated with great respect, and were nurtured and nursed by their family as they aged.'

'But they didn't age over such a long period as they do now, Leo,' countered Julia. While understanding his position, she was also anxious for Sylvie. 'Or in such a degree of infirmity. Once you were as sick as Sylvie's mum, you got pneumonia and died. You didn't hang on for months or years, still taking tablets for your blood pressure and your cholesterol, as if these mattered

172

while your neurological system was unravelling day by day. As a result, you were often saved from the final awful ravages of your disease by succumbing to a gentler, faster illness.'

'And your family was saved too,' remarked Stephen.

Sylvie ignored the others to look at Leo. 'So you think that I should do it then?' she asked very faintly.

'Take a break from your job and go back to Melbourne?'

'Yes. To nurse my mother in her own home until she dies.' She looked at him steadily, reading his face closely, waiting for his words. Leo hesitated, and Julia knew he was thinking of Sandra and how awful it would be for her to face the next few months alone.

'No, I do not think you should do it.' Relief flickered briefly on Sylvie's face, but Leo wasn't finished. 'However, I do not think that it is unreasonable of your mother to want it.'

'I certainly wouldn't do it, Sylvie,' intervened Julia quickly, her loyalty divided. 'But I would continue to go down on weekends as you have been doing. If your not being there every day means that she'll have to go into a nursing home, then that's what has to be. It's probably not going to be for very long anyway, if her deterioration continues as fast as it has been.'

Sylvie was wretched. 'Isn't that then an argument for being with her? If it's not going to be very long?'

Leo's mobile phone rang and he excused himself to attend the delivery of a patient. Soon after, Stephen looked at his watch, noted that it was past four o'clock and declared that he likewise should go. Stacey and the kids were waiting for him at Whale Beach. 'That was a great lunch,' he said, standing up and patting his stomach as he tucked in his shirt which had ridden up slightly.

'It's a pity we can't do it more than once a year,' said Sylvie, clearly enjoying the opportunity to have more than just snatched moments with her colleagues.

'Yes, it is,' agreed Stephen. 'Good luck with your mother, Sylvie,' he added sympathetically. 'Don't make any rash decisions, but remember that we can cover you if you need it.'

Sylvie nodded, appreciative of his support.

'And good luck with Tony,' he said, turning to Julia. 'I'm sure it'll be all right. Wish the old bugger happy Christmas from me.'

After Stephen left, Sylvie moved to his chair, since it had the best view of the bay. Julia turned hers slightly as well and they sat side by side, mesmerised by the water as it glinted in the late afternoon sunlight.

'I suppose we'd better go soon too,' said Sylvie lazily, sinking deeper into her chair. Her plane was to depart at much the same time as Tony's arrived, and Julia was giving her a lift to the airport after they'd collected Emma. But they had time to spare and were lost in their respective thoughts of Christmas.

Julia had nothing left to protect her; no intervening distractions remained. No exam results, no final operating list, no last session of patients in the surgery, no cocktail party, no partners' lunch. There was nothing that now separated her from Tony's arrival. As she allowed her unshielded mind to finally dwell on him, she found a pain so fresh it made her gasp.

'Are you all right, Julia?' Sylvie swung around in concern.

'Yes, yes, I'm fine.' She forced a smile. 'I hope your Christmas is not too bad,' she said. The way Gerda made Sylvie feel upset Julia greatly. Life wasn't fair, she thought, contrasting her colleague's lot with her own situation of loving father, gorgeous daughter and wonderful boyfriend. She reached into her bag, pulled out a large, brightly wrapped gift and handed it over. 'Happy Christmas.'

Sylvie was embarrassed as she slowly unwrapped a book of jokes.

'You're to read ten pages, three times a day,' Julia instructed.

'It's just what I need. Thanks. But I thought we'd agreed, no presents.'

'It's not a present, silly. It's a prescription.'

Chapter 19

Scruuunch . . . The sound was familiar, it was only the object she'd scraped her car against that was different. She got out to inspect the damage. She'd been going slowly, but the parking space was tight and the pylon obviously closer than she'd judged. And the accident inevitable given how she felt. She ran both her eye and her finger along the scratch. It wasn't too bad; the pylon and the car were the same colour. Still, thirty centimetres further back would have been better. The duco there was already damaged.

She dragged herself to the domestic terminal. Sylvie would be boarding now, while Emma was no doubt excitedly scanning the arrivals board for her father's flight. They'd been told it was delayed when they'd rung; Julia found herself hoping it wouldn't come at all.

Emma was waiting for her, face bright. 'He'll be here in ten minutes.'

'Great.' Julia's tone was ambiguous as she suppressed her irritability with her daughter. Why couldn't Emma have just gone to Brisbane as planned? Why did she have to put her in this position? It was the last thing she needed at the moment. At any time, really.

She cast a longing glance at the bar as they passed; a shot of liquid courage would be welcome, but she was driving. Besides, she was going to need her self-control.

As the plane taxied to its allocated gate and the hostess in the arrival lounge opened the door, Emma moved forward while Julia stepped back and slid into a chair. This was it. Seven years of living with betrayal and loss of confidence, of revisiting cruel comments, of recalling needless public ridicule. Now she was to come face to face with the author of her pain. She hoped she could be civil, for Em's sake, could conceal her resentment and leave unspoken the bitter words buried deep in her soul. Sitting there, she felt them surge up, and resolutely squashed them down again. Then, as Emma said, 'Mum, he's here,' she stood up and stepped forward to greet a man she didn't recognise.

'Happy Christmas, Julia. And thank you for letting me come.'

Julia was at the kitchen sink early on Christmas morning as Tony walked in, preceded by an alerting cough. She was wearing an old summer dressing gown while he was fully dressed. Even so, she could tell it was he who felt the more ill at ease. Certainly more than he'd expected to feel when he'd accepted the invitation to stay.

'Do you mind if I use the phone?' Tony was awkward, clearly not wanting to impose upon her further but having little choice. 'I forgot to charge my mobile, and I promised Antonio I'd ring him early this morning.'

Julia turned to him. She was still surprised at the reaction he'd evoked in her last night. For years she'd carted the memory of what he'd done like an open black umbrella above her, forever shading her into dim, cold bitterness. Expecting to be awash with anger and hurt and resentment all over again, she'd instead felt sorry for him. When he'd emerged at the airport so thin and sad and grateful to her for inviting him, she'd found her long-nurtured bitterness towards him had nowhere to go. It had become a habit for her, hating him, but now as she looked at him, she realised she could no longer focus that hatred on the man who stood before her.

'You never were very good with technological things, Tony,' she chided mildly. 'You can use the phone on one condition.'

'Oh?' he asked cautiously.

'That you clean the barbecue before lunch. I haven't used it for weeks, and I'm scared of what I'll find growing on it.'

'Might add to the flavour,' he offered, trying to make her smile.

'Barramundi doesn't need that sort of flavour.'

'If I did it, I'd be entitled to a very long phone call.'

'You would indeed, but it is my experience that three-year-olds can't manage more than sixty seconds on the phone. Especially when they have new toys to get back to.'

'This is my son you're talking about,' Tony joked, only then realising what he had said.

'In that case I'll revise my estimate to thirty seconds,' Julia rejoined lightly, hiding her wound.

While Tony went into the hall to make his call, Julia pondered what she knew about Cecilia. While it wasn't much, it was a lot more than she'd known a week ago; Emma had given her a crash course. Tony had met Cecilia, a graphic designer now in her mid-thirties, through mutual friends five years before. Apparently they'd taken to each other immediately; they married within six months.

The first few years were blissful but, after the birth of Antonio, they'd started to grow apart. Emma wasn't sure of the details but knew that at least part of the problem related to Cecilia's obsession with her body. Despite being lean and in great condition, she'd apparently decided that pregnancy had ruined her physique. Reducing her body fat and improving her muscle definition had become very important, so important she'd taken to spending six hours a day at the gym, with Antonio in the facility's creche. She'd also stopped cooking, since she wasn't eating.

On one of the weekends she'd visited, Emma had come home

with her father and found Cecilia in bed at five o'clock, resting before she went out with a crowd from her pump class while Antonio was wet and hungry in his playpen in front of the television. Tony wouldn't say, but from comments Cecilia had made to Emma, it appeared he'd suggested she seek help for her eating disorder and she'd laughed in his face. Brisbane was full of fatties – they were the ones who needed counselling.

Over the past twelve months, Tony had taken to dropping Antonio at his sister Anna's or his mother's on the way to work. Both also cooked Tony a meal in the evening when he went to collect his son. Though invited, Cecilia wouldn't join them; she wouldn't be caught dead eating such oily food. Then, six months ago, she'd announced that she was leaving Tony for Curtis, a twenty-five-year-old body-builder at the gym who understood her needs far better than he ever had. And she wanted custody of Antonio.

'How was he?' Julia asked when Tony returned. She'd moved to the table in the back room, and now sat beside a large pot of fresh tea, considering the drizzly weather and wondering if they would be able to eat lunch outside on the deck as she'd planned.

'As you thought,' Tony replied. 'Very caught up in all his booty.'

'What did you give him?'

'An electric train set.'

'I'm sure he'll love that.' A small smile crossed her face. 'Emma always loved hers.'

'I know.' They sat lost in the memories for a moment.

While Tony took his place at the table across from her, Julia poured tea for them.

'You look well,' he said.

She pulled her dressing gown selfconsciously about her but did not return the compliment. Misery emanated from him, suffering writing its battle history in the lines on his face. He was obviously desperate about Cecilia and Antonio; he'd probably expected that Christmas without them would be no worse than any other weekend, and now found that it was, that making do with a phone call and a photo of Antonio with Santa was a very poor substitute for the real thing.

'Do you want to talk about it?' she asked gently.

'I thought I was supposed to be the shrink.' It was a feeble joke.

'No one has a monopoly on listening.'

Before they could proceed further, the phone rang. Emma answered. 'Mum, it's for you,' she called. 'It's Patrick.'

'Tell him I'll take it upstairs,' said Julia, excusing herself to Tony.

Emma came to join her father at the table, giving him a hug as she did so.

'How are you, possum?' he asked.

'Fine, Dad. Happy Christmas.' She sat down in the chair her mother had vacated. 'Have you rung Antonio yet?'

'Just a few minutes ago.'

She frowned. 'You should have told me, Dad. I wanted to wish him happy Christmas too.'

Tony, pleased that she took an interest in the half-brother she'd met only a dozen times, was chastened by her complaint. 'Sorry, darling, but you were still in your room. And besides, it was all I could do to get him to leave his toys and speak to me. I'm sure he'd love to hear from you though. We'll ring again tomorrow.'

He told her about the need to clean the barbecue and, as they moved out to the wet deck, asked her what was planned for the day.

'Not much.' She handed him the scraper and followed with the paper towels. It was just a small Christmas this year, positively tiny when you compared it with a Cabrini Christmas. Grandpa was coming up from Wollongong for the day, and they were going to have barbecued seafood for lunch. Just the four of them. Maybe only three if Julia had to go to the hospital. She had already been in during the night.

'Isn't Leo covering for the holidays?'

'He is, but you know Mum. She has a couple of doctor-patients due, and somebody special's daughter, and a nurse she used to work with, and maybe a couple of others, and she's promised them all that she'll be there for their deliveries.'

'She hasn't changed then,' said Tony, amused.

'It's the job, Dad,' Emma defended. 'It doesn't give her much choice. Then this evening, Grandpa will go home, and it will be just us. Mum's new boyfriend, Patrick, the one on the phone, was supposed to come for dinner with his son Ryan, but that's changed now.' She paused before adding, 'Jason might come over.'

While it was Julia's new boyfriend that Tony wanted to inquire about, he asked about Emma's instead.

'Jason's got a band too, you said?'

'Yeah, and they're pretty good. Although not as good as us.' Emma was suddenly uncertain if this constituted disloyalty. 'You won't tell him I said that, will you, Dad? Not even joking. I'll kill you if you do.'

Tony laughed. 'Of course not. I'll only tell his friends.'

'Dad!'

By the time Julia joined them again it was after nine. She had showered, blow-dried her hair and dressed in a new lilac linen shirt worn over a pair of white cotton trousers, with lilac sandals. The outfit was her Christmas present to herself. She had lost a few kilos in the last couple of months, but unfortunately not her bulge, and the shirt worn loose gave her a much better line than it did tucked in.

'Happy Christmas, Mum,' said Emma, standing up to kiss her. 'We thought you must have gone to the hospital, you were so long,' she teased. 'Were you on the phone all that time, or just in the shower?'

'Those are the sorts of questions that it is permissible for parents to ask their children, but not vice versa, Miss Stickybeak. As a matter of fact, I lay down for half an hour. I had two phone calls during the night before finally going in for a delivery at three. And then, when I came home, I just couldn't get back to sleep. So, when I finished on the phone and the bed looked so inviting, I climbed back in.'

Julia could feel Tony appraising her while she spoke; once again she hoped she hadn't changed as much as he had. He asked if she minded if Emma took him for a walk down to the beach and around the point, then up the hill and back through the old cemetery. The weather was a bit grim, but it was years since he'd done that walk, and he wanted to have a look around.

'It would be nice if you could come too,' he added hopefully.

Julia thought she should stay. The hospital might call. And she had a few things still to sort out for lunch. And then she might lie down again for a while. She didn't add that after the emotional upheaval of the last few days, she needed some time on her own.

She turned to Emma, smiling at her daughter's obvious excitement at retracing the track she'd so often taken as a child with her father. 'Make sure you show him the refurbishment of the Icebergs' Club. And Jamie Packer's apartment.'

'I will.'

'And where they've widened the pavement on Campbell Parade to allow for all those new restaurants.'

'Okay.'

'And the Mediterranean-style villas that are going up everywhere.'

Tony laughed. 'Sounds as if there'll be nothing that I'll recognise.'

'The traffic will be pretty familiar,' Julia observed drily. 'Take your time, have a good look around, but don't forget you promised to clean the barbecue before lunch.'

She could have sworn Tony winked at Emma.

Julia finished her lunch preparations quickly. Unlike Angie, she was not a wizard in the kitchen. Rather, she had a talent for finding easy recipes and making them her own. She'd decided last week that an entree of fresh prawns on a bed of coriander and chilli noodles would be a nice start, while with the barra-mundi there were lime leaves and grilled summer vegetables. For dessert she had made a mango mousse, not recalling until later that it was one of Tony's favourites.

There being nothing more she could do until the lighting of the barbecue, which thankfully was under cover, it was time to put her feet up for a while. After brief consideration, she chose not to go back to bed. While her limbs ached and it was definitely dozing weather, she knew she wouldn't be able to sleep. Not with her brain discharging enough pulses to light the Christmas tree on its own. She settled instead on the couch and looked out over the deck and down to the ocean. She couldn't see that far, however, the view being dulled by the heavy rain which had just started up again. Anxious for her father, she unfurled herself from the couch and padded to the front door. Peering through the downpour to the street beyond, she hoped he would arrive soon. His eyesight was not as good as he pretended, and she knew he wouldn't enjoy driving in this weather.

Returning to the couch, she picked up the new book Emma had given her and started to read. And stopped again. Her overloaded mind saw only print; comprehension was beyond her. She should have been grateful, she mused with a defeated sigh, that her preoccupation with Tony and Patrick had for the moment pushed thoughts of her looming lawsuit from her mind. But she was unconvinced of the benefit.

As the rain fell like sheets of silvery metal, she pondered again her unexpected response to Tony. Anticipating an earthquake of emotions to swallow her at his appearance, last night she'd seen him amble back into her life without a single seismic shudder.

She was happier now, that was part of it, her confidence at least partly restored by Patrick's adoration. And time had done some of it. While she'd held the sharp lines of the negative in her mind all these years, the print had actually faded; at Tony's emergence, she'd found her emotions could no longer generate the intensity her memory demanded. And finally it was Tony himself, his appearance so altered it had stripped away whatever residuum of resentment still remained. He seemed much older than she remembered, his face creviced, his curly black hair colonised by corkscrews of grey. It was only when his smile sent light to his beautiful eyes that she saw the old Tony. But he wasn't smiling much. It was obviously a difficult time for him.

She had spoken to him little on the way back from the airport, preferring to listen as father and daughter caught up. And she had been taken aback. It was as if Tony had simply been away for a week on business, the detail he knew of Emma's life. He asked all the right questions about Jade and the band, could name the new songs they had written, and realised that Brad had been replaced by Jason. He was well aware of her exam results and those of her friends, and even knew about someone called Stan, a zany new colleague at the music store where Em worked, whom Julia had never heard of.

With a twinge of unexpected ambivalence, she had left them happily chatting while she went to visit Patrick. A few hours on Christmas Eve was the last the lovers would have for two weeks, and she'd refused to give them up. Tony had, after all, come to see Emma.

Patrick had been waiting for her when she arrived, his arms seeming to sense she needed nurturing, his lips soon on hers. Ryan was singing Christmas carols up and down the neighbourhood with a clutch of local children and would not be home for an hour. They had moved quickly to the bedroom and, in the moments of intimacy, Julia resolved to tell him about Tony's visit. Their relationship was too important to permit dishonesty, however oblique.

'Patrick, there is something I need to speak to you about,' she said quietly. They were dressed now, and in the kitchen, Julia watching while he opened a bottle of champagne. Ryan was not yet home.

'You can't imagine lasting a fortnight without making love to me? In that case, come to the farm,' he said, engaging her with the sultry gaze he knew she could never resist, and bending over to kiss her softly. He lifted his glass. 'To my beautiful Julia.'

'To my wonderful Patrick.' As they strolled into the living room, the fine sheen of perspiration appearing on her palms made it hard for Julia to hold her glass and she put it down. She turned to Patrick and waited anxiously for him to inquire what it was she had to tell him, hoping he would still love her when he heard. But, as they took a seat near the Christmas tree, Patrick had moved on. To Ryan and his work and his family.

'I hope you don't mind me letting you down tomorrow night, Julia.' He took her hand.

It was a perfect cue to introduce Tony, and Julia had said the first three words when the phone rang. It was one of Genevieve's sisters, upset, calling to make sure Patrick was all right. It was only the second Christmas since the accident. Once the call had been concluded, Patrick's mind was on his wife and daughter as he sadly recalled Christmases past. Julia waited, not wanting to interrupt his memories. Then, as they moved on to happier subjects, she tried several times to lead into an admission of her ex-husband's presence in her house. Having determined to speak about it, she was now desperate to do so, to have it out in the open, not a needless secret between them. She waited for her moment, but found that each time she began, Patrick diverted her to something else. Until, with Ryan's excited arrival, it was too late.

And she had driven away without mentioning Tony.

She looked out the front door for her father's arrival several more times, wishing he was less stubborn about not having a mobile phone. At least then he could have rung if there was a problem. But he hadn't wanted a 'newfangled intrusion' in his life. Growing progressively more worried, she decided that eleven was a reasonable hour, and poured herself a glass of wine. Returning to the couch, she was disconcerted to discover that, despite the deluge of other preoccupations, her mind would not leave her litigation alone completely. It always hovered just outside her consciousness, waiting for the slit of an opening to fly in.

She found herself carried back to Tony's trial. The past two months had made her reluctantly appreciate a few fragments of what he must have gone through. Curled around her Christmas drink, she saw more. In her consternation that she may have unwittingly contributed to Brendan Edwards' suffering, she caught glimpses of the agony of failed responsibility Tony must have experienced following the death of his patient. And recognised that such horrific distress could lead to errors of judgement; her own past few months were proof enough of this.

To escape the confrontation of her thoughts, she flicked on the television and found herself in the mindless cheer of the Bing Crosby perennial. Involuntarily her lips curled into a smile as the movie pulled from the attic of her memory the picture of Christmas a decade ago. They were just back from their two years in Europe and Emma, then six, had been quite put out at the absence of snow. Tony had leapt up, singing that he was 'dreaming of a white Christmas' and disappeared mysteriously into the bathroom. When he returned, the three of them had liberally iced the Christmas tree with talcum powder.

Her smile dissolved into tears. In the brooding, bitter years since Joseph's death and their divorce, she'd forgotten how happy they'd once been and how much fun they'd had. Sadness flooded her that it had all been destroyed.

Just then, the doorbell rang.

She dashed to the kitchen, sliced a large onion in two, and carried it with the knife to the front door. It was her father. 'Come in, Dad. I'm so glad you're here safely,' she sniffled, wrapping her arms around him in relief. 'Let me finish with this onion and I'll be with you.'

'Don't rush, princess, I've another armful to fetch from the car.'

Julia opened him a beer and found a bowl for the gardenias he'd brought. Finished with his unpacking, George looked around expectantly for Emma and Tony. Julia told him where they were. His look suggested he thought it unlikely weather for a walk.

They sat for a while catching up. Gracie Marsden from next door had broken her hip and he was minding her cat, while Mr Stubbs from across the street was in his usual rude health and had been over for some Christmas cake this morning. 'And what about you, princess? How are you?'

'I'm great, Dad. Things couldn't be better. Would you like another beer?'

Tony and Emma were nearly home when the front door opened and George emerged, keys in hand. 'Grandpa!' exclaimed Emma, running to him and flinging her arms around his neck.

'My little scallywag, how are you?' he said, returning her

hug, and then holding her at arm's-length for a full appraisal. 'Have you grown again?'

'Grandpa, I haven't grown in over three years.'

'Maybe you're just fatter then,' he teased, instinctively putting his hands up to protect himself.

'I'm glad you've got your keys, Grandpa, 'cause you're leaving now,' Emma replied, clobbering him as expected, and propelling him towards his car.

'I've got my keys, young lady, because I forgot to bring your Christmas present into the house.'

'Oh, a present?' she asked with feigned consideration. 'In that case, maybe you can stay.'

'Just let me say hello to my son-in-law first,' he said, extending his hand to Tony, who had hung back while Emma and George carried out their pantomime.

'It's good to see you, George,' Tony said, shaking the older man's hand.

'Likewise, Tony. I've missed you.'

Tony and George talked for hours after lunch. The rain and clouds cleared in the mid-afternoon and, as the sun hit the front porch, so did they. The women left them to it.

Julia rang Angie at her sister's. Behind the brightness, she could hear the strain in her friend's voice, the intonation which bespoke her fear that this might be her last Christmas with her family intact. Julia wished her luck and promised to ring again tomorrow. She then thought to call Leo, who would be having an equally grim day. But it was not usual for her to do so and Sandra would immediately know that he'd told her.

Awaiting a call from the hospital, she took the opportunity to stretch out on the couch for a while. Emma came to sit beside her, fresh from dancing to the new CD Grandpa had given her. 'Thanks so much for having Dad to stay, Mum. It's been the best Christmas ever. Grandpa obviously thinks so too.'

'I'm glad you're enjoying it, Em,' said Julia, happy for her daughter.

Emma's inflection changed. 'Mum, do you think you were fair to Dad?'

'Fair? Fair in what way?' asked Julia, slowly sitting up.

'In leaving him after his trial.'

Emma and her father had spoken about that time on their walk. Emma had been vaguely aware of the story, of course, mostly from playground comments, but had never quite understood how her father's trial had led to his sudden departure, her parents' divorce, and her mother's desire never to see him again. Over the years, she'd asked her mother about it several times, but Julia had always deflected her. Now that her father was divorcing again, it seemed a reasonable time to ask him. And he had told her.

'I'm just not sure why you had to leave him after the charges were all dropped.'

Julia was furious. How dare Tony discuss this without asking her first. He was a guest in her house, for God's sake. Why was he undermining her with her daughter?

Oblivious, Emma went on. 'Dad said he wasn't sure if it was his story you couldn't believe, or his stupidity.'

Julia's eyes became hard as granite. 'I'm sorry, Em, but I'd rather not talk about it. It was a painful time. The worst. It's best left in the past.'

Emma nodded, unenlightened, but said nothing more.

Chapter 20

Like Boxing Day yesterday, the morning was sunny and still, the rains of Christmas now evident only in the growth of the grass. Julia was making tea while, beside her, Emma picked distractedly at the remaining nuts in the jar on the bench, still far too excited to eat anything more substantial. Julia grinned at the sight of her. 'I suppose you were all rather pleased at how it went?'

Emma was outrageously pleased, but asking gave her the chance to talk about it all over again. 'It was wonderful, wasn't it, Mum? So exciting, even more than the last concert. They didn't want us to leave the stage, did they?'

Emma's band had been one of seven participating in the previous afternoon's beach concert. They'd played before a huge crowd, drawn by the weather, the location and the public holiday. Growing in assurance over the past couple of months, the girls had turned in their best performance so far, and Julia knew her daughter had lain awake most of the night replaying the entire bracket over in her mind, bar by bar. 'Yes, darling, it was wonderful, it really was. Your father has been singing "Party Pooper" ever since. I could hear him in the shower belting it out just a while ago. I think you might have a new member for your band.'

'I hope not,' Emma grimaced comically. It was not from Tony that she derived her musical talent.

They took their mugs out onto the deck.

'Which song did you like best, Mum?'

Knowing which of the two new original compositions Emma had largely written on her own, Julia considered her reply. 'I like "Party Pooper" too, Em. It's catchy and has a great beat, but I think "It's Cold Comfort" is better. It's got a more complex melody and fabulous lyrics.'

Her daughter flushed with pride.

Later in the morning, after Emma had gone to work at the music store, Tony and Julia sat on the deck in the mild sunshine. Tony flicked distractedly through the newspaper, thin as it was, before finally starting on the crossword, while Julia was absorbed in a book. A short while before they had breakfasted on ham with eggs, tomatoes, mushrooms and toast which Tony had cooked. He'd then cleaned up the kitchen, even sweeping the floor. Julia was only vaguely aware of his industriousness, so caught up was she in the last few chapters of her novel. She stopped briefly to eat, subsequently nodded yes to a cup of coffee, but was otherwise unreachable.

Finally she was finished and let out a satisfied sigh. 'Thanks, Tony. That's the best thing I've read all year. Except for Emma's school novels. Some of them were pretty good.'

'I thought you'd like it, even though war fiction isn't usually your style.'

She sat up in the deckchair, took off her sunglasses and looked at him. 'Isn't it?'

Tony was immediately defensive. 'I just meant that you always liked family sagas and offbeat comedies, and so I was a little hesitant in buying something so different.'

'My reading tastes are much broader than that. Always have been.'

189

She replaced her sunglasses and lay down on the deckchair again as he turned back to the crossword. They felt the chill as the sun went behind a cloud. Julia lay unmoving for several minutes before finally speaking. 'Sorry, Tony. I'm a bit irritable at the moment. Thank you for the book. And you're right, it's not at all my usual style, and it is something I would never have read if you hadn't given it to me.' The sun emerged from behind the cloud.

Tony looked relieved but said nothing for a few minutes. Then, very quietly, he asked, 'What are you irritable about?' She'd snapped at him and Emma several times over the past few days.

'Well, for starters, I'm pretty pissed off at you for talking to Emma about our divorce without consulting me first.' Her sudden aggression took them both by surprise.

'She asked me.'

'So? She's asked me plenty of times and I've told her I don't want to talk about it.'

That was the difference, of course, and she could see it in his edginess and the way his arteries pulsated at his temples; he *did* want to talk about it.

'What did you tell her, Tony?' she asked after a bit, her own heart now also quickening.

He hesitated. 'I told her the truth. From my point of view, of course.'

'You told her *everything*?'

'About Madeleine, yes,' he clarified with some embarrassment. He went on hastily, 'I could see no reason not to. She's heard snippets from lots of people over the years. I wanted her to hear the whole story from me.'

Julia said nothing, unable to fathom why Tony would want to discuss that dreadful time. She certainly didn't. It had been miserable enough living it once; she had no wish to revisit it. Especially with him. In truth, she was ready for him to go.

They had managed reasonably well in the few days he'd been here, better than she'd expected. But, with Emma back at work, the buffer between them was gone and the awkwardness more apparent. Her choice all along had been never to see him again, and the strain of his unexpected nearness was taking its toll, confusing and alarming her. After years of tightly held resentment, seeing him now so wounded himself and finding she didn't hate him any more had completely thrown her. His presence reminded her that she had once loved him desperately, a truth she had buried under years of bitter sadness. Digging it up again was too much for her.

She wanted him to go. And she wanted Patrick to come; he'd rung every day from the farm, and yesterday made her promise that they would soon have a holiday together. He was missing her so much. And she was gravely in need of his consolation.

She broke from her thoughts to look at Tony. 'It's fair enough, I suppose,' she said neutrally.

'I wouldn't have brought it up if she hadn't asked.' Tony still knew her well enough to recognise the distance in her tone. 'I also spoke to her about my divorce from Cecilia.'

Julia grabbed the change of subject. 'It must be very upsetting for you. Especially with Antonio.'

Tony nodded grimly. Although things had not been good for a while and he'd been regretting the marriage, he was still devastated when Cecilia said she didn't love him any more. And bewildered. No one else in his family had divorced, yet he had two failed marriages. His confidence was badly shaken. And he was worried about his son.

He told Julia about Cecilia, how she barely remembered to feed Antonio, let alone play with him; he could see changes in his child already. And what was most upsetting was that there seemed to be only one reason she wanted custody: money. His lawyer had explained that with custody, Cecilia would get the house, well over half the assets, and regular child support.

Julia sat up and took off her sunglasses. 'You aren't applying for custody, Tony?'

His dark eyes narrowed. He wanted to, more than anything in the world. He'd already had one child grow up without him, and couldn't bear the thought of doing it again. The pain washed across his face. He could easily cut his hours and, of course, there was his mother and Anna. His whole family loved his little boy.

'So what's the problem?'

'Do you have to ask, Julia? Do you really think that I could win a custody battle? With my past?'

She looked at him. That Madeleine Morgan was still casting her shadow over his life as well came as a shock. 'Is it relevant, Tony?'

'It's as relevant as Cecilia's lawyer would want to make it.'

The subject of lawyers now broached, it took little further questioning for Tony to learn of Julia's court case, the other reason she was so irritable. She gave an outline.

'Of course, it may not go to court,' she said finally, not really wanting to discuss it further with him. 'I won't know until next month.'

'They might settle?'

She refused to get her hopes up. 'Yes, they might.'

She then stood and announced her intention to have a shower; she'd had enough of talking to Tony. But she couldn't finish without giving him one last piece of advice. If he really believed it would be bad for Antonio to live with Cecilia and her boyfriend, he had to fight for custody. 'For the sake of your son.'

At her words, suddenly he was overcome. He wanted his son with him, desperately. But each time he contemplated the approach Cecilia's lawyer would take, he knew he couldn't do it, couldn't face those allegations all over again, not even for Antonio.

There was a long silence before he whispered the question to which she already knew the answer. 'Could you?'

Chapter 21

Julia and Patrick sat in peaceful, tired silence, their legs dangling over the wharf as the January sun set behind them. Quiet fishermen nursed their reels on either side, while yachts pulled up slowly, one by one disgorging their laughing, sunburnt cargo before moving off to moor nearby. It had been a magical few days of swimming and sailing and making love and, as it came to an end, Julia still marvelled that an entire weekend had been annexed to pleasure. It had been Patrick's doing, of course. Snuggling closer into his welcoming chest, she felt his fingers in her hair and thought for the thousandth time how unbelievable it all was. Just a few months ago, a weekend like this would have been unimaginable. But now she had Patrick and everything was possible.

Even through his grief, his zest for life still shone, his energy and enthusiasm battling the sadness thrust upon him, lifting Ryan up as well. It was one of the things Julia loved most – the way he cared for his son. After how he cared for her, of course. His gaze, his words, his touch all took her to a place where she was queen of the world. And that was before he made love to her. A sigh of contentment wisped quietly from her lips. There had been no one special in her life for such a long time, since Tony really, and she had forgotten the peculiar joys of being a couple. She could have sat on that wharf for the rest of her life.

Patrick moved his hand to stroke the skin of her thigh lightly, in small caressing circles. He knew it tickled and waited for her to push him away. When she did, he grabbed her hands and started stroking her palms, knowing they tickled also. She tried to wriggle up the wharf, but his arms were around her. His laughing eyes locked with hers. 'You didn't think I'd be letting you go, did you? Not when it took me so long to get you here?'

They walked back up to the hotel, the last of the sun's rays now saying goodbye. Julia took in the view for a final time. Turning to Patrick, she wrapped her arms around his neck. 'Thank you so much for bringing me here. It's one of the most beautiful places I've ever seen.'

This was all the opening he needed. 'So you won't mind that I've already booked another weekend next month? And while we're about it, I want you to come to the farm for a week at Easter with me. Mum and Dad insist on meeting you. They won't take no for an answer this time, not after everything I've told them.'

Julia knew she was smiling goofily at his generous words but couldn't stop; he was always doing this to her and it felt wonderful. She was delighted to have another chance to visit his parents after turning them down at Christmas. Although she probably couldn't manage a week. Leo might be needing time off by then. Patrick nodded, now very familiar with her work. A few days would be fine. 'Besides, you've got to save up your holidays for our grand overseas trip.'

'Oh?' Her enlarging eyes betrayed her excitement. Was there no end to his surprises?

Patrick grinned boyishly. He had been waiting for the right moment to speak of his plan. There was an architects' conference in Paris in August. He knew she was planning to catch up with Emma in Europe in July, and wanted her to stay on for a few weeks to travel with him as well. His look compelled her. She had half a year to sort out her patients and he was not going to accept any excuses. 'You're coming with me.'

Julia tingled at the thought of such a holiday with him. Of visiting palaces and cathedrals and art galleries in his company, his vast knowledge taking her beneath the surface of the treasures. And the timing was perfect, as he said. She planned to have three weeks with Emma, but surely she could wangle an extra fortnight to stay on with Patrick? Although August *was* when Stephen was thinking of having leave. And Sylvie after him. And of course, Leo could need time off as well. Still, if she started organising it now, she might just be able to swing it. She felt her temperature shoot up with the fever of it all.

And fall again. Who was she kidding? Her colleagues' holiday plans were far from the major consideration. It was Tracey Edwards who held that honour. If the case did not settle, if it went to trial, it could put paid to all her holiday dreams. Until she knew what was happening there, she couldn't plan a single thing. With Emma or with Patrick. And she wouldn't know that until Friday.

Suddenly she felt deflated. This wretched, horrible lawsuit could ruin everything. She went to tell Patrick about it, but stopped. Now was not the time. It would spoil the tenor of the weekend, the warmth of the evening. And maybe, maybe after Friday she wouldn't need to tell him at all.

She lifted her face up to his, her eyes aflame with appreciation. 'Thank you for asking me, Patrick. It sounds irresistible.'

Tired and hungry and happy to be finished, Julia gazed longingly at the Pacific, so inviting in the evening sunshine. Thank heavens she'd be down there for a swim shortly. Mind you, the day hadn't been too bad given that Marcia had squeezed a number of Sylvie's gynaecological patients, ones who simply couldn't wait, into an already fully booked session. Leo was currently seeing Sylvie's other patients, the pregnant ones.

Sylvie had not come back after Christmas, having made the decision to stay with her mother until she died. Her patient load should have been shared equally among her colleagues, but Stephen was too busy to help. Julia doubted he even realised Sylvie wasn't here, though he'd made a grand gesture of support before she left. Now booking over four hundred confinements a year to the others' two hundred, his fatigue and frenzy were such that he mostly didn't know which patient he was seeing or what day it was. Julia left him out of the equation, for the patients' sake as much as his own.

At the same time, Leo wanted to be with Sandra. He'd been hoping to have some time off while she was still well, and now found himself busier than ever. As a result, Julia had covertly instructed the staff to direct most of Sylvie's patients to her. But she couldn't possibly see them all.

It was Stephen's late night for consultations and, as Julia walked through the reception area on the way to her car, the press of patients and partners and children, as usual, spilt onto the front porch. Justine was on the phone sorting out an urgent appointment for tomorrow, while Erica and Cynthia and Marcia were hard at work with the waiting patients. Those arriving far outnumbered those leaving. Julia recognised several of Sylvie's patients among the multitude.

'Isn't Leo here?' she asked Cynthia. He'd gone to do a delivery but she'd expected him back long before this.

The secretary scowled. 'He's stuck in the labour ward at St Agatha's, and will be for some time.'

Poor Leo, he must be so exhausted. Julia had seen him age ten years in a few weeks; Sandra looked better than he did at the moment.

'Who's first, Cynthia? I'll see them for him.'

The secretary threw her a look of gratitude. 'Would you? That would be a huge help. Two of them have been here for over an hour and another two for nearly that long. And as you can see,' she indicated the assembled clientele, 'we've already run out of chairs.'

Julia picked up the first file and involuntarily braced herself as Sarah Mawson, now two days past the due date in her first pregnancy, lumbered awkwardly through the door, her equally lumpish mother in tow. Already a heavy young woman, she had gained double the recommended weight increase for pregnancy. Her hands and feet, swollen with the oedema of late pregnancy, were further grossly distorted by the humid mid-January days. She had removed her rings and could wear only thongs. She was uncomfortable, unhappy, and desperate to be done with it.

Julia had seen Sarah the previous week when, not even due, she had already been pushing for an induction. Her mother had had three inductions and thought all labours started with a drip. With considerable difficulty, Julia had prevailed upon Sarah to wait for nature to take its course. While the patient seemed to understand that this gave her the best chance of a normal delivery, the agreement to wait had been hard won. This week, even before the girl sat down, Julia knew her chances of extracting a further delay were slim. Especially with two against one. She was right.

The baby was large, but probably not too large for Sarah, although its head was still not in the pelvis. The cervix had not yet started to soften, and was long and unready for labour. Nothing was auspicious for an easy delivery. She conveyed all of this to Sarah and her mother. It didn't matter, they said. Just get it out. In her younger days Julia would have argued more vigorously in favour of the benefits of awaiting spontaneous labour, for one more week at least. Even last year she would have argued. But not now. Not after Tracey Edwards. If something went wrong they would blame her. Her patient could have what she wanted.

By seven-thirty Julia had seen all of the patients booked to see Leo and was attending to her correspondence. Having given up on her swim, she was forcing herself to deal first of all with the phone calls she didn't want to make and was presently struggling with Jane Steel, now nineteen weeks, who'd had her pregnancy ultrasound earlier in the day. Jane had been advised to leave the report unopened until she came for her visit tomorrow for exactly this reason. That she wouldn't understand what it meant, would therefore worry about it, and would ring to have it explained. Which she did.

Julia had been up since four and was keen to get home. She was starting to find Jane Steel irritating, but was at pains to conceal it. One by one, she dealt with the young woman's concerns, concluding early that there was nothing amiss.

'I don't think you need to be worried, Jane. I see that sort of report every day. It's perfectly normal.'

'But what about the fundal placenta? And the fact that the baby's leg measurements are equivalent to eighteen weeks while the head is measured at nineteen weeks?'

As Jane went on, Julia caught herself flipping through a pile of pap smear and blood test results in front of her on the desk, only half-listening to her patient's monologue. Breaking two of her own rules. Eventually, having gone over everything twice, it was time to end the conversation. She suggested to Jane that she probably wouldn't need to come in tomorrow, since the appointment had been made to go over the ultrasound report, and they'd done that already. Jane should ring in the morning when Marcia was in the surgery and make a new appointment for a month's time.

Julia smiled to herself, awaiting the protest. She knew that Jane would never agree to miss an appointment, but was unable to resist the opportunity to tease her slightly. She was rewarded by her patient's slightly taken-aback tone.

'The ultrasound is only one of the things we need to talk about, Dr Kent. I have many other things to discuss with you. I will be keeping my appointment tomorrow.'

As she replaced the phone, Julia recalled a conversation she'd had many years before with Mick Mullins, a fellow obstetrician at Eastside; she was still a registrar at the time, while he had been in private practice for about a year. He'd explained to her that the secret to a happy practice was to recognise that there were essentially two groups of people in the world. By far the bigger group, about ninety percent, was made up of people who were reasonable, considerate and essentially undemanding. The other ten percent were exacting, querulous and selfish. The important thing to realise was that this second group took up more of one's time and energy than the reasonable ninety per-cent. Not that they had any more problems; they just made more demands.

Whether at a parent–teacher meeting, in the sports club or at the hairdresser, the demanding group always sought more than their fair share of time and resources. They were fussy, critical and hard to please. Curiously, they were also the customers most likely to default on their bills.

The good thing, Mick had gone on, was that they were almost always identifiable early. They couldn't help themselves. Their selfishness always showed, which meant that the action plan, to get rid of them, could be enacted almost from the beginning. This was the secret to a happy practice, and Mick had perfected it. Every year a handful of patients who saw him were initially unimpressed as he strove at the first or second appointment to eliminate these demanding ones from his practice. Finding that he answered only ten of their fifty questions and returned only a handful of their twice-daily phone calls, they decided early on that he was not the doctor for them. With the remaining pool of reasonable patients, he was the delightful and charming Dr Mullins, whose popularity was well deserved.

Julia wondered how long Jane Steel would have lasted with Mick. Not this long, that was for sure. While agreeing with his theory, Julia could never implement his practice; it was not in her personality. She had learnt early, however, and had instructed the secretaries likewise, never *ever* to accept a patient who wanted to transfer from Dr Mullins' care to hers. Her own ten percent were enough.

She reached the call she had been saving till last. Grace Chan had been trying for a baby without success since she married nine years ago. She had badly damaged fallopian tubes, pre-sumably from an infection as a teenager. The cause of her infertility had long been established, but Grace was unable to accept that she wouldn't conceive without assistance, high-technology assistance. She kept hoping that it would happen naturally.

She'd taken every herbal, naturopathic, horoscopic and Chinese remedy available, but each month the period came. Without fail.

Julia had been her doctor from the beginning. She had suggested IVF, which allowed conception to bypass the damaged tubes, as soon as the problem was identified, but Grace had resisted until this year. Now thirty-six years old, she realised that if she didn't get pregnant soon, she never would. In desperation, she agreed to try anything that would help her have the baby she so dearly wanted. She had just completed her second cycle at the fertility clinic. Marcia's note said that Grace was pregnant.

'Grace? It's Julia Kent. Marcia told me the good news. Congratulations.'

'Thank you, Dr Kent. It's wonderful, isn't it? I still can't believe it, but the nurse at the IVF unit rang me this morning and said that it's definite. I'm finally pregnant after all these years.'

'That's fantastic, Grace. How do you feel?'

'It's funny, but I feel like I'm going to get a period, as a matter of fact, but more so. Sore breasts, bloated tummy. But perhaps some nausea as well, which they tell me is a good sign.'

'Nausea usually means the pregnancy is going well. I hope you're feeling very sick, very soon.'

They spoke a little longer and Grace made an appointment to see Julia in a fortnight. She would be six weeks then, and an ultrasound assessment of the pregnancy's progress would be undertaken. Neither of them mentioned the risk of ectopic pregnancy or miscarriage this evening; both had been discussed at length previously. For now, they would be keeping their fingers crossed.

Chapter 22

It seemed to Julia much longer than eight weeks since she had last sat in the spacious, comfortable reception area of the Doctors' Defence Organisation. At so many times in her life eight weeks had passed in the blink of an eye, but this was not one of them. She had lived each one of these fifty-odd slow days with the shadow of her medical malpractice case as her constant companion.

Not Emma's good exam results, nor Tony's visit, nor Sandra's illness, nor Angie's troubles with Geoff, not even her treasured relationship with Patrick, had separated her from her shadow for more than a few hours. On each of the slow days since November, she had been moving towards this appointment, this meeting. The one where they would tell her they had settled her case with money and privacy, closed the file, signed off on it forever.

Or reveal that they had decided to fight it, to throw her person and her reputation into the jeering, deadly pit of a public courtroom. And see if she emerged alive.

In the chill of the reception area, a layer of perspiration coated her. Fumbling for a tissue to wipe her face, she forced herself to remember that less than ten percent of medico-legal cases went to court. Often nearer five percent. They were good odds. The majority of cases either went away for lack of evidence, or were settled out of court and never heard of again. Was it too much to hope for?

As the traffic through the reception area picked up, she slid her body lower in the couch, turned up the collar of her jacket and screened her face with a magazine she'd already read. Only four people were aware she was here – Marcia and Leo, who were covering for her in different ways, Angie, who had known since the beginning, and Tony, whom she had promised herself she wouldn't tell, but who had prised it from her on the day after Boxing Day with no difficulty at all. In retrospect, she acknowledged, Tony's effortless extraction wasn't really a surprise. He'd always had that special skill; it was what made him such a successful psychiatrist.

She looked at her watch. Again. It was just before eleven. Hopefully the meeting would start on time. That's if there needed to be a meeting. Maybe someone would just pop out and tell her it was all settled and she could go. What a relief that would be, and not only for her. Poor Leo was covering both her and Sylvie today and it was not proving easy for him, as she'd learned when she rang a little while ago. One of her own patients was in labour at St Agatha's, one of Sylvie's at Eastside, while Leo himself was in the middle of a long and challenging operating list. He'd bravely laughed it off when she expressed concern; it was just like the good old days. He sounded a little stretched nevertheless.

'Julia?'

She pulled back from her thoughts as Jennifer Pereira approached, smiling.

'Sorry to keep you waiting. I got caught with a long phone call. I'm sure you understand.' She smiled conspiratorially and held out her hand. Julia, momentarily uncertain if she was being offered assistance in getting up from the depths she'd sunk to on the lounge, realised in time that it was a handshake that was being extended.

The claims manager was looking well, she thought, although perhaps she'd gained a little weight over Christmas. Scrutinising Jennifer's demeanour closely for a hint of the critical decision, Julia took her cheerful manner to be an encouraging sign. They had decided to settle. The case was finished. There would be no court hearing. She would never need to come here again.

Jennifer showed her through the large frosted glass door which led from the waiting area into the wide central corridor off which smaller corridors branched, and along which employees laden with heavy files scurried. Julia was familiar with this part of the suite. But instead of turning down the first corridor on the left which led to Richard's office, or the next, which led to her own, Jennifer continued along the main passage, not deviating until the corridor ended at a vast wall of glass. As she tossed an unseeing glance over the lush park and magnificent harbour, Julia grew progressively less hopeful. Taking a turn to the right, her heart sank and she had to stop herself biting her lip. Off the corridor was a conference room. In it was a long table, covered from one end to the other with papers. At the table sat not only Richard Tripp but a much larger, much older man whom Julia knew immediately was the barrister.

They were going to court.

Both men stood up as Julia inched selfconsciously into the room. Richard Tripp came forward and greeted her warmly. 'Come in. How are you?'

For Pete's sake, couldn't he guess? 'I'm fine, Richard, thank you. Did you have a nice break?' Julia thought he must have had. He looked rested. And younger than thirty again.

'It was great, Julia, thank you. And you?'

'I had a few days off, but babies don't realise that it's Christmas,' she said, immediately regretting her whingey tone.

Richard introduced the large man beside him. He was Gordon St Jude QC, the barrister the DDO had retained for her case. He was apparently very experienced in matters such as hers. Julia had vaguely heard of him, which she supposed was a good thing. It probably meant he was successful. It almost certainly meant he was expensive. Still, she was not paying, at least not directly.

Everything about Gordon St Jude was oversized. He was tall and heavy-set, like a former front-row forward now under-trained and overfed. His face was large and confident. Even his hair, which was grey and thinning, seemed more abundant than it was. He held out one of his enormous hands for her to shake, and when he spoke, his voice was big as well. Julia found his age and size reassuring.

They sat down. She shifted uncomfortably in her chair and moved to the front of the seat, knees together, businesslike. Seeking a more relaxed pose, she then slid back, curled her spine into the soft leather and crossed her legs. And rotated slightly to the right. Then the left. Assailed by the prospect of an onslaught of tears, she wondered what they'd think if she hid her face behind her hands while they spoke.

Finally, Richard started. After long and detailed considera-tion, the DDO had decided not to settle the matter of Tracey and Brendan Edwards. Certainly not for the ten or so million dollars the plaintiffs wanted. All of the preliminary reports were now in, and he and Jennifer had gone over them in great detail. Their experts did not know why Brendan Edwards was severely handicapped, but did not believe that his lawyers would be able to show it was due to negligence on the part of Dr Julia Kent.

'So, we are going to court?' Julia asked fearfully, wanting it spelled out exactly.

'We have no choice, I'm afraid. If we do not fight this case, then lawyers for every impaired child in the country will be blaming the problem on birth asphyxia. It's a policy decision.'

'But won't that also happen if we go to court and lose?'

Going to court sent a different message, Richard explained. It showed that the DDO was prepared to fight these cases one by one, and expected to win most of them. One loss in one court was much better for them than settling cases that had no merit.

Julia nodded impassively as the solicitor spoke. While out-wardly serene, privately she mocked her own naive foolishness. How could she *ever* have thought this matter would go away and leave her in peace? She really had lost her judgement.

Richard then launched into what was probably a standard

spiel at this point, designed to make the doctor before him feel better. Julia already knew most of it. They were going to court not because the DDO thought she was negligent, but for exactly the opposite reason. Richard developed the line a bit, adding that every day he saw cases in which the doctor had been negligent and provable harm had been done to a patient. Most were minor claims, but some involved serious and permanent handicap. Those cases did not go to court; they got settled and no one ever heard about them. There were dozens of them. DDO figures showed that every one of her obstetric colleagues would, on average, have a claim against them every five years. Some would have more than one. And yet doctors had never been more careful. Unfortunately, the bottom line was that they were human and made mistakes. And patients were more ready to sue.

'I'm sorry, Julia. I know this is not the decision you'd have preferred.'

Still reeling, Julia said nothing.

Richard went on. 'One of the reasons we decided to fight is you yourself. In a case like this, where the cause of the poor medical outcome is unclear, the demeanour of the doctor being sued is a substantial influence on the judge. Jennifer and I think you will make a good witness; your composure will be an asset at your trial.' He smiled at her as if bestowing a prize.

Felled further by this unhelpful piece of information, Julia did not smile in return. If only she'd gone to pieces the last time she'd seen them, they might have decided to settle. Couldn't she do anything right?

Rescuing her lip from her teeth, she asked how long the court hearing would take. With a judge, about four weeks, Richard said. With a jury, more than double.

Julia gasped. 'Eight weeks?'

'That's with a jury. We don't expect this to be a jury case.'

'You don't? Why not?'

'Time, money, and the absence of a written decision.'

Gordon St Jude, urbane and assured, took over at this stage to expand on what Richard meant. Cases like hers were usually

205

heard by a single Supreme Court judge. However, he added, either side could requisition a jury. This rarely happened for the reasons that Richard had given. Jury cases took twice as long and cost twice as much. At least. And in the end, there was no written decision. The jury announced its conclusion, nominated its compensation if the plaintiff had won, and then went home. A judge, on the other hand, was required to detail his findings and document the reasons why he had found in favour of one side over the other. Aside from adding to the body of law, this also leant itself far more easily to appeal. And, since lawyers on both sides were always looking to appeal a decision to a higher court, they generally preferred a judge over a jury.

Julia felt her heart lift slightly at this information. All along she'd simply assumed there would be a jury, could already feel their horrified stares piercing her as they learned of the callous and careless way she had destroyed the life of little Brendan Edwards, while the small boy groaned before them in his wheelchair. To know that there might not be a jury after all went some way to reducing the pressure.

Not only that, a jury would mean eight weeks away from her practice. As it was, four weeks was going to be impossible. Four weeks. She had not for a moment thought it could take so long. Tony's case had taken less than two weeks and, since hers was more straightforward, she had assumed it would last about a week.

Anger hit her suddenly. Anger and indignation that her clinical judgement and professional standing were to be publicly challenged, her reputation damaged even if she won. Already, before she got anywhere near the court, her life was being destroyed. She had lost her nerve, was inconsistent and capricious in her management of patients, had the midwives confused by her behaviour. She could see their amazement at her decisions, their surprise at her irritability and impatience. The staff at the surgery had noticed the change in her too.

And if all that was not enough, her entire annual leave was now up in smoke. All wasted. She, who had not even managed a proper break over Christmas, was now expected to squander

206

four weeks of leave fighting a case which her lawyers claimed had no merit. Her time in Europe with her daughter, her trip to Paris with Patrick, both would have to be cancelled. It was all she could do not to burst out crying.

Gordon St Jude was still speaking. Pitching from frustration to disappointment, Julia realised that she had missed his last few sentences, but from the tone deduced that they had been in the nature of general comments rather than something she needed to know. Steadying herself she prepared to learn the worst. 'When is the matter likely to be heard?'

Gordon's face was black; she had interrupted him. She'd thought he was finished but he was simply pausing for effect. She had a lot to learn about him. 'We are not yet sure, Dr Kent, but it's unlikely to be before August.'

'August?' she choked. It was still only January. She fought her tears once more.

'At the earliest, Dr Kent. This is the Supreme Court, you know, and we are looking for four consecutive vacant weeks. Maybe more.'

Julia sat silently before them, the large room closing in on her. Her whole year was going to be ruined; that's if she survived the next few weeks.

'When do you think you'll know the date of the trial?' she asked faintly.

Gordon St Jude's chest expanded. He was working on that right now. Trying to pull a few strings. She'd be informed in due course.

There was perhaps one glimmer of hope, she thought, desperately trying not to drown in misery. If the trial was going to be delayed that long, perhaps it would be possible to run it in September, at the time of all the football grand finals.

'Whatever for?' spluttered Mr St Jude.

He must have tickets, she thought, refusing to be defeated. 'That would be the best time to minimise the chance of attracting publicity.'

The barrister bathed her in his disdain. 'My dear Dr Kent. This sort of case is unlikely to get any publicity. We run these matters all the time. They are almost never reported.' He seemed disappointed.

'Really?' Julia's heart lifted for the second time that morning.

'To be reported,' he continued, 'a case has to be newsworthy. People have to want to hear about it, either because it breaks new ground or because it deals with an issue that is intrinsically interesting to the public. This case does neither.'

'Thank heavens for that.' Relief surged in Julia. 'The last thing I want is to be of interest to the public.'

'There are exceptions, of course,' the barrister added casually.

Julia turned to him sharply, her pardon revoked.

'Those are the cases, Dr Kent, where the participants themselves are of interest to the public, even though the case is not.'

Chapter 23

At four in the morning on the day after the DDO meeting, the phone rang.

'Dr Kent, it's Rosie at St Agatha's delivery suite. Mrs Barbara Pollak has come in. She's a patient of Dr Berger. This is her second baby. The first was a caesarean at six centimetres for foetal distress. Her card says that she is to have a trial of labour. She's four centimetres dilated with membranes intact and is labouring well, having three in ten moderate contractions. She would like an epidural, if that's all right with you.'

'That's fine, Rosie. Is the foetal heart okay?'

'The baby's very happy, Dr Kent.'

'Are you sure? This is a trial of scar. Foetal distress could be the first sign of the old caesarean wound rupturing.'

'I'm aware of that,' the midwife replied patiently, although Julia could imagine her pulling a face at the other nurses at the desk. 'And yes, Dr Kent, I'm sure the baby's fine.'

'And you think she's contracting well?'

'It's only early but, yes, the contractions are becoming quite strong.'

'But not too strong?'

'No. I think they're just right.'

Julia could sense her grimacing again. 'Good. Thanks, Rosie.'

She replaced the phone. A previous caesarean section always meant a risky subsequent labour. The old scar could open during a contraction and, if not detected early, could cause the baby to die. It was a rare event, but Julia had seen it several times. Remembering the most recent occasion, she swung her legs out of bed and leapt up, preparing to rush to the hospital to ensure everything really was all right. Then she halted. No, she wouldn't go. She had to stop doing this, stop anticipating disaster. Rosie was a good midwife and she had to trust her.

Reluctantly she lay back down and instead calculated when she should do her rounds. There were patients who wanted to go home this morning and would need to be seen before ten. If Barbara Pollak dilated at an average rate, she would deliver at about eleven, while if she laboured quickly, she might deliver before eight. On the other hand, if she went slowly and required an oxytocin drip to make her contractions stronger, she wouldn't deliver until the afternoon and might even require a caesarean section like last time. Julia abandoned the calculations as hopeless. Labour was unpredictable. She would do her rounds at nine and just hope that they fitted in with the delivery.

She rolled onto her side and looked out at the moon, knowing with cheerless certainty that she would not be the only one lying awake. Angie had been back to see the private detective yesterday. And found Ritzy Rainer's research very thorough.

Not only did the detective have pictures of Geoff's current liaison, she had pictures of *two* current liaisons. One was the forty-year-old wife of a close university associate, and the other a twenty-seven-year-old post-doctoral researcher in his own department. Ritzy believed that the affair with the older woman was probably in the denouement phase while the second had only started a few months ago. As well as those two, Ritzy had a photo suggesting that he was also a little too close to one of his students.

Moving to the second file labelled 'past relationships', there

210

was anecdotal evidence of at least one other affair with a faculty colleague, and one with an aerobics instructor at the university gym. And that was just the past five years. Ritzy could go back further if Mrs Summers wished her to. Angie, thinking that she would cry, had instead started to laugh. But in the end, her laughter had given way to tears as she'd related the news to Julia.

'He's been cheating on me for years, possibly my entire marriage, and I had no idea. Am I blind?'

'Just trusting. You're not supposed to cheat in marriage, so why should you expect it?'

'Why does he cheat on me?' Angie was crushed. 'What's wrong with me that my husband needs to sleep with every woman in town?'

Desperate for an explanation, she wondered whether her long working hours had forced Geoff into the arms of other women. Or her habit of letting him sometimes go on his own to university functions. By nature she was not nearly as gregarious as he was and she was happy for him to socialise without her occasionally. Her nights off were precious, and she mostly chose to spend them with her sons. She'd always been grateful that it never seemed to bother Geoff. Now she knew why.

Julia was furious at the suggestion that Angie was in any way to blame. For years she'd envied her friend's ability to arrange her work around her family and admired the happy home she'd created for her sons. Angie always went to the trouble of cooking a fabulous evening meal, made sure she was there to help Ben and Richie with their homework, had their friends over to stay, and involved herself in their sports. And she was likewise loving and unselfish with Geoff, her occasional absence from a boring university shindig notwithstanding.

'It's not what's wrong with you, although it might take you a long time to see it,' Julia insisted while Angie sobbed in her arms. 'It's what's wrong with Geoff.'

As the sky began to lighten, Julia looked at the clock again. It was nearly five. This time yesterday she had still been clinging to the hope that her malpractice litigation would be settled out of court and the misery of a trial averted. What a silly hope it now seemed. Not that she had been the only one who held it.

Tony had rung last night to see how things had gone. She'd not spoken to him since Christmas, when he'd left five days early, aware of her discomfort at his presence. Only later did she learn he'd spent the rest of his time fishing on the Shoalhaven River with her father.

Still, she was not overly surprised it was him on the phone, intent on learning how she'd fared with the DDO. While it was weeks since she'd mentioned the meeting and the possibility of settlement, it was entirely like Tony to have remembered. He had been tentative, embarrassed to be calling, but determined to find out what had happened. He'd even apologised, as if it was his fault Tracey Edwards was suing her. Appreciating what he meant, Julia had been grateful.

After he'd commiserated with her about the DDO's decision, he asked after Angie, and she'd told him the private investigator's awful news. It was only as she put the phone down that she recalled Angie asking her to tell no one about Geoff. Cringing, she'd cursed her thoughtlessness; Angie would never do that to her. She consoled herself with the wry thought that Tony had a proven ability to keep a confidence.

Barbara Pollak's delivery and the rounds coincided after all. The epidural was still working well when Julia arrived, and the patient was in little discomfort. Propped up on pillows, hips and knees bent in a reclining squat, Barbara peered intently into the mirror at the end of the bed. She could see the reflection of the visible part of her baby's head with its scant fair hair straining her perineum as she awaited the next wave of pain. Julia spoke a few words of encouragement as the contraction built. With a final push, Barbara was rewarded for her efforts, watching as first the head, then the forehead, then the nose, and finally the chin of her son slipped out of her vagina.

Julia completed the data entry out at the main desk before

returning to the delivery room to check on the Pollaks. To her surprise, Barbara, who had been robust and laughing only minutes before, was now pale and sweaty. Aside from the baby, silent but awake in the cot beside the bed, she was alone. The midwife had taken the placenta and soiled drapes to the waste room, while her husband Mike had gone to fetch his parents.

'Are you all right, Barbara?'

'I feel very faint, Dr Kent,' the patient replied weakly.

'I think you could be bleeding,' said Julia as she lifted the sheet.

Between Barbara's legs was a growing pool of red. Julia pressed the nurse-call button, and then, while Barbara groaned in protest, she proceeded to firmly massage the fundus of the uterus which was large and soft and boggy. After a short while the midwife appeared.

'Was the oxytocin given at delivery, Roxanne?'

'Yes, Dr Kent, I gave it with the birth of the anterior shoulder, as usual.'

Only new to midwifery, the nurse came closer to the patient. 'Is she bleeding?'

'She's lost nearly a litre. And still haemorrhaging rapidly. The placenta was complete, there were no lacerations, so I think it must be coming from the uterus. It was very atonic and slack when I came in, but it's starting to firm up with the massage. If you could take over rubbing it for me, Roxanne, I'll quickly put a drip in, so we can get an oxytocin infusion going.'

Julia pushed the nurse-call button again to secure an extra pair of hands for the emergency.

By the time Mike returned, still unaware of the drama, everything was under control. Blood had been cross-matched but would hopefully not be needed, the infusion was running well, the uterus was nicely contracted, and the bleeding had settled. Barbara's sheets and gown had been changed and, while pale and weary, she was looking a lot better. Nearly ninety minutes after the delivery, Julia finally prepared to leave.

'Thanks, doc,' said Mike as he ushered his parents into the room. 'Mind you, you didn't have to do much. Not like Dr Berger with the caesarean last time.'

'That's the way I like it, Mike,' Julia replied, stealing a smile at Barbara as she departed.

Emma was home, thought Julia happily as familiar music greeted her arrival. They had not seen much of each other in the past few days, both of them busy and preoccupied, and in two months her daughter would be gone. Resolving to grab what was left of the afternoon, she sprang open the door expectantly. And stopped.

There, in the middle of the lounge room, dancing in a line to the pulsating rhythm of Kylie Minogue, were Emma, Jade and Jason. And Tony. They had obviously been at it for a while; even Tony knew the steps to the dance routine Em had been working on all week. He lost his place briefly at the sight of Julia, but his daughter insisted he finish the song before they turned off the music.

'I had nothing better to do,' he explained, not quite to Julia's satisfaction. They were briefly alone, the three teenagers having set off for Jason's to retrieve a CD. Julia inspected him as he drank his tea, and concluded that he was looking better than he had a month ago. He'd gained some weight and the sadness was less deeply etched on the topography of his face.

'I just thought I'd come down and see how everyone is,' he continued.

'Everyone?'

'Emma and you, of course. And Angie.'

'Angie?'

'After you told me about Geoff last night, I felt awful for her. So I called and asked what she was doing for dinner tonight.'

'You called her from Brisbane and asked her what she was doing for dinner in Sydney?'

'Is it so strange? It's only an hour by plane. I could imagine how terrible she must be feeling and I remembered how wonderful she was to us, both of us, during our troubles. And so I thought that, if Geoff was not around tonight and she was not busy with the boys or work, she might like to have dinner with me.'

214

His tone was less confident than his words but Julia, focused on her own concern, did not notice. 'Did Angie sound upset that I had told you?'

He hesitated before telling the truth. 'Initially. But then she didn't seem to mind. She said she would have told me herself if I'd been around.'

Julia hoped Angie would forgive her.

Tony was staying at the Pacific Hotel, as he usually did when he came to Sydney for conferences or to see Emma. He wasn't sure where they were having dinner; Angie was taking care of the booking.

Julia felt oddly left out.

Tony looked at her. 'I told Emma I'd be back in the morning to take her somewhere for breakfast. Would you like to come?'

'Thanks, Tony, but I'm on call for the practice this weekend,' Julia replied abruptly. 'I doubt I'll have time for breakfast.'

'I'll be here at about ten if you get lucky.'

'Thanks.'

Julia parked her car and proceeded a little nervously up the meandering but well-lit path towards the party noises issuing through Patrick's open front door. She had just assisted at the delivery of a beautiful baby girl to the proud parents of four boys. The two older brothers had been present to witness the birth of their tiny sister. It had been a joyous event and Julia was on a high. There were two other patients in labour this evening, but for a while she had time to party.

As she made her way through the front rooms she was shy. She'd met the people from his office, of course, and some of the parents from Ryan's school, but knew none of them well. It was a happy, well-lubricated crowd and she was glad she'd made it. Patrick had organised the party a month ago when this weekend was rostered as Sylvie's.

She found him in the kitchen surrounded by a group of his work colleagues. His gaze widened at the sight of her. Excusing himself to his friends, he came to her.

'Hi, gorgeous,' he said softly, his voice sending a tiny charge through her as it always did. Locking her eyes with his, he stroked her cheek and murmured, 'Now you're here, I think I might send everyone home and hold a private party.' For a moment Julia forgot where she was.

They reluctantly separated. Patrick filled a plate for her and took her to meet his guests. It seemed everyone had heard the sad news that she was working, and commiserated with her accordingly. One was Natalie, the young architecture student Julia had met at the Christmas party. The two women were just catching up when the hospital rang.

Patrick saw her to her car. He was disappointed she had to go but delighted he'd had the chance to show her off. He pulled her close in the dark and purred, 'Don't be long, darling.'

She swooned at his touch. If she didn't leave soon, she would be incapable of driving. 'I'll hurry,' she promised.

Chapter 24

It was unusual to have a day off mid-week, and a pity not to be using it for fun. But when Sylvie had rung to say her mother had passed away and the funeral was on Tuesday, Julia knew she had to go. Sylvie's brave decision to stay with her mother had to be supported. It was a small gesture really and, in truth, the worst of it fell to the secretaries, whose job it was to tell the patients.

She took a taxi from the airport and gave the driver the name of the crematorium, trusting that he knew where he was going. Cheerful and chatty in the mid-morning traffic, he asked, 'Someone in your family?'

'No. The mother of my friend.'

'You knew her well?'

'Not at all. I'm here for my friend.'

'Oh.'

They finally pulled in to the long road leading up through the beautiful gardens and manicured lawns to the crematorium buildings. Julia was struck by the large crowd and the number of cars ahead of them, snaking slowly, looking for a place to park.

'She was famous, your friend's mother?' asked the driver, suitably impressed.

'I don't think so.' Julia was now unsure.

He pulled in to the undercover area adjacent to the administration building. It was getting quite hot and Julia appreciated the shade. She thanked him and paid, giving a generous tip. He looked at her eagerly. A fare from here to the airport was not to be passed up. 'Do you want me to come back?'

'Thank you, but I'll be having lunch with my friend.'

He shrugged equably, smiled and was gone.

Julia stood uncertainly for a moment, looking to get her bearings. She realised now that the crowd was actually two crowds, the bigger one heading to the East Chapel, and the smaller one to the North Chapel. She recognised no one in either group and was just about to inquire at administration when her name was called.

Sylvie engulfed her in a hug. 'Julia, you're here. Thank you so much for coming.'

Julia suddenly realised how much she'd missed her younger colleague. 'It was an honour to come, Sylvie. And everyone at Waratah House sends their love.'

Sylvie was looking well, Julia thought with relief. She'd been worried about the toll all this would take on her friend, nursing the mother she'd never got on with and watching her die. But Sylvie looked fantastic. She'd lost weight and had done something with her hair that accentuated her cheekbones and eyes. And she was wearing a new cream suit which really flattered her.

Beside Sylvie stood a tall, heavy young man, unmistakably her brother. Julia held out her hand as Sylvie introduced him. 'It's nice to meet you, Friedrich, after hearing so much about you.'

'Likewise.' He was a man of few words.

Sylvie turned to the small Asian woman hanging politely behind. 'And this is Malu, my mother's nurse and my saviour.'

The woman, in late middle age, stepped forward to greet Sylvie's colleague from Sydney. 'Pleased to meet you,' she said, her eyes smiling. 'She needed no saving, of course.'

They followed neither the large crowd to the East Chapel, nor the smaller one to the North Chapel, but made their way to a tiny room deep inside the crematorium. The coffin was already in place and they took their seats, just the four of them, and waited the few minutes for the pastor to arrive.

'So, tell me what's been happening,' Sylvie demanded as she and Julia walked through the department store, scanning the merchandise for a present for Malu.

Julia gave her a brief run-down about her patients, the practice and the staff. 'Everyone has been missing you, of course, but we've managed well.'

'My patients weren't too upset about my absence for the last six weeks?'

Julia tossed her a comforting smile as they paused at a display of silk scarves. 'They were very disappointed not to have you for their deliveries, of course, but they understood. Most were very sympathetic to your decision to stay with your mum at this time.'

'Most?'

Julia immediately rued her choice of words. 'Really, they all were.'

'Even Aveline Simmons?'

Julia laughed. 'Actually she was the one I was thinking of when I said "most". Aveline was rather put out that your mother had chosen such a thoughtless time to get sick.'

'That sounds like her. Did she deliver okay?'

'She surprised herself by having a short and easy labour with no stitches. After which she told Leo that since she hadn't needed him at all, she couldn't see why she should pay his bill.'

'She won't either,' responded Sylvie knowingly.

Already Julia could see that there was a change in Sylvie. It was not just the weight loss, the attractive suit and the nicely shaped hair. It was something more than externals.

'How have you been?' she asked carefully as they moved on to the handbags. 'Was it as awful as you expected?'

219

Sylvie hesitated before she replied. 'It was. But it was good too.'

Julia waited, subconsciously expecting from Sylvie a tale of reconciliation and liberation. Of mother and daughter finally understanding and appreciating each other in the last few weeks of Gerda's life. The story Sylvie told was completely different.

She had indeed been liberated, but not by her mother's approval. Even after all the nursing and nurturing, night and day, over the past six weeks, the old woman would not give it. Rather, Sylvie had been liberated by the knowledge that it was not she who had failed.

After she arrived on Christmas Eve, it had taken only a couple of days to understand the reason why her mother was facing transfer to a nursing home. It was not because of her deteriorating health but because, one by one, the nurses who cared for her declined to come any more. There were so many patients needing home-care that the nurses could pick and choose. And they chose the patients who didn't snarl and sneer and whinge and insult. And hiss. They each told their agencies and local councils that they would not be seeing 'Adolf Berger' any more.

Except Malu. The grey-haired Filipina grandmother, the one Gerda said she couldn't understand, thankfully couldn't understand her either. Or at least pretended not to. She had been nursing Gerda for several months and was the only one still coming in December.

To Sylvie's surprise, Malu, seemingly unaware that her patient's daughter would be there, had come on Christmas morning to gently bathe and dress the old woman, bringing with her a small box of brightly wrapped chocolates and a card. Gerda had barely nodded thanks but Sylvie, already despairing after only twelve hours and still undecided as to what to do, had been flooded with gratitude. She told Malu not to come on Boxing Day, but had desperately looked out for her the day after. She then watched in embarrassment as her mother repaid the nurse's kindness and tenderness with snarls and grunts, the larger invalided woman even striking the smaller helping one as she turned her in the bed.

'Your mother was obviously suffering a lot,' offered Julia.

Sylvie shrugged. 'She probably was, but that's no excuse. You and I see patients sick and in pain all the time. In labour, after surgery. We see them dying. Only a tiny number behave like my mother did. And we know what sort of people they are.'

Julia nodded but said nothing.

Sylvie continued. 'Malu simply accepted it. Not in a subservient way. Rather with a kind of compassionate strength. And a sense of humour. I asked her why she hadn't given up like the others. She laughed and said Mother was a challenge and she was not going to be defeated by her. She could see the funny side of her determined misery. Something I had always been too close to see.'

Sylvie paused while a sales assistant offered them some help which they declined. They took the escalator up to household appliances.

'When did you decide that you would stay?' asked Julia as they arrived at the juice extractors.

'When I realised that I couldn't leave it all to Malu. Despite her stoicism and humour, I could see that she was getting tired. She's sixty-two herself, and still working a full week.'

'Was she pleased?'

'My mother or Malu?'

'Your mother.'

'I don't know, she never really said. She seemed to think it was her due. She treated me much the same as Malu, in fact. Nothing I did was right – the soup was too hot, the pureed fruit too sweet, the pillows too high or too low, the television too loud or she couldn't hear it, the room too bright or too dark. If I'd been on my own it would have been unbearable, but with Malu it was almost enjoyable. She'd mimic my mother's tone and say, "What are you making today, Sylvie, soup that's too hot or too cold?"'

Sylvie smiled at the memory. She then asked how Julia was.

Looking up from the sandwich-makers, Julia decided to tell her. 'I've got a bit of a problem, actually.' She explained about Brendan Edwards and his mother, and Jennifer and Richard and Gordon St Jude.

Sylvie was outraged and loyal. How could anyone sue Julia? She'd never known a doctor so careful. Julia told her she too

221

would probably be sued sometime. 'You just have to hope you're clearly negligent.' With a grim laugh, she explained the paradox.

Sylvie asked when the trial would be held. That was part of the problem, Julia said. No one knew. But whenever it was, it was going to take four weeks.

'Four weeks? Away from work? For a court case?' Sylvie was stunned.

'Awful, isn't it? And with a jury, it could be eight,' Julia added miserably, wondering whether a new kettle would cheer her up.

Sylvie's heart went out to her; it was so unfair. Well, whenever the trial was, and however long it took, Julia could count on her help.

Thanking her, Julia said she wished she could be as sure of Stephen's support; he'd already lived through one court case involving her, and been singularly unimpressed with the adverse publicity.

'What did he say when you told him?' Sylvie asked gently.

Julia pulled a wry face. She hadn't actually told him yet.

'Oh.' Sylvie was not especially surprised.

'I'm sure he'll be fine about it,' Julia amended hastily, fearing she'd been disloyal.

They were in the home entertainment section now, and Sylvie asked how Leo was.

'So you know?'

Sylvie nodded. He'd rung her last week, after he'd told his children.

He was a mess, Julia said. Sandra was the most important thing in his life, and the thought of living without her was unbearable for him to contemplate. He was barely sleeping or eating. 'You'll be shocked when you see him, Sylvie. He's turned into an old man overnight.'

On the plane going home Julia's thoughts hovered between two sorrows. The enduring sadness of Sylvie's relationship with her mother, and the impending death of Sandra Steiner.

Sandra had been Julia's friend for more than seven years now, since she and Leo had gone out of their way to show support and kindness during Tony's trial. Afterwards, Sandra had become Julia's patient, coming regularly for a breast check and pap smear. She was one of the most wonderful people Julia knew, vibrant and generous and loving. In every one of Julia's recollections of her, she was smiling. It was impossible to think of her no longer being around, to contemplate not being able to see her cheerful face or hear her riotous laugh.

And then there was Sylvie, a great doctor and a good person, low on self-esteem but large on compassion, who had tried all her life to please her selfish, exacting mother, and had failed.

Julia looked out the window while the plane started its early evening descent into Sydney. As the cabin's energy level rose in preparation for disembarkation, she shifted her focus to her own family. She recalled her own mother Helen, indefatigable and irrepressible, her oven always baking, her bench cluttered with bulbs and cuttings, her home always open to visitors. A mother who had given her an expansive, exciting childhood. And whom she'd then seen almost nothing of in the last ten years of her life. Too frantic with study and work. Always promising to get down next month. Away in London for two years. And then choosing to make her home in Sydney, in direct contradiction of her promise.

Of course, her neglect didn't end there. There was also her wonderful father, warm and uncritical, whom she barely made time to ring, let alone visit, allowing his undemanding nature to excuse her irresponsibility.

And finally there was her very special daughter, thoughtful and mature, to whom she owed her survival after her divorce. And who, since primary school, had made her own transport arrangements because she could never rely on her mother.

Julia was immobile in the face of her own accusations.

'Are you all right?' asked the flight attendant, wondering if she should call a doctor. Everyone else had left the plane while this woman remained fixed in her seat.

'No, I'm not sure that I am,' said Julia quietly.

She couldn't wait to get home, chafing with impatience as the taxi inched along in the snarling traffic. She'd rung Emma from the airport to tell her to freshen up. Her mother was taking her out to dinner, anywhere she wanted. Julia would even eat KFC if she had to. Just to be with her daughter. To sit and listen to everything she had to say, to make up for the times she'd been unavailable.

She alighted from the taxi and almost sprinted to her front door, her heart light with anticipation. The phone rang as she turned her key in the lock. She heard Emma answer it and tell the caller he'd have to try the mobile. 'Hang on, she's just coming in the door.'

It was the gynaecology registrar. Mrs Grace Chan had come into the emergency department about thirty minutes before. Just under six weeks pregnant, she had been bleeding since this morning. A few hours ago she'd developed severe lower abdominal pain and by the time she'd arrived at the hospital was very pale with a distended abdomen, rapid pulse and falling blood pressure.

'I think she has an ectopic pregnancy, Dr Kent.'

'A textbook description, I'd say,' responded Julia dejectedly.

Poor Grace. Finally pregnant after nine years, and this is what happens. Her desperately wanted pregnancy stuck uselessly in the fallopian tube and haemorrhaging rapidly, when it should have been resting safely in the uterus.

'Theatre's ready when you are, Dr Kent, and the blood bank will have four units available soon,' finished the keen young doctor.

'Thanks, Trevor. Please get Mrs Chan up to theatre and I'll meet you there in ten minutes.'

Emma had been leaning against the wall next to her mother throughout the conversation. She'd showered and washed her hair and was wearing a clean white t-shirt and her best jeans. Julia could hardly bear to face her as she replaced the receiver. 'Oh, Em, I'm so sorry. I can't tell you how much I was looking forward to an evening together. Just the two of us.'

Emma came to hug her, disappointed but resigned. 'I know, Mum. It's not your fault. Mrs Chan needs you.'

Julia shrugged hopelessly. 'It's been such a bad week.'
'All your weeks are like this, Mum,' replied Emma honestly.
'That's not entirely true, Em.' Julia was suddenly defensive.
'It's mostly true, and you know it.'

Chapter 25

It was a beautiful mid-February afternoon and, to do it full justice, it was Friday. After four days of rain, the clouds had finally cleared, revealing a city that, having showered, was ready to party. Nowhere was this more so than on the coast, where the sun was like a magnet and the freshly washed streets were thronged with would-be revellers.

Sylvie had been back for ten days and was covering the weekend for Leo and Julia. She had done the previous one as well, but no one had argued too strenuously against her doing another. As a result, her colleagues were finishing early, although not Stephen of course. He was still hard at work at Eastside doing a forceps delivery, while a caesarean awaited him at St Agatha's. His home renovations were still not finished and Stacey had added a gym and sauna to the downstairs rumpus room. He would be working all weekend.

Julia walked out with Leo, who looked worn as he always did these days, his face falling in folds where once had been strong flesh. Sandra was much sicker now as the melanoma lived up to its fearsome reputation. Tumour now in her lungs made the excursion of each breath difficult while, in the past week, a CT scan had confirmed that the pressure in her head was due to secondaries there as well. She, of course, continued to make light of her illness, refusing to talk about it, to 'give it oxygen'. Instead, each time Julia visited, she would make tea and offer food and talk about her children and grandchildren and ask about Emma and Patrick, as if nothing had changed. Julia saw that she fumbled with the teapot and had difficulty opening the packet of biscuits and could stand for only a minute before needing a chair. But she remained determinedly cheerful.

At home Leo tried to match her brave stoicism, but with Julia he poured out his heart. Staring bleakly at a future without his wife of forty years, he could hardly see the point of living himself. The retirement they had so excitedly planned for the year after next would now never happen. Until Sandra got sick, they'd been poring over maps for their trip around Australia, giggling like children about the golf they would play (Leo was not good with balls) and the sailing they would try (Sandra hated getting wet). They'd been listing all the movies they would finally get to see and, most of all, dreaming about the leisurely sleep-ins and uninterrupted meals they would have in each other's company.

Julia touched his arm but had no words that could console. The overwhelming love Leo felt for Sandra made his loss so much greater. But it was also sustaining him. 'Anything new on the treatment front?' she asked. Sandra had seen her oncologist yesterday.

There wasn't. Only palliative care. Leo's children were dismayed by the lack of therapy. They wanted him to fly Sandra to America and seek another opinion. 'They can't believe there's nothing anyone can do.' He couldn't believe it himself.

Julia understood how they felt. Leo's daughter, Alex, had quizzed her at length when she'd come for her first pregnancy visit the week before. She'd always been close to her mother, and was beside herself at the thought that Sandra mightn't live to see her baby.

'I should have retired five years ago,' said Leo mournfully. 'I could have afforded to. But I love the work so much. And Sandra wasn't in a hurry. She said I should take my time and do what I wanted. So we agreed on the end of next year. And now it's too late.'

'But you didn't know, Leo.'

'No, I didn't. But I'm telling everyone I love not to make the same mistake.' His sad eyes looked into hers. 'That includes you, Julia.'

Julia walked into an empty house. Emma was at the music store but would be home shortly. She was having an 'in-night', which meant videos and pizza and Jason. She was following this with an 'in-morning' tomorrow. There were only six Saturdays on the calendar until she left for Europe, only two when neither she nor her mother would be working. Tomorrow was one, and Emma was cooking breakfast for them both. 'And I don't expect you to do rounds in the middle of it, Mum, do you hear?' she'd commanded before leaving this morning.

Flinching slightly at the memory of her daughter's edict, Julia changed, poured herself a glass of wine, collected her hat and sunglasses, and strode deliberately past the large pile of unopened mail on the living room table. Arriving on the deck, she settled lazily in the warm afternoon sunshine and looked down towards the Pacific. It was the right name for her ocean, she concluded, as a wave of peace reached her.

It was a recent peace. Death had a way of diminishing lesser threats. Sylvie's mother's death and Sandra's impending fate had shot into stark relief the trivial smallness of her own concerns. Gerda Berger's funeral, bleak and brief, had made her pause. If ever there was a woman who focused only on negatives, all the while squandering the potential joys of her life, it was Sylvie's mother. Sitting in the small, barren chapel of the crematorium, Julia had resolved not to be like her.

And then there was Sandra, who squeezed every drop from the joys which came her way, watering the lives of those around her as she did so. The most vital person Julia knew, she would soon be dead. But at least she had lived.

Since her trip to Melbourne, Julia had forced herself to look at her own existence and confront a few truths.

It was not the threat of a month in court that was ruining her life; it was her response to it. While understandable, nothing positive could come from her anxious obsession. Rather, it generated its own basket of negatives – headaches, insomnia, poor judgement, irritability. She could not go on like this, especially with the case not likely to be heard for another six months, maybe even twelve. And the judge's decision delayed even beyond that. It could be two years before it was over. It was a long time to live with a headache. She had forbidden herself to brood on her trial until it was imminent. That took care of one problem. The other was much harder. She'd been aware of it for years, of course, but had successfully pushed it to the back of her mind and closed the door.

She had allowed work to become a substitute for life. Especially since her divorce, work had been her refuge. Refuge from the trauma of betrayal. From the sniggering and rejection which did not end in the courtroom. From the grief and guilt over her son's death. And most of all, from the great gaping hole that the loss of Tony had left in her life. A hole that had seemed unfillable, but that she shovelled full of work. It had been easy to do. Hers was the most exhilarating, satisfying job in the world, absorbing and challenging and enormously rewarding.

But it was also the most greedy and unreasonable and anti-social and never-ending, gobbling up lives whole, leaving no time for loved ones, or friends, or weekends away, or concerts, or exercise. It left no time for anything, really. Which was what she'd wanted. Then.

The astringent taste of comprehension made her wince. She'd given herself over to her patients and their babies in the belief that here was a safe haven. That work at least couldn't hurt her. How wrong could she be? But this was about much more than just Tracey Edwards. The litigation was simply the final pain, the one that made her pause. But before it had wounded her so obviously, hiding in her work had been injuring her for years, contracting her life, allowing her no time to think, rendering her unavailable to those who might want a part of her. Including her father and Emma. And more recently Patrick.

What a waste. It was time she did something about it.

'Mum?'

Julia had fallen asleep and had not heard Emma come in. While after seven, it was still sunny and warm. She opened her eyes but otherwise made no attempt to move, although her mouth widened in a broad smile at the sight of her daughter.

'Hi, darling.'

Emma kissed her mother's inert form, kicked off her sandals, and took her place on the other lounge. 'Thank goodness the sun is back.'

'It's only been gone for four days, Em, and weekdays at that. You really can't complain.'

'Summer's nearly over, Mum. Every day counts.'

'But you'll be having a northern summer this year as well, Em, so you'll get your fair share.'

They were lost in their thoughts for a while and Julia waited for Emma to speak.

'Are you seeing Dad this weekend, Mum?'

'Dad?'

'You know Dad, the tall thin dark one from Brisbane. Tony Cabrini.'

'I think I know who he is, Em, I simply wasn't sure why you were asking.'

'He's coming down tomorrow morning.'

'He is?'

'Yes,' replied Emma. 'He said he had some things to do in Sydney, but I think he's mostly coming to see me.'

'Oh? Is he still coming next weekend for your birthday too?'

Emma would be eighteen next week. She was not having the party Julia had offered, instead opting for money to help with her trip. But her parents, together with Jason and George, were taking her out to dinner to celebrate.

'Yeah, he's coming next weekend as well. It's just that he

230

thought Antonio should see me a couple of times before I go away. So he's bringing him down.' They were to stay at the Pacific, Emma explained. She would meet them for lunch tomorrow at Coogee, followed by a swim. And sandcastles, of course. Jason would join them after he finished work. Then, in the evening, Tony was having dinner with someone.

'He's asked me to mind Antonio.'

Julia was surprised. 'Do you think he'll remember you, Em? He's only a little boy, and you haven't seen him in more than six months.'

Emma had the confidence of youth. Her father had been showing Antonio her picture and talking to him about his 'sister'. And he was used to being with lots of different people. 'I'm sure it will be fine, Mum.'

'Of course it will,' back-pedalled Julia. 'I think it's lovely for him to come and see you.'

'There is one other thing, Mum.' Emma's face was full of uncertainty. 'I was thinking that it might be nicer to mind him here rather than at the hotel. Easier, you know.'

Before she'd even realised, Julia had agreed that Tony's son could come and stay the night in her house.

She finally decided on the loose, long, sleeveless black dress which suited her colouring and slimmed her lines. Patrick always noticed what she wore. But while his compliments were intended to affirm her, paradoxically they fed her insecurity. Ill at ease about her body, she would have felt more attractive with someone less observant. And while Patrick insisted he loved the way she looked, once or twice lately he'd run his hands over her too-soft belly or eyed her less than perfect derrière in such a way as to suggest that any plans she might have for diet and exercise should be upgraded to urgent.

She took extra care with her hair and make-up and was finally happy, especially once she exchanged the honest glare of the bathroom for the more subtle lighting of her bedroom. Not that there was any need to hurry. Patrick had rung to say he'd finished later in the office than expected and would go home to change before picking her up at eight-thirty.

A pang of expectant pleasure went through her. How lovely it was to have someone, how quickly life could bloom. In just a few months, Patrick had become so much a part of who she was that the time before he existed barely existed either, the years in front of the television, her only outing to collect Emma or rush to the hospital, now someone else's past.

Not that she'd completely overcome her insecurities; she doubted she ever would. But each week she could feel her confidence growing, to the point that she no longer waited for the words which said he was ending their relationship; sorry, he'd made a mistake. Beyond that, however, she didn't dare to plan.

As she put on her bracelet and simmered with excitement at the coming evening, only half-consciously did she admit that her anticipation of the dinner itself was more blunted. She adored restaurant food and was particularly fond of fried entrees, rich creamy sauces and wicked desserts, especially on a Friday night at the end of a long and demanding week. Dining with Patrick did not easily allow that sort of indulgence.

His father and grandfather had both died in their early fifties from heart disease and Patrick was determined not to follow suit. He lived a low-fat, high-vegetable, no-dessert diet, and had done for so long that it was beyond him to contemplate most of the items on a menu, let alone order them. Julia doubted he even saw the creamy sauces any more. His eyes zoomed in on the dishes he could just as easily have had at home, almost without fail ordering grilled fish or lean meat, steamed vegetables, undressed salad, and a fruit-based dessert. For both of them.

It wasn't quite that bad, of course, but after their first meals together when she had chosen exactly what she wanted, Patrick had told her it discomforted him to see her eat 'unhealthily'. His disapproval, gentle as it was, had spoilt her pleasure and exaggerated her anxieties about her body.

Taking one last glance in the mirror, a memory popped up from the recesses of her mind of Friday nights long ago. She and Tony and little Emma had a regular booking at the local trattoria, where all meat was crumbed, the servings were enormous and the desserts were piled high with cream. She actually laughed aloud as she recalled the desserts; Tony would always order several. Thin and unconcerned about his mortality, he ate what he pleased. But the truth was, the desserts were for her. Recognising her 'too-full' protests for what they were, he would select what he knew she wanted. And ask for two spoons.

As she came downstairs, she could hear Jason and Emma talking. They were in the music room at the front of the house, her daughter seated at the piano and Jason leaning near her, looking at the score she was scribbling on. As Julia came to the door, he was also taking the opportunity to plant little kisses on Emma's neck.

Unembarrassed, he looked up. 'You look rather swish tonight, Mrs C,' he said appreciatively.

Professionally Julia was Dr Kent, but with Emma's school and friends, she was always Mrs Cabrini. Even after the divorce. It made sense, especially with the teachers; it was hard enough for them to remember one surname for each child.

'Thanks, Jason. You can come around any time you like.'

She hadn't known him long, but in the past three months she'd taken to Jason McKenzie and could see why her daughter liked him. He was not at first glance anything special, but he was so cheerful and funny, cheeky and irreverent, that he soon had people thinking he was gorgeous. At the same time, he seemed to know when to be respectful and responsible.

Emma swivelled on her piano stool and looked at her mother appraisingly. 'You do look lovely, Mum. That dress really suits you.'

'Thanks, darling. What have you got planned for the evening?'

'We're working on a new song. And then we might watch the videos Jason brought.'

The doorbell rang. Julia hurried to answer it, thinking it would be Patrick. Instead, it was a pizza delivery boy with Emma and Jason's dinner. She paid and carted the cardboard boxes down the hall and into the kitchen. Opening the top one

233

to see what they had ordered, she was hit with the smell of fresh hot pizza. Until that moment she had not realised how hungry she was. Unable to resist, she took a sharp knife and cut just a small sliver of the Hawaiian. Then another larger sliver. She moved to the other box and sampled the 'meat-lovers' pizza, before attacking the Hawaiian again. Just as she finished her fourth slice, the doorbell rang once more. She panicked. Patrick would smell the pizza on her. Replacing the lid, she threw the knife in the sink and grabbed some peppermints from her bag.

Emma showed Patrick into the kitchen. He was very buoyant. 'I'm sorry I'm so late, darling, but I've had a very exciting afternoon. I'll tell you all about it over dinner.' He looked derisively at the pizza boxes. 'Aren't you glad you're not stuck with that for dinner?'

Julia settled onto Patrick's couch and slipped off her shoes, watching him while he brought in the coffee. He was wearing a short-sleeved, dark green, open-necked shirt which went well with his lightly tanned skin, while his hair, overdue for a cut, gave him a slightly roguish air. As he looked over and smiled at her, she loved him.

He was only now winding down after the afternoon's news. A cluster of ugly, unpopular shops about a kilometre from Bondi Beach had been sold to Bruce Rogerson, a developer with a well-deserved reputation for tasteful low-rise luxury apartments. His usual architect, made wealthy by their association, had recently retired, and he was in the market for a new one. Impressed with what Patrick had done at Vaucluse Manor, he'd sought him out some time ago and invited him to submit some sketches for the Bondi site.

They had met again this afternoon, the developer, his builder, his accountant and Patrick, and the meeting had gone well. They were quite taken with his preliminary sketches, and had contracted him for the job, with the possibility of another if things went well. Work for architects had been slow recently and

Patrick and his partners were feeling the pinch. A contract like this was invaluable. Apart from the money, it gave them an unrivalled opportunity to demonstrate what they could do in the modern as well as the period style.

All evening he'd buzzed with his good fortune. As they'd taken their seats in the restaurant, Julia had asked what he had in mind. Immediately he'd pulled out his pen, turned over first his menu and then hers, and filled the pages with his ideas; he'd hardly bothered to eat. It was only now they were back at his place that he asked Julia about her day.

She told him about Grace Chan, who had been in for a post-ectopic visit, crushed that her desire for a child had been cruelly dashed once more. At the mention of children, Patrick was suddenly downcast; he was thinking of Miranda, Julia knew. He mentioned her less often than before but she was always on his mind. He would occasionally come to a sudden halt in the street and, following his gaze, she would see a lively pre-teen who resembled his little girl.

'Would you like another child, Julia?' he asked, sitting next to her on the couch.

'Another child?' she stammered, spilling her coffee.

'Yes. A child with me.' Patrick looked at her tenderly. 'I'd like a child with you.'

A sudden gust of emotions threatened to topple her – giddiness at the unexpected extent of Patrick's love, exultation at the thought of a baby with him, distress at the memory of Joseph, and rigid fear at the possibility of another loss.

'You wouldn't want a child with me?' he prompted eventually.

'Oh, Patrick, I would love one.' She trembled, her heart unsteady, her mind a maze where she was fast getting lost. 'But I . . . I might be too old.' While this was true, it was irrelevant to her concerns.

'You're younger than Cherie Blair,' he persisted.

She reluctantly conceded his point.

'So you're saying no?' He was hurt.

Touched beyond belief at his request, Julia couldn't speak. There was nothing in the world she wanted more than a baby with him. But if something went wrong, she knew with equal surety, she would splinter into a million pieces.

She struggled to find the right words. 'I'd love to have a child with you, Patrick. I'm just not sure I'm ready yet.'

'But you'll think about it?'

'Yes, darling,' she appeased, squeezing his hand and fighting back tears. 'I will think about it.'

They went upstairs to practise.

Julia did not stay the night at Patrick's, wanting to be home for breakfast in the morning with Emma. There were not many nights when Ryan was away and Patrick's disappointment was easy to read. He was so sombre as he lay on the bed, turning away while she dressed, that Julia wondered if she should stay after all. She was tossing it up in her mind when he asked her to sit down for a minute; he needed to talk to her.

Caught by his mood, she perched nervously on the edge of the mattress.

He took her nearer hand in both of his. He'd meant what he said about the baby. And there was something else as well.

Julia gazed into his unusually serious eyes and waited, uncertain.

'I want to marry you,' he completed.

She gaped in amazement, his declaration so unexpected that, for the second time in a few hours, she was without words. They'd known each other for several years, of course, but this more special relationship was very new. And while, from the beginning, she'd been certain of her own feelings, she'd not been so sure of his. Not for any concrete reason – he was always wonderful to her. Just because it would be too good to be true.

She forgot to breathe, and her heart seemed to stop as well. But at the same time she was confused. She thought he hated all the phone calls, the uncertainty, the interruptions. He did hate them, he admitted, but he had come to realise that they were a part of her. At least if she lived here, he could have her the rest of the time.

Julia couldn't look at him for a moment; she'd had no idea he felt so strongly, and she struggled to contain her amazement. He took her silence for reluctance, and began to lose confidence. 'Don't you want to do it, Julia? To marry me?'

Immediately she turned to him. 'I would love to, Patrick. And thank you.' As she bent to kiss him, he pulled her down onto the bed again, crushing her dress.

She laughed. 'But it might be too exhausting!'

Chapter 26

They were all on the floor. Even Julia. Antonio had insisted that she be a dog too, and so she was crouched next to Jason and Emma as they chased the squealing three-year-old from room to room, barking.

'Catch me, catch me,' he implored each time they stopped for a break.

Finally even he had had enough, and they were able to get up.

'Would you like a drink?' Julia asked as he followed her into the kitchen.

'Duce.'

'Apple or orange?'

'Blackcuwwant.'

Julia explained that there was no blackcurrant. Antonio asked if he could mix the apple and orange together.

'Just try a little bit first and see if you like it.'

He finished his drink, which he pronounced okay but not as good as blackcuwwant, and opened the cupboard he had seen Emma at earlier.

'Wanna biscuit.'

'Please,' Julia prompted.

Antonio nodded.

Julia explained. 'Antonio, you have to say "please" before I can give you a biscuit.'

'Please Ju-ya, wanna biscuit.'

'Which one would you like?'

He pointed to the chocolate ones. She gave him two and made him sit at the table to eat them. He was a talkative little boy and sat happily for a while giving her snippets about his plane trip, and his cousins, and his toy train set.

Then, from being cheerful, he became apprehensive. 'Where's Daddy?'

'He's having dinner with a friend.'

'Who?'

'A friend called Angie. She's a friend of mine too.' Julia was not sure why the fact that it was Angie that Tony was having dinner with again should disturb her, especially today. But it did.

'Is he coming back?'

'Not tonight. He's coming back in the morning. You're staying with us tonight.'

Julia looked at his distressed face and decided it was time to become a dog again.

'Would you like a cup of tea, Dad?' asked Emma, showing Tony into the back living room. It was ten on Sunday morning.

'That would be great, Em.'

He could hear Antonio laughing upstairs. 'How did it go last night?' he asked, gesturing towards the shouts of delight.

'Good.' She pulled a sheepish face. 'Actually, Dad, Jason and I took advantage of Mum being home, and went out for a while.'

'Oh?' Tony was embarrassed. He thought Julia might be sensitive about Antonio and had only agreed to have Emma mind him here on the assumption Julia would be out for most of the evening.

'Mum didn't mind. She wasn't doing anything else,' Emma said with teenage disregard.

'She wasn't going out with her boyfriend?'

'Patrick and Ryan had a father and son thing at scouts.'

'I see,' said Tony awkwardly. 'So how did they get on?'

'Great. Antonio followed her around all evening apparently, took every shoe out of her cupboard to try on, and sampled all her perfumes. He then insisted on sleeping with her rather than on the camper bed in my room. And he hasn't left her alone since he got up this morning. He even did the washing with her.' Emma laughed. 'He'll never let you do your whites and coloureds together again, Dad.'

She paused as they heard the excited squeals again. 'Mum's giving him a bath at the moment. I think she's used an entire bottle of bubble bath because he kept saying the bubbles weren't "nuff". I doubt he'll go home with you.'

Patrick was on the phone to Henry in the other room, discussing a new idea for the Rogerson project, an idea too exciting to wait until tomorrow. They had eaten and cleaned up, and now Julia and Ryan sat at the table constructing a balsawood aeroplane from a kit. The ten-year-old was good with his hands, methodical and exact. Which was lucky, thought Julia, since tonight she was none of these. She just put glue over all the wrong pieces, which Ryan then patiently wiped off.

'How was the scouts' barbecue last night?' she asked.

His face lit up at her question. 'It was funny. They made us tie all the fathers up with ropes to see if they could undo our knots.' He laughed. 'And Dad got so tangled up that he fell over.'

'Did any women go?' she teased.

'Of course not,' he replied disdainfully. 'It was just for men.'

He was happy enough to talk to a woman about it, however, and cheerfully described the games and songs and the big bonfire. As they worked steadily, piecing together first the body of the plane and then the wings, Julia noted that, for the second night in a row, she was playing games with a young boy.

Joseph would have been ten this year.

Patrick was a long time on the phone and they had finished the glider by the time he rejoined them. He was flushed with excitement at his own project and generous in his praise of theirs. 'I think Ryan might be a builder when he grows up,' he said proudly. 'And then we could work together.'

'But I want to be a pilot, Dad,' Ryan replied, zooming his plane around in wide arcs. 'An airforce pilot. And Julia's going to be my engineer,' he added with a nod in her direction.

As Julia prepared for bed, she could hear Jason and Emma downstairs playing music and trying to be quiet. Not that they need have worried; there was no way she'd be getting much sleep tonight.

Just before she'd left Patrick this evening, he had repeated his proposal. He thought they should reverse the order of things and have their honeymoon in Paris in August, and then get married when Emma came back at the end of the year. And not only was Patrick desperate for this, Ryan had been consulted and was keen as well. They could build an entire airforce together, he'd said. And maybe a navy.

Julia wondered where her fairy godmother had been until now.

As she listened to the giggles from the music room, she also wondered how Emma would feel. She doubted her daughter would want to move into Patrick's house on her return from overseas, although she too was invited; she would probably prefer to stay here on her own. Suddenly, Julia was torn. While Emma was at an age when children commonly left their parents, her mother felt much less comfortable being the one doing the leaving. It had been just the two of them for so long.

There was that other problem too, of course: Tracey Edwards. Julia realised that she couldn't possibly marry Patrick until the court case was over, whenever that was. She knew only too well how it felt to be collateral damage, and refused to inflict it upon him.

Which brought her to the fact that she still hadn't told him anything about it.

Partly, it was shame. Patrick was proud of her career, its irritations notwithstanding, and she felt extreme embarrassment at the thought of telling him that a heartbroken young mother and a flock of medical experts believed *her* responsible for the destruction of a little boy's life. But, awful as it was, that discomfort was nothing beside the other reason for her silence.

If Patrick *had* to know she was being sued, it was imperative he not dismiss it as just a professional hiccup. For someone else it might be, but not for her, not with what she'd gone through last time. Patrick had to understand how damaged she'd been and how terrified she now was of having to relive it all again, dreading the thought of the old case being dredged up to embroider the new. And he could only understand all this if she told him about Tony. And Madeleine Morgan.

Even now, after four months of exquisite intimacy in which they'd talked and argued and laughed and cried about every topic under the sun, they had never once spoken about Tony. Patrick had never asked; and she had never volunteered. She wasn't sure why he didn't ask, but she knew quite definitely why *she* never mentioned her ex-husband. The belief that she was soiled.

In that part of her brain responsible for rational thought she recognised that Patrick wouldn't care about her past; none of it had been her fault anyway. He knew who she was, and he loved her enough to marry her. But in an inaccessible alcove of neurons, where the rules of logic held no sway, she feared him suddenly looking at her in a new way. She'd done it herself, met someone and liked them, and then learnt something unexpected about them, and from that time viewed them differently, the original estimation forever altered. Well, she didn't want that happening to her. She couldn't bear it if Patrick stared at her with the prurient curiosity of the other men she'd known since her divorce, their mean appraisal laying to waste her already shattered confidence. And so she'd kept quiet.

But now he'd asked her to marry him, she knew she had no choice; she had to tell him everything.

Chapter 27

'I 'd like to have my tubes tied, Julia.'

'Would you, Louise?' Julia raised her eyebrows as she flipped through the patient's file. She'd made the same request before her third child and before her fourth, now cradled in her arms. Both times she'd cancelled because her husband was seeing his own doctor to take care of the matter.

'I thought Edward was going to have a vasectomy.'

Louise laughed. 'He's still going to, Julia. He's going to, he's going to, he's definitely going to . . .'

'I see.'

Julia was thankful that most of the morning's consultations were simple. She couldn't have managed otherwise, her concentration buffeted by a maelstrom of conflicting emotions which commandeered her mind and dragged it from her patients' concerns to her own. Luckily, her resolve to reduce her working hours and book fewer patients was slowly starting to impact and, by mid-morning, she had earned a quick break. She found Leo alone in his office, his silent slouch telling her all she needed to know. He was only working half-days at the moment, but had someone in labour today. She offered to cover so that he could get away, but he declined. He wanted to do the delivery himself; it would take his mind off other things. And he didn't feel like talking about Sandra. Instead, he enquired about Julia's progress with her court case.

She felt a little awkward discussing such a relatively unimportant matter, but did need his advice. The DDO had set up a meeting for her with her barrister, Gordon St Jude, in his chambers earlier in the week. Although they still did not have the court dates, the malpractice insurer felt it was important to continue the preparation for the trial.

Richard Tripp was supposed to have been there but had been called away at short notice, and Julia had seen the barrister alone. During their meeting Mr St Jude had taken three prolonged phone calls on unrelated matters, buzzed his secretary for a cappuccino while Julia was in the middle of her explanation of the monitoring options in labour, and read the form guide for the mid-week horse races while pretending to look in a drawer for a file. He had yawned when she tried to explain the tests available in late pregnancy to assess foetal wellbeing, and scratched his crotch when she described the difference between a healthy small baby and an unhealthy one.

But worst of all, he had still not read the painstaking and detailed report she'd written about the events surrounding Tracey Edwards' pregnancy and delivery. His questions made it obvious he knew nothing of what had gone on. When she'd hesitantly challenged him about this, he'd simply waved his hands dismissively. He'd seen it all before, he said, and could run these cases with his eyes closed.

Leo was shocked. Perhaps she should ring Jennifer Pereira. But Julia felt ill at ease. She was in a weak position, the 'guilty party'. She was also the newcomer to their circle. Jennifer and Richard and their predecessors at the DDO had been briefing Gordon St Jude QC for years. Who was she to challenge them?

'I wouldn't leave it, Julia,' Leo persisted. 'This trial is much more important to you than it is to them. You should at least register your surprise and disappointment at Mr St Jude's professional conduct. There are hundreds of barristers in Sydney. It would not be unreasonable to ask for another one.' He looked at her protectively. 'You've got a lot at stake here, Julia.'

'I know,' she said glumly. Much more even than dear Leo realised.

She took a phone call from Patrick just before lunch.

'How's my beautiful fiancee?' he purred.

She found she was rather taken with her new designation. 'I'm fine, darling.'

'All set for tonight?' he asked eagerly. He had booked at an exclusive new restaurant, wanting something extra special for their first night out as a 'nearly married' couple.

'I can't wait, Patrick.'

'Please, Julia, don't use the word "wait". We've waited two days as it is. You might jinx us again,' he said, with a low chuckle. The original booking had been for Tuesday, but she had been called away to an emergency just as they were sitting down. And last night, Ryan had a thing at school. And so their engagement celebration was to be tonight. Just over one hundred hours since Patrick had asked her to marry him.

She'd arranged for Sylvie to cover her, determined that nothing would spoil their evening this time. Or interrupt it. She needed Patrick's complete focus on what she had to tell him.

'So I'll pick you up at seven-thirty?' he confirmed.

'I'll be waiting,' she said.

Just as she hung up the phone Marcia came into her office, the confinements book in one hand and a cup of tea for Julia in the other. She closed the door behind her and took the patient's chair across the desk from her boss. She was far from happy. Since the DDO meeting last month, Julia had instructed that all patients wanting her to deliver their babies from August onwards were to be rejected. Without explanation. Having cancelled the August and September babies, Marcia was currently knocking back those due in October. The patients were becoming increasingly upset. Several had asked if Dr Kent was retiring.

Julia shook her head hopelessly. She wasn't sure what else she could do. She felt dishonest agreeing to deliver someone's baby and not mentioning she might be unavailable; she had never practised like that. All the patients booked for July and early August had long been told that she might be in Europe on holiday. But those due after that were not being told anything. They were just being rejected.

Marcia nodded, understanding the decision. She then pulled out a piece of paper and reeled off the names of the women who'd been instructed to choose another obstetrician. Among them were some of Julia's longest-standing and dearest patients, many of whom she'd cared for over several pregnancies, and some of whom had also brought their family and friends to see her.

She paled visibly.

The secretary continued. 'These are only the old patients I've rejected over the past month. There are quite a number of new patients who want you to deliver their babies at that time, but I didn't bother to record their names. Although I do recall Leo's daughter, Alex, was knocked back the first time she rang.'

'Oh no!'

'I'm afraid so. Leo fixed that up, of course.'

Marcia gazed sympathetically at her boss. What they needed were definite dates for the court case so they could do away with all this guesswork. Did she have any idea? Julia shook her head. The DDO didn't know either; she had spoken to Jennifer Pereira only yesterday. In that case, said the secretary firmly, they should book pregnant patients as normal. Julia would just have to take a month's leave when the trial started.

Julia was stricken. 'But what am I going to say to the patients I have to let down?'

'You won't have to say anything. I'll tell them that you are unavailable for "personal reasons".'

'They'll think I'm having an operation. Or a breakdown,' Julia argued limply.

246

'Let them think what they like,' countered Marcia, recognising the concession and pushing her advantage. 'It is the best way. Best for you. Best for the patients. And best for the staff.'

'The staff?'

'Cynthia and Justine and Patricia book your patients too. I had to tell them your instructions.'

'Did you tell them about my court case?' Panic shrivelled Julia's features.

'Of course not. I've been saying that you are hoping to join Emma overseas at about that time, but have not yet finalised the details.'

'Thanks, Marcia,' said Julia gratefully.

If only that was the reason.

Julia was now running twenty minutes late. It didn't sound like much, but as it flowed through the rest of the day, it could mean the difference between doing the last case on her list this afternoon, or having it cancelled by Sister Aboud. And that was if it stayed at just twenty minutes; running late had a habit of compounding itself. As she looked at the list of patients still to be seen, she was not optimistic.

Marina Sorensen, a well-known public relations and major functions mogul whose multi-million dollar company was rumoured to be listing on the stock exchange next year, came back into the room having done another urine sample. She finished a call on her phone as she entered. Forty years old, this was her first pregnancy. At her last visit, a week ago, her blood pressure had been starting to creep up. This week it was even higher and there was now protein in her urine. The blood tests confirmed mild kidney impairment. These features, taken together, suggested that she was developing pre-eclampsia. There was evidence that the baby's growth was falling behind as well, and she wasn't yet thirty weeks pregnant.

Julia explained the implications of Marina's tests and outlined her proposed plan of management.

Marina rejected the first suggestion. 'I'm sorry, Julia, but there is no way I can go into hospital for monitoring and rest.' She had her diary open now. Apart from the fact that Sven didn't like it when she was away, her program was fully booked until the end of April. She flicked the pages with one of her elegantly manicured nails. There was the Autumn Fashion Week, the Bailey's Ball, the opening of Peter Rickard's new restaurant. 'As you can see, Julia, I'm fully booked until after the Easter Racing Carnival in late April.'

'The baby is due in the first week of May, Marina. Have you noted that in your diary too?'

Without embarrassment, Marina turned the pages to check. It was there. The third of May. 'I'm free that week. That's one of the reasons I planned to have the baby in May. It's a quiet month for me.'

Having just explained the seriousness of Marina's condition, Julia struggled to contain her frustration and amazement. Patiently starting from the beginning, she went over it all again. Slowly. In the midst of the discussion, she noticed Marina glance at her watch.

'Do you have to go?'

'I'm supposed to be at the Hilton at twelve to discuss the flowers and lighting for a fashion parade next week.'

'Would you like to ring them and let them know you will be late?'

Marina nodded and pulled out her phone. Julia pretended to be busy with a file on her desk while her patient embarked upon a long conversation with Hugo from Brilliant Bouquets who, it appeared, would not be able to wait until she arrived. Unperturbed, Marina conducted the proposed meeting over the phone, describing her floral requirements in great detail and emphasising how important it was that the colours perfectly complemented the theme of the designer's autumn and winter collections.

After some minutes Julia stole a look at the time, not really wanting to know how late she was by now. She indicated to Marina that perhaps the phone call should come to an end.

Finally resuming the interrupted consultation, it was obvious that alternative management strategies had to be offered. Just as Marina was too busy for hospital, in the same vein it would be impossible for her to manage a brief daily visit to the surgery for assessment of her and her baby's health by the midwife.

'Every day? Do you know how hard it is to park around here?'

Julia realised that subtlety was lost on her patient. Pre-eclampsia could and still did kill both babies and mothers every year. Even wealthy ones. She looked at her patient directly.

'Marina, it would seem to me that one of the reasons you are so successful is that you are very efficient.'

Marina nodded, pleased, although Julia could tell her mind was already on her afternoon engagements. Clearly she was unprepared for Julia's next comments, and ignorant of her doctor's own pain as she uttered them.

'It would be very inefficient to invest seven or eight months in a pregnancy and end up without a baby, don't you think?'

As Marina's face darkened with shock, Julia finally had her attention. She went on. The condition Marina had was very serious. If it worsened much more, it would be a threat to both her and her baby. Eventually they reached a compromise.

Erica would instruct Marina on how to check her own blood pressure three times a day and her urine twice. She would have a blood test to check kidney function on Mondays and Thursdays at her local pathologist, and come in to see Julia on Tuesdays and Fridays to discuss the result.

'Will I have to do this for the next ten weeks?'

'No.' Julia continued quickly, before Marina could become encouraged. 'Your pre-eclampsia looks like it will progress rapidly. My feeling is that we will have to deliver the baby soon, probably within a few weeks.'

She then put it in language Marina understood. 'Before Autumn Fashion Week.'

At first, Julia didn't recognise that it was Angie who walked ahead of her along the dimly lit corridor from the lowest level of the hospital to the doctors' car park. They hadn't seen each other out of gown, hat and mask for several weeks, and Julia didn't realise the changes Angie had made; only the build was similar. Her flyaway, fine, light brown hair, for many years a shoulder-length, raggedy mess, had been cut very short and coloured a bold copper. It looked stunning.

'Dr Russell, is that you?' Julia asked playfully as she caught up to her friend. Outfitted in a new suit, Angie was even wearing make-up. Julia was amazed. No wonder Tony had commented on how gorgeous she was looking.

'Hi, Julia,' said Angie, enfolding her in a big hug. 'Actually, I was just going to give you a call and offer my congratulations.'

Thunderstruck, Julia stopped walking. How did Angie know? She'd been dying to tell her all week, but hadn't. She had to tell Emma first, and didn't want to do that until after her birthday.

Angie went on excitedly. 'So where are you going for the celebration dinner?'

'Dinner?' mumbled Julia. 'Tonight?'

'I thought it was tomorrow night.' Angie was suddenly confused.

'Oh,' said Julia, finally catching on. Emma's birthday dinner. Of course. Colouring deeply, she told Angie about the arrangements.

'Make sure you wish her all the best from me,' said her disconcerted friend.

Julia quickly moved the conversation to the meeting from which Angie was just returning. She was over the moon. The long-awaited audit had confirmed that Dr de Bruin's complication and length-of-stay rates were double the national average. Together with the adverse coroner's report on Jacob Newton, the hospital now had enough ammunition to force his resignation.

'Will he fight?' Julia asked, her interest keen.

'Even his hide's not that thick.'

As Angie laughed, Julia looked at her friend admiringly once more. 'Have you been through a makeover machine? You look fabulous, Angie.'

'Do I?' Angie asked, selfconsciously touching her hair. 'You don't think it's too bright?'

'Not at all. You look beautiful. What does Geoff think?'

'He accused me of having an affair.'

'And are you?'

'Not yet.'

Julia considered her dear friend closely. Ever since she'd known her, Angie's entire wardrobe was built around a basic black combo. Years ago, someone at uni had told her that if you didn't want to spend time or money on clothes, that was the safest way to go, with scarves and belts added for colour. The problem was, Angie mostly forgot to add the scarves and belts, and unrelieved black did little for her.

Curiously, Angie's transformation had occurred at Ritzy Rainer's suggestion. At their meeting last month, the detective had made two critical summations about Geoff's behaviour. Not that it was her place to do so, but Ritzy prided herself on being a 'full-service' professional.

First, she had kindly explained that the adequacy of the wife was mostly irrelevant in cases of compulsive infidelity. Some men, especially attractive but insecure ones like Geoff, needed serial conquests. For them, the chase was more important than the actual affair, the life span of which could usually be measured in weeks as they leapt to the next challenge. Angie felt bleakly cheered by this, although Ritzy's references to Bill Clinton and Mick Jagger were not especially comforting.

The second point was less kind. Fixing Angie with a serious gaze, the detective had explained that, despite her former comments, the characteristics of the wife were sometimes very relevant. Fearing Angie wouldn't comprehend her meaning, Ritzy had spelled it out for her. Geoff was a particularly handsome man who obviously liked stylish companions. All his lovers were not only good-looking, but also glamorous; women who obviously took pride in their appearance. Ritzy had suggested Angie take a look in the mirror.

Since that fateful meeting, Angie had undergone a dramatic transformation. She'd been to a new hairdresser, seen a stylist, had her colours done, and bought a new wardrobe. She was now arrayed in a loose-fitting pantsuit which gave her a fuller shape, the fabric in olive which suited her skin toning and her new hair colour.

Angie admitted she'd made the changes in an attempt to win back her husband's affection. But the result had been the opposite of what she'd expected. Not Geoff's reaction, which had been predictably positive. It was *her own* response that had been the surprise. Instead of being thrilled at her husband's new passion for her, she found herself recoiling from his touch. His delighted comments about her appearance actually made her loathe him. She thought of all the other women he'd said the same things to, and she despised him.

Julia asked gently if she'd told him what she knew.

Angie hadn't; she couldn't face it yet. And she wasn't planning to say anything until she'd worked out what she was going to do. Sadness overtook her. 'I think my marriage is probably over.'

Julia pulled up beside Stephen's BMW, pleased he was still at the surgery; she'd come back especially to speak to him. He'd recently asked when she was taking holidays this year, having heard from the secretaries that she was planning to travel overseas to join Emma. She had told him that she wasn't yet sure. While her answer was honest, it was not completely so, and she felt uncomfortable about not telling him the truth. Leo and Sylvie already knew; he had a right to know too, especially since any adverse publicity would reflect on the practice. That was the problem, of course. Stephen's reputation as the most expensive, the busiest and, in his mind at least, the best eastern suburbs obstetrician was very important to him. Particularly as he struggled to get on top of an increasing level of debt. Julia knew that he would not feel favourably towards anything, or anyone, who threatened it.

She could not put it off any longer. Gathering her bag and operation notes, she made her way into the dimly lit surgery, calling out as she came through. When he didn't answer she went to his room. His bag was there, and some open files on his

252

desk, but no Stephen. She checked the tea room, and the bathroom, but couldn't locate him. Hearing a faint noise coming from Erica's room, she looked in there. And found him, fast asleep on the midwife's examination couch, the rug pulled almost over his head. She stood watching long enough to be sure that he was all right before tiptoeing out. Their conversation clearly wasn't going to happen today.

The bayside restaurant was full but cleverly intimate, with indirect lighting and well-spaced tables and soft, rich furnishings to mute the noise. As Julia and Patrick took their seats, they looked at each other and laughed, remembering her rushed exit from this very spot earlier in the week. She took his hand across the table and gave it a small squeeze.

'I won't be going anywhere tonight.'

Cheerfully, he squeezed her hand back. He coped better with her disappearing acts these days, she thought. And there would be fewer of them in the future as the cuts to her hours and patients worked their way fully through the system.

They ordered. Patrick splashed out and chose steak with a red wine sauce on a bed of mashed potato but Julia, under his loving gaze, was abstemious and made do with grilled fish and a plain salad. They ate slowly as they exchanged the details of their day, a frisson of joyful expectancy travelling in their glances. This was the start of their lives together.

Julia looked at Patrick, loving him for his enthusiasm and imagination, watching the fall of his hair accentuate the elegant curve of his jaw. She was still in a dream state, the depth of his feeling having completely bowled her over. The solitary time she'd been facing once Emma left was now filled with joyful anticipation.

She just had to speak to him about her court case. Having failed to inform Stephen, she was even more determined to tell Patrick. She waited until he'd finished the latest instalment in the saga of Mrs Chalmers, whose chronic indecision was turning her modest three-room renovation into a bigger job than the Sydney Opera House.

Finally, she started. 'Darling, I was wondering, do clients ever sue architects? Say, for not realising the potential of a site?'

It did happen sometimes, he agreed. Especially if there were cost overruns. Or the builder had not been supervised closely enough. But it wasn't common, not if you were careful. He knew of a couple of architects who'd been sued and, in his opinion, they'd got what they deserved. If they had listened to their client and been meticulous with their work, they wouldn't have come to grief. 'We've never had any complaints,' he added proudly.

The conversation wasn't going exactly as Julia planned. Without inflection she said, 'Doctors get sued quite often, of course.'

'And so they should.' Patrick had been very upset with a local medico who'd failed to diagnose Miranda's middle ear infection before the eardrum had ruptured when she was two. And he had friends with similar tales of missed appendicitis and even cancers.

Julia countered that it was more difficult than Patrick realised to make a correct diagnosis. It could be nearly impossible to look into the ears of an irritable, unwell two-year-old. And, out of many thousands of children with tummy pain, only one or two had appendicitis; they couldn't all have an operation. And with cancer, of course patients looked back once the diagnosis was made and thought that the bit of tiredness or vague twinge they'd mentioned to their doctor should have alerted him earlier, but every patient who walked into a surgery had a similar complaint and most were better a few days later. You couldn't run a battery of tests on them all; quite apart from the discomfort and expense, some investigations carried complications. Heavens, even the simple act of prescribing antibiotics was not without risk. And yes, there were genuine mistakes; human beings tended to make them. But a lot of the time, it was the patient's medical condition – or their unrealistic expectations – that was the problem. Not the doctor.

As they passed the topic back and forth, Julia was surprised at Patrick's keenness for litigation against her profession. Gingerly, she asked if he would ever sue his own doctor. He might, he said, if the consequences of a mistake were serious. But he was very happy with his current practitioner; Dr Howard was not the sort to make an error.

Disturbed by his comments, she anxiously contemplated her coffee and searched for the courage to finally tell him about Tracey Edwards. As she began, her voice was little more than a whisper. 'Actually, Patrick, it's not just bad doctors who get sued. Sometimes –'

Just then a loud male voice cut across hers. 'Well, well, look who's eating at the newest place in town.' It was Henry from Patrick's firm, with his wife Lara. They had been at a large table in another room and were just leaving. 'And congratulations on your engagement, Julia,' Henry added, kissing her. 'I told the bugger he should have asked you months ago.'

Julia was speechless, her tortured words about Tracey Edwards suspended not just by Henry's interruption but by her pique at Patrick's breach of trust. They had agreed not to tell anyone except Ryan until she'd spoken to her daughter this weekend. She hadn't even let Angie in on the secret.

'Sorry, darling,' Patrick grinned. 'I was bursting with the excitement of it. I *had* to tell someone. And Henry's promised to keep it to himself.' He looked up at his friend, who nodded somewhat guiltily.

Henry called for champagne and pulled two more chairs to their table. As he and Lara toasted the prospective bride and groom, and Patrick circled his arm proudly around Julia, all discussion of her trial receded completely.

Chapter 28

Julia looked at her sleeping daughter, an adult today, and smiled. Eighteen years, so full of detail and yet so brief. She thought of waiting for her to wake, but it was Emma's day off and she had been out very late. Instead, she quietly left the birthday card on the pillow, but kept the bracelet. She'd give it to her tonight.

She did her hospital rounds quickly and got to the surgery early. The day was only lightly booked – she had been unreservedly ruthless – and she would see the last of her patients by mid-afternoon. The secretaries were under strict instruction that she was unavailable for emergencies. No matter what. She perused the appointment book and nodded with satisfaction. Even with the extra phone calls and results Friday always brought, she would easily be home by five. There would be plenty of time for a swim with Emma, and then a leisurely shower before they were joined by Tony, Jason and George at seven for champagne.

She realised she was excited.

Jane Steel, now twenty-six weeks pregnant, had arrived for yet another extra appointment, this time clutching a small portfolio. She launched into the problem immediately. Since having the diabetes test two weeks ago, she'd been thinking a lot about her diet, wanting it to be as perfect as possible for the baby. Julia reminded her that her sugar test had been normal; they'd discussed it last week. At length. Jane nodded; she knew that, but now she wanted to improve upon any natural advantage in order to make things perfect for the baby. Julia nodded resignedly as Jane opened the portfolio.

'As a result, I've written down everything I've eaten in the last fortnight.'

'You have? Everything?'

'Yes, everything.' Jane looked sharply at Julia. Was her doctor implying the record was incomplete? She turned to her notes again. 'I want you to look at what I've recorded and make sure that my diet is nutritionally balanced. Meal by meal.'

'You do?' quailed Julia.

Julia was just finishing with Mrs Boyd, a middle-aged woman who had come for her annual pap smear and breast check, when the phone rang. It was Patricia and she was hesitant.

'Julia, I'm sorry to interrupt you, but there's a bit of a problem.' The practice manager paused, aware of today's carefully planned timetable. 'One of the nurses from the operating theatre at St Agatha's just rang. Sylvie's in the middle of a difficult hysterectomy. The patient's pelvis is apparently a terrible mess with dense adhesions and a lot of bleeding, and Sylvie asked if you could come and give her a hand.' Patricia inhaled audibly. 'The nurse sounded pretty worried.'

By now Julia was behind, not much, but enough to have made her conscious of the time. It was twelve-thirty. She looked at the list of morning patients still to be seen.

'Leo can't go?' she asked anxiously. She knew he was in today.

Patricia sensed her distress. 'He's doing a caesarean at Eastside. He's only just started it.'

'And Stephen?'

'She asked for you,' replied the practice manager diplomatically.

Julia sighed. She would go immediately, of course, but Patricia must speak to the last three morning patients about what had happened, and rebook them for the following week.

The practice manager hesitated again. Rebooking the patients was not going to be easy; they were already here. Two of them had come together and could only come on Fridays. And Julia was going to a conference next Friday.

'Put them on the Friday after.'

'They'll both have their period then. They've timed their visit to avoid that.'

'And the following Friday?'

Patricia was prepared. Stephen was having that day off, and Julia had agreed to see his complicated pregnant patients for him. The day was already bulging, and she would be hours late by lunchtime. 'I wouldn't recommend it.'

The practice manager listened to the silence at the other end of the phone. She knew how badly Julia wanted to finish early today, but perhaps the easiest thing would be for the patients to go and have lunch and come back this afternoon. 'They shouldn't take long,' Patricia encouraged.

'You've just guaranteed that they will,' retorted Julia mildly, her afternoon swim with her newly adult daughter now jettisoned. 'But all right. I'll see those two at the end. But move the other one to next week.'

Patricia was sorry, but there was a problem with her too. Her appointment was supposed to be next month, but she had rung every day this week desperate for an earlier one. She had been squeezed into a spot today. Patricia lowered her voice. The woman was already here, an hour early, and was very upset about something. She looked awful.

'I don't think she's going to leave until she's seen you.'

Julia recognised defeat. 'Oh well, just do what you have to,' she said with resignation. 'Maybe someone will cancel.'

'We can only hope.'

Julia turned her attention to the patient across the desk. 'I'm sorry, Mrs Boyd, but there seems to be a bit of a problem at the hospital, and I'm going to have to go.' She found she was speaking in her slow, deliberate voice, the one she always used when there was an emergency and she needed to act quickly. She was never sure if it was more for herself or the patients, but either way the effect was calming.

By now she was in a hurry to get to St Agatha's and help Sylvie. She'd been in this situation herself and knew how frightening it could be. Even more, she knew that every minute counted. But she had to finish with her current patient without seeming to rush her. 'Do you need any scripts before I go?'

The patient was already standing and moving towards the door. 'If I do, Dr Kent, I can always get my nephew, the doctor, to fix me up. You run along. It sounds as though someone needs you much more than I do.'

'Thanks,' Julia replied, grateful.

'Thank you for coming, Julia.'

Sylvie's relief was shared by the hospital resident who was assisting at the operation, the anaesthetist, the scrub nurse, the scout nurse, the ADN in charge of theatres, and most especially the blood bank, which was fast running out of A negative blood.

Julia, now gowned and gloved, displaced the hospital resident as she took her place on the right of the patient, opposite Sylvie. She looked into the pelvis. 'No doubt about it, Sylvie, this is an awful mess. I've had a few cases like this, and each one ages me five years.'

She took the sucker from the resident. After a few minutes probing the pelvis, she felt no better. Blood was pouring from everywhere and she could hardly distinguish the uterus for all the adhesions, and couldn't see the ovaries at all. Bowel was stuck to everything. No wonder the poor woman had been in so much pain.

'This is as far as I've got after nearly two hours freeing up adhesions,' Sylvie confessed. When she'd first opened the abdomen, she could see nothing at all, unable to distinguish bowel and nerves from scar tissue, and uncertain what could safely be cut.

'Severe endometriosis with a history of previous surgery. These are the worst operations we ever do,' pronounced Julia. 'Worse even than cancer.'

While the patient continued to bleed heavily, Julia tried to identify the proper surgical planes for further dissection. Before she made a decision, she turned to the anaesthetist to ask about the estimated blood loss, only to find that it was Angie. Immediately she felt better. Angie thought the patient was down about two litres. She was putting in the fourth bag of packed cells at the moment, but more would probably be needed before the operation was finished.

'Unfortunately, her haemoglobin was already a little low even before we started,' Sylvie admitted. 'Her recent periods have been very heavy as well as painful.'

'How low?'

'Ten point four.'

Julia tried to put the best spin on the situation. It might actually be a good thing for the patient's body to be used to a bit of anaemia.

'It might,' replied Sylvie doubtfully.

The operation, already in progress for nearly two hours, was not finished for another two, but at least by then the uterus and ovaries were out and the bleeding had ceased.

Sylvie sat on the bench in the change room while Julia dressed in her street clothes. Very quietly she said, 'I can't thank you enough. I think she would have died if you hadn't come.'

'I'm sure that's not so,' replied Julia, unconvinced by her own words. 'You were doing well. What you really needed was an expert assistant, someone who knew exactly what you were going to do next.'

In cases like these it was always a good idea to have two surgeons with experience; once or twice a year, she and Leo arranged to operate together when they anticipated a horrible pelvis. It made the operation safer, faster and less bloody. 'And less stressful for everyone, especially us,' Julia added knowingly.

Sylvie, very frightened by the experience, shook her head in disbelief. She hadn't realised how quickly a patient could lose so much blood. She'd never seen such adhesions before and it hadn't occurred to her that she might need help. She probably wouldn't have called for assistance when she did, except that Angie had suggested it.

'Well,' Julia grinned. 'Angie's been my anaesthetist for years. She knows a terrible pelvis when she sees one.'

Sylvie was not mollified. It wasn't easy though, was it, calling someone in? Everyone was already so busy they hardly had time for lunch, without her asking them to help with an operation she couldn't manage by herself. 'Look at you, Julia. You're going to be three hours late because of this.'

'Maybe I will, but that's not unusual, is it?'

'That's not the point,' Sylvie insisted dejectedly.

Julia sat down on the bench beside her. 'Sylvie, this is one of the reasons we're in a group practice. To have each other to call on. And it's not as if this sort of thing happens very often.'

'Thank God.' Sylvie was very embarrassed, muttering that the nurses would think she was a hopeless surgeon. Everyone would hear what had happened, and would laugh about her incompetence. She was starting to sound like the old Sylvie.

'What absolute nonsense,' Julia replied with exaggerated irritation. She reminded Sylvie that she was one of the youngest gynaecologists on the staff, and that her surgical patients did very well. The nurses were always saying that. 'This was a bloody awful case, Sylvie. There's not a surgeon I know who would have found it any easier.'

'You managed to find the planes, identify the ovaries, tie off the major arteries, and get the uterus out pretty slickly, Julia.'

'Yes, and I've been in practice for seven years longer than you, and I had *you* for an assistant. A big difference from the hospital resident.'

'Maybe.' Sylvie's confidence was returning.

'It's not maybe. It's the truth. And if I need a hysterectomy, Sylvie, I'll be coming to see you.'

The younger gynaecologist smiled gratefully.

It was six-thirty by the time Julia saw out her last patient and returned to her desk to pack up her things. Stephen was on call for the practice for the weekend and, while Julia was happy to have the two days free, she was beginning to doubt the advisability of having him care for her patients any more. Chronically overworked and exhausted, she suspected he was taking short cuts and making mistakes. Leo and Sylvie also had misgivings, but unfortunately no one else could do this weekend.

Julia rang her daughter to apologise for her tardiness.

Emma was furious. 'Why didn't you call me earlier? I could have gone to the beach with Jade. Instead I've been sitting here waiting for you.'

Julia was distraught, only now realising that, in her rush to make up lost time, she'd forgotten to ring her daughter about their aborted swim. 'Oh, darling. I'm so sorry.'

She could hear Emma's angry shrug. 'Just don't be late tonight, Mum. Please. Not tonight.'

'I'm leaving in a few minutes. I promise.'

Forlornly returning the phone to its cradle, Julia looked at her watch and then glanced at the results and messages in two piles on her desk; even the urgent one was big. They can wait, she thought, standing up and resolutely collecting her bag. She would not even look at them; she knew too well what would happen if she started. Well, tonight she wasn't going to do it. She was simply going to walk out the door.

And then she caught sight of a name in the urgent pile. Olivia Milton. She moved the paper slightly so that she could see more of the note in Marcia's generous hand. Olivia Milton was bleeding very heavily and her mother needed to know what to do. Julia had prescribed medication to prevent the periods but it wasn't working. Olivia was fifteen. She had acute leukemia and was on chemotherapy. Even one period could kill her, so thin was her blood. Julia knew she'd have to call.

As she stood beside her desk speaking with Mrs Milton, she could not help seeing the other notes in the urgent pile. Jean Priestly had a terrible rash since starting the antibiotics Julia prescribed yesterday. Thuy Nguyen's hysterectomy wound was badly infected. Sally Khan had forgotten which day to start her fertility tablets and thought it was today. Fatma Ali's baby was still very jaundiced and becoming drowsy.

As well, Brittany Dunlop's pap smear was very abnormal, and Shalini Kumar's mildly so. Both had been told that they'd have a result by today, and indeed both had rung while Julia was operating with Sylvie and had been assured that Dr Kent would ring them back today. Brittany in particular would be waiting for the call. Of the other results, Nicole Salmon's husband's sperm count was very low, while Bridget Grier's husband's was okay. They'd also been told that they'd have the result by today. Julia knew them both. They would be staying home tonight until they heard from her.

She worked her way methodically through the calls, her panic rising as the time got away and she recalled her promise to Emma. She tried to deal with matters quickly but, having called, found it hard to get off the phone. Everyone wanted to talk.

'I don't know why it's low, Mr Salmon. These things are very common, and it could be temporary. We always recommend having a repeat test before making any decisions.' She listened to his response for a long time before continuing: 'Yes, it could be related to your job, but that isn't a usual finding.' She listened again, looking at the clock with concern. She sought to wind up the conversation. 'I think that the best thing is for you and Nicole to ring on Monday and make an appointment to see me next week. Then we can go over it all in detail.' She listened again, curbing her impatience. If she were him, she'd be concerned too. 'I realise that you have a lot of questions, and I am more than happy to answer them. The best thing would be for you to write them all down on a piece of paper so that you don't forget anything when you come for your appointment.'

Finally finished with the urgent matters, she stood up and put on her jacket. As she packed up the non-urgent messages to deal with later in the weekend, she noticed something sticking out, clearly in the wrong pile. A pathology report, faxed late this afternoon.

Enid Jones, the sixty-two-year-old woman she'd curetted

yesterday because of recent vaginal bleeding did indeed have a cancer in her uterus, a nasty one. This was not unexpected, and Julia had thought to tell Mrs Jones of its likelihood before she discharged her from hospital last evening, but had decided instead to wait for today's result. The patient lived alone and her husband had died of cancer himself last year. She did not need unnecessary worry, although the possibility of cancer would no doubt have occurred to her already. She was an intelligent woman. Julia sat down again and dialled the number anxiously. Enid Jones would have been sitting by her phone all afternoon.

'Enid? It's Julia Kent.'

'I thought it would be you, doctor. Bad news, is it?'

'Not exactly,' Julia said, her heart pounding. She hated giving patients unpleasant results.

'It is cancer, Enid, but if you've got to get a cancer, getting it in the uterus is one of the best places. We can cure most of them. A hysterectomy will probably fix you up,' she added, hoping it was true.

'When could you do this hysterectomy, Dr Kent?'

'Within the next month. You should come and see me next week to discuss it further.'

'I will.'

As Julia went to hang up, she realised that Enid was still on the line.

'Was there something else, Enid?'

The woman hesitated. She was not one to bother people. 'My daughter is here tonight. I was wondering if you could tell her what you've just told me?'

As Julia finally walked towards her car, her mobile rang.

'Mum?'

'Hi, Emma. Did Tony and Grandpa arrive?'

'They've been here for over an hour. As has Jason. It's nearly eight-fifteen, Mum. Where are you?'

'Oh, darling, I'm sorry. I'm so sorry. I've had an awful day, and I didn't realise how late it was. I've been ploughing my way through the phone calls and results.'

Emma exploded. 'Couldn't they wait, Mum? Just this once? We didn't even know whether to open the champagne.'

Julia was devastated. 'I'm sorry, Em. So sorry.'

'Do you want to just meet us at the restaurant, then?' Emma asked crossly.

'What time did you book for?'

'Eight o'clock.'

'It doesn't look like we have any other choice, does it? You'd better ring them and tell them we're running late.'

'I think they already know what we're like, Mum. Everyone does.'

'Sorry, Em. I'll see you soon.'

Julia sat in her car and wept. To have let her daughter down again, today of all days, was unforgivable. But her weeks of careful planning had been demolished in one fell swoop. She sobbed with disappointment; if she hadn't gone to help Sylvie, it would only be just after five.

The restaurant was buzzing when Julia arrived. She saw that they had a verandah table, and was pleased. It was not only cooler outside, but much quieter. They were laughing as she approached, raising their glasses in a spontaneous toast to Emma. Even George had champagne, he who was suspicious of anything but beer. He was looking scrubbed and lovable in his well-worn sports coat, while next to him Jason was dressed in his smart charcoal shirt and maroon tie. Beside them, Tony appeared rather wild in the exotic shirt his daughter had given him for Christmas. For her part, leaning in close to him as she laughed, Emma was wearing a strappy, yellow sundress, her hair highlighted with glitter. She was wearing enormous yellow earrings to match the dress, and looked exactly as one should on one's eighteenth birthday.

They were still laughing as Julia reached the table. 'I'm sorry I'm so late,' she said brightly, hoping her eyes were no longer red. 'But at least I'm not on call.'

Emma looked at her severely. 'Even so, I'll bet you've got a bag full of patients' files in your car.'

About to sit down, Julia stalled. After a moment, Emma relented, bestowing a small smile.

'For light reading only,' confessed Julia.

They finally stopped talking and laughing long enough to order. The waiter had approached and been politely waved away several times. Finally he light-heartedly insisted that they make a selection before the kitchen closed. Julia hesitated, hovering between the crisp-skinned duck and the rack of lamb.

'I wonder if the duck would be too rich?' she asked of no one in particular.

'It's supposed to be rich,' replied Tony.

'I'm trying to watch what I eat,' she added, patting her belly by way of explanation.

'If you have the duck, then I will watch what you eat,' he joked.

At Tony's urging she had chosen not only the duck for her main course but had preceded it with the ginger prawns for entree, and followed it with lemon tart smothered in cream *and* ice cream for dessert. It had all been glorious, although she felt somewhat guilty at the end. Remaining at the table with Tony to settle the bill, she put on her jacket so that she could discreetly undo the top button of her skirt. She exhaled gratefully.

'I really shouldn't have had all that food.'

Tony looked up from signing the chit. 'You feel sick?'

'Only because I won't be able to do up my clothes all week.'

'Get some new ones.'

She looked at him, suddenly interested in his opinion; he'd seemed to watch her closely during the evening. 'You don't think I'm getting too fat?'

An enigmatic smile played on his lips. 'I don't think it's a serious problem, Julia.'

Chapter 29

Marcia popped her head into Julia's room between consultations, frowning. Jennifer Pereira had just rung. 'She wants you to call her when you're free.'

Julia nodded mutely, apprehension suffusing her face. This is it, she thought. The dates. Her ribs were whalebone around her chest as she dialled.

Jennifer was apologetic. 'Sorry, Julia. I didn't want to bother you in the middle of seeing patients, but I needed to speak to you about the case.'

Julia's voice was faint. 'You have the dates?'

'No, I don't. But I might have something better.' The plaintiffs' team had approached the DDO about the possibility of settling the case. They had asked for a settlement conference.

Julia exhaled slowly, waiting for the other doctor to continue.

'They've seen our experts' reports now and probably realise their case isn't as strong as they thought,' said Jennifer.

Julia's heart lifted hopefully. 'Do you think they'll drop the claim?'

Jennifer was careful. They might decide to do that, but it was more likely they wanted to find out what the DDO's bottom line was, in terms of settlement dollars. They were probably hoping to get some money and save themselves going to court.

'We'd give them money to settle?' Julia was confused. She thought the whole point about fighting the matter was that the DDO didn't think Tracey's claim was worth any money.

That was right, agreed Jennifer. The DDO didn't want to settle, but it could be a commercial decision. It was going to cost half a million dollars just to run the case. If they lost, it could be another ten million on top of that. They at least had to listen to offers from the other side.

Julia again expressed her disquiet. Richard had said that fighting the claim was a policy decision. To discourage spurious cases. He'd said that if they simply settled, any child with a neurological disability would make a claim that it was due to birth asphyxia.

'That still applies, Julia.'

'So is there any point in agreeing to a settlement conference?'

Jennifer thought there was. Firstly, because the plaintiff had asked them to and secondly, because the DDO were interested in how low Tracey's lawyers were prepared to go.

Julia resisted the obvious reply and instead asked what the bottom line was. It was confidential. And not necessarily fixed. The DDO would need to see how plausible Tracey Edwards was. Her manner as a witness would go a long way to influencing the judge in a case like this.

'We'd like to see how she handles herself, Julia. Especially when she has to face you.'

Julia's heart sank. 'Does this mean I have to go?'

'I'm afraid it does. We're hoping your presence might influence Tracey. If her lawyers have already told her the case is not strong, maybe seeing you will be enough to persuade her to drop it.'

'That's if I don't scream at her and claw her face,' said Julia mildly, overtaken by wretchedness. For a month now she'd succeeded in confining the lawsuit to the less frequently logged-on sites in her mind. And seen the benefit immediately. And here the bloody thing was back on her home page again.

'Yes, of course.' Jennifer was familiar with defendants' power-less anger, especially as the impending weeks in court became a reality. She described what was involved in a settlement conference.

As the claims officer spoke, an appreciation of what the meeting could signify slowly crept over Julia. If the DDO agreed to settle, it would mean the end of her ordeal. 'When is the conference?' she asked with sudden eagerness.

'Next Monday morning. Nine o'clock.'

'Monday?'

'Is there a problem with Monday?'

There was a problem with any day, but Monday was especially tricky. Julia was operating. It was not a big list, and she would be finished by two o'clock, but she could not really cancel the patients at this late stage. Several of them had arranged with their work and families to have six weeks' convalescence. It simply wouldn't be fair to change the arrangements now.

Jennifer understood that asking busy specialists to cancel patients increased their already keen frustration and distress. She always kept meetings to a minimum and tried where possible to fit in with a doctor's schedule. But, she explained, she was just a small cog in the settlement conference wheel. The key players, the solicitors and barristers for both parties, had nominated the earliest time that suited them. And that was Monday morning.

'It could be our last chance to settle,' said the DDO doctor gently.

Julia sighed. It was probably one more false hope, but it was all she had.

'I'll be there.'

She drove carelessly in the late afternoon traffic to Patrick's. As the possibility of settling her case sank in, her mind began to soar with the hope that it might all be over by next week, despatched with unanticipated suddenness. The humiliation of court, the battering of her confidence, the wasting of her annual leave, all taken care of by a signature on a cheque. She wouldn't have to tell Patrick about being sued after all; his comments about negligent doctors had unnerved her. And she wouldn't have to talk to him about Tony and Madeleine either. She could leave all that in the past where it belonged. Instead, she could stride happily into the future and begin organising her holiday in Europe and her wedding at the end of the year.

But she still had to get through Monday.

Icicles of dread splintered down her spine at the thought of it. She hoped Brendan wouldn't be there.

She arrived at the same time as Patrick.

'Hi, darling.' He grinned as he opened her car door for her, bulging plastic bags in hand.

'Hi,' she said, cheered at the sight of him. 'Been shopping, I see.'

'The best of the day's king prawns and the choicest of blue-eyed cod, for madame.' As he bowed she giggled, and thought again how lucky she was.

Her cheerfulness slipped once or twice during the evening, but Patrick did not seem to notice. He was on a high about the latest developments with the Rogerson apartments. His words almost tumbled over themselves as he explained how well things were going. Julia struggled to listen to him. Her mind brimming with Jennifer Pereira's momentous news, she managed the effort of asking interested questions, but barely heard his answers.

Finally she needed to be alone, and made a move to go. Patrick's face betrayed his surprise. 'I was hoping you might stay,' he said, his hands softly playing with her hair. Ryan was away.

She deflected him gently. 'I'm feeling a little unwell tonight, actually. I think I should probably go home.'

'Maybe I can make you feel better,' he suggested, moving his hand down to stroke her nipple.

She smiled. 'If anyone could, it would be you. I should be home for Emma as well. I've only got her for two more weeks.'

Patrick drew her to him, disappointed. 'After she's gone I expect you to move in here with me. I'm not going to put up with being apart from you any longer.'

'That would be wonderful, darling,' she said.

Anything might be possible after Monday.

Emma and Jason were in the music room struggling with a new song. They'd gone beyond vexation and were laughing when Julia arrived.

'I've told him we'll have to leave it till I get back from overseas,' teased Emma. 'I might have some new musical ideas. European ideas.'

'And I've told her I'll complete it with my new girlfriend while she's away,' countered Jason. 'Australian girlfriend.'

'And I've said that in the time it would take him to find a new girlfriend, the song will be out of date.'

'And I've told her that by the time she gets back from overseas, everything will be out of date.' He looked more doleful than cheeky at this stage, and Julia felt for him.

She left them still sparring and ran herself a bath. It was where she did her best worrying.

Chapter 30

Julia was late. Not enough to hold things up, just enough to put her in a terrible state. She woke with an uneasy start; there was too much light for her alarm not to have gone off. Spinning her head towards the clock, she saw it flashing 3:25, and howled. The power must have gone off for a while during the night. Launching herself out of bed, she tripped over a shoe and arrived at her dressing table on her knees. And saw the dial of her watch. Just after eight. An elephant in its death throes couldn't have matched the sound that followed.

Her shower broke all water conservation records but, as she towelled her hair on the way to her bedroom, she became aware of an unfamiliar slickness to it. She'd left the conditioner in. Emerging from the shower a second time, she reached for a clean towel, only then recalling that the others were downstairs in the wash. Damply dragging on her new stockings, she laddered the right leg just below the knee with the hangnail she'd been too distracted to file.

Slow down, she breathed to herself, sit for a minute; you'll collapse if you don't have something to eat. She then fed a bowl of muesli to her lap, and had to change into a considerably tighter skirt. When the taxi hooted, she released a small sigh: she was just going to make it. And she would have. Except at that point she couldn't find her house keys, although she'd had them just a second before. Emptying her bag revealed the nail file, but no keys, and there followed ten frantic minutes of upended drawers and tossed cushions before they turned up. Already in the front door.

Finding the well-appointed offices of ABJ, AtkinsBrisden-James, the major Sydney law firm handling Tracey Edwards' case, was relatively easy after everything else, although once inside, Julia could have mistaken it for an art gallery. Those not lucky enough to have suites overlooking the harbour still had beauty to feast their eyes on.

A self-important secretary showed her to the conference room and, as she inched nervously through the door, she saw that everyone else was already there. From the way the pre-meeting chatter suddenly stilled, it was obvious they'd been waiting for her. It wasn't my fault, she wailed silently, recognising that if the reason she was here was to persuade Tracey to drop her claim, she'd better get her act together quickly. Richard stood up and smiled at her, but Gordon remained seated, quite taken with his watch. An acid taste filled Julia's mouth at the sight of her barrister. What did he have to complain about if she was late? He'd just made two hundred dollars for nothing.

In the few months she'd known Gordon St Jude, Julia had come close to loathing him. As far as she could see, he was a man with all of the worst features of privilege, and little of the charm. Two weeks before, finally rebelling at the thought of her career in his hands, she'd taken Leo's advice and rung Jennifer Pereira. Wasn't there another senior counsel they could use? She wasn't comfortable with Mr St Jude and, to be honest, not all that confident of her defence in his hands. The insurance doctor had been astonished at Julia's request, reassuring her that Gordon was one of the most experienced medico-legal barristers in Sydney. The DDO had specifically sought him for her case.

Upon being further challenged, Jennifer had conceded, albeit reluctantly, that thoroughness in preparation was probably not Mr St Jude's forte. Julia had replied that that was exactly what she needed – someone arguing her defence without even reading what she and the DDO's expert witnesses had written.

'Relax, Julia. Gordon's value is his court presence. The junior barrister, Roger Corrigan, will make sure that the preparation is done properly.'

Julia hadn't met Roger yet but Jennifer had told her he was famous for his thoroughness. 'Why not scrap St Jude and just have Corrigan then?' Julia had demanded. 'You'd save a heap of money, and spare me the unpleasantness of dealing with the old bore.'

'Unfortunately Roger is a junior counsel. We need a senior too.'

'Whatever for?'

'That's just the way the legal system works.'

Edging towards the conference table now, Julia took in the short, plump, balding man in his late thirties seated beside Richard and Gordon, and currently absorbed in making notes on a legal pad. He must be Roger Corrigan. He didn't look all that impressive, but Jennifer Pereira had spoken highly of him. Not that her recommendation was necessarily reliable; she'd spoken highly of Gordon St Jude as well, and Julia had yet to see anything to warrant that.

The junior counsel eventually registered Julia's presence. He stood up and extended his hand. 'Dr Kent, I'm Roger Corrigan. I'm very pleased to meet you.' He indicated that she should seat herself beside him and, when she did, whispered, 'I know you're probably nervous, but it'll be okay.'

She felt the tautness of her facial muscles soften at his kindness.

Upon Julia's arrival, the parties were introduced to one another. Tracey's team consisted of her solicitor, Louise Craig, a partner in ABJ who was fortyish, trim and efficient-looking, together with a senior barrister, Ernestine Hillier, who looked like someone's grandmother. The junior counsel, Michael Lethbridge, was not able to make it this morning and had sent his apologies.

Julia couldn't help stealing a look at Tracey, seated at the far end of the table, beside her two lawyers. Her former patient studiously avoided returning the gaze. She was smaller than Julia remembered and older, of course, lines starting to form around her eyes and mouth. Dressed in a simple cheap blouse and skirt, she looked exactly what she was: a single mother living in public housing.

For a moment Julia was taken aback when Tracey's mother, Norma, was introduced. She wondered if she too should have brought someone. But who? No one she knew could take a Monday off in mid-March. They were all back in the thick of work, making up for the lazy days of summer.

Having dreaded all weekend the prospect of seeing Brendan, she noted with relief that he was not present. Her relaxation was short-lived. Ms Craig, who seemed to be in charge of proceedings, explained that the child was currently with a nurse elsewhere on the floor, and would be joining them shortly. The ABJ partner then outlined the proceedings.

Firstly, a video of Brendan would be shown. It had been made recently and showed various aspects of his life as edited over several days. Most of it had been taken at the Malabar Home for Disabled Children where he had lived almost since birth. The last few minutes of the tape showed him with Tracey and Norma last month.

When the tape finished Brendan would be brought in by Nurse Wendy Sullivan, who had known him since he had gone to Malabar at the age of three months, and was one of his principal carers. She would describe what he was like, what his potential had been assessed as, and why she thought he would be better off living with his mother and grandmother. After that, Tracey would be given an opportunity to discuss why it was important to her to have her son at home. They would then break for lunch, after which it would be time for the legal negotiations.

Ms Craig's bald professional summary in no way prepared Julia for the horror that was to confront her.

At five years of age, Brendan Edwards was confined to a life spent in nappies and lived in a wheelchair. His lolling head looked bigger than it was, mounted, above a supporting neck brace, on his small, wasted body. Dribble constantly escaped lips that wouldn't quite close. His tiny, shrivelled limbs had little movement, twitches only. He could not stand, or crawl, or feed himself, or even wipe away his own spittle. He certainly couldn't climb or kick a football as other five-year-olds did. And he never would.

In case the fates had underdealt his hand, the child also suffered from violent seizures which jackhammered his helpless frame nearly every hour. According to Nurse Sullivan, a new medication had seen an improvement; he'd fitted only twice so far today.

His mental age had been assessed as that of a twelve-month-old baby. As such, he had little understanding of language and no words, although he made a constant stream of low-pitched noises, the tone of which seemed to indicate that he might be in pain. Nurse Sullivan said they couldn't know for sure, but didn't think he was. Even so, his every groan let off a bunger in Julia's brain.

But it was his unexpectedly beautiful smile that nearly brought her undone. While she'd pictured him in her mind a few miserable times, she'd never anticipated the sweet gurgle, generous and expectant: a baby's smile. And while, like a baby, he returned anyone's grin, there was no doubt that his readiest delight was for his mother. His response to her presence was obvious. And she was clearly besotted with him, lovingly wiping the moisture from his chin and murmuring softly to him during the proceedings. Julia turned away, unable to watch any more. Oh please, don't let this be because of her.

After Brendan had been taken from the room, Ms Craig invited Tracey to describe how she felt about her pregnancy and labour, to outline her feelings for her son and explain why she wanted him home with her. As she spoke, Julia forced herself to turn again and face her opponent. Now thirty-one, Tracey was not ageing well. Years of smoking didn't help, but it was more than that. A lifetime of hardship was etched in her face. Growing up fatherless and impoverished, leaving school early, drifting from job to job until she found she had a talent for hairdressing, her young life had been difficult. Until, at the age of twenty-four, she had met Brendan's father. He was two years older than her.

Tracey told the assembled conference that Brett Halsted had been a wonderful boyfriend, kind-hearted and thoughtful, hard-working and frugal. He had been in the army since he was eighteen. It was a good place for a poor boy to get an education, and he was doing well. He had been good to Tracey, a change from the boyfriends she was used to. He took care of his body and his money and had a plan for their future. They had been living together for over a year, Tracey explained, when she had fallen pregnant.

Although unplanned, a baby was not unwelcome. Initially Brett seemed even more pleased than she was and they intended to marry after the birth. As the pregnancy progressed, however, he had become less certain that having a child was a good idea. In the middle months, especially, he seemed anxious and moody. Tracey, who knew how awful his own father had been, was sympathetic to his concerns about being an adequate parent. Reassured by her love and faith in him, Brett had picked up as the pregnancy progressed towards term, and in the last weeks seemed as excited as Tracey.

Throughout the labour he had held her hand, wiped her brow and fed her iced water. Tracey described how he willingly got drenched each time she headed back to the shower for pain relief, just so he could be with her. He encouraged her through the worst of the pains in the ways he had learned at the antenatal classes, not one of which he had missed. He calmed her when foetal distress was diagnosed and the baby delivered with forceps, and comforted her in the first few days when it was hoped that there would be an improvement in the baby's condition.

But, he was unable to help her at all when it was obvious that their baby was going to be severely and permanently braindamaged. He simply buried himself in his work, applied for an extraordinary amount of overtime, and barely spoke to her when he came home.

Tracey had been discharged from hospital after four days

while Brendan remained behind in intensive care. He was unable to suck at either the breast or the bottle, and was fed via a thin tube passed down his nose into his stomach. Having been told that breast milk was the best thing for her tiny son, Tracey spent hours expressing and carrying her precious supplies back to the hospital for him. She would then sit endlessly beside his plastic cot, stroking his arm, talking to him, and looking for small signs of improvement in his condition. Her mother Norma often came with her, as did her sister Donna, and some of her friends. But not Brett.

He never visited his son, nor asked about him. He barely spoke at all. At the end of a month, he told Tracey that he was being transferred to Darwin. Tracey had protested that Brendan couldn't go to a small place like Darwin. Brett said he wasn't taking him. Or her either.

Tracey had never seen Brett again. For a while he rang occasionally, but since they could not speak about Brendan, their conversations were stilted. He hadn't rung in over four years and she did not know where he was. She wasn't even sure if he was still in the army. While the actual words were left unuttered, those assembled were in no doubt that Tracey Edwards believed Julia Kent had robbed her not only of a healthy child, but also of the love of Brett Halsted.

Tracey went on to describe what her life had been like since she'd had Brendan. She was on a pension, which she supplemented with part-time hairdressing. She lived with her mother Norma and daughter Bianca in a two-bedroom flat on the fifth floor of a dilapidated public housing block where the lift seldom worked. Her mother had given up her job as a library assistant to help Tracey with the care of two-year-old Bianca. Tracey spent three days a week with Brendan at the Malabar Home where she attended to his needs, massaged his atrophied limbs, shampooed his hair, sang to him and read to him, and took him around the garden. She could see that he benefited from her attention and, in recent months, she had taken the bold step of bringing him home for the weekend. But he was getting too heavy for her to carry up the stairs. And she couldn't manage his care without assistance.

Since separating from Bianca's father, Tracey had not had a boyfriend; in fact she did not have a social life, having accepted that it was impossible for a new partner to appreciate the importance of Brendan in her life. As well, she could not really afford to go out, instead spending what little spare money she had on buying things to make Brendan more comfortable. Whilst the staff at the home did their best, it was a public institution where the patient to staff ratio was high and the facilities poor. It provided little stimulation to children such as Brendan, and was not a place in which he would flourish. He would do much better at home with her and her mother. Over the past year, Tracey had become even more sure of that and was determined to make it happen.

When Tracey finished, Ms Craig announced a thirty-minute break for lunch. Julia sat crumpled in her chair, ravaged by the morning. She had confronted Tracey Edwards and lost, before she'd even uttered a word.

Chapter 31

Staggering from the conference room at midday, Julia hurled herself towards the exit. Not required for the negotiations, her driving thought was to get as far away as possible. As she scuttled through the plush foyer, she nearly walked past the familiar person sitting on one of a bank of soft leather chairs on the way to the lifts. 'What are you doing here?' she gasped.

'I didn't have anything better to do.' Angie stood up to hug her. 'And I thought it might be awful for you, seeing that little boy.'

At the sight of Angie, Julia nearly broke down. Having clung tightly to her composure all morning, the presence, among all these strangers, of someone who loved her was her final undoing. Ushering Angie hurriedly into the lift and away from the curious gaze of the self-important secretary, she fell into her friend's arms and sobbed.

'It was terrible, Angie, unbelievably terrible. And to think that it might be all my fault.'

'That's exactly why I am here, Julia,' said Angie unemotionally.

'I knew you would blame yourself, so I thought I'd better be here to nip that idea in the bud while it's still in its formative stages. Rather than having to deal with it as an entrenched belief next week.'

'So you're here for yourself, really?' Julia tried to smile.

'Of course. And for lunch. Now, where are you taking me?'

That they could go for lunch was entirely due to Angie's foresight. Quickly scuttling Julia's initial suggestion that they still operate this afternoon, Angie had arranged for the list to be done the previous Friday. Julia's face told her it had been the right decision.

They decided to eat walking around Cockle Bay. Julia forlornly hoped that if she kept moving, maybe she could shake off some of her gloom. So far, it wasn't working. She told Angie about the morning, her face drooping with despair as she recalled the shrivelled, groaning, fitting bundle that was Brendan Edwards. 'He's trapped for life, Angie, it's so unfair. But at least Tracey makes it a little better for him. I think we should just give her the money and let her get on with it.'

'Will the DDO do that?' Angie looked at her expectantly.

Julia didn't know. She had left before the discussions. All of a sudden her lip quivered and her eyes became blurred as fear overwhelmed her once more. 'What if it really is all because of me, Angie?'

'We've been over this many times, Julia.' Angie's script was prepared. 'You and I both know that this case is not really about you and your management. It never has been. It is a financial quest on Tracey's part. This is the only way she can ever get the money to have her son at home. It is not personal.'

'It feels personal, Angie. A roomful of lawyers arguing about *me*, a mountain of documents with *my* name on them, four weeks in the Supreme Court to judge *my* competence. Couldn't feel more personal, actually.'

Forced to stop their promenade for a few minutes while the old bridge opened to let a tall boat pass, Julia left Brendan behind and asked Angie about Geoff. He'd become unusually attentive, Angie said, without satisfaction. Partly it was her new look, but mostly it was because he genuinely thought she was having an affair. 'Can you believe it?' she scoffed. '*He* challenged *me* about an affair.'

Julia wasn't at all surprised. 'To someone like Geoff, your having an affair is not so improbable, is it? He obviously knows a lot of women who do.' She pondered for a minute. 'On the other hand, do you think perhaps he's trying to establish whether you know about *his* affairs by accusing you of the same thing?'

Angie didn't think so. No, it was the threat to his comfortable existence that had him worried. If she had a lover, she might leave him. And take with her her salary which, at three times his, provided him with a quality of life he could not otherwise afford. Overnight he'd become extremely solicitous of her feelings and considerate of her comforts. He'd even started leaving lights on for her when she came in late, something he'd never remembered to do in the past. 'And he's home by five every day.'

'You're not even a little bit pleased about all that?'

Angie faltered. If he was doing it because he loved her again, she'd be in raptures, but he wasn't. He was doing it to keep the cash cow happy. All she could see, every time he did something thoughtful, was what was behind it. Quietly certain, she said, 'I won't be able to stay with him much longer.'

With the bridge now passable again, they resumed their walk and moved on to happier subjects. Julia spoke about Emma's preparations for her trip. Just about everything was organised, at least for the first month. She was flying to Naples where an old university friend of Julia's would meet her. It was, Julia admitted, a big relief to know that she wouldn't be alone. She would see Pompeii and Mt Vesuvius before meeting up with some Cabrini relatives in Rome for Easter.

'What a great way to spend Easter,' enthused Angie.

'Isn't it?' agreed Julia, wishing for all the world she could be there too. 'After Easter, she's going to travel around Italy for a month or so before going to Paris and Berlin. It's all pretty flexible and depends on how much fun she's having and if her money lasts. She'll probably be away six months.'

'Do you think you'll be able to go?' Angie asked delicately. Julia's plans for her July visit to her daughter and her August holiday with Patrick were still on hold. Not that either of them knew it yet.

Julia gave a pathetic shrug. She couldn't make any decisions until she got the court dates. And given Sandra Steiner was so ill, she couldn't possibly go early. Besides, with four weeks committed to the trial, she wasn't going to have any leave left anyway. 'The chances are between Buckley's and nil.'

'At least Tony will be catching up with her in Italy,' Angie comforted.

'Is he going?' Julia was surprised, although she saw immediately that she shouldn't be. She wondered vaguely how Angie knew.

They decided to have a second ice cream. They'd had one after lunch but, as Julia pointed out, that was an hour ago. And there were another thirteen flavours to try.

'I shouldn't, of course,' she said, as always recently. She'd regained the few kilos she had lost before Christmas but simply couldn't deny herself at the moment. As she ordered a large scoop of both the strawberry ripple and the butterscotch cream, she looked like a naughty child. 'At least Patrick isn't here to tell me I'll never fit into my wedding dress.'

'You've chosen one already?' Angie's eyebrows shot up. 'Good heavens, you've barely been engaged a month.'

'Of course I haven't. He just means that if I keep eating like this, I won't be able to fit into anything at all.'

Angie nodded but seemed to think it best to say nothing in reply. Instead she asked what Emma thought about it all.

Julia stopped licking her ice cream. To be honest, she wasn't sure what to make of her daughter's response. Certainly Emma had been shocked at the precipitousness of it all, which was understandable; Julia had been taken by surprise herself. But she'd expected more enthusiasm from her daughter who, after all, had been encouraging her to date for years. But now, when she'd finally found someone she really liked, Emma seemed strangely unhappy.

'Do you think it's because you'll be moving to Patrick's?' probed Angie.

Julia thought it must be. Emma said she wouldn't be coming with her, which was fair enough but disappointing. 'And she made me promise not to do anything until she comes back. Which I wouldn't, of course. Patrick and I had already agreed about that.'

'And how is the bridegroom-to-be?' asked Angie indulgently.

Julia became flushed as she enumerated her beloved's virtues: he was fantastic, interesting, intelligent and fun. She effused in a similar vein for several minutes without embarrassment. 'And he's such a good cook.'

'Sounds like someone out of the personal ads,' teased Angie.

'He's not perfect, of course,' Julia amended, now mildly abashed. 'But he comes close. The only other man I've ever felt like this about was Tony.'

It was time to make their way home. Sipping coffee as they ambled towards the taxi rank, their minds returned to Julia's court case and to the deliberations now taking place between the two sets of lawyers. Angie asked whether Patrick knew about Tracey Edwards yet. He didn't. Not that Julia hadn't tried to tell him. Several times. But something always got in the way.

'Anyway,' she said, her voice lifting hopefully, 'after today there might not be anything to tell.'

As Angie gave an insightful nod, Julia acknowledged the unsatisfactory state of affairs. 'I know, I know. To tell the truth, I feel as if I'm keeping secrets from everyone. I haven't told Emma about my trial. I haven't told most of the staff or Stephen about it either. I haven't told anyone except you and Emma that I'm getting married in a few months. And I haven't told Patrick about my trial – or anything about my murky past.'

'At least he knows you're getting married,' twinkled Angie.

'Are you sure?' Julia managed to laugh.

Then she was gloomy again. She longed to tell Patrick what she was going through, was desperate to have him console her. They shared so much of their lives. Except this.

Julia had only to wait until the next afternoon to hear the outcome of the settlement conference. Richard Tripp rang to tell her the news. Since Tracey's mission was to have her son at home, and to care for him for the next fifty years with the assistance of regular shifts of nurses, she was not really in a position to negotiate a reduction in her claim. It did not take complicated mathematical calculations to realise that her dream would cost millions of dollars. About ten million dollars in today's terms if future inflation was not to eat it up before the end of Brendan's life.

The DDO had offered two million dollars. Tracey wouldn't even consider it. After a few years the money would be gone, and she would be in the same situation as now. Her own lawyers had tried to get her to consider making a counter-offer of five million, but again Tracey had shaken her head.

'Thanks for letting me know, Richard. I must say I didn't hold out too much hope,' Julia lied, her spirits plunging.

'Neither did we, but when the other side wants to talk, it's foolish not to listen.'

Julia again mused on how the DDO could reconcile their offer of two million dollars with their stated policy of not settling spurious claims. Since it no longer mattered, she left it alone.

'Oh well, it's roll on August then,' she said, sighing loudly as she looked at her desk calendar. Another five months, at least. Probably more. It was far enough away for her to be able to resume her strategy of trying not to think about it, of focusing on the wonderful things in her life instead, of making time for the people she loved. She would not worry about the weeks in court until they were upon her.

The heats were over; she was in the rest break before the final.

'Actually, Julia, it's not going to be August after all.'

Julia started. October? November? Was it going to ruin another Christmas? 'You have the dates?' she gulped.

'We do. We got them this morning. There has been an early settlement in a big case, and we've been allocated the vacated Supreme Court time.'

'When?'

'May.'

'May? This May?'

'Starting the last Monday of May, and set down for the next four weeks. So, most of June, really.'

'Oh.' Julia felt winded. Glancing at her desk calendar again she recalculated. Less than eleven weeks. She could forget the interim rest period: this *was* the finals.

Glumly she trawled her mind through the dozens of patients Marcia had already rejected for August, September and October. For nothing. A sudden spark of frustration and anger shot through her. Her life was being mucked around in so many ways by this case, and there seemed nothing she could do about it.

'These dates are absolutely definite, Richard? No more changes? We go to court starting the twenty-ninth of May?'

'Julia, these are the first dates we've given you,' he replied reasonably in his gentle style. 'These are also the first dates we've been given. And they are definite. Previously, I know, we gave you an estimate, based on our experience, of when the case would be likely to go to court. We said we did not think that it would be before August. We were wrong.'

He paused for a moment. When he continued, he sounded hurt. He'd thought she'd be pleased, getting it all over sooner. Gordon had knocked back a rather high-profile brief in order to be free for her case at this time. If he hadn't, they would have had to wait for a much later date, probably November or December given the court's current backlog. They had put a lot of pressure on him to decline the other case.

Julia stiffened. They knew how she felt about Gordon. They should have let him go. She would feel much more confident with a different barrister.

'We probably wouldn't have been able to get another QC at such short notice,' said Richard. 'I know you have some problems with him, but we've used him a lot and are happy with his work.' Richard waited for her response. When nothing came, he pushed on. 'I didn't want to let the May dates go, Julia. I realise what a strain these cases are and, to be quite honest, I thought you'd jump at the chance to go early.'

There was a long silence during which tears made their way down Julia's cheeks. So this was it. The weeks in court that she'd subconsciously hoped would never actually arrive were just around the corner. Her sobs grew increasingly noisy. Richard was doing his best for her; she knew that, and was grateful for his efforts and concern. And he was probably right in saying it was better to go early. But a June trial was too soon. What was she going to do about her patients? Those wanting appointments in the office in June would wait until July. Those wanting surgery in June would wait until July. But her patients having babies in June couldn't wait until July.

'Whatever am I going to tell them?'

'I thought you had partners to cover you, Julia?' Richard ventured bravely.

'I do, for the weekends,' she conceded, sniffling. 'But even then, not all weekends.' She delivered most of her patients herself. And if a patient was delivered by one of her partners, she always visited them as soon as she could, and looked after them until they went home from hospital. They were her patients, not the patients of a group practice. And all the women she had due in May and June had been told she was not taking leave at that time. They were expecting her to care for them over the last weeks of their pregnancies, and to be there for the birth of their babies.

'What do I say to them, Richard?' she whispered.

'Would you prefer a date in November?'

Chapter 32

Julia went straight to Angie's.

'What's happened?' exclaimed her friend, opening the door in her apron, the potato peeler still in her hand. She was shocked at Julia's face.

'I've got the dates,' Julia croaked. 'The twenty-ninth of May.'

'This May?' asked Angie.

'Yes, *this* May,' Julia almost shouted, terrified at the imminence of it all.

Angie chose her words carefully: 'It is a surprise, Julia, but don't you think there might be an upside to having it sooner rather than later?'

'If there is, I'm sure you'll point it out to me,' Julia moaned despondently.

Angie was not deterred. As they sat at the kitchen table, she patiently listed the advantages of an early hearing. Firstly, Emma would be away. Her getting caught up in any possible publicity was something Julia had been dreading. Secondly, with the trial over early, she might still manage some time in Europe. Thirdly, it had been hanging over her since October and was

288

affecting her badly. If it had to happen, let it happen soon and be done with.

'And finally,' Angie concluded, reaching out for Julia's hand, 'as you said only yesterday, it is interfering with you and Patrick. Even though he doesn't know about it. With it behind you, you can be free to really enjoy your relationship with him. And plan your future together.'

Julia looked at her dear friend and smiled weakly. 'Would you like to be my lawyer, Angie? If you can argue my case like you argued the advantages of a May hearing, I'd get off on the first day.'

Julia left Angie's resolving to speak to Patrick immediately about her problems, to get everything out into the open. Once she'd explained to him about this case, and the last one, and he'd taken her in his strong arms and told her he'd be there for her all the way, she would feel vastly better. And she'd be able to focus her emotions on the trial itself. She felt a surge of anticipatory relief.

Patrick was on the phone when she arrived, pen in hand. He waved her in and blew a kiss but remained on the line for a long time. Earlier in the afternoon he'd undertaken an urgent review of a large block of land in Randwick that Bruce Rogerson was thinking of buying. The developer wanted an idea of what Patrick could do with the site before he made an offer at the auction on Friday. During dinner, as Julia sought her moment, there was another long phone call about Randwick, and then two about the Bondi project.

Patrick was apologetic. 'I'm sorry, darling, but while I'm thinking about Randwick, we're also trying to finalise our preliminary plans for Bondi for Rogerson's builder to cost. Next week is the deadline. Natalie's working flat-out on the final specifications.'

'Natalie?'

'You know. Natalie Anderson. From the office.'

'I know who she is, Patrick. It's just that I thought she finished up in January. I spoke to her at your party and she was looking for a job.'

'Well, we gave her one,' he said proudly. 'When we got this

big contract we had the money to keep her. She's working on the Bondi project exclusively. Doing some of the more tedious bits, and doing them sensationally.'

The phone rang again as they finished dinner, and Patrick excused himself once more. Julia and Ryan spent half an hour doing maths homework. Long division was defeating him. Julia hoped it was clearer after her explanation, but his brow was still furrowed. 'Do you ever use long division, Julia?'

'Actually, Ryan, for these sorts of sums I would use a calculator. But I could do it if I had to,' she added hastily.

She could hear Patrick in the other room speaking technically and with some urgency on the phone and realised that tonight was not the night for one of the most important conversations they would ever have. Nor would any time in the next week be appropriate; she needed his undivided attention.

She made a decision. She would leave it a fortnight. By then, Patrick's deadline would be met. And Emma would be gone. They could give the trials of her life their full consideration.

Clothes were strewn all over Emma's bedroom as she made preliminary attempts at packing. Over the past week it had become obvious that only a fraction of what she'd laid out to take would actually fit in her bag. Julia walked in as she was throwing a minor tantrum, unable to decide between her jackets, and quite petulant that so many of her fabulous clothes would have to remain behind. Julia laughingly offered her daughter some advice.

'When you can only take a limited number of things, Em, you have to apply the "this goes with that" principle.'

'So I'd better ditch the bottle green jacket?'

'If you're intending to wear it with either the brown or the burgundy pants, yes, perhaps you should.'

'Did you want me to put the retractor over the bladder, Dr Kent?' asked the young resident who was assisting at Marina Sorensen's caesarean. The PR mogul's blood pressure and kidney impairment had progressed to the point where delivery could no longer be avoided. She was thirty-three weeks pregnant. 'Don't worry about Autumn Fashion Week,' she'd said when she signed the consent form. 'Just as long as I'm back on deck for the Bailey's Ball.'

'What?' asked Julia of the resident, her mind a million miles away.

'The retractor, Dr Kent. Do you want it in the pelvis now?'

'Yes, of course. I'm about to open the uterus.'

Thank God the operation was going well; she doubted she'd cope if it wasn't. She'd been like this for days now, completely unable to concentrate. Emma was about to go, the court case was about to come, and sometime later this year she was getting married. There wasn't room in her brain for anything else.

Marina's tiny baby daughter safely in neonatal intensive care, Julia exited the hospital via the labour ward and found Sylvie there, having just finished a delivery. 'How are things?' Julia asked, taking a seat while Sylvie punched the data into the computer.

'Not too bad,' replied the younger obstetrician, although she was clearly less vibrant than she'd been on her return from Melbourne last month. 'And you?'

'Not so good, I'm afraid.' Julia couldn't see the point of pretending any more.

Sylvie turned from the screen to look at her colleague.

'That case,' Julia continued grimly, 'the one I told you about in Melbourne. It's back.'

'The Edwards' case?' Sylvie forgot nothing. She registered immediately what Julia was saying. 'You've got the court dates?'

Julia frowned. 'Yes. From the twenty-ninth of May for four weeks.'

'This May? Ten weeks away?' Obstetricians could always calculate weeks faster than anyone else. 'I thought it was supposed to be the end of the year?'

'So did I.'

They sat for a minute saying nothing.

Eventually Sylvie asked, 'What preparations have you made, Julia?'

'For what?'

'For your case.'

'Like slitting my wrists, or stocking up on pills to overdose with?'

Sylvie didn't smile. 'How do you intend to fight the claim?'

Julia looked tired. 'I thought I'd let my lawyers work that out.'

Julia stared vacantly at the flickering images on the television screen. She couldn't have said what the movie was about, but it was colourful and fast. And it helped her avoid what she should have been doing, but couldn't.

Sylvie was right. She needed to plough her way through the medical literature, systematically collecting the data on which to build her defence, amassing the evidence to support the decisions she had taken in the pregnancy and labour of Tracey Edwards. She recalled Sylvie's surprise this afternoon when she'd said she hadn't even started. Indeed, Jennifer Pereira had asked her to do it months ago. But just thinking about it made her sick.

Her mind went back to Tony's trial and she recalled her own frustration, and the disbelief of the DDO solicitor, at his inability to produce a report about Madeleine Morgan. What had he said? That he simply couldn't face it.

Julia finally understood what he meant.

Maybe if she had someone to help, to comfort and cajole her through it all, she might be able to manage. But since she was now an immobilised, frantic mess, the support she required was immense. At the very least she needed to be told every second that Brendan Edwards was not her fault, reminded every minute that she was not a careless doctor, assured hourly that there would be no publicity, and promised daily that this would never, *ever* happen to her again.

Emma, she couldn't tell. And she would never reveal the depths of her despair to Patrick. Despite his love for her, she would feel ashamed. And while Sylvie and Leo and Angie were pouring kindness and encouragement over her already, they could be burdened no further; they had more important things in their lives to deal with. She needed someone who could hold her hand and not let it go until the whole thing was finished. And there was no one who could do that.

The phone rang.

Julia hoped it wasn't Stephen. She'd left a message for him to call her tonight if he had time, but had spinelessly added that it wasn't urgent; she still hadn't had the chance to tell him about her court case. She picked up the phone apprehensively.

It was Tony.

'Hi, how are you?' he asked so casually that she knew immediately he'd heard about the dates.

'I'm fine, fine. And Emma is out, I'm afraid.'

'I've called to speak to you.'

'You've heard about the trial then?'

'Yes,' he admitted. 'Angie told me. It's much sooner than you expected, isn't it?'

'Yes. Much. But probably all for the best,' she said without conviction, knowing it was what Angie would have said to him, and not wanting to reveal the canyons of her dread.

They spoke for two hours.

Tony asked about the settlement conference. She told him how desolate it had been. He inquired about the DDO personnel and she told him of her dislike for Gordon St Jude. He suggested she request a substitute. She had, she said. Fruitlessly.

His concern for her was palpable. 'It's a bit worrying, Julia, the preparation of your defence being so far behind.'

'It's not all Gordon St Jude's fault, actually,' she confessed, her voice very soft. 'I haven't done what I was supposed to do either.'

Tony said nothing but, in his silence, she knew he understood. He concluded carefully. 'You probably don't need me to say this, but whatever the outcome of this case, it doesn't change the fact that you are one of the best doctors I've ever known. And I want you to remember, if you need any help from me, at any time, please ask.'

'Thanks, Tony,' she said, over-bright, denying the tears which now puddled and spilled. 'I'll probably need the name of a good psychiatrist when it's all over.'

The front door opened and Julia heard Jason and Emma quietly say goodnight. Her daughter came in and plonked herself down on the couch. 'Hi, Mum. What are you watching?'

'Whatever it is, I think it's watching me, Em.' Julia pressed the off-button on the television remote. 'Did you have a nice time?'

Emma had. She and Jason had been out to watch other bands again; there were some great ones around at the moment and Emma was having misgivings about her trip, now less than two weeks away. Maybe she should cancel it, stay in Sydney and concentrate on her music. And Jason, of course. 'What do you think, Mum?'

Julia was alarmed. The last thing she wanted was to see Emma mangled in the fallout of her trial. She'd protected her last time, and would do so now. She spoke very quickly. 'You'd be mad not to go, Em. You've had this holiday planned for a long time and you'll only be away for a few months. Go, do all the things you want to do, and then come back to Jason and the band.'

Emma returned impishly, 'Of course, Mum, if I stayed, you could get married sooner.'

'I can wait, darling.' Julia forced a smile. 'I want you to go. You'll have a wonderful time. And you'll be back before you know it.'

'I suppose you're right.' Emma still sounded doubtful.

Julia seized the concession. 'Of course I am. By the way,' she added, moving on. 'Your father rang. He can't get down this weekend. He's very disappointed and asked me to apologise to you, but he's on call for the hospital and his cover has fallen through.'

Emma was predictably dismayed. The band's final gig was on Saturday and she'd wanted Tony to be there.

'I'm off this weekend, Em,' Julia ventured humbly.

'I know you are, Mum, but I wanted you both.' She shrugged with customary resignation. 'By the way, what did Dad say about your wedding?' Julia had permitted Emma to tell her father about the engagement.

'He didn't mention it, darling. It wouldn't be important to him.'

As she settled into bed, Julia's thoughts kept drifting to Tony. Speaking with him this evening had been good for her, his slow, deliberate questioning uncovering fears she'd been hiding even from herself. Confronting each in turn, she'd found herself less intimidated. Maybe she could now start to deal with them.

Chapter 33

Above the music and the laughter, Julia thought she heard Antonio calling her, although at first she couldn't see him. He was so small among the throng of adults, but his voice was loud and he was determined to find her. He'd been with her all day while they set up, his happy chatter keeping her company while she cleaned, his excitement building as first streamers and then balloons filled the back room.

'Ju-ya,' he exclaimed, running into her legs. She picked him up and smiled into his eager face.

'Can you dance, Ju-ya?'

Sixty of Emma's friends had gathered to say farewell before she left tomorrow. It was a deferred birthday party as well. Money for a holiday was an inadequate acknowledgement of an only child turning eighteen and leaving school. Something more was needed to properly celebrate; a surprise farewell party was the perfect solution.

Emma seemed genuinely astonished and was radiant as she moved from group to group, excited and vivacious. Jade and Jason had done the inviting. There were friends from school and from the local bands. There was even Stan from the music store.

Julia finished her dance with Antonio and, while he was irresistibly enthusiastic, decided against asking him to help her with the food. She looked for Tony and found him where the crowd had spilt onto the deck. He was with her father and Angie. They were talking about fish, the two men how to catch them, and Angie the best ways to cook the various types. Julia was pleased her father had come. This was the second time he had been in Sydney in a month, and he was having a ball. He'd even been dancing to the music Jason had compiled. Julia thought how nice it would have been if Grandma Cabrini could have made it too, but her arthritis was bothering her badly and the trip was beyond her. Emma had been up to Brisbane to see her twice since Christmas, and had promised to send her a postcard from every Italian city she visited.

'Would anyone care to dance with this wonderful young man, Antonio Vincente Cabrini, for a little while?' Julia asked, bowing as she introduced him to the group. 'I need to hand around some of the hot food.'

'I can help, Ju-ya,' he insisted, turning back, reluctant to leave her.

'You can help me later, Antonio. I think you should dance with your father first.'

Angie and Julia edged carefully through the crowd bearing trays laden with food. Angie indicated Emma, who was laughing with Jason and Jade. 'It's a wonderful party, Julia. You can see how delighted she is.'

'She is, isn't she? I'm glad we decided to do it.' Julia was glowing herself. The party's organisation had been a good distraction from her case, now nine weeks away. But more, it had been a distraction from the fact that Emma was leaving.

Angie said she'd deal with the desserts, freeing Julia to seek out Patrick who had arrived a few minutes before, pleased to finally be included in a family do. Julia knew he was bewildered by her request to keep plans of their wedding relatively private for a while. Over the moon himself, he wanted to let everyone in on his good fortune, and was noticeably nonplussed that she didn't seem to feel the same. This week, she would explain it to him.

She located Patrick out on the deck with Tony and was gratified at how easily the two men had found each other. She wanted this encounter. Tony had been a big part of her life and, although there had been a hiatus of seven years when she hadn't seen him, he had not been gone from her mind. Quite the opposite. Each of those two and a half thousand days had seen her hating and resenting and regretting and missing him. And now, in a development that still astounded her, they were becoming friends again. It was important to her that Tony like Patrick.

She also wanted Patrick to warm to Tony. It would make what she was about to tell him so much easier.

As she approached she could see that her future husband was holding forth while her ex-husband listened intently. A typical pose for each, she thought with a small upturn of her mouth. Patrick was a great conversationalist, captivating and amusing. But there was no denying Tony was the better audience.

The two men, naturally awkward, had found safe common ground in the artistic and architectural treasures of Italy. Patrick was enunciating the ones Emma should make sure she didn't miss while Tony appeared to be in agreement. Patrick grinned as Julia approached and he put his arm proprietarily around her. 'We'll be seeing them ourselves soon, won't we, darling?'

Julia smiled weakly; she doubted she'd be getting there.

She hadn't anticipated how bad Monday was going to be. She knew she should have gone early, done breakfast rounds at the hospitals, and caught up on what had happened to her patients over the weekend. But she simply couldn't locate the energy. She dragged herself downstairs to the kitchen and parked at the table, still in her pyjamas, her chin resting on her folded arms as she looked through the window to the morning which moved on without her. Her daughter had been gone only sixteen hours but already she was missing her dreadfully.

298

She thought about the party and how magnificent it had been. A determined group of carousers, Emma and her grandfather among them, had still been dancing at breakfast. Tony had taken Antonio back to the hotel just before midnight and, after seeing them off, Julia had then wanted to dance with Patrick, only to find him preparing to leave also. He was very tired, he said. Though disappointed, she was not really surprised, given how hard he was working. She'd taken him out to his car and bid him goodbye with a promise to call in on her way back from the airport.

As the kitchen clock ticked on, Julia finally dragged herself upstairs to the shower. It was illusory progress. She leaned against the tiled wall, the hot water a balm to her wounds, and thought about the airport farewell and how unsatisfactory it had been. Her excited, adult daughter had been surrounded by a noisy crowd of her friends, as she should have been. But to Julia it seemed there had been no chance to say a proper goodbye before Emma was gone, swallowed by the customs barrier. Not to be seen again for months. They had privately said their farewells at home, of course, as she helped with the last of the packing, and had indeed been saying goodbye in little ways for weeks. But somehow at the end it was all too fast.

Julia adjusted the taps, turning up the heat of the water even more.

Tony and Antonio had been next to depart. She and Tony had said little as they transferred to the domestic terminal in her father's car, but Antonio was chirpy at the prospect of an aeroplane adventure. He was encouraged by George, who pointed out the planes already in the sky. As Julia helped the small child with his backpack, he looked at her hopefully.

'Come wif us, Ju-ya?'

'I'm afraid I can't, Antonio. I have to go to work tomorrow.'

'Can work wif Daddy.'

Since the airport was on the way to Wollongong and taxis were plentiful, Julia had resisted her father's determination to drive her home again, and bade him farewell too. Once home, she had rung Patrick but only reached his answering service.

Wondering for a minute where he could be, she left a message saying that she would not be coming over after all, but would call in tomorrow night after work instead. She did not mention that she had something important to tell him.

When the hot water eventually ran out she traipsed to her bedroom; now she found it impossible to get dressed. Sitting on the side of the bed, she slumped forward, unable even to open the cupboard and take out her clothes.

By lunchtime, however, with the support of Angie and the operating theatre nurses, she was marginally brighter. Tony rang to commiserate with her. He was feeling blue too but, as a psychiatrist, he at least had a name for it. Acute reactive depression. He promised that by the end of the week she would start to feel better. After she hung up Julia thought that even if she didn't, at least she would be too busy to notice. It was her weekend on call.

'There's something I need to talk to you about,' Julia said. Ryan was at a soccer camp overnight, and they were alone. Patrick had been vague all evening, his mind on his projects, his ear mostly to the phone as first Henry and then Natalie had rung, but she had put this off for months and could keep it to herself no longer.

'There is?' He looked at her with interest.

Julia chewed her lower lip before spitting the words out. 'Someone is suing me. A patient. For malpractice. The matter is going to be in court for four weeks. From the end of May. The Supreme Court.'

'Why are they suing you?'

'Because they want ten million dollars.'

'What?' he spluttered into his wine, spilling it on his trousers. 'Ten million dollars from you?'

'I don't have to pay the money personally. My insurance covers it.' She observed his relief. It wasn't completely true about the money, of course. Obstetricians' insurance premiums now exceeded one hundred thousand dollars a year so as to cover cases like hers.

She explained in more detail about the case, pointing out that it would have been settled six months ago if the DDO thought she truly had been negligent.

'So you think you'll win?' he asked carefully.

That was the problem; no one knew. The DDO didn't think Tracey's case was strong, which was why they were fighting it. But so much came down to just one person. The judge. And to what he thought.

'Especially what he thinks of me,' Julia said humbly.

'You'll win then,' Patrick said. 'How could he think you were anything other than a good doctor?'

Holding his gaze she reminded him of his recent pronouncement that most people who got sued probably deserved it. And even if she didn't deserve it, judges made findings against good doctors all the time; their sympathy was naturally with the plaintiff. No one could look at Brendan Edwards and not want to give him money to make his life better. Which was why Tracey Edwards' legal team was continuing with the litigation. 'Even though the DDO's lawyers assure me Tracey's case isn't particularly strong,' she concluded, downcast.

'And you're worried about it? Going to court?'

Her face answered his question. She was terrified. Who wouldn't be? How would he like to sit in a courtroom every day for four weeks, listening to experts argue that he was negligent and incompetent and responsible for a little boy's ruined life? She was paralysed at the thought of it. Absolutely paralysed.

If she'd expected Patrick to take her in his arms at this point and wrap her in his reassurance, it was not what happened. Instead, he was sombre. 'How long have you known about this case, Julia?'

'The case itself or the dates for the court hearing?'

'Both.'

'I learnt that she was suing me last year but I kept hoping we would settle. All chance of that finally disappeared about two weeks ago. I got the court dates at the same time.'

'Does Angie know about this case?'

'Yes.'

'And Tony?'

'Yes.'

'And your work colleagues?'

'Yes,' she replied, remembering the disappointing exchange she'd had with Stephen last week.

Before she could continue, they were interrupted by a phone call from Natalie.

'How did you get on with Rogerson's builder?' Julia asked on his return, relieved to change the subject.

Patrick's face glowed. 'At the risk of sounding smug, I think he was really impressed with our final ideas for Bondi. He's recommended very few alterations to our design. Natalie's working on them at the moment.'

As the evening wore on, Julia waited for him to ask her to stay as he usually did when Ryan was away. With all of the upheaval in her life, she needed to be with him tonight, and had come prepared. She did not want to be alone. But Patrick remained distant and preoccupied, distracted by his work. She stood up to leave. He hesitated momentarily and then saw her out.

'Don't worry too much, Julia. I'm sure it will turn out all right.'

'Thanks,' she replied as she got into her car. She heard his phone ring again.

'You go. We'll catch up tomorrow.'

Chapter 34

Midwife Liz Ellison spoke into the phone to Julia. 'Mrs Benjamin is seven centimetres dilated and labouring well, but I don't like the CTG. The dips are quite deep, and slow to recover.'

'Do you think she needs a caesarean?'

'No, I do not,' the midwife said sharply.

Julia recoiled at her tone. She'd overheard Liz and the other midwives earlier in the week complaining about her, grumbling about her panicky, inconsistent approach. Sally Stevens had been particularly disappointed. She'd chosen Julia to deliver her own three children because she had such a low intervention rate. Sally had said she would choose almost anyone else now. Julia had been shocked to learn that the latest stats showed her caesarean rate to be approaching forty percent. It had always been half that.

Liz went on. 'The head is low and the water around the baby still clear. She doesn't need a caesarean, she just needs your review.'

Julia felt her anxiety rise. She was in an impossible situation:

about to do an urgent forceps delivery at St Agatha's while Mrs Benjamin was at Eastside.

'I can't come to Eastside for about an hour,' she said, unable to keep the shrillness from her voice.

'What would you like me to do, Dr Kent?'

'I don't know,' whined Julia. Sorting out a problem like this was beyond her these days. 'I've got to go. Could you try Dr Berger? Or Dr Steiner? Sorry.'

Sylvie was sitting at the desk entering the data into the computer as Julia arrived at Eastside to catch up with Mrs Benjamin. She was not in theatre attire, suggesting that a caesarean had indeed not been necessary. In fact, Sylvie explained cheerfully, by the time she'd arrived to review the CTG, it was back to normal. She'd stayed and read the newspaper while waiting for an hour or so until her patient was fully dilated, and then assisted her to the normal delivery of a beautiful baby girl. The cause of the earlier abnormal trace was not apparent. Julia apologised for interrupting Sylvie's Saturday.

'It couldn't be helped, could it?' said Sylvie. 'Besides, I wasn't doing much.'

Julia caught the inflection; Sylvie was lonely. 'Have you had lunch yet?'

Sylvie hadn't and it was obvious she'd like some company.

'Should we pop somewhere for a quick bite, then? Things look like being quiet for a while.'

Sylvie looked at her watch. She had been planning to look at a couple of townhouses this afternoon. One was open for inspection at two, the other at three. She'd recently realised that she hated her flat; it was noisy and cold and looked directly onto the block next door. 'It's time for me to move. Would you come and look at them with me?'

Julia hesitated. What she really wanted to do was call in at Overton Oval where Patrick would be watching Ryan's soccer match. It had been a strange week for them. Patrick had been preoccupied and uncommunicative, offhand even. She knew he was worried about the new Rogerson project at Randwick, and the unreasonable deadlines attached to it, but had been too fixated on her own concerns to offer him her full support. She now felt badly about it and was keen to catch up with him this weekend. This afternoon was the best opportunity; he was going to a party at Henry's tonight and would be working all day tomorrow.

Torn, she looked at her lonely colleague. She knew a bit more about loneliness now that Emma had gone. 'That would be great, Sylvie. I love looking at other people's houses. There's almost nothing better than an "open for inspection". Except for the auction, of course. They're always a bit of fun,' she joked.

'In that case, you can bid for me next week if I decide to buy one of them.'

After reviewing the properties, which did not live up to expectations, they parted briefly, Julia to make some purchases for the early dinner they'd decided to have in lieu of their missed lunch, and Sylvie to return to her flat to collect something she wished to show her friend.

Julia rang Patrick, who was just home from the soccer. Ryan's team had won, and he had scored two goals. Patrick was fairly crowing. She offered her congratulations.

'Are you coming to Henry's tonight, Julia?'

'I don't think I will, darling. I'm on call and I've got this court case hanging over me. I'm not really in the mood to party.'

'Are you sure?'

'Yes. In fact, Sylvie is going to come over for dinner. She helped me out in a crisis this morning, and she's a bit short of company, so I asked her over. We'll just have a quiet night. Sorry, darling.'

'I understand,' he said softly.

Sylvie walked into Julia's house carrying a large box which she placed on the dining table. Julia raised her eyebrows. Was she clearing out her flat already?

'Leo and I have been doing some research for your case.' Sylvie was both diffident and proud.

'Oh?'

Julia approached as her colleague unpacked a large pile of photocopied documents. There were journal articles, College of Obstetricians policy statements, international reports, and chapters from books. Hundreds and hundreds of pages of them.

'This is only a start, of course,' said Sylvie bashfully. She knew Julia had a meeting with the DDO shortly and thought it would be good to show her what they'd found so far. 'It might help your lawyers prepare your defence.'

Julia was speechless with gratitude. Despite her recent hope that she might be able to confront the preparation for her trial, it remained beyond her. The task was simply too massive and too daunting. And now Sylvie and Leo had done it for her. It must have taken every spare moment they had, which couldn't have been many. Julia's eyes stung; she hoped she wasn't about to make a fool of herself.

'Thank you so much, Sylvie. I just haven't been able to face it. It makes me terrified, just the thought of it.' Her face was grey with the misery of it all.

Sylvie understood. She also comprehended that the only way to overcome Julia's incapacitating mental block was to meet it head on. 'I'm going to cook, Julia. And you're going to go through the box. I suggest you start with the journal articles in the green folder, the ones about monitoring in labour.'

Julia couldn't sleep, her mind brimming with her court case. Sylvie had stayed for six liberating hours, guiding her through studies about small babies, arguments about electronic monitoring, debates about the role of birth asphyxia in cerebral palsy. Thinking of the great mass of material, Julia shivered. If she'd had any idea of the sheer volume, she'd have been even more intimidated than she already was. But Sylvie had distilled the essence of it and made it easy. Maybe there was a chance for her after all.

Some time later, the phone rang. One of Leo's patients, booked for an elective caesarean the following week because of two previous caesareans, had presented to St Agatha's in early labour.

'Does she want an epidural or a general anaesthetic, Jenny?'

'An epidural, Dr Kent. We're trying to reach the anaesthetist on the other line.'

When Julia arrived ten minutes later, she found the nursing staff trying to find a replacement anaesthetist for Dr McMahon, who was unwell. By now the patient was quite distressed with the pain and the operation was becoming urgent. Unlike the public hospital, the private one did not have an anaesthetic registrar on site after hours. When the midwives couldn't find anyone else, Julia dialled Angie's number. It took a long time for the phone to be answered, and when it was, it was Geoff on the line.

'Geoff, it's Julia. I'm sorry to call you at this time, but I need Angie's help with an operation.'

'Angie's not here. She's in Brisbane for the weekend at a conference. She won't be back till tomorrow night.'

'Sorry, Geoff. I didn't know she was away. I'll call someone else.'

The caesarean over, Julia drove home wondering about Angie. The anaesthetist who'd done the operation knew nothing about a conference in Brisbane, while Julia had spoken to Angie every day this week and she'd not mentioned going away for the weekend.

She cast her mind back over recent months and Tony's increasingly frequent visits to Sydney. She'd taken it for granted that he'd mostly been coming to see his daughter, but that no longer provided the whole answer. That he'd often met up with Angie while he was down she already knew; it was nice for both of them. But now it hit her. Angie wasn't just someone Tony slotted into his visits; he'd been coming *expressly* to see her.

Julia was staggered at the thought of it, then staggered she hadn't thought of it before. Why shouldn't Tony and Angie get together? They were wonderful, attractive people who'd always

307

liked each other. Tony was available, and Angie potentially so, and they were both looking for some happiness. She was delighted for them, of course. Although what she felt was more complicated than that.

Over the last few months Tony's phone calls had become a regular part of Julia's evenings. Although he mainly called for his daughter, he made a point of speaking to her as well. Sometimes he even rang when he must have known Emma would be out. He always asked about her life and her work and especially her litigation. And he remembered what she told him. Their nightly chats had been of great benefit to her, more even than she'd realised. Until, with Emma's departure last weekend, they'd largely stopped.

She felt a pang of something resembling jealousy.

She slept fitfully until eleven. Still unnerved by her suspicions about Tony and Angie, and not wanting to rattle around her empty house alone, she decided to surprise Patrick by picking up some things at the deli and calling in on him for lunch. Ryan was away at a birthday party while Patrick would be working hard on the Rogerson plans all day. He would be too busy to think about lunch. It was time she pampered him as a good wife would.

After only one week on her own, the appeal of moving in with him had grown enormously. He was right. If they lived in the same place they would see much more of each other and their lives would run more easily. Especially now that he was so busy as well. She'd explained last Monday, when she told him about her court case, that she would move in as soon as her trial was over.

She rang the doorbell and heard his footsteps.

'Surprise,' she laughed as he opened the door, her arms laden with her delicacies and wine and flowers. 'I thought you might like some lunch.'

He looked taken aback. 'Julia, hi. I wasn't expecting you.'

'That's why it's a surprise, silly.' She stood for a minute. 'Can I come in?'

Patrick hesitated. Just then Natalie Anderson, dressed in one of his nightshirts, emerged from the bathroom, unaware the front door was open.

'Julia, I think that we need to have a talk.'

She did not recall driving home, but found herself there anyway. She did not recall phoning Sylvie but found that she had. Her colleague would cover her for the rest of the Sunday.

'Is there a problem, Julia?'

'There is, I'm afraid.'

Sylvie waited, unsure. Finally Julia replied, 'I'm having a bit of trouble with my heart.'

'Oh.'

What was it he had said? That she didn't need him. She sobbed into her pillow at the falsity of it. Not need him? She had never needed anyone more.

'How do you need me, Julia?' he asked gently, walking her to her car. 'You are the most independent person I've ever met. You have your work, your colleagues, your daughter, your house. Your life is so full you barely have time to fit me in. How do you need me?'

She articulated it as best she could. She needed him for all those other things to be worthwhile. It didn't matter what she said, of course. The protests of the abandoned party never did. Her whole body ached at the betrayal.

'Even before you told me it was over, you slept with her?' she croaked.

'I didn't mean it to happen like this, Julia.' He was genuinely distressed. 'I've known Natalie for over a year now, and there's been nothing special between us until the past few weeks. Working on the project together has changed things. And reminded me how a relationship is supposed to be,' he added.

'How is that, Patrick?' Julia asked quietly.

He didn't want to make comparisons, but Natalie made him feel that he was the most important thing in her life. He realised that her circumstances made it easier; maybe that was why she appealed to him. She had the time to make a relationship with him a priority. She wanted to be with him all the time; she phoned him just to say hello; she made him feel that she needed him.

'And she's young and beautiful.'

'Julia, if it was just that, I would have started a relationship with her a year ago. That's not what this is about. It's that she's shown me how complete a new relationship can be.' He looked at her directly. 'And she doesn't keep things from me.'

At Emma's farewell party the weekend before, he'd learned that Tony had stayed over Christmas at the very time Patrick had asked Julia to visit his parents and she'd been unavailable. And then, on Monday, he'd found out that she had been grappling with the trauma of major litigation for five months and hadn't told him. She'd even had the court dates for two weeks, but had said nothing. And yet half a dozen other people knew.

Julia started to explain but realised that it was pointless and stopped. 'So it's over for us then, Patrick?'

'I think that it is,' he replied sadly, his words leaving a suggestion of hope where in fact there was none.

She sobbed until she thought no more tears could possibly come. Then she cried again as she recognised the truth in what Patrick had said. Her life *hadn't* easily accommodated a new lover; she could see that. There had been nothing but Emma and work for so long, it took a while to make the adjustments. But she *was* making them, slowly reducing her workload and reordering her priorities so that she could be with Patrick more. It was what she desperately wanted. At the same time, her responsibilities to her patients and colleagues didn't end because she loved him; she couldn't just walk away from them. Her work was an important part of her life, and always would be. But it would no longer be a substitute for a life. For months now she'd recognised the imbalance. And been fixing it.

As for Tony's visit at Christmas and the Tracey Edwards lawsuit, had her silence been an act of deliberate concealment? A gross breach of Patrick's trust, as he claimed? She supposed in retrospect it had. But it was not how events had unfolded at the time, or what she'd ever intended.

Chapter 35

Julia approached the offices of the DDO for her first formal meeting with her lawyers since the dates of the case had been allocated. There had been a number of phone discussions with Jennifer and Richard in the interim, but today the whole team would be assembled, and they would be planning their strategy in detail. The trial was only six weeks away, but now, even while she was dreading it, she wanted it to come; and to be finished. Whatever the outcome, she could not live with it hanging over her any longer.

It had been a miserable few weeks and she was still in a state of shock about Patrick. Every time she thought about him, her heart seemed to break again. Confusion abounded. How could he have seemed to love her so much and yet discard her so easily?

She had driven past his house on several occasions, daring herself to knock on his door and ask for an explanation. And to offer one. She had picked up the phone a thousand times in the same way. But this was not her first broken heart, and she was old enough to know that the incoherent pleadings of the discarded only further alienated the beloved.

The timing was appalling, of course.

While Patrick dumping her was clearly the worst of it, Emma being away made it doubly unbearable. There was no one at home to commiserate with, no one to keep her company during the lonely evenings. All by herself she faced the inexorable march towards a trial which would make no allowances for her crippled state. She ached from the inside out.

She didn't know what she would have done without her friends. Leo and Sylvie had been extraordinary towers of strength, both at the surgery and in their efforts for her trial. She couldn't understand how they found the time; they were always slipping her new articles they'd unearthed which supported her case, or tossing back and forth fresh arguments for her defence. Their spontaneous and unwavering support had dragged her through the past few weeks.

And then there was Angie, thoughtful as always, helping her in so many little ways like shopping and cooking and just keeping her going. At the same time, there was now an unspoken strain in their friendship. To the point that she'd felt uncomfortable telling Angie what had happened with Patrick.

As she walked briskly to her meeting, Julia changed her brief-case to the other hand. Reaching the lobby of the DDO building, she put it down altogether. It was heavy, packed with the best of the research they'd collected. Sylvie had done the bulk of it, nearly driving the medical librarians mad with her demands for articles, while Leo had made time late at night to edit and cull what Sylvie compiled, methodically isolating the research which was most helpful to her defence.

Embarrassed, Julia had urged Leo to leave it alone for now. Visiting Sandra every few days, she could not believe the rate of her friend's deterioration, her once inquisitive, alert face now swollen from the steroids she was taking to reduce the pressure of secondaries in her brain, while the rest of her body was shrunken. She was weaker each day, and could only whisper, but smiled in thanks for the flowers Julia brought.

When Leo had seen her out yesterday, his anguished face creased with the toll of his wife's suffering, Julia had again thanked him for his help. It had made such a difference to her. But perhaps he should stop for a while now. It didn't seem right that he spend his spare time on her case, not when Sandra needed him so badly. Leo disagreed; he enjoyed the escape it provided. And he felt it was important she win. Important for all of them. 'At least I can help *you*,' he concluded sadly. His wife was disappearing before his eyes, and there was nothing he could do.

'You're helping Sandra just by being with her, Leo. She told me.'

Julia waited in the DDO reception area, slung low on the couch with her face concealed as usual. Even so, thanks to Leo and Sylvie she felt much less insecure than the last time she'd been here. She was eager to show the dossier to Jennifer and Richard, knowing how helpful it would be in their preparation of her defence.

The claims manager, as usual, came out to collect her personally. As she approached, Julia realised belatedly that Jennifer was pregnant. Quite pregnant. She laughed to herself, remembering the post-Christmas podginess she'd noticed at the January visit and realising that her subsequent dealings with Jennifer had been on the phone. She stood up, greeting the claims manager warmly.

'How many weeks are you?'

'Can't you tell? You're the expert.'

'Thirty?' It was always much harder to tell standing up.

'Twenty-eight.'

Julia did a quick calculation. Her case would be finished in ten weeks. 'So you'll be around for my trial?' she asked hopefully.

'Actually, no.' The DDO doctor explained the trouble she was having with her blood pressure. Her mother had nearly died in her first pregnancy with a similar problem and had lost the baby. Jennifer's obstetrician had advised her to stop work next week. She looked at Julia regretfully. 'I'm really disappointed that I won't be here to help.'

'I'm sorry too, but you should do exactly what your obstetrician recommends,' said Julia, her confidence ebbing slightly.

'I've handed over your case to another of our claims managers.' Jennifer hesitated. 'Dr Mason-Fraser.'

'Clarissa Mason-Fraser?'

'Yes. Do you know her?'

'I do,' replied Julia, her confidence disappearing altogether.

As a junior resident, Dr Clarissa Mason-Fraser had done a three-month rotation through the department of obstetrics and gynaecology at Royal Eastside about seven years before. She had quickly become known as a doctor who was unreliable and dangerous. While Julia had not worked with her directly, she'd heard all about her from both the nurses and the registrars. Women had complained far more than men; Clarissa Mason-Fraser was gorgeous, aware of it, and not backward in using it to her advantage.

She had never been known to do her own overtime, and barely even managed to do her daytime work. A string of male residents and registrars covered for her. It was not clear what they got in return, for her favours at that time were apparently reserved for a Royal Eastside cardiologist whose help she was enlisting to secure a place on the highly competitive Physicians Training Scheme. Apparently she fancied the idea of becoming a cardiologist herself, although no one knew why, since her ambitions seemed confined to partying often, travelling widely, and marrying well.

She had obtained the training position, not to anyone's surprise but to the anger of many, including the ambitious young doctor whose place she had taken. In her fourth year of training, again not to anyone's surprise, she had failed the exams and, having decided that to pass required more than contacts and favours, had belatedly dropped out. She'd turned her hand to general practice for a while, but found it also demanded more work than she was capable of. Last year she had secured a job as a claims manager at the Doctors' Defence Organisation, apparently without an interview.

While Julia considered how she could tactfully ask why the DDO would employ someone as demonstrably hopeless as Clarissa Mason-Fraser, Jennifer leaned over and whispered in her ear: 'Her father is a director here.'

314

Clarissa's father was the famous Angus Mason-Fraser, a very successful and wealthy ophthalmologist who was currently the federal president of the College of Surgeons. He was also on the hospital board of Royal Eastside and several private hospitals. He was a powerful man.

With a sinking heart, Julia entered the conference room behind Jennifer. Richard Tripp and Gordon St Jude were deep in conversation about a matter obviously unrelated to Julia's case. They stood as she entered, but Gordon did not interrupt what he was saying. Dr Mason-Fraser was not present. Julia's spirits rose. But nor was Roger Corrigan. Her spirits sank again. She knew an explanation would be forthcoming.

Richard invited her to sit down, indicating a chair across the table from where he and Gordon sat side by side. 'I gather Jennifer has told you she is leaving us. Although no one could begin to replace her, you are not to worry. Your file has been handed to Dr Clarissa Mason-Fraser, who will be with us presently.' He beamed.

Jennifer was short. 'Clarissa knew the meeting was at nine-thirty, Richard. Do you know where she is?'

'She rang a few minutes ago to say that she was delayed with another matter,' Richard said defensively. 'She will be here as soon as she can.'

The fledgling hope Julia nursed that Clarissa might have changed evaporated with that exchange. Still never where she should be, her female colleagues continued to peg her early as workshy and unreliable, while the men remained bewitched by her.

Since no one was offering an explanation for Roger Corrigan's absence, Julia asked. Richard was apologetic. 'I'm afraid we've lost Roger also. When the matter was brought forward, he found he was already committed to another case. We are looking for a new junior barrister.'

'Oh.' The chair threatened to give way beneath her.

As Richard assembled the papers into the order he intended to follow this morning, Jennifer left the room to collect a missing document. Gordon, briefly busy with his phone, finally turned his attention to Julia.

'Good morning,' he said in his smug, self-satisfied way.

Julia immediately stood up, the shocking news of first Jennifer's and then Roger's loss overcoming her. 'Excuse me a moment.'

Saying nothing more, she picked up her handbag and briefcase and walked with composure from the room, down the corridor, and towards the main foyer. With equal composure she opened the door to the ladies' bathroom, entered a cubicle, closed the door, fell against the wall, and cried.

How could they do this to her? For six months she had been living with the dread of this trial and one of the only things keeping her going on her darkest days was the belief that the DDO knew what they were doing. The knowledge that her defence was in the hands of competent and experienced doctors and lawyers had sustained her.

But now, instead of Jennifer and the hard-working Roger, she was left with the ludicrous Clarissa and the slothful, careless Gordon St Jude. She leaned her forehead against the cool of the marble, and cried and cried.

She lugged her briefcase through the city crowds down Pitt Street to Circular Quay and from there around to the Opera House. She sat at a small cafe, staring at a coffee she didn't want and trying desperately not to bawl again. She was grateful for her sunglasses, though the day was overcast and the cafe dimly lit, and had no intention of taking them off.

Whatever was she going to do?

She had slipped out of the DDO offices without returning to the conference room. She wasn't going to let that pompous patronising bastard see her until her composure returned and, since it would not be coming back today, she had left, turning her phone off as she did.

She looked at the briefcase beside her, the one that should now have been empty, and started to weep again. The hard work of her friends would be dissipated in the hands of her defence team. Neither Clarissa nor Gordon would ever take the time to read more than a few pages, while Richard was too weak to withstand the combined incompetence of the other two.

Julia reached for her phone and instinctively pressed Patrick's number. Then she remembered and began to cry again. Her pain was enormous. Now, more than at any time in the past few weeks, she needed to talk to him, needed his comfort and love. She should forget her foolish pride and ring him. Beg him to reconsider, to take her back. Apologise for how busy and pre-occupied she had been. Make him see the changes already happening in her working life because of him. Explain why she'd kept things from him, why she'd tried to protect their precious new love not only from the publicity of her upcoming trial, but also from the demons in her past.

She put the phone back in her bag. Until now she'd thought of this year as the second worst in her life. It had moved up a notch.

Unable to face Sylvie and Leo at the office after the disastrous DDO meeting, and not wanting to return to her empty house, she went to a movie, to escape for a few hours before facing her tribulations again. Later, she could not remember what it was called, but it made her laugh once or twice. When it finished she almost hoped the hospital would page her for an emergency, but no one did. She wandered around the shops for a while before finally catching a taxi home, dragging her heavy briefcase with her.

Ignoring the flashing answering machine, she took off her clothes, ran herself a bubble bath and lay in the hot soothing water for over an hour. She flicked through a magazine while she soaked, momentarily distracting herself with the dramas in other people's lives.

She was just deciding what to do about dinner when Sylvie arrived. Unable to reach her friend on the phone, and eager to hear how the research had been received, Sylvie called in on her way home. She was dismayed to learn what had happened.

Julia made no attempt to hide her distress. 'More than any-one, Sylvie, you realise how critical good preparation is in a matter like this. I could lose my case because of incompetent lawyers and that stupid Clarissa.'

'I'm sure things are not as bad as you think,' her colleague soothed. While this St Jude fellow was arrogant and lazy, he wouldn't have got where he was by being a lousy lawyer. And, remember, she'd always had a lot of respect for Richard. It was just the shock of losing both Jennifer and Roger on the same day that had rocked her.

While Sylvie's words were calm, her face was dark and determined. 'Don't worry, Julia. Things will fall into place. You'll see.'

Chapter 36

Winter came early and one of the most miserable May evenings on record hurried Sydneysiders indoors. Julia closed all the curtains and turned up the heat, but still the rain and wind and plummeting temperature resonated with the chill in her heart. Tomorrow was the first day of her trial.

The weeks and months of dread were over, the hours of research and preparation finished, any hope of a late settlement long gone. The time had come to face Tracey and Brendan Edwards, to meet their allegations with her defence, and let the judge decide.

It was nine weeks since Emma had left and, although Julia was relieved her daughter was away, she missed her badly. Emma was having a ball and was still in Italy, in love with the people, the food and the architecture. She rang at least once a week and wrote surprisingly often, jaunty little postcards with her trademark squiggles.

And it was eight weeks since Patrick had said he didn't love her any more. Eight miserable, lonely, aching weeks during which she had played and replayed their relationship over in her mind, daily seeing more clearly the mistakes she had made. She should have put him first, right from the beginning, cut her hours as soon as he'd declared his love, not assumed she could just squeeze him into her already cluttered life. Granted, with Sylvie away for six weeks and then Sandra so sick, it would have been difficult, but she could have tried harder. No wonder he thought he didn't matter to her.

And she should have trusted him more, should have known that he would not think less of her because she was being sued. Or abandon her because her ex-husband was once charged with complicity in the death of a patient. It seemed so clear now.

Angie saw it differently, of course, loyally pointing out that Patrick had known she had a daughter and her own home and a busy career when they first got together. Why did he require immediate changes in her life? It had been less than six months, after all. And if he'd taken the time to leave aside his own concerns and inquire about hers once in a while, he would have learned about her problems. Like her other friends had.

Though grateful, Julia did not concede any points to Angie, recognising now that her friend hadn't liked Patrick much. But Angie hadn't known him, hadn't bathed in the heat of his love. Angie hadn't seen his face light up at her presence, hadn't heard his low laugh as they talked, hadn't felt like precious china at his touch, hadn't heard his soft murmurings as he loved her.

Julia wiped her eyes automatically, barely aware of her tears, the unpredictable torrents that flowed each time a remembrance of Patrick intruded. She'd have expected them to lessen by now, but they hadn't. Still, there was one consolation. Amid the heartache and remorse, Patrick's action had spurred her to finally confront her trial head-on, to throw her heart and soul into defeating the allegations against her and defending her reputation. She could not afford to lose anything more.

Her broken heart was not the only spur to action. The terrifying thought of leaving her defence in the hands of Clarissa Mason-Fraser and Gordon St Jude was also a powerful incentive. From the day of the disastrous DDO meeting, Julia had immersed herself in the arguments for her case. Where only weeks before she'd been unable to open a journal, now she was driven to pursue the evidence that would exonerate her. Harnessing every spare minute, she'd built on the groundwork of Leo and Sylvie. Not that they were through helping her; daily they had more information, more suggestions.

Dear Leo, she didn't know how he managed. Sandra was in the terminal phase of cancer; it had been so fast. The headaches and nausea were continuous now and, although she struggled to be cheerful, she could no longer conceal her suffering. She was frail and pale and often barely conscious. Leo had taken the last month off to be with her, but would be returning to work tomorrow so that Julia could go to court.

The alarm clock buzzed and Julia immediately reached out and turned it off. It was still dark. She took in the cold glow of the street light and shivered. This was it, her day of reckoning.

As she stumbled to the shower, the phone rang. It was Angie.

'Hi, Julia. I won't ask how you slept, since I can guess. I'm just calling to say I'll be around at seven-fifteen for breakfast. I'll bring the croissants, you put on the coffee.'

'What?'

'I'm coming with you today. Thought I'd tag along for a bit of free entertainment.'

'Oh,' said Julia inadequately, tears welling.

'I think you should wear one of your smartest suits,' Angie continued. 'It will give you a psychological advantage. The peach, or maybe the lemon.'

No matter how awful she felt, Julia had to smile at this sort of advice coming from Angie. 'Perhaps you should tell me what you're wearing so we don't clash.'

The weather only worsened and, as they alighted from the taxi outside the court just after nine, they were met not only by rain, but a blustery wind that hurled itself through the streets of the legal district. Julia directed Angie up the steps which led into the New South Wales Supreme Court, the highest court in the state apart from the Court of Appeal.

'This is it?' Angie was incredulous.

There was nothing court-like about the building, no sandstone or timber, no grandeur or majesty. Aside from the court crest, it could have been any one of the characterless modern, glass, steel and concrete buildings of which Sydney was unfortunately full. The lower levels of the building were devoted to administrative matters, while the higher ones housed the courts. Functional and modern, most of the courtrooms were little bigger than classrooms.

'I'm afraid it is,' said Julia in reply. Acting on the advice of Richard Tripp, she had made a preliminary excursion here a month ago. Coming alone, she had felt nauseous and nervous as she toured the building, but this morning was grateful she'd done it. Getting lost was the one outcome she needn't fear.

They advanced to the large boards in the massive vaulted foyer where rows of pages outlining the day's proceedings and court allocations were pinned. Such ordinary-looking pieces of paper for such significant matters. The court lists for Monday came out on Friday afternoon and, with them, the name of the judge allocated to the case.

Julia was well aware how important the selection of the judge was. He or she was the only person who had to be convinced whether she had been negligent or otherwise. And not beyond reasonable doubt. Simply convinced on the balance of probabilities, the standard required in civil claims. Which was why medical negligence claims favoured the plaintiff. While often unfair to the doctor, it made sense that a judge's natural sympathy would lie with an injured patient, especially one as pitiful as Brendan Edwards. Richard had explained many times that all Brendan's lawyers had to do was give the judge a little bit of help to justify his existing inclination to find in the child's favour.

With a single judge, there was a significant element of chance in the outcome. Whenever more than one judge sat on a case, it was never an even number. A panel of judges could rarely agree. In the High Court in Canberra, there were seven judges. For them to decide seven-nil about a matter was uncommon. Six-one or five-two were more usual. Sometimes they split four-three. It followed that, with only one judge, the element of luck was considerable.

Richard Tripp had rung Julia on the weekend with the news that her case would be heard in Court 9G by Judge Percival Owen. Richard seemed quite happy with the allocation. Judge Owen was in his mid-sixties and had been appointed to the Supreme Court ten years before, after many years as a successful senior barrister. During his career as a courtroom lawyer, he had appeared perhaps more for plaintiffs than defendants, but was widely considered to be impartial. He was apparently a lot better for their case than many other judges they could have drawn.

'I see you got here all right.'

Julia turned from the pressing crush of fellow litigants to look into Richard's boyish face. 'Yes I did, but I guess even with this weather, getting here is the easy part.' She introduced Angie. 'We usually do a surgical list together on Mondays, so Angie thought she'd spend the day with me here instead of St Agatha's. Same team, different operation.' She laughed nervously.

Richard shook Angie's hand. 'Pleased to have you here with us,' he said in his slightly formal manner. 'It always makes a defendant feel better to have supporters in the court. And it looks better to the judge. Thank you for coming.'

Gordon St Jude was waiting for them in one of the small lawyers' rooms adjacent to each of the seven courtrooms on the ninth floor. The door was open and he was lounging on a chair barely big enough to contain his bulk, speaking into his mobile phone. Typically, he was talking loudly enough to be heard even as they emerged from the lift. As his unmistakable, hearty laugh reached them, interrupting all other conversations on the floor, Julia felt her distaste for him escalate. How dare he be so jauntily cheerful when she was so miserable. How dare he be so brazenly insensitive when the whole floor was full of people who were worn out and worried from suing or being sued.

Gordon terminated his phone call as she and Richard entered the small room, leaving Angie to read the newspaper outside. He stood up to greet them.

323

'Good morning, Julia, Richard,' he said, shaking their hands, his large face beaming with the gleeful enthusiasm one usually associated with a football match. Litigation was obviously his favourite sport. 'I hope you're both ready for the big day ahead,' he added jovially.

Julia immediately felt unready. And foolish. For weeks she'd lectured herself not to feel threatened by the process she was about to endure; that the right attitude would see her through. What idiocy. No one could fail to be threatened by a month on trial in the Supreme Court. In desperation, she tried to mimic her barrister's attitude. 'Ready as we'll ever be, I suppose.' But the words came out rather too offhand, failing to convey the mature confidence she'd intended.

As Gordon packed up his papers to move into the courtroom, Julia looked at her watch and realised that it was nearly ten o'clock. Suddenly needing the bathroom, she excused herself.

Angie joined her as they made, not for the ninth floor bathroom, but for the lifts, electing to use the facilities on a different floor for the duration of the case. Julia hoped that this would lessen the chance of an informal and awkward encounter with Tracey Edwards and her lawyers. Luckily, the bathroom on the twelfth floor was empty.

'I'm not going back down there, Angie,' said Julia, losing the battle to restrain her tears as she slumped next to the hand-drier. 'I can't face it, I just can't. I can't sit day after day for four weeks listening to a parade of people say how incompetent I am. And if there's even one journalist writing it down, I'll die.'

Angie patiently went over it again. Everyone who worked with Julia knew she was far from incompetent. Patients waited for months to get an appointment. Doctors hassled her secretaries to have their patients, or even their wives, jump the queue. The nurses discharged her patients early because they did so well. Julia knew all of this. Just as she knew, deep down, that this same case could have happened to any of her colleagues. It was just bad luck it had happened to her. Angie looked at her friend compassionately. 'It will all be over in a few weeks, Julia, and forgotten soon after. We just have to get to the other side of it.'

As she spoke, Angie furtively glanced at her watch. It was now after ten, but she did not wish to rush her already distressed friend. At that moment, the door swung open and they held their breath.

It was Ming Tan. Ming was the new junior barrister, the one who had replaced Roger Corrigan. Now twenty-eight, she had spent several years doing a Masters of Law and some academic work before admitting to herself that she really wanted to stand up in court and argue. Since starting at the bar six months ago, she had done a few small matters but this was her first major trial. Despite her youth and lack of experience, Roger Corrigan had recommended her without hesitation when Jennifer Pereira rang him to suggest a replacement in the *Edwards v Kent* matter. The DDO's senior claims officer was insistent that he provide the name of the hardest-working, best-organised junior barrister in town, those being the words the relentless Sylvie Berger had used during her unscheduled, long and demanding meeting with the claims officer. And in half a dozen steely phone calls since. The words perfectly described Ming Tan.

As she came into the bathroom, the junior counsel looked stern. It was no time to indulge the defendant. 'You girls sure know how to give someone the slip. Don't you know what time it is? I've been to every bathroom in the entire building. Do you want the hearing moved up here to the twelfth floor toilet, Julia? I could speak to the judge, if you like.'

They were ten minutes late, but Judge Percival Owen had not yet taken his place on the bench when Julia, Angie and Ming entered Court 9G. It was one of the smaller courts, painted cream, panelled in modest pine, and carpeted in a serviceable light brown wool-nylon blend, which was no doubt easy to vacuum. It didn't need to be any bigger or grander, but Julia felt keenly that its ordinariness was at odds with a ten million dollar lawsuit and the months of preparation and pain that went with it.

Two long lawyers' tables, one behind the other, faced the judge's bench and witness box. The table nearer the judge, the bar table, was for the barristers of both teams, while the second was for the solicitors. Julia and Tracey would also be sitting at the second table for the duration of the proceedings. Behind the tables was a slim railing which separated the thirty seats for onlookers, fifteen on each side in three rows of five.

Julia apprehensively took her seat at the solicitors' table while Angie settled in the public seating immediately behind her and Ming went to join Gordon and Richard, who were still standing, deep in conversation, next to the bar table. Richard nodded as Julia arrived, but Gordon seemed not to have seen her. As the lawyers conferred, making last minute tactical decisions, Julia furtively scanned the courtroom. It appeared that everyone except the judge was present. Certainly Tracey Edwards, her supporters, and her legal team looked like they had been here for days. She noted with relief that Brendan was not yet in the courtroom.

At this stage she could see no one who was obviously from the press; the thought alone sent a tremor through her lower bowel.

At the other end of the bar table, senior counsel Ernestine Hillier had turned her chair to face the solicitors' table and was speaking intently to Tracey Edwards. After her opening statement to the judge, she would be calling Tracey as her first witness and was outlining, for the final time, the questions she would be asked.

Julia stole a glance at them; she knew a fair bit about Tracey's senior lawyer now.

Ernestine was fifty-eight. She had come late to the bar, having given up the law not long out of university in order to raise her six children. Her husband, also a barrister, was killed in a car accident shortly after they both turned forty. A clever man and an able practitioner of the law, he was, however, neglectful about matters such as annual life insurance premiums. With her children to support and the encouragement of her many friends, Ernestine returned to work, and flourished. She quickly built up a practice in what she unashamedly called 'female law', in particular medical negligence and high-profile divorce cases. She had been promoted to senior counsel a few years ago.

She looked like a grandmother, which indeed she was, grey,

plump, and bespectacled. She wore no make-up, made no attempt to dress smartly, and smiled warmly at all parties. Ming had told Julia she did this in the belief that her benign appearance lent itself to complacence, and ultimately carelessness, in her opponents. Her clients were said to love and trust her, but other lawyers tended to be dismissive. Even on her own side, the junior counsel and solicitors were inclined to underestimate her. Ming said the smart ones only did it once.

Julia turned her gaze to the junior counsel for the plaintiff. Michael Lethbridge was off to one side, talking quietly on a mobile phone. From the look on his face, it was pleasure not business. An up-and-coming lawyer in his mid-thirties, he was apparently renowned for his ability to argue his client's case with a single-mindedness that was awe-inspiring. Like Gordon St Jude, he was a performer rather than a researcher, although he would probably get little chance to show his talents in this case. Ming had thought this might irk him a bit.

Just along the table from Julia and appearing rather more anxious than either of her barristers was Tracey's solicitor, the efficient Louise Craig. Immaculately dressed as always, she was working her way down the witness and document lists checking that everything was in order. Watching her, Julia had no doubt that it would be.

Julia saw Ernestine finish with Tracey and then survey the seat where Roger Corrigan should have been sitting. She was aware that Ernestine had worked both against and with Roger and knew how formidable a barrister he was. The tiny wisp of triumph that crossed her face suggested relief at his absence. Julia saw her countenance then become puzzled at the appearance of Ming; it was clear she didn't know the new lawyer. Her puzzlement slowly yielded to satisfaction as she watched Ming and Gordon together. Standing beside her senior counsel, Ming looked like a child, weighing little more than forty kilograms to his one hundred and twenty, and barely coming up to his shoulder. He could look right past her, which Julia had no doubt he intended to do. She saw Ernestine register this as well, her suppressed smile suggesting that she thought things were looking good.

At that moment the judge's associate, Mabel Appleton, entered the small courtroom. Both legal teams stopped what they were doing and assumed their allocated places. Then the door at the side of the judge's bench opened, and through it appeared Justice Percival Owen. He made his way to the middle of the bench, nodded to the assembled courtroom, and sat down. As the barristers and solicitors introduced themselves to His Honour, Julia took a close look at the man who would decide the fate of the case.

He was completely different from what she had expected. A short man, portly, florid and bald, he walked with a noticeable limp as a result of an arthritic knee, but otherwise had no particular distinguishing features. Until he opened his mouth. Then, his deep and resonant tones commanded immediate attention. He invited Mrs Hillier to outline her case.

The senior counsel proceeded for the next sixty minutes to list the plaintiffs' allegations of Dr Kent's negligence and how her culpability would be proved. Angie, knowing how her friend must feel, moved closer to the railing which separated them. Julia meanwhile stared steadfastly ahead, unable to look at Ernestine Hillier while she spoke, and wishing she could block her ears. It was all she could do not to slide to the floor in a faint. To think that everyone in this room was here because of her.

She distracted herself by counting them up. There was the judge, his associate, the stenographer, the clerk of the court, six lawyers, herself and Tracey Edwards. Twelve constants. Maybe thirteen if Clarissa Mason-Fraser was counted. The claims manager had previously said she'd be here, but Richard explained that she was hectically busy with two lesser matters in the District Court and a dozen cases in the process of settling back at the office, and probably wouldn't make it today. Thank God, thought Julia.

She then looked at the cast of extras. Out of the corner of her eye she could see that supporters for Tracey at this stage numbered eight and included her mother Norma, sister Donna, and a number of friends. For herself there was only one. She glanced around gratefully at Angie, grimly noting that her supporters would drop to zero tomorrow. Aside from her practice colleagues and Tony, she had told no one else about her case. Except Patrick, of course, she thought sadly.

Deep down she'd nursed the ridiculous hope that he might turn up out of the blue to wish her luck. Or at least send a card. But he hadn't. In fact, she hadn't heard from him at all since he'd ended their relationship. He certainly wouldn't be coming to offer his support. Julia continued her count, looking at the list of proposed witnesses, twelve for them, four for her. In all, there would be thirty-nine people gathered together over four weeks because of her. She'd probably have fewer at her funeral.

She had diverted her attention well, and found that Mrs Hillier had concluded her opening address and was now calling her first and principal witness to the stand. It was eleven-thirty. If court was to sit for five working hours each day, three before lunch and two after, for twenty working days, that would be one hundred court hours in total. Of course there was a public holiday in June, but still, it was an easy denominator. Julia quickly calculated that they were now one point five percent of the way through the case, and so far nothing terrible had happened. The thought cheered her; at least for the few minutes it took Tracey Edwards to enter the witness box.

Chapter 37

Tracey Edwards swore an oath to tell the truth. She was wearing a dark brown polyester suit which did not flatter her, but did make her look sympathetic. Sitting in the witness box, nervous but determined, she was taken through the main part of her evidence known as the examination in chief. While none of what she had to tell was new, Ernestine Hillier brought out the story in an evocative and moving way, leading her client through the months of the pregnancy and asking her to relate how she and Brett had prepared for the baby. Tracey told how they'd played the video of the ultrasound over and over, often pausing at the bit where Brendan seemed to be waving at them so that they could wave back and call out that they loved him. For they knew it was a boy, after the ultrasonographer had inadvertently let it slip. By the middle of the pregnancy they had decided to call him Brendan as a hybrid of Brett, for his dad, and Dan, for Tracey's deceased father.

Tracey described how, as the pregnancy advanced into the final months, she would lie in bed at night watching her stomach change shape as the baby moved. She came to know her son's personality and love him even before he was born.

She described the labour and how she'd spent much of it in the shower, thinking that everything was going well until the end, when the midwife, Monica, told her that the waters around the baby were soiled, and that the baby's heart rate seemed to be dropping very low. She'd then moved back onto the bed where the midwife had undertaken a vaginal examination, pronounced her as nearly fully dilated and applied a small clip to the baby's head to monitor the heart rate via the CTG machine. This confirmed that the baby was now in some distress. Tracey recalled her rising panic as the midwife's face betrayed anxiety. Another senior midwife was called into the room to look at the trace as well, and she also was very worried.

Tracey was told that the baby was in trouble and that Dr Kent was on her way. She was given oxygen and moved onto her left side in an attempt to improve the baby's heart trace. When that didn't help, she was then moved onto her right side. All the while, the sound of her baby's heartbeat seemed very slow. She had heard the baby's heart at every visit to Dr Kent, and never before had it been so slow. It had seemed to Tracey that it might stop completely before Dr Kent arrived.

All this time the contractions built in relentless intensity as the second stage of labour approached. The gas she was given did not relieve the awful pains and she started to cry out with them. They were much worse than when she had been standing in the shower, and she wanted to get off the bed into an upright position to deal with them better. This was not allowed. She had to stay on the bed, wearing the oxygen mask, and await Dr Kent. As each pain receded she looked hopefully at the door, willing her doctor's arrival. It seemed ages before she came.

When she did, the room was suddenly full of people Tracey did not know and who were not introduced. She had since learnt that there were three midwives and a paediatric registrar, together with an anaesthetic registrar who had called in briefly in case he was needed.

Her intimate and precious birth experience, to be shared only with Brett, Dr Kent and the midwife, had turned into a public emergency in which she was a bit-player, no longer in control.

331

Dr Kent looked at the baby's heart monitor for a few seconds. She then examined Tracey and told her that she needed to lift the baby out with forceps. The midwives tied her legs up into the stirrups, after which Dr Kent gave her an injection of anaesthetic in the vaginal area. She had then placed large steel forceps blades inside Tracey and dragged Brendan out. His cord was clamped and he was immediately given over to the paediatrician waiting beside the resuscitation trolley.

'How was Brendan when he was born?' asked Ernestine Hillier.

'At first I didn't know,' replied Tracey forlornly. 'I couldn't even see him. I was flat on my back with both legs tied to the stirrup posts while Dr Kent put in some stitches. Brendan was on a resuscitation trolley to my right. The paediatrician and two nurses were between him and me, leaning over the trolley. I couldn't see him.'

'Did he cry?'

'No.'

'What were the staff doing to him?'

'I couldn't see. They were in my way. That's what made it so awful. I couldn't see him, and yet I knew he needed me. I was still tied to the horrible stirrups.'

'How did you feel at this point?'

'I thought that my baby was going to die before I'd even held him.'

'How long was it before he was taken from the room to the neonatal intensive care unit?'

'At the time I didn't know, but I later found out that it was about fifteen minutes.'

Ernestine then took Tracey through the next few weeks as she sat with her baby in intensive care, weeks in which, with growing understanding, she realised that he was seriously and permanently damaged. Tracey told how the intensive care staff were quite optimistic at first, and how this falsely raised her hopes. The nurses told her that they often cared for babies who'd suffered some distress in labour and how they mostly improved quickly. Nearly all were discharged out of the unit after a few days, and grew up to be perfectly normal.

But Tracey's optimism faded as Brendan failed to recover. She was almost inaudible as she explained how she sat by his crib daily while one specialist after another came to look at her son. Everyone in the courtroom leaned forward, straining to hear her words. Julia wondered if Ernestine had advised her to speak quietly at this point for dramatic effect. If so, she had advised her badly.

Ming had done some research on Judge Owen since Friday. One of the things she'd learned from speaking to her legal friends was that the judge was becoming hard of hearing. She'd told Julia that, although he concealed it well, it was problematic enough that he was considering hearing aids. Given he was in his mid-sixties, such difficulty was not unusual, but in his job, where hearing was everything, it was more than a minor problem. It irked him enormously when witnesses whispered.

'Ms Edwards, it would be of great help to all present in this courtroom if you would speak up,' Judge Owen intoned loudly. 'Now, could you please repeat the last answer that you gave.'

Tracey glanced at Ernestine.

Julia watched them closely, noticing the senior counsel's almost imperceptible nod to her witness and realising that the older woman had silently catalogued the judge's difficulty in hearing for inquiry later. Which was more than Gordon St Jude had done.

Julia looked at her own senior counsel at the table in front of her. He had been scribbling furiously since Tracey's testimony began and had filled several entire pages. Since none of what the first witness had to say was unexpected or contentious, Julia was surprised. Especially since Ming had barely jotted down a word. She wondered what he was writing. From her angle she could make out only a few of the words, mostly names. None was familiar. At first she was puzzled, but then it dawned on her. Gordon St Jude was writing a legal opinion for *another* client on *another* matter, and had been for most of the time that Tracey Edwards was speaking. She made a note to ask Ming if this was usual.

Ernestine was bringing Tracey to the end of her testimony

about the early weeks of Brendan's life. It was just before lunch on the first day. Tracey would be in the witness stand for the rest of the day and most of tomorrow. She would be asked to describe her relationship with her son and interrogated on the reasons she thought he would be better off at home with her. She would also be taken over particular aspects of Dr Kent's management of the labour and delivery.

For now, however, Ernestine was concentrating on the psychological effects that the birth of a brain-damaged baby had had on her. Demonstrating a mother's 'nervous shock' increased the payout significantly.

'When did you realise that Brendan would not be coming home? That he was not going to get better?'

'It was quite a long time.' Tracey was speaking softly again, forcing Ernestine to ask her own questions in a louder voice than usual.

'Weeks? Months?'

Tracey responded more audibly, although the effort was obvious. It had been in the second month. She was in a daze in the beginning, of course. As the days and weeks passed and her son made no progress, she became increasingly distressed. Every day a new doctor would come to see him, but they didn't say much to her. It was obvious that something was terribly wrong but that the doctors couldn't agree what it was.

After about three weeks, the director of the neonatal intensive care unit, Dr Julius Tong, had called Tracey into his office to discuss Brendan. The doctors had formed the opinion that there was little hope of him ever improving, Dr Tong said. He had a serious neurological problem that would be permanent. He would most likely never walk or talk or care for himself, and he would probably need twenty-four hour nursing care for the rest of his life.

Dr Tong explained that Brendan was to be moved from intensive care to the less intensive Special Care nursery and, from there, would eventually be discharged from the hospital. The social worker would discuss the arrangements with her.

'And did you see the social worker?' asked Ernestine.

Tracey nodded sadly. She'd had several long meetings with her. Until this point Tracey had expected that her son would be coming home with her. As a *mother* would, she said, choking slightly on the word. The social worker, however, suggested that Brendan would be better cared for in a home. It was her job to place him in one. She spoke of 'placement' as if that would be the end of the matter. For her, of course, it would be. When Tracey asked if she could have a say in the choice of home for her son, she was told that there really wasn't a choice; where Brendan went depended on where there was a vacancy.

'How did this make you feel?'

'That my son was a name on a list. He was to be "placed", and then crossed off.'

'What happened after that?'

'I collapsed.'

'Would you like to tell the court about it?'

Tracey looked embarrassed. She was meeting with the social worker for the third time. She'd been so numb during the first two meetings she'd taken little in. She still wasn't sure why Brendan had to go to a home, why she couldn't care for him herself. The social worker told her about other families whose children had similar problems. She explained that while looking after her son as a tiny baby would be difficult, as he grew it would be almost impossible. She described how it would be when he was a man, seventy kilograms in weight but unable to walk or talk or wash or feed himself, still in nappies, still in a wheelchair.

'At that moment, I suddenly realised that this was it. This was the life my child would be living. And it would not get better. It would be forever.'

'What happened at that point?'

'It was like I'd had a stroke. I couldn't move. The social worker had to get a wheelchair to move me downstairs and put me in a taxi to take me home. Afterwards I slept for nearly twenty-four hours. But when I woke up, nothing had changed.'

Tracey was clearly exhausted by her testimony. Ernestine waited a few moments for her to recover before returning to

Tracey's conversations with the director of the neonatal intensive care unit.

'Did Dr Tong tell you why this had happened to Brendan?'

'He said they didn't know.'

'Did anyone tell you why it had happened?'

'Only the deputy-director of the unit, Dr Menzies. She said it was because of the foetal distress Brendan had suffered in labour. She said Brendan was damaged because of birth asphyxia.'

Judge Owen looked at the clock, which was approaching one, and announced the lunch adjournment. Tracey Edwards would resume her testimony this afternoon. As everyone stood for the judge's departure, Julia saw Gordon carefully place the legal opinion for his other client in a folder, no doubt to be typed up by his secretary and despatched, with the bill, this afternoon. At the same time she saw him look derisively at Ming's pad, which contained half a page of notes. Mustn't have a very good memory, she could hear him think, his own pad now clean.

Soon, only Julia, Angie and the three defence lawyers remained in the courtroom. They gathered around the bar table, waiting for direction from Gordon. He gestured dismissively to the witness box. 'There's nothing new in the testimony so far. In fact it's been a complete waste of a morning. Everyone knows that women look forward to the birth of a baby, and that any mother whose baby is a vegetable is not going to be too happy about it. Why go over it? The court should just accept as given that the plaintiff has suffered nervous shock, and get on with the nitty-gritty of whose fault it is.'

Ming, who, like Julia, knew where his mind had been, challenged him. 'You aren't going to cross-examine her on this?'

'What's there to cross?'

'Maybe the fact that the pregnancy was not actually planned, her relationship with her partner was not as stable as she maintains, and that she continued to smoke while pregnant. Things that show Brendan was never going to be born into the ideal situation she's trying to paint.'

Gordon looked at her for a moment as if trying to place who

336

she was. 'Half of all pregnancies are unplanned, Ming. We make ourselves look like moral police if we bring that up. If we mention the ex-boyfriend, she can say Julia's negligence cost her not only a normal child, but a loving relationship as well.'

Ming nodded, as if acknowledging his reasoning. She was, however, arranging her counter-arguments while letting the senior counsel continue.

'As for the smoking, old Judge Owen is a bit of a smoker himself.'

'An ex-smoker,' Ming corrected. 'He stopped over twelve months ago and is rather proud of himself. Wonders why others can't quit too.'

Gordon seemed taken aback.

The younger lawyer pushed her advantage. 'And he made a judgement in February against a smoker who claimed his lung disease was due to workplace dusts rather than tobacco.'

'Maybe,' said Gordon, who knew nothing about the judgement. But it was not a concession. If they spent time cross-examining about irrelevant matters, the four weeks would be up and the case wouldn't be finished. They had to keep things moving along. He looked at his watch and walked towards the door of the courtroom. He was going back to his chambers for a while. They would meet back here just before two o'clock.

'Perhaps you and Richard can show Julia and her friend where to have lunch,' he added to Ming as an afterthought. With that he was off.

Despite the weather, which remained cold, wet and windy, the defence team chose to avoid the restaurant in the Supreme Court building. The plaintiff and her lawyers would likely be there. Instead they ventured out to a small and cosy Italian cafe, Gianni's, around the corner from the court. Julia went to place the orders at the counter, leaving Richard and Ming with Angie. Waiting for the coffees she heard laughter behind her and turned to see Angie and Ming in a state of unsuppressed merriment. Given that Richard was trying not to laugh, it seemed that the joke was at the expense of Gordon St Jude.

Julia smiled. Angie might not have met Richard before today, but she knew Ming well now. On several occasions in the past month the three of them, together with Sylvie and Leo, had met to discuss Julia's defence. The meticulous Ming had come to the meetings already well-versed in relevant legal decisions, obviously taking the job of defending Julia very seriously. The four doctors had exhaled collectively, and Sylvie had quietly congratulated herself. Ming, for her part, said she was equally impressed by them.

After they finished their pasta, it was time for business. Richard started, addressing Ming. 'How do you think Tracey is coming across on the stand? Do you think the judge likes her?'

He liked her better forte than pianissimo, of course. Apart from that, Ming thought Tracey was quite impressive. After discussing the morning's testimony in detail, the young barrister turned to Julia. 'How are you finding it so far?'

Julia grimaced, but made an attempt at nonchalance. She felt disturbed listening to Tracey, of course, but so far it was not too bad. 'I think I survived the first three percent.'

Ernestine spent until lunch the next day on her examination in chief of Tracey. She led her through her relationship with Brendan, her concerns about the standard of care at the Malabar Home for Disabled Children and her belief that not only would her son be more comfortable with her, he would make better progress.

Ernestine then changed tack and took her witness through the last weeks of the pregnancy. Tracey had been worried when Dr Kent said that the baby was small and that further tests were needed. She remained worried even when told that the tests were normal. As it turned out, the baby was much smaller than expected. Dr Kent should have known this.

Similarly, Dr Kent had never suggested that Brendan was at increased risk of foetal distress in labour because of his size. At no time was continuous electronic monitoring recommended. Tracey had been led to believe that intermittent listening with the small hand-held Doppler was perfectly adequate.

Finally, it was Gordon St Jude's turn. He stood up slowly, allowing his height and bulk to indicate to all present that he was a force to be reckoned with. He then took longer than necessary to look over the notes in his hand before turning his attention to the witness where she sat, tired but resolute, in the witness box. Julia saw Ernestine curb her impatience at his delay and was unsurprised. She'd heard that the older woman did not have much time for Gordon, that her opinion of him was at little variance with Julia's own.

Gordon's first questions were about Tracey's relationship with Brett Halsted; he'd been persuaded to use the information Ming had uncovered from a former hairdressing colleague of Tracey's. Gordon had not reached his current pre-eminent position by failing to utilise the talents of those around him.

'You've told the court that Brendan's father was very supportive through your pregnancy and labour.'

'Yes he was.'

'And you believe you would still be together if Brendan had not been disabled?'

'Yes we would.'

'What makes you say that?'

'Because it was only after Brendan was born that the troubles in our relationship started.'

'But he'd left you before, hadn't he?'

Tracey was surprised. 'What do you mean?'

'What I mean, Ms Edwards, is that before he left you permanently after the birth of Brendan, Brett Halsted had left you previously, hadn't he?'

'Yes.' Almost inaudible.

'Could you tell the court when this was?'

Tracey looked at her hands in her lap. 'When I was about halfway through the pregnancy.'

'At about the time you said that you and he were replaying the pregnancy video over and over?'

'Before that. He left when I was about twenty weeks pregnant, and came back a month later. He did not leave again until after it was obvious that Brendan would be permanently impaired.'

'I see.' Gordon St Jude waited, hoping that the judge would also see. He continued his attack.

'You have already told us that it took a number of weeks before you realised that Brendan would not improve. During that time, Brett Halsted never visited his son, did he?'

'No.'

'Not even once?'

'No.'

'So the picture you painted for the court of a perfect relationship spoiled only by the birth of a severely disabled child is not entirely true, is it? Your relationship with Brendan's father was shaky before the diagnosis of permanent impairment was made. It was shaky long before Brendan was born, wasn't it?'

'That's not true,' replied Tracey quietly.

'It doesn't seem that way to me, Ms Edwards.'

Gordon St Jude continued: 'May I ask you how tall you are?'

Tracey looked surprised and glanced momentarily at her lawyers before answering.

'I'm one hundred and fifty-five centimetres.'

'And how much do you weigh?'

'Forty-six kilograms.'

'For the older people in the room, that's just five feet one inch and seven stone three pounds. Isn't it, Ms Edwards?'

'Yes. I think so.' She sounded uncertain.

'You said that Brendan was small when he was born. How much did he weigh?'

'Two point four kilograms.'

'And did Dr Kent tell you that she thought he was going to be small?'

'Yes. But not that small. The intensive care staff told me Brendan's birth weight was below the fifth centile. That's very small. Dr Kent should have known that.'

'How small did she say he was going to be?'

Tracey hesitated. 'She didn't, exactly.'

'But she thought he was small enough to warrant a number of tests?'

'Yes.'

'And the results of the tests showed what?'

'That everything seemed to be normal.'

'Did she ask you how much you weighed when you were born?'

'Yes.'

'And what did you tell her?'

'That I was about five and a half pounds.'

'Which is about two point five kilograms, isn't it?'

'I don't know.'

'It is. Did she tell you that the mother's own birth weight was one of the major predictors of the size of a baby?'

'I can't remember.'

'Ms Edwards, let me remind you that you are under oath. I will ask you the question again.' Gordon St Jude drew himself up to his full height and stared at her fiercely. 'When Dr Kent asked you your own birth weight, was she asking because it was related to the weight of your baby?'

Tracey said nothing for a moment, and then a small sound escaped her. 'Yes.'

Gordon glanced at the bench to see if the judge had heard the answer. It appeared he hadn't. 'Was that yes, Ms Edwards?' Gordon clarified.

Tracey dropped her head. 'Yes.'

Gordon then moved on to the question of Tracey's smoking during her pregnancy, again with no hint of embarrassment. She conceded that she'd smoked while carrying her son, but had tried hard to give up, limiting her cigarettes to less than eight per day. She reluctantly admitted that she had continued to smoke even after learning that Brendan was small. She had also smoked during her next pregnancy, and was a smoker even now, although she would desperately love to give up.

'Do you know that smoking is harmful to small children in the home?'

'Yes. That is why I always smoke outside.'

'But there is no "outside" for the baby when you smoke in pregnancy, is there?'

He did not wait for an answer.

'You accuse Dr Kent of harming your son, and yet you knowingly harmed him yourself, didn't you, Ms Edwards?'

'I know that women shouldn't smoke in pregnancy,' Tracey conceded pitifully. 'I tried very hard to stop, especially with Brett encouraging me, but I couldn't give up completely. Just getting my cigarettes down from thirty to less than ten a day required an enormous effort. I was nearly down to five by the time Brendan was born. If things had gone well for me since then I think I would probably be off them altogether. That's what I want.' She looked down at her lap again.

Gordon St Jude concluded by dealing with the monitoring during labour. He handed Tracey a copy of Dr Kent's notes, and of the hospital record made by the midwife. In both it was mentioned that Tracey felt strongly about unnecessary intervention in labour. She wanted everything to be as natural as possible. Dr Kent had recorded this request on three separate occasions during the pregnancy.

'Did you go to the antenatal classes, Ms Edwards?'

'Yes.'

'Did you go to them all?'

'Yes.'

'Then you knew about the options for monitoring a baby in labour, didn't you?'

'A bit.'

'You certainly knew that you couldn't have continuous electronic monitoring in the shower, didn't you?' When Tracey did not reply, he went on: 'It is spelt out quite clearly in the classes, isn't it?'

'Yes.'

'And you had discussed it with your obstetrician?'

'Yes.'

'And so Dr Kent was trying to give you the sort of labour you wanted, with your preferred pain relief being the hot water of the shower, wasn't she?'

Tracey protested. 'I wouldn't have wanted it if I thought it was going to hurt my baby.'

'It has not been established that it did hurt your baby. What

342

has been established is that you requested not once, but many times, to have a very low-intervention labour, and that Dr Kent tried to help you have what you so badly desired. Isn't that so?'

Tracey desolately shook her head.

Judge Owen directed her to answer the question. Eventually she acknowledged that it was largely true.

Ernestine Hillier spent the initial hour of Wednesday morning in re-examination of her first witness. She was at pains to reaffirm the extent of Tracey's anguish and Dr Kent's negligence. Julia thought she seemed reasonably happy as her witness left the stand, but there was no doubt she'd been caught unawares about Brett Halsted leaving during the pregnancy. Ernestine had looked sharply at Gordon when he'd scored that point, her expression suggesting that perhaps she'd underestimated him.

Chapter 38

All in all, Julia thought when she woke on Saturday morning, the first week had not gone badly for her. As Ming had explained, the initial few days were largely about presenting Brendan to the court, documenting his disabilities and life expectancy, demonstrating that he would be better off with his mother, and estimating what it would cost to achieve this.

The bottom line, allowing for inflation, was very close to the ten million dollars the DDO had predicted. Julia's defence team had no argument with the cost estimate or what would be best for Brendan. Only with who should pay for it.

Julia looked at the clock; it was still only five-thirty. Snuggling under the warmth of her blankets, she was thankful she'd let Stephen know she couldn't work today. Before the trial began, she had rashly committed herself to covering her colleagues for twenty-four hours each Saturday; she'd wanted to give them a break. Yesterday, she realised she couldn't do it.

It was not just how she felt after the first week in court, or even the difficulties she'd had coping at work over recent months. It was also a strategic move. Given that she'd been missing all week, both the nurses and her patients would ask where she'd been. They would also assume that she was back from wherever it was, which meant that next week, when she was missing again, there would be even more questions. It was silly not to have realised this earlier, but she'd been desperate to hang on to her normal life as much as possible.

She'd rung Stephen last evening to inform him of her change of heart. He would have to cover her. Stacey had answered the phone, very cool. 'How's the case going? There doesn't seem to be any publicity yet.' To Julia's ears, she sounded almost disappointed.

'It's been okay so far, Stacey. And there has been no media presence, mercifully. These cases are very common. Mostly they are of no interest to the press.' Even so, Julia had spent the week constantly looking around the courtroom to assure herself of this.

'Are they really that common? Stephen said he didn't know of any other colleague who'd got into the sort of trouble that saw them in court.'

Julia felt betrayed. Stephen knew that she was only in court because her actions were defensible. Had he been implying something else to his wife? As she pondered, Stephen came on the line. Stacey had handed the phone over without so much as a 'good luck'. Even if she didn't mean it, it would have been nice to hear.

Stephen, her practice partner and closest obstetric colleague for over ten years, was a little more sympathetic. He understood if she could not do the weekend. It was obvious that she was not coping well at the moment, a reference Julia did not entirely understand, but which seemed to imply that he had been talking to the nurses. He finished with a 'good luck' and 'if there's anything else I can do to help'. At least he got the platitudes right.

It was a pity the first weekend was Stephen's, since Leo and Sylvie would already have known that she was incapable of honouring her foolhardy promise. They'd seen what she was going through.

After the comforting presence of Angie on Monday, behind

her in court and beside her during the breaks, Julia had not been looking forward to being alone for the rest of the week. Especially since the Edwards' side was full of supporters. On Tuesday morning she had been so focused on Tracey's testimony that she did not hear Sylvie slip into the court and take the seat behind her. When the lunch break was announced, she turned and saw her colleague. And realised that she wasn't even surprised. Sylvie had been such a help to her in the last few months, she was part of the case now. After court, she had come back to Julia's for coffee.

She expressed admiration of Julia's calm demeanour in the courtroom. 'If it was me going through all this I'd be a mess.'

'Trust me, Sylvie, it's not calmness, it's exhaustion. I'm worn out with the worry of it all.'

Julia could tell Sylvie understood. After all, Sylvie had watched her struggle with the trial preparation, seen her lose her confidence at work, listened while she expressed her fear of what people would say when they found out. As a result, Sylvie was becoming a bit worn out and worried herself. And terrified of being sued. Julia knew she now scanned her in-tray with trepidation.

'Have you made up your mind yet?' Sylvie asked softly.

'About obstetrics?'

'Yes. About whether you'll give it up at the end of the year.'

As the trial had drawn nearer, Julia's dread of being publicly humiliated, of seeing her good reputation torn to shreds, had escalated enormously. Upsetting her most of all was the fact that she would be irrevocably damaged *even* if she won. Knowing she could never go through this again, she'd told Sylvie last month that she could see no alternative. She would have to stop delivering babies after this year.

As Sylvie waited for her answer, Julia regarded the younger doctor closely, fully aware that her response would influence Sylvie's own plans for the future. She chose her words carefully. 'I still haven't quite decided but, yes, it's likely I'll stop. Lots of our colleagues are giving up, after all, and most of them haven't as good an excuse as I have.' She tossed a small smile to her friend. 'Whatever I decide, Sylvie, I promise you'll be the first to know.'

When Leo showed up at the court on Wednesday and Marcia on Thursday, Julia finally recognised that their attendance was not spontaneous; there was a roster. Someone would be with her every day.

She was therefore disappointed that no one had come by late morning on Friday. It must have been allocated to Stephen, she thought sadly. He would have a hundred things to do before he could get here. In fact, he probably hadn't even wanted to be included, but was too embarrassed to say so. Better to agree, and then be unavoidably delayed. She felt disappointed, not only at his absence now, but at his entire lack of support. She realised he was busy and accepted that he was tired, but they had been close colleagues for a long time and a simple word of encouragement from him would have meant a great deal to her.

She also understood his concern that adverse publicity from her trial might damage his reputation and income. She worried about that herself, not only for him but for Leo and Sylvie too. Not that they were bothered by such fears, bless them.

It was late on the Friday morning, at the point where Judge Owen was asking Mr St Jude whether he would be finished with Nurse Sullivan before lunch, that she heard a familiar cough. Turning around she saw her father, carefully dressed in his one suit. The same one he had worn to her wedding eighteen years before.

'Angie told me Friday was a good day to come,' he said in the lunch break.

'Angie?'

'Yes. She said she had the other days covered.'

Julia was stunned. She had not wanted her father to know about her case, and had deliberately kept it from him. She was ashamed to have him hear the awful things that were being said about her, he who was so proud of her. But even so, she was overjoyed to see his kindly face.

'When did you find out about the case, Dad?'

'I can't quite remember. A while ago.'

'Who told you? Angie?'

'No.'

Julia waited. He had no choice but to tell her. 'It was Tony.'

Julia could hear her father moving about in the kitchen; he was always up early. He'd needed no prompting to stay with her last night, indeed had intended to, having brought his bag with him. It appeared that he had plans for the weekend in Sydney which, looking at his gear, had something to do with fishing. She heard a low tap on the front door. He answered it immediately. She then heard voices, a number of them, all male, all of which she recognised. She got out of bed and peeked through her door, which was just ajar. Sure enough, moving along the hall to her kitchen at six o'clock in the morning, all dressed for fishing, were Geoff and young Richie, and Tony with little Antonio. She heard them laugh, and then try to be quiet, and then laugh again. She contemplated joining them, but instead retreated to her bed in a state of perplexity, pretending to be asleep until they left.

She waited until nine o'clock before ringing Angie to confirm what she had seen. Angie would probably have been woken by the departure of her husband and younger son but, with luck, may have gone back to sleep. Heaven knew, she deserved it. She'd spent Monday with Julia and had rung her every day since. She'd organised a daily companion for her in court, even enlisting Julia's father's help. And it now appeared she had arranged some fishing for George to do while he was in Sydney. At the same time, Angie had worked a full week after Monday, been on call Tuesday and Thursday nights, and had given a lecture to the trainee anaesthetists yesterday afternoon. She should have been exhausted. Knowing Angie, however, right now she was probably jogging down to the beach while a casserole cooked slowly in the oven.

'Hi, Angie, it's Julia.'

'Hi, Julia. I was going to call, but thought you might still be asleep.'

'Maybe I am. I've certainly had the strangest dream.' Julia related the tale.

Angie laughed. 'They've gone to Little Bay for the morning. When Tony heard that George was coming to Sydney, he insisted that they go fishing.'

'But why is Tony in Sydney? And with Antonio?' And no one told me? As far as Julia knew, he hadn't been down since Emma left.

Angie was a bit hesitant. 'He just wanted a weekend away. He's having some problems with Cecilia.'

Cecilia was making Tony's access to his son difficult, deliberately getting arrangements wrong, and then telling Antonio that Daddy hadn't come. It was part of a financial strategy. She was trying to wear Tony down in her push for the house, the new car, and an enormous amount of child support. She wanted almost everything Tony earned. 'In fact, she nearly wouldn't let him bring Antonio this time.'

Julia was distressed at the news. In spite of what Tony had done to her all those years ago, he did not deserve something like this. He was a wonderful father; you only had to look at how much Emma loved him to see that. He would not want this conflict in Antonio's life and would appease Cecilia to limit it. Which she obviously knew.

'Would you like to come over for lunch, Julia?' Angie said. 'The boys insist they'll be bringing a fine catch back with them, but in case they don't, I've prepared a few things. I know everyone wants to see you.'

Julia was at a loss for words. Her father, her ex-husband and his son were all having lunch at Angie's and this was the first she'd heard about it. She felt strangely left out, as she had several times since the friendship between Angie and Tony had blossomed. But this was even stranger. Tony was staying in Geoff's house. She wondered how he'd feel if he knew.

'Julia?'

'Sorry, Angie. I was just thinking about what my plans were today.'

'Are you still on call?'

'No. I took your advice and asked Stephen to take over.'

'Good.' Angie was patient. She knew the strain her friend was under. 'Why don't you think about it for a while, and let me know. Or just turn up. Twelvish.'

'Thanks.'

Julia wandered aimlessly through her house, finally occupying herself with a load of washing. She even got out the vacuum cleaner, but had had enough after one room. She ironed a few shirts for the following week; she'd never had to worry about her appearance so much. Luckily Angie had lent her a couple of smart new scarves and accessories to help vary her outfits. She could see why barristers wore gowns.

Going into the kitchen to make a cup of tea, she picked up the postcard that had arrived from Emma yesterday. It was the second this week, and there'd been a letter also. If her daughter had this much time to write, it must be raining in Venice. Although, Julia thought knowingly, if it was raining Em would have complained about it. She'd been gone ten weeks now, all of it in Italy but she was planning to fly to Paris tomorrow. She was obviously having a wonderful time, and there was no mention of when she might be coming home. Sadly, she'd stopped asking when her mother might be joining her. Not that Julia could have said.

She sat at the table and looked down to the Pacific. It was a nice winter's day, still and sunny, and the temperature would probably nudge the low twenties by the early afternoon. She should go to Angie's. It would seem strange if she didn't. Besides, she wasn't the only one in need of support right now: Tony had his troubles with Antonio, and Angie herself was facing a big decision about Geoff.

Last week Angie had told her that Geoff was again coming home at irregular times. No longer worried she was having an affair, he had gone back to his old ways. Angie had learned that his liaison with his colleague's wife was now over, while that with his post-doctoral researcher continued, albeit at a more subdued pace. She didn't need Ritzy Rainer to tell her that her husband was probably right now casting around for his next conquest.

Angie was annihilated by the extent of her husband's betrayal, but still didn't know what to do about it. It seemed there were three options. She could remain silent and stay. She could insist that Geoff change his ways, and stay. Or she could leave.

She told Julia that she'd already abandoned the second option as hopeless. Geoff's infidelity was so ingrained that it would be well-nigh impossible for him to change now. Angie would just spend the rest of her life checking up on him. It would be a joyless existence. No, she either had to accept things as they were, or go.

She had listed the arguments for staying. The biggest by far were Ben and Richie. Despite what he was doing to her, Geoff remained a good father. He encouraged his sons in their endeavours and, although he could have been more available sometimes, he was generally quite keenly involved in their lives. Their sons were secure and happy and Angie didn't want to see that change. Nor did she want to lose custody of them, which might happen if they were allowed to choose. They were boys, after all.

Also in support of staying, Angie conceded, was the argument that nothing had really changed in her relationship with her husband. Only her ignorance. Geoff was still pleasant and charming and easy to live with. He didn't beat her or shout at her, he wasn't boorish or boring, he didn't make a mess with the toothpaste or drop his socks on the floor or turn the television up too loud.

On the other hand, Angie had sobbed, her impassivity finally giving way to tears, there was a very good reason why she wouldn't be able to stay in her marriage much longer. Julia had frozen immediately, thinking she was going to hear Angie confess her love for Tony. But she hadn't. It was how Angie felt about Geoff that was going to make her leave. As the sham life she'd been so happy with was ripped away, and with it her confidence, and, as she saw her husband's attentiveness wax when he felt under threat and wane when he didn't, Angie's realisation had deepened. She was beginning to hate him.

While she dressed, Julia reflected on Angie and Tony, the plight each currently faced, and the comfort they were finding in each other. Today was the first time she'd see them together. Julia could think of no one more entitled to good fortune than her best friend; and Tony had also had his share of woe. She knew without doubt they would make each other happy and the more generous part of her nature was thrilled they'd found each other.

But, in alarm, her more selfish side registered a completely different emotion.

She left the car at home and walked the two kilometres to Angie's in the winter warmth. Just getting outside and seeing that ordinary people were still doing ordinary things – walking dogs and washing cars, chasing kids and kicking balls, laughing and lunching – was an antidote to a week spent cloistered in a windowless courtroom. By the time she arrived, she felt quite cheerful.

Angie and Tony were in the kitchen standing very close as she came in. Tony was looking sheepish, while Angie was unable to control her mirth. Julia wasn't able to piece together exactly what had happened, since each time Angie tried to explain, she was convulsed with laughter. And Tony was too embarrassed to say. It seemed to be something to do with Tony mistaking a very pungent fish sauce for balsamic vinegar and ruining the magnificent green salad by applying it liberally.

Luckily Angie had arrayed a veritable feast of salads, a smorgasbord for the eyes as well as the palate, and the loss of the green salad could easily be borne. Julia hadn't seen either of them laugh so much in ages. She smiled in spite of herself.

Angie was looking lovely in a caramel cardigan and cream pants. With her height, new haircut, and striking appearance, she looked like she belonged beside Tony, who was wearing a russet jumper over dark woollen trousers and was a touch sunburned from the morning's outing. His thick dark hair, which Julia had always loved, contained a few new curls of grey in its just-washed fullness. His amused guilt at devastating Angie's salad gave him a slightly vulnerable appearance. Together they made a long, lean, elegant pair, which left Julia feeling even more squat than usual.

She forced herself to be cheerful as she kissed them both, put her wine in the fridge, and made her way to where her father was holding forth in the backyard. He was standing with Geoff beside an old garden table, showing an amazed Antonio, and a somewhat repulsed Richie, what was to be found inside a freshly caught fish. They had done well with their catch, and had four respectable flathead to show for their endeavours.

Antonio ran to her as she came down the back steps. 'Ju-ya. Ju-ya. Come see the fish.'

She picked him up and swung him around. 'Oh, Antonio, it's wonderful to see you. I've missed you.' Still holding the child, she turned to her father.

'I see you put the morning to good use, Dad.'

'I did, princess, but I was not alone. I had these young men here to help me,' he said, using the hand holding the half-gutted fish, rather than the one with the knife, to point to the boys. Antonio giggled while Richie promptly went inside.

It was a wonderful lunch and they sat laughing in the sun for hours, around a table laden with food and wine and flowers from the garden. If Geoff had any misgivings about Tony, they were not apparent. Not surprisingly, Angie's husband had few male friends, but he seemed pleased to have Tony and Antonio stay. While Geoff might not see it, to Julia it was disquietingly obvious that Tony and Angie's feelings for each other had moved well beyond friendship. They sought each other's glances, made excuses to go into the house at the same time, and were noticeably attentive when the other spoke. Julia even saw Tony place his hand on Angie's shoulder a couple of times.

She felt winded at the sight of them and had to remind herself to smile. She had not expected such an intense reaction and could not exactly pinpoint its cause. Was it their obvious happiness? Or her exclusion from it? Or was it something else?

She could not bear to think what else it could be.

353

Neither Julia nor her father had their cars, which did not matter since neither would have driven after an afternoon of drinking. The darkness fell quickly after five and, as they made to go home, Angie, who never drank much, offered to take them. But the winter's evening was mild and they said they'd like to walk. George was in the habit of trekking five kilometres daily anyway. Tony decided to come part of the way with them since Angie had, with mock fear, declined his offer of assistance with the cleaning up.

Protesting that it was not a proper walk if you didn't get up a sweat, George went on ahead, leaving Julia and Tony to proceed at a more leisurely pace.

It was eight years since they'd strolled anywhere together. The darkness lent a special intimacy and Julia felt strangely nervous. She sensed Tony ease his stride to match hers and could almost feel his cool breath on her face as he inclined his head towards her when she spoke. Acutely conscious of his nearness, she moved away; she did not want to accidentally brush against him.

'So, how's it going?' he asked quietly. Better than anyone, he comprehended how awful it was.

It was not too bad, she admitted, so far at least, but it had been mostly preliminaries. Next week would be worse.

'Their experts?' He knew how these things ran.

'Yes.'

They walked on in silence for a hundred metres, watching with detachment as people readied themselves for Saturday night. Tony asked about the presence of journalists. It was what they both dreaded most.

'So far, so good,' Julia said, but without much relief. 'I keep expecting great hordes of them to turn up.' And crucify me. Like they did you.

Tony shrugged sadly in the dark. 'It will probably be okay, Julia. It's a low-profile matter.'

She hoped he was right.

'Have you heard much from Emma?' he asked, after a bit.

'She's writing at least twice a week.' Julia was amazed. Over the past two weeks she'd received three postcards and two letters.

'She's wonderful,' Tony agreed, pleased. His own ration of mail had been cut accordingly.

As they ambled slowly towards her house, Julia was desperate to ask about his relationship with Angie. She had a right to know, given her closeness to them both and the impact their friendship would have on her. She'd already felt excluded at lunch. It was more than just a feeling of being left out, she admitted to herself, only dimly aware of what it was.

Leaving it alone, she instead asked Tony whether he still intended travelling to Europe to see their daughter.

He was noncommittal. It depended on a lot of things, including Antonio.

Julia looked at him with sympathy. Antonio was such a lovely child; being apart from him so much must be awful.

It was, Tony agreed sadly, clearly struggling to keep his head above the misery of it all. Leaving his son with Cecilia and her boyfriend was slowly killing him with worry. And it was even worse now that Cecilia was mucking around with his access. Having her change arrangements at the last minute made him so angry he nearly lost control. And it confused Antonio. This was not what he wanted for his son, parents who hated each other. And that was what Cecilia was counting on. 'She doesn't really want him, you know. It's just about screwing me for money.'

'You're still not going to fight her for custody, Tony?'

Tony gave a short laugh. 'We've had this conversation before, Julia. Do you really think the Family Court would consider me over Cecilia? Can't you hear them jeering when they recall why my name is so familiar? No, I have to accept that she'd get custody. What I have to do is maximise my access. And the only way I can do that is to give her everything she's asking for. Which is the house, the car and seventy percent of my income for the next fifteen years.'

'What? That's ridiculous. She came to the marriage with nothing and you're going to let her walk away with everything?'

'It doesn't matter to me, Julia. I'd happily give her the lot as long as, in return, I could have Antonio.'

'And?'

'She won't even consider it. Says she couldn't bear to be away from him. But, if I sign the financial agreement, she'll let me see him several times a week.'

Astounded at Cecilia's avarice, Julia asked, 'And if you don't sign?'

Even in the dimness she saw his face blacken. 'Then she's going to tell the court to look into my record, that they'll see it backs up her claim that I'm an unsuitable parent. And that I should have no access *at all* to my son.'

'But that's outrageous.'

'It is,' he agreed bleakly. 'And she'll probably fail. But she'll then make things as difficult and nasty as possible. And the person who'll suffer is Antonio.'

Julia had to restrain herself from touching him. How dare that cruel, greedy woman try to blackmail Tony like this. As Julia had recently come to realise once again, he was a gentle, generous person. Antonio was clearly besotted with him, as was Emma. He didn't deserve something like this.

Overtaken by a blistering fury, she said, 'Call her bluff, Tony. Go to the Family Court. Fight her for custody. It mightn't be as bad as you think.'

They stopped walking for a moment and regarded each other under the embracing glow of the street light. Tony's beautiful dark eyes shimmered with pain and Julia immediately knew what he was going to say. He'd done it once before, believed in the rightness of his position and taken on the legal system. He wasn't about to make the same mistake again.

As she held his tortured gaze, Julia ached for him. 'For a dead person, she casts a long shadow.'

'Madeleine Morgan?'

'Who else?'

It was hard to believe, after all this time, that she could still injure them both. If her name was connected to Julia's by a resourceful journalist, the newspapers would have a field day; she'd be Mrs Scandal once more and they'd be a husband and wife team of negligent doctors. And if Madeleine's name was linked to Tony's by Cecilia's lawyers, the Family Court would decide against his custody application, and might even deny him visitation rights.

They were at her gate now, both worn out by their short walk. As Julia anguished about Tony's plight, she saw him likewise look at her with concern, then consciously shift to a brighter mien. 'I'm sure it will be all right this week, Julia. But good luck anyway.'

'Thanks. And good luck to you too.'

Tony turned and walked back to Angie's.

Chapter 39

Waiting for Angie to finish a phone call, Julia observed the drift of people into the Supreme Court building: bored clerical staff snatching one final puff, confident lawyers mentally refining their arguments, frowning plaintiffs now doubting their decision to sue, and weary defendants wondering when it would all be over. Not that Julia could really tell who was who but, as each group passed and she took in the stride and the set of the shoulders and the look in the eyes, she thought she knew. Were they doing the same to her?

She straightened up and forced an expression of indifference. Maybe that would fool them. Fat chance, she admitted derisively. A two-year-old could tell that her knees were barely hinged, her stomach about to rebel, a concrete pour had taken place in her brain. It was going to be a dreadful week.

She felt her eyes drawn to a woman across the road who'd propped for a minute and opened a newspaper, and she gave in and thought about the dream that had disturbed her night, the dream about Meredith Henderson, a girl from primary school. Their friendship had broken down in high school when Julia, academically more able, was placed in the advanced stream. Highly competitive, Meredith had always resented this. In the dream, she wore an enormous sneer as she read a front page newspaper report about Julia's disgraceful court appearance.

'Ha! Look at this. Look at the trouble Julia Kent's in this time. I always knew she wasn't as good as she made out and that it would only be a matter of time before she fell flat on her face. But twice in eight years? Unbelievable. Wait till I tell all the others.'

A tired sigh escaped her. She hadn't seen Meredith for twenty years, hadn't thought of her for ten, and here the girl was, tormenting her while she slept. She forced the dream from her mind and accepted Angie's offer of a soothing coffee. And braced herself for the clutch of medical experts who would this week lay the blame for Brendan Edwards' sad existence at her feet.

Tracey's legal team and supporters were already in place when Julia and Angie walked into the court. Ernestine and her junior, Michael Lethbridge, were going through the final instruction of their first expert medical witness, while solicitor Louise Craig was on her phone ensuring that the second witness would definitely be available after lunch. Beside them, Tracey stared vacantly at the empty judge's bench, while behind her, Norma and Donna whisperingly pointed things out to friends who had come to court for the first time today.

Ming and Richard were buried in a pile of papers, readying their questions for cross-examination of the plaintiff witnesses. They smiled encouragingly at Julia, but did not interrupt their work. Julia and Angie took their seats as the clock showed ten, at which point Gordon made his appearance, breathlessly rushing to the bar table as Judge Owen limped to his place behind Mabel Appleton. They were ready to begin.

Ernestine Hillier looked down at her notes. Watching her, Julia recalled what Ming had said; the plaintiffs' case would be moulded around three tenets. Firstly, Brendan Edwards' neurological condition was due to birth asphyxia. Secondly, the asphyxia was entirely preventable by proper obstetric care. And thirdly, Julia had failed to provide that care and was therefore liable to compensate him for his disabilities. The plaintiffs' witnesses were ordered in that sequence and Julia surrendered to a small shudder of trepidation as Ernestine called the first to the stand.

Dr Adam Elliott was Brendan Edwards' neurologist. He had been consulted by the neonatal intensive care unit about Brendan's condition in the first week of the child's life, and had been looking after him ever since. He was in his late thirties, handsome and neatly bearded, his intelligent green eyes magnified by a large pair of spectacles. He clearly had no misgivings about his testimony, thought Julia glumly as she followed the trajectory of his bold gaze over the courtroom.

Ernestine took him briefly over Brendan's level of impairment. The nurses had described it in detail the previous week, but a medical opinion added import. She made sure to focus on the child's abilities as well as his disabilities, confirming previous opinions that the child recognised different people, and experienced emotional pain when separated from people he knew. The size of the 'general damages' component of any payout depended on this. The more the child could be shown to suffer, the more money Tracey would get for his care.

Dr Elliott was in little doubt that Brendan's problems were due to birth asphyxia. The child was damaged because of hypoxia – lack of oxygen – late in pregnancy or during labour. He had first made the diagnosis when Brendan was a week old, and had stuck with it ever since. He enunciated his reasons compellingly.

As Gordon St Jude stood to address the witness, Julia noted that Adam Elliott displayed no obvious anxiety at the prospect of cross-examination. Ernestine had probably told him that Gordon's bark was worse than his bite and the first question seemed to be one he'd been expecting.

'Dr Elliott, could you tell me how many children with major neurological disabilities you have under your care?'

'At the present time, over a hundred.'

'What are the common causes of neurological abnormalities which date from birth?'

'The major ones are inherited conditions, birth asphyxia, head injuries sustained while in the uterus, metabolic conditions, damage from drug usage by the mother. There's also a large group of "unexplained", about twenty-five percent.'

'What percent are made up by birth asphyxia?'

'About ten percent.'

The barrister looked suitably perplexed. 'On what basis, Dr Elliott, do you put Brendan into the birth asphyxia group and not the much larger "unexplained" group?'

'The seizures and the history.'

'What history?'

'The history of birth asphyxia. There was foetal distress, meconium-stained liquor, a low Apgar score at five minutes, and then a neonatal period consistent with birth asphyxia. It therefore seems reasonable to make a diagnosis of neurological damage as a result of asphyxia.'

'Would other paediatric neurologists agree with you?'

'Not all. No group of doctors ever agrees on everything, but I believe that many would.'

'The ones who disagreed, what would they say?'

'You'd have to ask them,' the neurologist replied, his tiny glance in Ernestine's direction telling Julia that the question had been anticipated and the answer supplied. He was not going to fall into any traps.

Gordon St Jude moved on to the question of the seizures. 'Doctor Elliott, could you tell us when Brendan's seizures first started?'

'They were first noted on the fifth day.'

'Could you tell us when seizures due to birth asphyxia typically begin?'

'Mostly within the first forty-eight hours.'

Gordon nodded. This was the answer he expected. 'Could you please tell the court how you reconcile these two facts?'

The doctor could. The seizures were first noted on the fifth day. Since Brendan was relatively floppy at that stage, it was possible that he was having seizures before this time which were not apparent because of his lack of tone. As well, while asphyxial seizures usually began early, the neurologist felt strongly that there were occasional exceptions. He believed Brendan Edwards was one of those.

Gordon countered. 'We have a number of expert reports from neurologists which state categorically that seizures commencing on day five would be considered far too late to attribute to asphyxia. What do you say to that?'

'They are entitled to their opinion, Mr St Jude,' the neurologist replied confidently. 'I am not changing mine.'

Dr Elliott's cross-examination finished just after three and Judge Owen decided not to begin with the next expert witness until tomorrow. No one objected. Not Gordon, who had a client waiting in his office, nor Ernestine, who was happy with the day, nor Ming, who wanted to work on later aspects of the case, nor Julia, who had had enough. She and Angie walked out with the junior counsel.

'That didn't go very well,' Julia moaned, feeling fragile.

'It wasn't that bad.' Ming was not concerned. 'I think he might have been a little too smug. Let's hope he irritated the judge.'

'And this week is their experts, Julia,' added Angie sensibly. 'You have to expect them to score a few points.

'Do I?' Julia asked, her voice small.

Sylvie picked Julia up and drove her to court the next morning. Julia was embarrassed. Her colleague should really have been at the surgery helping Leo. 'You don't have to come every Tuesday, Sylvie. I'm okay on my own.'

Sylvie smiled. Leo had been adamant; someone was to be with Julia every day. Besides, it was the nights when Sandra really needed him, and Sylvie was already covering them.

'I'm going back to help him this afternoon,' she assured Julia. 'But until then, I'll be staying with you.'

Julia nodded, mute with gratitude.

———

Ernestine Hillier called her second expert witness, Dr Pauline Menzies, a paediatrician who specialised in newborn babies. She had been the deputy-director of the neonatal intensive care unit during Brendan's stay there and was now head of neonatal services at a large private hospital on the north shore of Sydney.

Like Dr Elliott, she was firmly of the view that Brendan's condition was due to birth asphyxia. She had put it as her diagnosis when she completed the Interim Discharge Summary upon Brendan's transfer from intensive care to the Special Care nursery. As Ernestine took her through her testimony, Dr Menzies argued convincingly and with authority that Brendan Edwards demonstrated enough features of oxygen deprivation and birth asphyxia to accept this as the principal diagnosis of his condition.

Gordon St Jude spoke deliberately and slowly. 'Dr Menzies, are you aware of the existence of a confidential survey among obstetricians at Northern Private Hospital last year? A survey recording their feelings about the quality of paediatric care you provide?'

'Objection, Your Honour.' Ernestine Hillier was on her feet. 'We are dealing with a baby born at Royal Eastside over five years ago, not at Northern Private Hospital last year. What possible relevance could this question have?'

Julia looked from the opposing senior counsel to her own junior barrister who nodded slightly. The speed of Ernestine's objection confirmed Ming's suspicion: Ernestine knew about the survey and was in no doubt that it damaged her witness's credibility. That she still decided to use the paediatrician was not a surprise either. Ming had said there was really no choice. As the doctor who had prepared the Interim Discharge Summary, Pauline Menzies was perhaps the most important witness the plaintiffs had. Not calling her would greatly weaken their case. And raise suspicions. Ernestine must have assumed that the defence team wouldn't know about the survey, a reasonable assumption if Gordon was in charge. And if Leo Steiner hadn't suggested which of his Northern Private colleagues would be delighted to speak with Ms Tan.

Judge Owen looked at Gordon. 'There is an explanation, I trust?'

'There is, Your Honour. It goes to the credibility of Dr Menzies as an expert witness. The defence maintains – and the survey shows – that she is well known among her colleagues for attributing almost every adverse neonatal outcome to obstetrician incompetence and birth asphyxia. Even when there is evidence that the problem was caused by a virus, an infection, or even a congenital abnormality. The survey addresses such claims in detail.'

'Can you verify the authenticity of this survey, Mr St Jude?'

'I can, Your Honour. I can also provide every one of the eleven obstetricians at Northern Private as witnesses at short notice.' This was far from true, but Gordon would never be called upon to confirm his claim.

'I will allow it, Mr St Jude. But in future, such irregular tactics should be cleared with me first. I would like a copy of the survey. Now.'

'I have several right here, Your Honour. I had intended handing one up to you this morning.'

'I should have had it last week, Mr St Jude.'

'Yes, Your Honour,' said Gordon meekly.

Once the survey was tendered, Gordon St Jude had few questions for Dr Menzies. He did not want to lose the advantage he had gained.

In her re-examination, Ernestine tried to repair the damage done to the neonatologist's reputation. She again took Dr Menzies slowly over why she felt that Brendan Edwards, in particular, demonstrated a neonatal course consistent with birth asphyxia. The paediatrician sounded much less convincing the second time.

Chapter 40

Gianni's Cafe was the defence team's refuge during the recesses of the trial. With the changing array of witnesses and supporters, it made sense to have a regular place to meet. It was enough that the food was good; it was a bonus that the coffee was great.

It was here that Leo found Julia. She was just finishing breakfast and had ordered a second cappuccino. Engrossed in a newspaper, she did not notice him approach.

'Good morning,' he whispered, slipping into the seat opposite her.

'I thought I told you not to come.'

'Sandra insisted. She wants me to help you. Leonie and little Louis are there this morning. And Ruth Levy, her doctor, will be coming shortly too.'

'Shouldn't you be there as well? To speak to Ruth?'

Leo was honest. 'What is there to say?'

Julia had last visited Sandra on Monday evening. It was clear she would not live to see the birth of Alex's baby; she would probably not even last out the trial. 'How is she?'

'Another bad night, I'm afraid.' For him as well. 'Luckily she's only semiconscious much of the time because the nausea's now impossible to control and the headaches are almost continuous.'

Julia put her hand over the back of his where it rested on the table. She had never been so appreciative of anything in her life. If he and Sylvie hadn't come to her rescue, especially after Patrick abandoned her and her legal team collapsed, she'd have just thrown in the towel. She held his hand tightly. She understood what it was costing him, helping her at this time. She knew the long hours he was working, he and Sylvie both. Not just covering her patients for her, but covering each other so that one of them could be with her. And she would never forget it.

Leo's mouth formed a small smile. He had been pleased to help. And it had given Sylvie a new purpose in life. He chuckled, thinking of his co-worker's dogged persistence, her determination to win Julia's case by sheer bulk of paperwork if nothing else. He accepted Julia's thanks graciously but admitted that, with the court attendance at least, he and Sylvie felt they had no choice. They were always willing to do the research, of course, but after Tony said that the worst thing about his trial was having to sit through it alone, they couldn't let that happen to her.

'You spoke to Tony?'

'Not directly. He told Angie to tell us.'

Just then Richard and Ming joined them, coming in from the cold to be warmed by Gianni's coffee and to prepare for the third plaintiff expert. Clarissa was supposed to be with them. The glamorous DDO doctor had graced the trial only briefly, popping in one afternoon, making a big fuss of being available to help with whatever was needed, and promptly disappearing. Richard explained that she had been unavoidably delayed this morning. Ming simply raised her eyebrows.

They outlined for Leo the events of the past two days. The lawyers were delighted about Pauline Menzies, but not so confident regarding Adam Elliott's impression on the judge.

'It's probably one-all,' said Ming, not unhappily.

They spoke about today's expert, radiologist Dr Craig Harrison. In his written report the radiologist had claimed that there were changes on Brendan Edwards' brain ultrasounds which demonstrated that an injury had occurred, most likely during labour. The timing was critical, and it was strategically crucial that the defence not let his opinion stand. They discussed how Gordon should handle the expert.

Julia tried to concentrate on the conversation, but her mind kept straying to what Leo had said about Tony facing his trial on his own. She felt defensive. It was true, Tony had gone through his trial alone, but it had *seemed* to be his choice. He'd ignored the advice of his lawyers, rejected every suggestion she herself had made and deliberately concealed information about the tapes. He'd been determined to protect Madeleine Morgan at all costs. And he'd seemed like a man hellbent on self-destruction.

At the same time, Julia felt contrite. As she'd toiled at her preparation over the past two months, flanked by her keen lieutenants, she couldn't help but contrast how different it had been for Tony. With stirrings of guilt, she remembered how little support his colleagues had given him. It could even be argued that she'd been the worst, withdrawing from him completely at the end. His trial had been different, of course – sensational, salacious and sordid – and only he'd known where the truth lay. But few had given him the benefit of the doubt.

Including her. With growing shame, a tremor ran through her at the awful thought of Leo and Sylvie and Angie regarding her as an embarrassing pariah and withdrawing from her. Leaving her all alone.

Ernestine Hillier introduced Craig Harrison to the court. He was a senior radiologist at both Eastside Hospital and its attached Children's Hospital. A serious-looking man well into his fifties, he had reported on Brendan's head ultrasounds. The first one had been taken when the infant was one day old, and the second a month later. The purpose of comparing the two films, the specialist said, was that injuries to the brain, especially those due to lack of oxygen, often took three or four weeks to show up as visible changes in brain matter. If there were abnormalities already present at the time of birth, then the injury had occurred at least a few weeks earlier, perhaps as a result of a serious fall in pregnancy. But if the abnormalities were not present on the ultrasound taken on the first day yet showed up a month later, then the injury had occurred at around the time of birth.

Ernestine took her witness carefully through the significance of the timing. 'Is it your conclusion regarding Brendan Edwards that the damage to his brain occurred at about the time of his birth?'

Craig Harrison was quite authoritative. 'Yes it is. If you compare the normal films taken soon after birth with the abnormal ones taken a month later, it is obvious that something happened to cause damage to the brain of Brendan Edwards at about the time of his birth.'

Ernestine drove her final point home carefully. 'Dr Harrison, can you therefore assume that his brain was normal before labour started?'

'Not definitely, no.' He had an air of measured reasonableness. 'But I think it is very likely.'

They broke for lunch. Julia had found the radiologist's testimony troubling. She had not expected him to have such presence in the court, to sound so convincing. She could see what the lawyers said about the witness's demeanour being half the battle. If Dr Harrison's testimony that the damage to Brendan's brain occurred at around the time he was born was not effectively challenged, it would undermine her whole case. There were opposing radiological opinions, Ming assured her, but if the judge was left in much doubt, this issue alone could determine his decision.

Gordon St Jude began his cross-examination by asking the radiologist if he would please hand over the two sets of Brendan Edwards' X-ray films he'd referred to, so that the entire court could view them. Dr Harrison somewhat sheepishly replied that the films were the property of the hospital, and that he had only the reports in his possession. This was not a problem for the barrister; he knew that the radiologist did not have the films. Turning to his junior counsel, Ming Tan, he asked her to tender them into evidence. The young lawyer had collected them from the hospital the previous evening, rather surprised that Ernestine hadn't subpoenaed them herself.

Ming was very familiar with these films now. She had also borrowed them last month, and personally taken them to two eminent radiologists for their opinions. She was deeply shocked when, in the first days of being retained by the DDO, she'd realised that such an important matter hadn't been attended to. She'd challenged Richard about the omission. He'd explained that Clarissa, as the doctor on the case, was chasing up the medical evidence. She'd been so busy, he had added protectively, she'd not yet had time to finish everything.

Ming plugged in the backlit viewing screen she had also obtained, and set it up as directed by Judge Owen, near the witness box and facing him. The judge then invited the lawyers for both sides to approach so that they could clearly see the films. The defence senior counsel used the delay to address the radiologist jocularly. 'It's not that we don't trust you, doctor,' Gordon chortled, strongly implying otherwise. 'It's just that we'd like to see for ourselves.'

Dr Harrison maintained his composure. He was an experienced witness and familiar with the posturings of barristers. He had also been well briefed by Ernestine. Gordon asked him to identify the two sets of films. The radiologist agreed that they were of Brendan Edwards' brain, one day after birth, and a month later.

The defence counsel continued: 'Dr Harrison, could you please point out to the court the significant differences which you have identified between the two sets of films?'

There followed a detailed analysis. With the aid of a pointer, Dr Harrison demonstrated the 'white matter' changes between the earlier films, which he claimed were normal, and the later ones, which were abnormal.

Gordon challenged him. 'Dr Harrison, I am not a radiologist, but pardon me if I say that the differences are very subtle.'

The expert agreed. 'They are subtle, Mr St Jude, but you are not used to looking for them. I can assure you they are there. Which is why specialist radiologists take six years to complete their training,' he added smoothly.

Gordon St Jude nodded slowly, but he was not agreeing. He asked what a radiological artefact was. The expert remained confidently assured. An artefact was where a mark or shadow appearing on an X-ray or ultrasound film was not really there. It looked like something abnormal, but turned out to be a false shadow.

'And do you think that the whiter areas you have pointed out to us on the second set of films could be artefacts?'

'No I don't.'

'Why not?'

'Because of their configuration.' The expert elaborated.

The defence lawyer heard him out. He then looked at the radiologist directly. 'We have had these films reviewed by two other radiologists. They feel that there are no differences between the two sets. That the white shadows on the second set are due to differences in the angle and depth of beam penetration. That is, they are artefacts.' He paused. 'Our experts conclude that both sets of films are essentially normal.'

Both Julia and Ming sat forward in their chairs, one behind the other, sensing that a breakthrough was occurring. Julia was surprised at how easy it seemed. But a quick glance at Ming told her how hard it had been.

Dr Harrison began to look uncomfortable. 'With subtle changes, differences of interpretation are common among radiologists.'

'Even after six years of specialist training?'

'Yes.' He was not so self-satisfied now.

'To summarise then, Dr Harrison, the changes are so subtle that a number of radiologists might not agree with you about these films?'

'Yes. That's possible.'

Gordon was feeling very confident. He decided to up the ante.

'If we were to give these films to ten currently practising radiologists, how many would say that the findings were unchanged between the two sets of films?'

Julia saw Ming look up from her doodles, little squiggles she always drew at tense moments. She had only shown the films to two radiologists and clearly wondered what the hell Gordon was doing.

The now not-so-eminent radiologist seemed equally perturbed. Had the films been reviewed by so many others? What had they thought? Julia watched as he made a quick calculation and decided that now was not the time to change his testimony.

'Just the two you mentioned before,' Dr Harrison replied with an enormous show of bravado. 'The other eight would agree with me.'

Ming was clearly furious. Gordon St Jude's smug miscalculation had diverted the court's attention from the crucial fact that two respected radiologists believed Brendan Edwards' second head ultrasound to be as normal as his first. And that the child had not sustained any demonstrable damage during labour.

The young lawyer was so ropeable, Julia noticed she couldn't even look at Gordon as they packed up for the day. 'Will I now have to get another eight opinions?' she demanded angrily, once she and Julia were alone. She reached for her phone.

Chapter 41

The courtroom was empty when Julia arrived early on the Thursday of the second week of her trial. She wondered whether Gordon St Jude would dare turn up to court today. It might be a good time for him to get sick, and for Ming to officially take over. The young barrister had been running the show anyway. As Julia took her seat at the second legal table, she thought that if Gordon's ridiculous blunder had not been such a critical jettisoning of her advantage, she would have rejoiced at his comeuppance. As it was, she, Leo, Ming and Richard had been fixed to their seats, horrified and hostile. Julia later suggested that Richard deduct a compensation payment from the barrister's sizeable fees.

As the courtroom filled, Ernestine Hillier prepared to call the fourth of her medical witnesses. She wore a brave face, but Julia could guess how she would be feeling this morning. Gordon's miscalculation notwithstanding, Dr Harrison's radiological opinion had been convincingly challenged. Following on from the discrediting of Dr Pauline Menzies, it had put a big hole in the plaintiffs' case.

In the past forty-eight hours, Julia had allowed herself to feel more hopeful. Even so, Ming had told her enough about Ernestine's skill for her to be far from relaxed. She crept to the edge of her seat as the senior counsel called Monica Martin to the witness stand.

Monica Martin was a good midwife and a good person, and her testimony was honest and without artifice. She was neither a defendant nor an expert, and was therefore in the peculiarly neutral position which made telling the truth an easy option. To be sure, she was embarrassed to be appearing against Dr Kent, but her embarrassment was less because she now worked in Melbourne. In any case, she had been compelled to appear; it was not her choice. Still, she had not told any of her Sydney friends that she was here. She did not want them to think badly of her. Gently, Ernestine took her through her testimony. It was as they had done several times before, and Monica knew what to say. Tracey Edwards was in her first pregnancy, and had come into the Royal Eastside delivery suite in early labour. She was a day before full term.

She was a private patient of Dr Kent. Monica rang the doctor to notify her of her patient's admission. Dr Kent told her that the patient very much wanted a natural labour. Dr Kent did not give any other special orders and Monica had managed Tracey as a normal low-risk patient. She listened to the foetal heart with the hand-held Doppler machine through two contractions every thirty minutes as she had been taught. Tracey spent much of the labour in the shower; it helped greatly with her pain and she needed no other analgesia.

Things went well until an hour or so before delivery when the membranes ruptured in the shower revealing the green of meconium liquor. Monica listened closely with the Doppler and soon after heard foetal heart decelerations. She encouraged Tracey back onto the bed so she could attach an electronic monitor. The patient was nearly fully dilated at this stage. The decelerations continued. Dr Kent arrived and undertook a forceps delivery. The baby was born in poor condition, and did not improve over the next fifteen minutes. He was then transferred to intensive care.

'Do you know what Brendan's birth weight was, Ms Martin?'
Ernestine asked as she had several times in the practice sessions.

'He was about two point four kilograms.'

'Is this a common weight at term?'

'No, it's rather small.'

'Is there a name given to babies that are that small?'

'Yes. SGA. Small for Gestational Age.'

'Was Brendan Edwards SGA?'

'Yes.'

Ernestine asked the midwife what the difference was between a Doppler and an electronic monitor.

Monica explained that both picked up the foetal heartbeat. With the Doppler, a small machine about the size of a mobile phone, the heartbeat was only heard. The Doppler probe was held over the pregnant abdomen and the heartbeat listened to for a few minutes. It was used intermittently and ran off a small battery. It was extremely portable. An electronic monitor, on the other hand, was a large piece of equipment, about the size of a television, which was plugged into the power supply. With it, the baby's heartbeat was also heard but was, in addition, printed onto a piece of paper. The monitor probe was held in place by straps around the abdomen, and was left to run continuously.

'Ms Martin, could you tell the court why electronic foetal monitoring is so widely used in labour these days?'

Monica explained that one reason for the popularity of electronic monitoring was that it was easier. Once it was in place and recording properly, it required no further work. The midwife didn't have to find the foetal heart on each occasion. She didn't have to listen for five to ten minutes every half an hour. The monitor did all the work, recording the baby's heart from beat to beat and printing out a continuous record, revealing exactly what the pattern was over many hours.

Ernestine looked at the midwife. 'Is electronic monitoring safer than using a Doppler intermittently?'

Gordon's mind was elsewhere at this point and his reverie was rudely interrupted by a sharp poke in the ribs from his junior counsel. She was motioning for him to object. To what, he wondered? She glared at him, as did Richard Tripp from behind. He had no choice.

'Objection, Your Honour,' he said, standing slowly, giving himself time to read Ming's scribbled note. 'Many thousands of obstetric articles have been written over the past twenty years about the relative merits of intermittent versus continuous monitoring in labour. International experts remain in disagreement on the issue. How can Ms Martin possibly be expected to answer a question that the experts cannot?'

Judge Owen was not much given to accepting objections, and this was no exception. He would be happy to accept into evidence any of the articles referred to by Mr St Jude, but for now he would like to hear what the witness had to say. Ernestine repeated the question. Julia saw her lips curl slightly as she did.

'It's probably safer in some cases,' responded the midwife carefully, 'such as if the decelerations are shallow rather than deep. You wouldn't hear them on a Doppler. Or in cases where the beat-to-beat variability is poor. You can't tell that on a Doppler. Both can be signs of distress not identifiable on a Doppler.'

Julia heard her start to add that these were usually early signs of foetal stress, and that true foetal distress was almost always associated with prominent and clearly audible decelerations, but the barrister had left her behind.

'Ms Martin, is it possible that Brendan Edwards exhibited either of these inaudible signs of distress prior to the signs that were audible?'

'It's possible, but –'

'Thank you, Ms Martin.'

Julia remained precariously on the edge of her seat, wary about what was coming next. Ming had predicted that her alleged violation of the labour ward protocol would be a major plank in Ernestine's case.

'Ms Martin, Royal Eastside labour ward currently has a book of protocols for the management of various obstetric situations and emergencies,' said the plaintiffs' counsel, as anticipated. 'Was such a book in existence at the time of Brendan Edwards' birth?'

'Yes.'

'There is currently a protocol that says all Small for Gestational Age babies are to be continuously electronically monitored during labour. Was that protocol in place at the time of Brendan Edwards' birth?'

'Yes. It was.'

'Why do you think continuous electronic monitoring is recommended for SGA babies?'

'Because they are considered high-risk. High-risk pregnancies are always continuously electronically monitored.'

'Why?'

'To allow foetal distress to be picked up earlier.'

'Why didn't you continuously monitor Tracey Edwards?'

'Because Dr Kent didn't tell me to.'

'Thank you, Ms Martin.'

From the way Gordon looked at the clock, Julia could tell he thought now would be a good time to break for lunch. She knew he was not interested in cross-examining the midwife; he considered her largely irrelevant to the case and had said so several times. As he rose slowly to say that he had nothing to ask the witness, Ming handed him a sheet of paper with the questions she wanted put to the midwife. From Gordon's glare, Julia knew he thought it a waste of time. His favourite chant was 'let's keep things moving along'. But, while he would have liked to ignore his junior counsel, he did not want to upset Richard Tripp, who, it appeared, also wanted the witness cross-examined; the DDO solicitor was his entree to these easy and lucrative cases. He had no choice. He started.

'Ms Martin, why did you not ask Dr Kent if she wanted the patient continuously monitored?'

The midwife hesitated. Gordon waited.

'I suppose it was because she had said that the patient wanted a low intervention labour.'

'Do many patients want that?'

'They do.'

'Can you easily move around when continuously monitored?'

'Not with the older style of monitor we were using then.'

'Could you shower while attached to that style of monitor?'

'No.'

'During the labour, did you think that Tracey Edwards' baby was particularly small?'

Again she hesitated. 'No I didn't.'

'So the issue of continuous monitoring did not occur to you, did it?'

'No.'

'Ms Martin, are hand-held Dopplers widespread in labour wards?'

'Yes.'

'Do they work well?'

'Mostly, yes.'

'Mostly?'

'An occasional one needs new batteries, or needs replacing altogether.'

'I see. Was the Doppler you used on Tracey Edwards working properly?'

'As far as I can recall.'

'If it wasn't working well, what would you have done about it?' Gordon revealed his impatience.

'I would have changed to a better one.'

'So,' he asked condescendingly, 'we have established, have we, Ms Martin, that the Doppler you were using on Tracey Edwards was in optimal working order?'

Julia winced. It couldn't be a good tactic to patronise a witness, but Monica responded without rancour. 'Yes, it was. It was in good working order.'

'Good. Did you monitor Ms Edwards every half an hour?'

'Yes, I did.'

'There was never a time when you were too busy to do it?'

'No. I did it every half an hour.'

'Even when she was in the shower?'

'Yes.'

'Did you listen during and after two contractions each time?'

377

'I did.'

'Prior to the last time, did you at any earlier time detect foetal distress?'

'No.'

'What do you estimate was the longest period of foetal distress that Brendan Edwards could have sustained before detection?'

'Twenty to thirty minutes.'

Gordon St Jude paused for a minute to catch his breath and change direction. He was nearly at the end of Ming's list.

'Is foetal distress common in labour?'

'Yes.'

'Would you see it every day in an average labour ward?'

'Yes.'

'What is the usual outcome?'

'The baby is fine.'

'Were you surprised at the condition of Brendan Edwards?'

'Yes.'

'Why?'

'He was much sicker than I expected.'

'Why were you surprised at that?'

'He had been delivered so quickly after the distress was discovered, I expected he would be all right.'

'What was your first thought when you saw him?'

Monica hesitated, and Julia guessed immediately that this was not one of the questions she'd been over with Ernestine.

'That he might be abnormal.'

It was all Julia could do not to leap into the air; Monica obviously thought Brendan's problems were intrinsic. She wished Sylvie and Leo were here to observe how well their questions had gone. Even pompous Gordon St Jude must be able to see the benefit that had been gained. With immense relief she saw that he was not adding any of his own questions today.

Ernestine was not finished with Monica, however, and stood up to re-examine her witness. She hoped her urgency wasn't noticeable.

'Ms Martin, is it taught to midwives that SGA babies are less able to withstand the stresses of labour?'

'It is.'

'Is it possible then that it required only a short period of distress to cause Brendan Edwards' disabilities?'

'Objection,' interrupted Gordon St Jude, not requiring any prompting this time. 'Ms Martin is neither a neurologist nor a paediatrician. How can she possibly be expected to answer a question that even experts do not agree on?'

Percival Owen looked out over the top of his glasses and nodded. 'I'm afraid, Mrs Hillier, that I'm with Mr St Jude on this one.'

Chapter 42

Turning away from the mime artists who entertained the lunchtime crowd in Martin Place, Julia and Marcia sought a sunny spot to perch for a minute. Julia let out a small laugh as she sipped her juice. 'I don't know if I can bear to hear it, but you'd better tell me what's happening with Jane Steel.'

They had been deserted by the lawyers. Gordon was in his chambers dictating an advice on another matter, while Ming was working on the case and Richard had gone back to the DDO offices to sort out yet another problem Clarissa Mason-Fraser couldn't manage on her own.

'Before we get on to Jane Steel,' said Marcia, pausing between mouthfuls of lamb kebab, 'I've got some good news. Grace Chan is pregnant again. And it's in the uterus this time. I promised her I'd tell you.'

Julia was tickled pink. She knew Grace had been for another IVF cycle since the ectopic in February, but didn't know the outcome. She wondered if Grace wanted to know where her doctor was. She did, of course, and had been told that Dr Kent was away for a few weeks on personal business. Like all the other patients were being told. The rest of the practice staff knew about the trial now, and they were managing to make her absence sound mysterious enough that no one was game to ask any questions.

Julia was very thankful for the protection of her privacy. At the same time, she couldn't believe that Jane Steel was content not to ask any questions; she was a walking question, that woman. But every time Julia asked Leo and Sylvie what was happening with her, an odd look came over them.

A mysterious grin also passed across Marcia's face at the mention of Jane. The secretary was hard pressed to recall a more troublesome patient. Jane was due this week, yesterday to be exact. She'd seen Sylvie for her last visit and Leo for the one before and, since neither could tell her where her doctor was, she had a mind to change to another practice. Dr Kent had said nothing about being away when her baby was due. If she had, she would have booked with someone else.

'Did you recommend Mick Mullins?' asked Julia cheekily. 'I could write a letter of referral tonight.'

'Please, Julia, would you?'

Julia asked how Stephen was. Marcia shook her head. He was mad, the way he was working; he couldn't possibly keep it up. She'd found him asleep on the tea room couch at mid-morning last week. There were a dozen patients in the waiting room and she could barely rouse him. Later the same day, Stacey had rung from a car sales room. She was buying a new Mercedes four-wheel drive, with all the options, and wondered what colour he favoured.

Julia didn't know what to say. She felt sorry for Stephen, and worried about him, but the situation was of his own making. She was tempted to mention his entirely negative response to her trial, but kept quiet. Marcia worked for them all and it was not fair to ask her to take sides. She'd probably figured it out anyway.

'And how are you coping, Julia?' asked the older woman gently. She'd been with her boss for ten years, and seen the devastation Madeleine Morgan's death and the divorce from Tony had wreaked. She knew about the joy and sadness of

Patrick. And she understood how the past six months had taken their toll.

Julia gave a selfconscious shrug. 'Better than I thought, actually. It's nearly halfway and I'm still in one piece. Thanks to Ming and Leo and Sylvie.' Her pitch rose abruptly. 'But not to bloody Gordon St Jude, the lazy, condescending jerk. And to think they pay him five thousand dollars a day to represent me.'

'What?' Marcia choked on her last mouthful. She paled noticeably. 'Five thousand a day? It takes me two months to make that much.'

'I know. Sickening, isn't it? And you know what's even more sickening? He doesn't give a damn about me or Tracey Edwards or this case. All he cares about is getting the whole thing finished and collecting his fee, which will be over one hundred thousand dollars.'

Marcia was still choking.

Professor Christopher Jones, who took the stand after lunch, was a handsome man. It was a fact of which he was obviously aware, but which had not necessarily served him well. Now nearing fifty, he had been divorced three times, and was currently living with a young doctor barely out of medical school. She had been a student in his tutorial group the previous year. His family support payments for his five school-age children were crippling. His third wife had sought and won the family home near Clovelly Beach, while the previous two were also comfortably ensconced in the surrounding area. He swore that his kids did more extracurricular activities than were humanly possible. Certainly it was humanly impossible for him to afford them. By the time he paid the school fees and the extras, his living and food expenses, he was essentially broke.

For the past three years he had been reduced to renting a rather inferior apartment many miles from the beach, from which he ventured seldom, not having the money for restaurants and the theatre any more. This led him to two decisions. Firstly, he'd quietly undergone a vasectomy of which no one, including his young girlfriend, was aware, and secondly, he'd sought to supplement his professorial and private practice income by appearing as an expert witness in medico-legal cases.

Initially offering his services to both sides, he soon found that plaintiffs gave him more regular work than defendants, and he now appeared almost exclusively as a plaintiff witness. This compromised his independence, but his professional standing was such that his credibility had only just begun to suffer. The author of several textbooks, and a full professor at the University of Central Sydney, his reputation, at least on paper, was hard for defence counsel to break. His testimony was likewise hard to fracture. So practised was he at giving an opinion, he could happily state a blatant untruth without even knowing he had done it.

He took the stand, took the oath, and took an extraordinary amount of time recounting his CV. Ernestine led him slowly through it all, obviously wanting his stature to be as impressive and impenetrable as possible. She seemed confident that his testimony would demolish Dr Kent.

Professor Jones was happy to oblige. This was an easily identifiable high-risk pregnancy. Investigations of foetal wellbeing should have included a full biophysical profile. The patient should have been induced at thirty-eight weeks since the baby was not growing well inside the uterus, rather than letting it go on to the usual forty. Then, during the labour, the foetal heart should have been monitored continuously using electronic means and not intermittently using a hand-held Doppler. If this had been carried out – in accordance with the hospital protocol, he emphasised – the distress, which should have been anticipated in this case, would have been detected early. And the baby safely delivered before this awful and permanent neurological damage had occurred.

Gordon had a much harder time with the famous professor. His opinion was set in concrete and no concessions were to be made. His testimony was like a mantra. High-risk pregnancy. Biophysical profile. Induction at thirty-eight weeks. Continuous electronic monitoring. Breach of hospital protocol. He repeated his view, over and over, reaffirming his testimony irrespective of the question asked by the defence counsel.

Julia watched him in fascinated, horrified silence. When Doctors Elliott, Menzies and Harrison were testifying against her, she had been unable to face them, staring instead into the middle distance, but with Chris Jones she was unable to look away. He was someone she knew quite well, a fellow obstetrician, a member of the College of Obstetricians as she was. They'd chatted at conferences over the years, sat on committees together. While they hadn't been close, they'd been cordial. And now he was happy to destroy her career.

Judge Owen indicated the clock and asked Gordon if he was nearly finished with the witness. If so, they would continue for a short while past four o'clock in order to release the professor. If not, the witness would be required to return in the morning. Involuntarily, Gordon looked at Ming. She moved her head slightly. Hold the witness over. We must be able to do better than this.

As the court emptied for the day, Julia watched Tracey prepare to leave. She had missed the middle part of the professor's testimony, only returning towards the end of the day's proceedings. Her mother and daughter were both unwell and, with Donna minding them, no one had visited Brendan since Monday. He was having problems with a new medication and Tracey had left at lunchtime to go to him. That she was at her wits' end with worry and lack of sleep was obvious; all week she had smoked outside the court building, despite Ernestine's advice to at least go somewhere she couldn't be seen. But Tracey was beyond deception at this stage. Julia realised she herself was not the only one feeling the strain.

Finally, the courtroom was empty but for Gordon, Ming and Julia, Richard having once again been called away by Clarissa. The plaintiffs' lawyers had left with Professor Jones minutes before. Ernestine was quietly pleased with the afternoon, and it showed. She'd needed this witness to perform well, and he had. Even under cross-examination he'd left no doubt that, in his professional opinion, Dr Kent had failed to manage Tracey Edwards' pregnancy and labour with proper care.

Julia sighed. She'd known for months this was the testimony Chris Jones would give; even so, sitting through it was more harrowing than she'd anticipated. She dragged her attention to her lawyers. Gordon was packing up his papers briskly, in a hurry as always to be gone, while beside him, Ming rifled through the pile of black folders which the case and its months of preparation had generated. Her brow was corrugated into lines of perplexity.

Oblivious to his junior counsel's concerns, Gordon strode to the door. 'We've made a mistake holding him over,' he said. 'We should have just let the bastard go. The longer he's on the stand, the more trouble he's going to cause us. We've got our own experts next week. They'll be able to refute his testimony.'

Ming said nothing, still unable to find what she was looking for. 'Gordon, there was a document about Professor Jones and his obstetric profile, you know, his complication and caesarean rates. It was in here somewhere.'

'Was it?' Gordon seldom knew which documents were where. That's what junior counsel were for.

'Yes, of course it was. Richard assured me that Clarissa had compiled it . . .'

Ming didn't bother to finish the sentence.

Chapter 43

'I'm not doing it,' Gordon St Jude said emphatically, handing Ming back her questions. They were in the lawyers' room beside the court. 'It's just a lot of risky time-wasting. Let's get their people off the stand, and ours on. That's the best strategy. If we can finish with their Dr Willard from Melbourne today, we can start with our witnesses on Tuesday. It's a mistake to put Professor Jones back on the stand. He'll just do us more damage.'

Ming said nothing further, and took a seat beside Julia. They would see what Richard thought. And they would not give up until he agreed with them. Most of their night had been spent discussing the best approach to the professor. Sylvie, who had joined them after a delivery, was adamant that he be discredited. She and Julia hated what he did to their colleagues on a weekly basis with his casual denunciations, despised him for destroying people's careers and reputations for money. It took one phone call to establish that Clarissa Mason-Fraser had done none of the research she was allocated. Julia had immediately sat down to ring everyone she knew who'd ever worked with the self-righteous professor.

Sylvie had taken it a step further, driving to the birth unit at his hospital, Queen Victoria's. Laden with flowers and a pink balloon and pretending she was looking for a recently delivered patient, she took the time to ask the midwife at the desk about the facilities the unit offered. She was thinking of choosing the hospital for her next baby. It was a quiet evening and the nurse was only too happy to give her an unofficial tour.

When Richard joined them, Ming quietly closed the door to the small lawyers' room. After the blasting he'd received from her about poor Clarissa the previous evening, Richard was receptive to a strategy of appeasement. Ming put forward her reasons for asking Professor Jones a handful of new questions. Gordon argued against it; indeed, he refused to do it.

Richard sensed an unusual opportunity. 'Should we give Ms Tan one hour then?' he asked the senior counsel.

'One hour for what?' said the burly barrister testily.

'One hour to ask Professor Jones her questions?'

'What?' Gordon was stupefied. He nearly fell off the chair which was already struggling to accommodate him. 'Are you mad, Richard? She's just a child, barely out of law school. She's never cross-examined anyone, let alone a seasoned courtroom performer like him. We can't risk letting her loose with her scrap of paper.'

But Richard Tripp seemed inclined to favour the young barrister. It had not escaped his attention how hard she was working, and how effective her efforts had been so far. She couldn't do any worse with the professor than Gordon had, and it might be good for her to have a turn at being the front person. And to do so now, when there wasn't the time for her to get nervous.

Richard looked at her. She was white. 'Well, Ming? Would you like a chance to address your questions to the professor? Speak now or forever hold your peace.'

Ming swallowed hard and looked at Julia, who simply smiled.

The entire courtroom looked up in surprise when Ming stood at the bar table and introduced herself to Professor Jones. Ernestine and Michael exchanged glances, the younger lawyer speculating whether he too might get a chance to show what he could do, and the older one wondering if Gordon St Jude was hungover. She had never known him to showcase the talents of his juniors, especially not during cross-examination of a critical witness. She sat forward expectantly.

'Professor, I was wondering whether I should have some investigations done.' Ming began more confidently than she felt.

Everyone in the court looked at her. Always tiny, she managed to look smaller than ever. Judge Owen, already surprised at her active role, looked at her rather quizzically.

The professor was curt. 'I don't know what you mean, Ms Tan. What sort of investigations?'

'Investigations to see why I am so tiny. I'm barely one hundred and fifty centimetres. I weigh only forty-four kilograms. There must be something wrong, don't you think?'

The professor glanced at Ernestine, and sat silent.

Ming continued. 'Of course there isn't anything wrong with me, professor. I was meant to be small. My mother and sister are even smaller than I am, and my father only a little bigger. It would not surprise you that I was less than two point five kilograms at birth, would it, professor? As was my equally normal sister. We were both very vigorous, normal, small babies. We were meant to be small.'

Julia could tell Ernestine was thinking that she should ascertain the relevance of Ming's meanderings. Judge Owen did it for her. 'Are you asking a question of the professor, Ms Tan?'

'I am, Your Honour.' Turning back to the witness, she said, 'How does an obstetrician determine if a small baby is healthily small, like me, or unhealthily small? It's not a new question for obstetricians, is it, professor?'

Finally realising where she was heading, Christopher Jones relaxed. He smiled benignly. 'No it's not, and even these days it's still not possible to be absolutely certain. But there are some tests we can do to help us distinguish between the two.' He outlined the usual measures, with which the defence team were now very familiar.

388

'Dr Kent did all of those tests, didn't she, professor?'

'She did not do a full biophysical profile.'

'She checked the baby's growth, its movement, its heart tracing, the blood flow to the baby from the placenta, and the amount of water around it. Of all the tests to do, those are the most important ones, aren't they?'

The professor hesitated. His own textbook, which he saw on Ms Tan's table, said as much. 'All of the tests are important. The ones she didn't do could have added information.'

'But she did the most important tests, didn't she, professor?'

He grudgingly admitted that she did.

'Is a small baby always detected before birth?'

'Not always. No.'

'Have you ever missed one, professor?'

'Of course. Everyone has.'

'Dr Kent didn't miss that Brendan Edwards was small, did she, professor?'

'He was particularly small.'

'She didn't miss it, did she?'

'No.'

'Professor, you say that Dr Kent should have induced Ms Edwards' labour at thirty-eight weeks in order to remove Brendan from what you referred to as a hostile environment.'

'That's right,' he concurred.

'Let me ask you a hypothetical question. If Dr Kent had ordered every test imaginable, and they had all been normal, should she still have arranged an induction at thirty-eight weeks?'

'I believe so.'

'Why?'

'To minimise the risks to the foetus.'

'If all of the tests have shown the foetus to be well, what is the need?'

'To be on the safe side.'

'Could you please tell the court what an induction is, professor?'

'An induction is when we undertake to bring a woman into labour at a time before it happens spontaneously.'

'Before the uterus and the baby are ready for labour?'

The professor waited before answering. It was a troublesome question. 'Before labour has started spontaneously,' he corrected, 'but close to the time that it will.'

'Could you tell the court how an induction is carried out?'

He described the process whereby the sac around the baby was artificially punctured and the waters drained while at the same time an infusion of synthetic oxytocin was run into a drip to make the uterus contract.

'Is there any evidence, professor, that induced labour results in a higher caesarean section rate?'

'There is, but that is often related to the reason for the induction itself, such as high blood pressure, or a poorly grown baby.'

'Is there evidence, professor, that induced labour is associated with a higher rate of foetal distress?'

'There is, but again,' he said smoothly, as if giving a familiar lecture, 'the distress is probably related to the fact that the baby is already compromised.'

'But there is evidence, isn't there, professor, that even with perfectly healthy babies, the incidence of foetal distress is higher in induced labours?'

'There could be,' he replied, wary of this young woman and not wanting to be caught in an untruth.

'Why do you think that is?' asked Ming, capitalising on his admission.

'I'm not sure.'

She looked down at the bar table and picked up a pile of medical journal articles before facing him again. She looked bigger somehow.

'There is quite a body of research now,' she said, referring to the papers she held, 'that shows changes occur in the baby's circulation, particularly in the blood supply to the brain, in the days before spontaneous labour. Are you aware of this research, Professor?'

It was an impossible question. Either answer was risky. He went with the affirmative.

'It is thought, isn't it, professor, that these changes possibly protect the baby's brain during labour contractions?'

'That's one theory,' he replied, as dismissively as he could.

'Do these protective changes occur in induced labour?'

'Possibly not. But the research is in its early days.'

'The studies here suggest that these changes do not occur in induced labour,' she insisted, indicating the papers again. 'Allowing for that, professor, isn't there currently a rethinking occurring in obstetric circles about the place of induction of labour?'

'Only to a limited degree. There will always be a place for induction of labour.'

'But there is a rethinking, isn't there, because we now have an explanation for why induction of labour causes more foetal distress than spontaneous labour?'

'As I said, the research is in its early days.'

She ignored his response.

'Is it not so, professor, that Dr Kent, having reassured herself that Brendan Edwards was healthy, was at the cutting edge of modern obstetrics by awaiting the spontaneous onset of labour in order to reduce the chance of foetal distress?'

'No.'

Though the answer seemed unhelpful, Julia knew that Ming would not be unhappy; it accentuated Chris Jones's inflexible partiality. She could feel the silent awe of the courtroom as all around were mesmerised by the young barrister's performance. Percival Owen leaned forward so as not to miss a word while the look on Ernestine's face suggested she now understood why the defence was performing better than expected. Her junior, Michael, had a hopeful air; maybe a precedent had been set and he also would get a chance. And Richard glowed with the quiet vindication of his decision. Only Gordon seemed to be focused on something else altogether.

Ming continued her cross-examination. 'Professor, you work at Queen Victoria's Maternity Hospital in Sydney, don't you?'

'Yes.'

'How many delivery rooms do you have?'

'Ten.'

'And how many CTG machines for continuous electronic monitoring?'

'Seven.'

'Not ten?'

'We never need ten. It is almost unheard of to have ten patients labouring at the one time. And even if we did, many don't need a CTG. Not everyone needs to be continuously electronically monitored.'

'What percentage of labouring patients at your unit would be continuously monitored?'

'Possibly fifty percent.'

'If a woman is continuously monitored, she is pretty well confined to bed in her labour, isn't she?'

'Not necessarily. If she wishes, she can move around quite a lot.'

'Within what range?'

'About one metre.'

'That's quite a lot?'

There was laughter in the courtroom. Even Ernestine smiled, although Gordon appeared not to.

'Could she have a shower while attached to the monitor?'

'No.'

'Your hospital is part of a trial to see whether greater mobility in labour results in a lower forceps rate, isn't it?'

'Yes, we are part of many international and national trials,' he replied proudly.

'Are there any preliminary findings from this study?'

'No,' he said quickly.

Ming moved on, her hour nearly up.

'Your delivery suite last year underwent refurbishment, didn't it?'

'Yes.'

'Could you tell the court what the major cost component of that refurbishment was?'

'There was new painting, and flooring and equipment.'

She looked at him fiercely. 'I'll repeat the question. What was the major component of the cost?'

Professor Jones moved uncomfortably in the witness box. 'To provide a shower in each of the birthing rooms.'

392

'Oh?' Ming asked with feigned surprise. 'Is labour that dirty, professor? Or is there another reason for the showers?'

She waited.

He gave in. 'It is believed that the hot water provided by the shower provides some pain relief in labour.'

'And being up and about, using the shower for pain relief, contributes to a lower epidural rate, and consequently a lower forceps rate, doesn't it?' Ming persisted.

'Some people think so.'

'Since the refurbishment of your delivery suite cost over two million dollars, I would certainly hope that it's more than just "some", professor.'

There was laughter again. Ming waited for it to settle.

'You certainly believe in the benefits of showers in labour, don't you, professor?'

'I think that there is a limited place for them,' he said condescendingly.

The young barrister picked up a thick, bound document which she held aloft. 'Do you know what this is, professor?'

He made a show of squinting at the title page. 'It appears to be the refurbishment proposal for Queen Victoria's delivery suite.'

'It is. Would you like to read out for the court the submission you made to the Area Health Service when the refurbishment was first proposed?'

He did not need to read the submission. He admitted, with some prompting, that he had argued strongly, very strongly, for the presence of a shower in each delivery room, using exactly the arguments the lawyer had enunciated.

'Do you not believe what you wrote, professor?'

'Sometimes one has to embellish these things.' Anyone seeking funding knew that.

'Why?'

'To get the money.'

'You would embellish the truth for money?'

Ming was shaking as she sat down. Julia and Richard beamed at her, and George, who she'd met the previous Friday, gave her a gentlemanly nod. Only Gordon, deeply engrossed in the file in front of him, did not acknowledge her.

Ernestine had to be distressed but she was hiding it reasonably well, though the note she'd just received from Louise Craig couldn't have helped. Her final witness, Dr Robert Willard from Melbourne, had been delayed by a surgical emergency; he wouldn't be arriving in Sydney until the mid-afternoon. Since she could not promise he'd be present when they resumed at two o'clock, Judge Owen adjourned until Tuesday. And the testimony he took to the Queen's Birthday long weekend was that of Christopher Jones.

The court emptied quickly, with Gordon the first to depart. Julia watched as Tracey Edwards, exhausted and dejected, left with her lawyers. Julia had smiled at Tracey a few times over the past two weeks, but her former patient always looked away. If she truly believes I have damaged her son, she probably hates me, Julia thought, averting her gaze before Tracey thought she was smiling at her today.

Once Tracey left, however, she couldn't keep the smile off her face. The case was now halfway, the months of despair nearly over. Of the plaintiffs' experts, only the paediatric neurologist Elliott's testimony had done her any harm. Menzies, Harrison and Jones had barely touched her. And there was only one left. Robert Willard.

She hugged Ming with delight. 'You were fantastic! I can't wait to tell Sylvie how it went.'

The young barrister was pleased but modest. 'Thanks, Julia – but, remember, it was you and Sylvie who wrote the questions.'

'You were still wonderful,' insisted Julia, bubbling. 'I'm starting to think we might win.'

Before Ming could answer, Richard intervened. More experienced, he cautioned them against overconfidence. Judges often made surprising decisions. Things were definitely looking good, he conceded. But he had been in this position before and still lost.

Nothing he said could dampen Julia's spirits, however, and

she turned happily to kiss her father, who'd come to give his Friday support.

'Not staying up for the races this weekend, Dad?' He had no bag.

'Not this year. I've lined up some fishing with some old friends down the coast. But I might stay next weekend if that's all right with you.'

'You know it's all right, Dad,' she said. As an afterthought she asked, 'Will Tony be down next weekend then?'

'He very well might be, princess.' Her father then excused himself to attend to a few things around the city. He would join her at Gianni's in an hour for lunch.

Julia walked out with Ming. They arranged to meet at Sylvie's on Sunday night to prepare for their own witnesses next week. And for the cross-examination of the plaintiffs' final expert on Tuesday.

'*Your* cross-examination, Ming,' added Julia provocatively.

'You don't think the big G would let me have another go, do you?' giggled the young barrister as she departed.

Chapter 44

Julia's buoyancy lasted through until the holiday Monday, at which time it was replaced by a feeling of foreboding and emptiness. The light she now glimpsed at the end of the tunnel also illuminated how barren her life was soon to be. There would be no Patrick and, for a while at least, no Emma. And soon there would be no Sandra.

When she'd visited on Saturday, her old friend had been much weaker, lapsing in and out of consciousness, but she'd managed a wan smile. Sandra's two daughters were there, Alex now heavily pregnant and Leonie with young Louis. They were trying to be brave around their father, but it was not a successful charade. They asked about Julia's trial. Leo had told them that things were going well, and Julia agreed that so far it was better than expected. They spoke briefly about Alex's pregnancy, which was being attended to by Sylvie in Julia's absence; it was also going well. Sensing their need to be alone as a family, Julia left soon after.

She'd stayed home on Saturday night and enjoyed a quiet time with a couple of videos. Then on Sunday she'd joined

Sylvie and Ming to prepare for the coming week. Although heartened by the poor performance of the plaintiffs' witnesses, they were not resting on their laurels. After Ernestine's final expert on Tuesday, it would be the defence's turn to present witnesses. The first of these was to be Julia herself. It was expected she would take the stand on Tuesday afternoon.

Determined that nothing be left to chance, Ming insisted they once more go over the questions Gordon would ask her. They had covered this many times already and Julia was confident of her testimony. But she acquiesced to her lawyer, understanding only too well how critical her performance was to their case, how much influence it would have on the one person who mattered. Ming had watched the judge closely while the other witnesses were testifying, and she instructed Julia to speak slowly and clearly, to present as confident but not arrogant, assertive but not unbending.

Finally they were finished to the lawyer's satisfaction. 'I think you're going to be great, Julia. Judge Owen will be so impressed we probably won't even need to call our other witnesses,' she said gleefully.

'I hope you're right,' said Julia, pleased.

'I'm paid to be right.'

After the promising evening, Julia was hit with an unanticipated sense of disquiet on Monday. She regretted the extra holiday; she just wanted to be in court, getting the whole thing over. She needed to give her testimony, conclude the case, obtain a verdict, and reclaim her life. But, as she focused for the first time in months on the relative inadequacy of that life, she became quite despondent. She would have her patients back again, which would be wonderful, but that aside, her future was looking bleak.

The worst of it was Angie and Tony. Although she'd forbidden herself to think about them until her trial was over, their images colonised her mind. They were two of the most important people in her life and she couldn't bear to contemplate how she'd be displaced in both their affections. It wouldn't be intentional, of course, but over time she'd be progressively excluded from their lives. She felt it already.

She hadn't spoken to Tony since he'd walked her home last Saturday; this was not surprising. But she'd also barely spoken to Angie, which was unusual. Angie had been her court companion on Monday but, since then, there had only been one fleeting phone conversation. Angie was busy, of course, and faced serious problems of her own, and that might explain her not having the time to ring Julia. But it did not explain why Julia hadn't called her. The unspoken issue of Tony hovered between them, staying Julia's hand each time she went to phone.

Seeing them together last Saturday was the problem. She'd expected to feel little more than mild discomfort, but had found herself gutted, shaken by feelings of betrayal and jealousy. As if that was not enough, she'd then had to endure the taunts of her own meanness. No one in her life had been a better friend than Angie. How could she not want her to be with a man she knew would make her happy? But, after a week of roller coaster emotion, of battling her lesser self, she had given in. She did *not* want them to be a couple.

Which brought her to Tony. He'd been on her mind constantly since last weekend, the nearness of his lean, familiar body as they'd walked home in the dark, electric in her memory. But even if she'd not already been dwelling on him, Leo's disclosure would have led her to him. Tony cared enough about her to make sure she did not go through this ordeal on her own.

As he had. She recoiled sharply as the truth of this took hold.

Over the past six months, seeing so much of him once more, she had unconsciously come to the conclusion that there had been nothing improper in his relationship with Madeleine Morgan. In spite of herself, Julia had inched belatedly to the view that he'd simply been a victim of circumstance, hostage to his patient's unbalanced imagination and his own misguided integrity. They'd *both* been victims of circumstance, in fact, herself as well as Tony. Madeleine's death, coming so soon after the loss of Joseph and Tony's infidelity with Sybilla, had hit them both so hard, it had completely overwhelmed their judgement.

Tony had failed to see that his foolhardy attempt to mislead the Medical Tribunal in order to protect Madeleine's reputation would be the final straw for his wife and would destroy their marriage. While she, befuddled by her depression about Joseph and her hurt over Sybilla, had failed to recognise his foolish but honourable actions for what they were.

And had, as a result, abandoned him.

A knife pierced her brain as the awful implications dawned. Her separation from Tony and the miserable years of pain that followed had been completely unnecessary.

And now he loved Angie.

Feeling she would suffocate if she didn't get out, Julia strode down to the beach. But although she could escape her house, she could not run away from the tumult in her mind. She walked for hours back and forth across the sand, even venturing once or twice to let the chilly winter waves lick her toes. But the brisk breeze and icy water did not relieve the claustrophobia which oppressed her. Nor release her from the truth she would still not admit.

Defeated, she made her way home to prepare herself for the third week of her court case. Coming up her street she met Angie and her dog; they'd been to her house. At the sight of her friend, Julia felt guilty; she'd not had her interests at heart these past few hours. She invited Angie back.

They drank their tea in the fading afternoon light of the back room and discussed the neutral ground of the trial. Julia expressed her relief that the plaintiffs' experts were nearly finished. She was looking forward to the judge hearing her side of the story, although she was, naturally, nervous about being the first witness. She would probably take the stand tomorrow afternoon, she said, shivering slightly at the prospect. Angie warmly assured her she'd be fine; she always presented well, and the facts were on her side.

They sat awkwardly for a few moments, watching Smudge chase birds around the backyard. Julia decided she had to ask Angie about Tony, bring it all into the open. She'd go mad if she had to bottle it up much longer. But, as she marshalled her courage, Angie spoke instead. 'I've made up my mind about Geoff.'

Julia waited.

Angie had been back to see Ritzy Rainer and was going to ask Geoff for a divorce. Hardened by months of watching him deceive her, she was now determined to keep both her house and her sons. She had asked Ritzy to assemble a complete dossier on Geoff's liaisons.

There was no surprise in the decision for Julia. Angie had been aware of her husband's infidelities since January and, while she'd done nothing so far, her burgeoning relationship with Tony must have finally galvanised her.

'You don't think counselling might help?' Julia suggested, with little hope.

Angie shook her head sadly. She'd thought about it a lot, and come to the conclusion that her husband wouldn't change; he'd had his spots too long. It was she who had to resolve the situation. And she'd decided to move on.

Julia looked out the window. 'Do you know where you'll go?' She wondered if Angie would move to Brisbane immediately.

Angie's chin jutted forward in defiance. She didn't intend going anywhere. She would be asking Geoff to leave and was planning to buy out his share of the house. Her face softened. She was hoping the boys would stay with her. But if they wished to live with their father, she'd have to reconsider about the house. She didn't want them having to move.

After Angie left, Julia sat for hours looking down to where the ocean was slowly devoured by the night, pondering her friend's momentous words. She hadn't needed to ask Angie about Tony after all: the situation was obvious. If Angie was intending to stay in her house, Tony must be moving back to Sydney.

Julia carefully laid out her cream suit for the following day in court, the day she would finally take the stand and, after months of anguished preparation, have her chance to defend herself before the judge. Critically regarding the suit, she changed her

400

mind and took out the navy one instead. She was just about to change her mind back again when the phone interrupted her. It was Tony, ringing to wish her luck with her testimony.

Julia's heart nearly stopped at the sound of his voice, and in that moment she knew. She loved him.

'How did it go last week?' Tony asked, cutting across her struggle to breathe. From his tone, she gathered it was the second time he'd asked the question.

'Fine, fine. It was fine,' she rasped jaggedly.

He asked more questions about the case and she gave distracted, one-word answers. While he seemed keen to talk, she desperately needed to be alone. The clamour in her brain was deafening.

'Julia, I wondered if you would like me to come down tomorrow?'

'Whatever for?' she asked abruptly, caught off-guard.

'No special reason,' he said quickly. 'Just to be there. To give you support.'

Julia was enveloped in longing. Nothing would be nicer than Tony coming to look after her. But she couldn't bear to see him, now he loved Angie.

'I don't think it's necessary,' she said slowly, each word requiring its own breath. 'What I have to say is very straightforward.'

'Giving testimony in the Supreme Court is never straightforward, Julia. Especially when you're the person on trial.'

'I'm sure I'll be all right.' She tried to steady the quaver in her voice. 'Besides, what if there were some journalists who recognised you? You could blow my cover.' She'd meant it as a joke, but it came out harshly.

She had a point, he agreed, disappointed. Had there been any journalists? Not in her court, she admitted. There were always a few around, of course, but thankfully there were much more exciting matters than hers for them to report. Still, she always kept her head down.

Tony said nothing for a moment. 'Well, good luck, Julia. I'm sure you'll be fine.'

'Thanks, Tony. I'm sure I will too.'

She sat looking at the receiver for a long while, too shattered to move. It was a relief in one way – to finally admit how she felt about Tony – but in every other way it threatened to blow her apart. Angie and Tony together. She covered her face with her hands at the thought of them, as if she could block out her mind's eye as well. She knew she'd never be able to bear it, never. It would be like death on a rack, a slow painful turn every time she saw them together. It was too much to expect she'd be able to face it, not in the long term. If Tony was coming to Sydney, maybe she'd just have to go somewhere else. And give up both of them.

She groaned in frustration and misery. If only she'd realised how she felt a couple of months ago, maybe she could have tried to win Tony back before Angie knew she wanted him. But now it was too late. She had lost him for a second time.

There were thousands and thousands of them and they brought traffic to a standstill for miles in every direction. Police issued a warning to motorists to avoid the city centre. TV cameras rolled while commentators earnestly clutched their microphones and helicopters whirred overhead. Off to one side, taking notes and drawing pictures, was a bustle of journalists who smirked at her with malign intent.

The protesters were mostly women and children, many of the children in wheelchairs or on crutches or aided by guide dogs. They screamed that they had been misled and waved large placards communicating their tortured existence. They had thought they were in good hands, but now they were disabled and in constant pain, their lives in tatters. Because of her.

She fell as the crowd pressed upon her, their jeering loud in her ears, their lurching forms robbing the day of light, and knew this was it, she was going to be crushed to death.

In a sweat she woke, her heart pounding, the bedclothes twisted. For a moment she couldn't breathe. Then, urgently gulping the morning air, her gasping quickly turned to sobs.

It was not that the nightmare was any worse than the dozens

she'd had since the first letter from Tracey Edwards' solicitor last October. It was that it had come now, when things in her trial were going so well. As she slowly started to prepare for the day, a sense of dread descended over her.

Chapter 45

Ernestine Hillier's final witness was Dr Robert Willard, the head of obstetrics at Mother Mary Maternity Hospital in Melbourne. While he was not by title a professor, preferring a busy clinical practice to academia, he had the stature of one. His published medical research was widely acclaimed, and he was currently working on the seventh edition of his seminal textbook, *Australian Obstetric Practice*. He was active politically and was the current vice-president of the College of Obstetricians. He was a shoo-in for the presidency next year, and a place on the national honours list soon after.

He had trained in the 1970s, a time when obstetric practice was becoming more interventionist and patients unquestioningly did what their doctor recommended. This suited Robert Willard. He was known to hate it when things went wrong; he saw every pregnancy as high-risk until proven otherwise. His patients were well cared for but very closely monitored. Any minor deviation from normal was immediately assessed with a battery of investigations. In particular, he had championed the biophysical profile, a set of five tests scored out of ten points, as the pinnacle of foetal assessment. Indeed, his early reputation was made from dozens of publications regarding the reliability of the profile in predicting foetal compromise.

He was constantly alert to potential obstetric problems and had a high rate of both induction and caesarean section. All of his patients were continuously electronically monitored in labour. He saw his approach as the prevention of preventable mishaps. Some of his colleagues called it meddlesome midwifery. His practice suited his patients, but would not have suited Julia's.

As Dr Willard solemnly took his oath, Julia heard Sylvie sit down behind her. Still ragged from the events of the past twenty-four hours, she mouthed a feeble hello before turning back to watch the final plaintiff witness prepare to give his testimony.

Unlike Professor Jones, she did not know Robert Willard personally but felt she did, since she owned several editions of his textbook and referred to them often. Not only did he have an impressive medical reputation, Ming had heard that his forthright, confident manner gave his courtroom testimony added validity. He was a redoubtable final witness for the plaintiff and, as Julia waited apprehensively for Ernestine to begin, she fervently hoped he wouldn't do her too much damage.

Unsurprisingly, Dr Willard had a long and impressive CV. Ernestine took him carefully through it, nodding with overawed respect at the appropriate moments. She then asked Dr Willard about the management choices available when an obstetrician thought that a baby was small. His testimony was the same as Professor Jones. He recommended a biophysical profile, induction, continuous electronic monitoring in labour – as the hospital protocol advised – and early recourse to caesarean.

'Dr Willard, is it your opinion that Dr Kent should have carried out a full biophysical profile on Tracey Edwards when it was known that the baby was small?'

He answered in the affirmative at length, quoting studies from a number of obstetric journals which showed the superior results obtained when a full biophysical profile was added to other prenatal tests of foetal wellbeing.

'Is it your opinion that she was negligent not to have done so?'

The expert hesitated, not wanting to dent his reputation by use of careless language. 'I think that negligent is perhaps too harsh a word. I think that she would have gained more information if she had.'

'Could that information have influenced the outcome of Brendan Edwards' life?'

'It could.'

Gordon St Jude tried to stare down the witness. 'Dr Willard, you refer to biophysical profile as if Dr Kent barely investigated Tracey Edwards' baby. Of the five tests which make up this profile you refer to, Dr Kent ordered three. She investigated foetal movement, amniotic fluid volume, and the baby's heart tracing on several occasions and found them to be normal. There is a body of literature which confirms that these three are the most important tests.' He held aloft several hundred pages of Sylvie's photocopied research. 'Indeed, Professor Jones has already conceded as much to this court. What do you think would have been gained by investigating the other two components of the profile, those of foetal tone and foetal breathing?'

'Both would give a more complete picture of foetal well-being,' replied Dr Willard assuredly.

'Are they likely to be abnormal if the other tests are normal?'

'They could be.'

'But it's not likely, is it, Dr Willard?'

'They would not have been incorporated in the biophysical profile if they were not independent variables,' the expert replied stonily. He had made the decision himself in 1983.

'But in many hundreds of studies from major centres around the world, foetal tone and breathing are almost always normal if the other tests are normal, aren't they, Dr Willard?' The barrister could be just as mulish. He had the evidence to support his claim, but was seeking a concession from the plaintiffs' expert. He was not going to get it.

'As I have already said, they are independent tests; tests of considerable importance. If they always mimicked the other components, they would be redundant, wouldn't they?'

The barrister moved on. 'As well as assessing foetal

406

movement, heart tracing and amniotic fluid volume, Dr Kent did some other tests of foetal wellbeing, didn't she, Dr Willard? Could you tell us what tests they were?'

It was a nice tactical approach, and the witness was momentarily wrong-footed. He did not want to be putting the defendant's case, and looked at Ernestine for guidance.

Gordon St Jude seized upon his hesitation. 'I'm sorry, Dr Willard, I was under the impression that you had familiarised yourself with the entirety of the case. Would you like me to remind you which other tests Dr Kent ordered to reassure herself that Brendan Edwards was well?'

This was the only time Gordon St Jude had the upper hand with the Melbourne expert. Despite the exhaustive research of Julia, Sylvie and Leo, and the barrister's exemplary questioning, Robert Willard cast a large shadow of doubt over the adequacy of Julia's handling of Tracey Edwards' pregnancy. He repeatedly, categorically and convincingly argued that young Brendan Edward's disability was most likely due to events which occurred in the last few weeks of pregnancy or during labour. Events which could have been prevented by careful, indeed mainstream, obstetric management.

On re-examination, Ernestine closed strongly. 'Is it possible, Dr Willard, that Brendan Edwards is so damaged because the period of his distress in labour was in fact considerably longer than has been recognised?'

'Of course,' he asserted, tendering no evidence for his claim. 'That is why high-risk babies should always be monitored continuously in labour.'

As the final plaintiffs' witness was released and the court emptied for the lunch break, Julia sat wretchedly immobile. What if Robert Willard was right? Maybe she should have ordered those extra tests. Perhaps she ought to have induced. Maybe she should have continuously electronically monitored. Perhaps she ought to have done an elective caesarean section. Maybe any or all of these things could have prevented Brendan's awful damage.

If Robert Willard had convinced her, what effect must he have had on the judge?

She could barely eat lunch. In fact, she thought she was going to be sick. Sylvie encouraged her to at least have a couple of mouthfuls. 'You don't want to testify on an empty stomach, Julia.'

'At least I won't throw up all over the courtroom.'

They were strolling around the shops; Julia had been too restless to sit. Sensing her nervousness, Sylvie tried to comfort her. 'I don't think there's too much to worry about, really I don't. The case has gone very well so far, much better than we'd hoped.'

'Robert Willard didn't go well,' Julia disputed.

'So?' challenged Sylvie. 'That's only one. Their other experts have been very ordinary. On balance, you'd have to agree we're in front.'

'Maybe.' She was unconvinced.

Sylvie seized the grudging concession. 'It's not maybe, it's a fact. Now, I suggest you concentrate on your excellent obstetric standard and how you're going to knock the socks off the judge with what a wonderful doctor you are.'

As they walked back into the courtroom Julia tried to focus her mind as Sylvie instructed, but she was riven by doubt. Was her obstetric standard excellent? Could she defend it? Suddenly she wasn't so sure.

Gordon St Jude called the first witness for the defence, inviting an increasingly pale Dr Julia Kent to identify herself to the court, stating her full name, her qualifications and her present place of employment.

Julia turned slightly towards Judge Owen, and spoke clearly and slowly, reciting the details as they had told her to, and making sure to mention that she had graduated with an honours degree from the University of Central Sydney. She was currently working as a consultant obstetrician and gynaecologist in private practice. She had appointments at both a public and private hospital and was also an accredited lecturer of the university in its clinical school at Royal Eastside Hospital. The judge seemed to make a note of this.

Turning back to face Gordon St Jude, Julia noticed for the first time that there were two young men she'd never seen before, sitting in the public gallery next to Sylvie. Both held notepads and pens. Both were writing. Both looked up to meet her gaze, businesslike but not unfriendly. Julia lost her breath. She knew who they were. Journalists. Finally come to get her.

Finishing with the highlights of his witness's CV, Gordon moved on to her professional standing. 'Dr Kent, could you tell the court whether Royal Eastside Hospital collects data regarding perinatal outcomes for quality assurance purposes.'

'It does.' The words came out sharply. The young men looked up from their notes and smiled at her. Julia looked down, distraught.

'How long has it been doing this?'

'What?'

'The hospital, Dr Kent. How long has it been collecting these statistics?'

'Since before I first came as a registrar in training.' Julia coughed nervously, clearing her throat.

She saw the journalists' eyes dart from herself to their notes and back again, their fingers moving quickly. Writing. About her. Though she tried desperately not to look at them, they were the only thing in the courtroom that she saw. As the pressure built behind her eyes, she barely heard Gordon's question. She looked at the barrister hopelessly and he asked her again.

'What statistics about the outcome of babies born at Royal Eastside are collected by your department?'

'All deaths,' she caught her breath. 'All deaths of babies over twenty weeks' gestation are recorded and discussed at a meeting. A monthly meeting,' she clarified hoarsely.

'Is anything else discussed, Dr Kent?' prompted Gordon as Ming looked on, anxious and bewildered. They had been over these questions many times and this was the easy part, after all. Sylvie also watched in horror. She'd known Julia was nervous, but this was unbelievable. She was shocked at her friend's performance; it was totally unrecognisable from the assured confidence she'd displayed during their hours of practice.

'Discussed?' Julia croaked.

'Apart from the babies that have died, is anything else discussed at these monthly meetings?'

'Yes,' Julia said, finally remembering her script. 'All babies admitted to neonatal intensive care are discussed.'

Gordon St Jude asked if statistics were kept on each individual practitioner. They were, but not by name. Each practitioner was denoted only by a number in order to protect confidentiality and promote frank and honest discussion of mistakes and poor outcomes. Especially preventable poor outcomes. She said the last words with quiet selfconsciousness.

'Does anyone know which number denotes which practitioner?'

'Only the statistician who compiles the data.'

Gordon handed Julia a sheet of paper and asked her to identify it. She stole a desperate glance at the journalists behind him as she took it. She was frantic now, but responded to Ming's glare, though she could not lift her voice above a whisper. She understood why Tracey had been so inaudible.

'These are the data from the last five years' meetings, in columns for each practitioner as denoted by a number,' she gasped.

'These are the statistics you were speaking about?'

'Yes.' Her eyes darted everywhere, seeking escape.

'Do you know which number you are?'

'What?'

'The numbers, Dr Kent, do you know which one you are?'

'Oh,' she swallowed, her mouth parched. 'Yes, I know, I do know. I found out for the purposes of this hearing. I am,' she paused, picking up her glass and draining it of water. 'I am number six.'

Gordon continued to look at her for a moment before turning to the judge. He had in his possession a Statutory Declaration from the statistician who compiled the record. Dr Kent was indeed number six of the thirteen practitioners on the list.

The statistician had helpfully tabulated and graphed the data so that interpreting them was very simple. It could be seen at a glance that, in each year of the past five, Julia was in the best-performing quartile of the cohort on all measures of perinatal outcome. The graph in particular was compelling.

Although the data spoke for themselves, Gordon was to have taken Julia through them to emphasise her excellent clinical standards. Ming shook her head. Instead, Gordon addressed the judge as he held the graph aloft, affirming loudly and proudly that it clearly demonstrated that Dr Kent's obstetric practice was consistently associated with a very low rate of poor outcome. Even more importantly, he stressed, Dr Kent scored an almost negligible rate of preventable poor outcome, as judged by her peers.

Julia was desperate to be out of the witness box, out of the court. Her distress was increasing every minute. The young journalists seemed unmoved by her torment. They now looked very stern and refused to return her glance when it came their way. They'd clearly made up their minds and were going to denounce her. She started to panic.

As all faces turned to her expectantly, she realised that she had not heard Gordon St Jude's question. She tried to ask him to repeat it but could not move her mouth. The words would not come out. She just closed her eyes, dropped her head and struggled to breathe, fully aware that this was not the image she was supposed to project, but unable to do anything about it.

'Are you all right, Dr Kent?' asked Judge Percival Owen.

'No,' she replied truthfully.

'In that case, I think that this would be a good place to conclude for the day, Mr St Jude. We will continue with Dr Kent's testimony in the morning.'

Julia sat mutely in the witness box, unable to move until Tracey's team departed the court some minutes after the judge. Gordon St Jude left soon after, disappointed in his witness's performance, but a little self-righteous as well. He knew how critically Julia viewed him, and wasn't displeased to see her falter. The journalists were also gone, and only Sylvie and Ming remained.

Ming helped Julia down.

411

'Are you feeling any better?' She was completely baffled at the change in her client.

'I'm okay,' Julia smiled feebly, still ashen. 'I'm just glad they've gone.'

'Who've gone?' asked Ming uncertainly.

'The journalists.'

Ming glanced around. 'Which journalists, Julia?'

'The ones who were sitting next to Sylvie.'

'You mean Brad and Andy?' The penny finally dropped for Ming. She shook her head miserably. 'Oh, Julia, I'm so sorry. I should have mentioned them to you. They're not journalists, they're law students. They're doing an assignment on the Supreme Court and they asked me if they could sit in. And I said they could. I'm so sorry.'

Julia looked more relieved than upset, still unaware how badly she'd performed and how dearly it had cost her in the eyes of the judge. 'So they're definitely not journalists?' she asked breathlessly.

'No, they're law students.'

'There weren't any journalists in the courtroom at all?' she repeated, needing to be certain.

'No, Julia. None.'

'Oh.'

Chapter 46

Ming was relieved to see Julia looking a little better the following morning, noting the extra care she'd taken with her dress and make-up, and hoping it signalled a turn-around in her testimony. For her part, Julia doubted the facade would translate into a better performance. As the relief at her mistake about the journalists had faded, glum appreciation of how unprofessional her collapse on the stand must have looked to Judge Owen had replaced it. But, rather than being motivated to repair the damage, she was simply worn out. She just wanted her testimony over.

She smiled bravely as she approached Leo, who'd arrived early, fully briefed by an overwrought Sylvie about yesterday's events. It was obvious he'd had another bad night with Sandra. There couldn't be more than a few weeks left, Julia thought sadly. 'It's not right, Leo. You should be at home.'

'Sandra insisted I come, Julia. It was one of the few lucid things she said all night.' Julia could tell his heart was breaking.

Gordon St Jude resumed the questioning which had been prematurely terminated the previous day. 'Dr Kent, could you please take us through Tracey Edwards' pregnancy, from her first visit when she was ten weeks' pregnant, until her labour.'

The barrister, under instruction from Richard and heavily influenced by Ming, was taking this slowly. They'd insisted he do it this way to allow Julia to regain her confidence. Her voice, initially tremulous, became stronger as she dealt with the familiar details.

The barrister continued: 'Could you explain the tests which you ordered during the last month of Tracey's pregnancy, after you noticed that Brendan was small?'

There had been three ultrasounds over five weeks, demonstrating a small but normally growing baby. Plotted on a graph, it could easily be seen that his growth followed the normal curve. The ultrasounds also showed that there was a normal amount of amniotic fluid around him. This was a reassuring sign of foetal health. There had also been three normal 'flow studies', special ultrasounds which assessed the amount of blood flowing to the baby from the placenta, and three normal CTGs or heart tracings.

'Is it normal to order this many tests late in pregnancy, Dr Kent?'

'No it isn't. These tests were only done because I had noticed that the baby was small. Usually I don't order any tests at this stage of pregnancy.'

Gordon St Jude drew to his full height to ask the next, very important question. 'Dr Kent, if Brendan already had severe neurological abnormalities at the time you ordered these tests, why didn't they show up?'

'Because problems such as Brendan's are not easily detected until after the baby is born.'

'Could you explain this further to the court?'

Julia noticed Percival Owen lean forward, and strove to speak loudly and slowly. She tried to sound impressive, but after the shock of yesterday, her words came out flat.

The tests that were available in late pregnancy essentially demonstrated whether a baby looked normal, which Brendan did, and whether it was getting enough blood and oxygen, which Brendan was. The tests didn't pick up neurological abnormalities.

414

This was because a baby didn't have to do anything inside the uterus except roll around a bit. He didn't have to sit, or crawl, or walk, or feed himself. He didn't have to do any of the things which would show up this sort of impairment.

'So he could easily have had these severe neurological problems and still have normal tests?'

'Yes.'

They moved on to the labour. Gordon St Jude went directly to the question of continuous electronic monitoring. Julia replied that, having assured herself that the baby was not oxygen deprived and, with an excellent midwife available, she did not think that continuous monitoring offered any benefit. Her decision was only partly influenced by Tracey Edwards' express wish to have an intervention-free labour. She simply did not think that tying her patient to the CTG machine was necessary.

'When would you use continuous electronic monitoring?' asked Mr St Jude.

'In a case such as this, with spontaneous labour and an experienced midwife, not very often. Probably only if the midwife was having difficulty hearing the foetal heart, such as occurs in obese patients.' Instinctively, many eyes went to the slight form of Tracey Edwards. 'Or if the midwife thought the heartbeat was abnormal. Or if she had another patient to care for as well, so that she could not stay with my patient as much as she needed to listen to the heartbeat regularly.'

'Are patients often left unattended in labour?'

'There are times when it's unavoidable.' Staffing levels were based on an average number of patients. Sometimes there was no one at all in labour, while at other times there was double the average. On those occasions each midwife, of necessity, had to care for more than one patient. Inadequate staffing was one of the major reasons for the increased use of electronic monitoring in labour.

'You feel that electronic monitoring is overused?'

'I do. Very much so. Hook the patient up, confine her to bed, and leave her alone. It's cheaper than paying more midwives. It's easier for everyone.' She paused. This was something she believed in strongly and it rallied her. 'Except the patient, of course.'

415

Gordon St Jude nodded.

'Was Tracey Edwards left unattended in labour?'

'According to the statement by the midwife, she was left only briefly, a few minutes here and there, and only when Monica needed to fetch things or report to the charge midwife about her patient's progress.'

'So conditions were optimal for regular, intermittent listening to the foetal heart with the Doppler?'

'Yes.'

'And your patient was able to have the natural labour she had repeatedly requested?'

'She was.'

Gordon took Julia through the recognition of foetal distress and the delivery with forceps soon after. With his guidance Julia emphasised to the court how frequent a problem foetal distress in labour was, a daily problem indeed, and how quickly Brendan Edwards had been delivered after an abnormally slow heartbeat was detected. So quickly, Julia explained, that in the ordinary course of events, he should have been fine.

Whilst her answers were the truth, her manner was halting and diffident, unconvincing, even insincere. The strain of each question creased her face. Every answer demanded an effort of concentration that was almost beyond her. As her testimony progressed, her head felt as if it was filling with cotton wool. Unable to fully process what Gordon St Jude was asking, she instead relied on her memory of what she had said at the practice sessions. The effect was one of rehearsed disingenuousness.

In the break for lunch, Julia and Ming bought sushi at a stall and walked several blocks to the park in search of elusive winter sunshine. Leo had gone home to check on Sandra and the two women were alone. The lawyer congratulated her client on her performance this morning, though both knew it was lacklustre. Julia recognised that Ming was trying to bolster her confidence before she faced Ernestine's cross-examination this afternoon.

They spoke about Tracey. She was looking better this week, they

416

agreed, and seemed to be smoking less. But she was clearly desperate for it all to end; it had been much harder than she'd expected.

'Especially doing it on her own,' added Julia. 'Without a husband to help her, I mean.'

Ming nodded. Julia had touched on something that had been quietly bothering the young barrister. 'It's funny, you know, Brendan's father not turning up at all. He hasn't even put in a claim.'

Julia was confused. 'He hasn't been involved for five years, Ming. Why would he turn up now?'

'For the money,' the young lawyer replied.

'What money?' Julia was completely lost.

'Pain and suffering. Mental trauma. All the errant fathers turn up when there's money on the table.'

'Really?'

The barrister explained that there had even been a case where the father was not only not involved with his disabled child, he had actually changed his name so that he could not be found for child support payments. For nine years. But, once the mother looked like getting some compensation, up he popped. Not seen for all that time, and there he was, large as life, seeking his share of the compensation.

'Did he get it?' Julia was incredulous.

'Fifty thousand dollars! He'd suffered dreadfully, you know.' Ming laughed. 'That's why it strikes me as strange that Brett Halsted hasn't turned up for his cut of the action.'

'Hopefully there's not going to be anything to have a cut of,' replied Julia, mildly put out.

'Even so,' persisted Ming. 'The fathers usually show.'

As Ernestine stood up to cross-examine her, Julia sat rigidly, watching the grandmotherly barrister weigh up her approach. She must be delighted with how badly I've done so far, she thought, giving in to her bitterness. I'll bet she's trying to work out how best to take advantage of it without alienating Judge Owen by pushing too hard. It came as no surprise when Ernestine went first to the issue of electronic monitoring.

417

'What are these, Dr Kent?' Ernestine indicated three large black folders with the Royal Eastside insignia on them.

'The labour ward protocols.'

Ernestine handed her one of the volumes. 'Could you turn to the chapter on Small for Gestational Age babies.'

Julia located it easily.

'Could you please read out the section on the management of labour in such babies.'

Julia obliged. 'SGA babies should be continuously electronically monitored in labour.'

'Brendan Edwards was an SGA baby, wasn't he, Dr Kent?'

Julia was suddenly feisty. 'Yes and no. He was small, but a large number of tests over five weeks amply demonstrated that he was not oxygen deprived. As such, he could be expected to withstand labour reasonably well.'

'He fell under the classification of SGA, didn't he, Dr Kent? Being only two point four kilograms?'

'It is a pretty crude classification, Mrs Hillier, based as it is solely on size rather than wellbeing. It is a classification that was developed when weight was the only thing we could assess about a baby. We now have a much fuller understanding about foetal wellbeing.'

Ernestine hesitated, perhaps surprised at the change in the witness but unwilling to leave matters where they stood. 'These protocols are updated every two years, Dr Kent, and the most recent one still insists that SGA babies be continuously monitored in labour.'

'It does. But the protocols are drawn up with the least experienced practitioner in mind, people such as student midwives and junior residents. People new to the practice of obstetrics. At consultant level, the protocols are simply guidelines, discretionary recommendations which can be set aside if there is judged to be a better way to manage a patient.'

'The way you managed Brendan Edwards was not necessarily better, was it, Dr Kent?'

'You have yet to establish that, Mrs Hillier,' Julia replied, grateful for Ming's coaching.

Chapter 47

Ming and Julia went down in the lift together, saying little. Even though the cross-examination had landed few punches, there was no doubt that the big impression everyone had assumed Julia would make on the judge had failed to eventuate. As the reality slowly sank in that her time on the stand was now over, Julia thought she might cry. Not principally because she'd damaged her chance of winning. It was letting Sylvie and Leo down that tormented her. They had given up months of their time for her, expecting that she, in return, would impress Judge Owen with a demonstration of her professionalism and competence. Especially under pressure. And she had squandered it.

'I'm sorry I went to pieces, Ming,' she said as they reached the street and were about to part.

Her lawyer, still kicking herself for her own unwitting role in Julia's poor performance, sought to console her. 'You were fine, Julia. Giving testimony on the stand is always harder than people expect. Certainly harder than doing it around a kitchen table.'

'You can say that again,' Julia agreed weakly.

There were no lights flashing on the answering machine when Julia walked into her house. It was funny how on the good days there had always been a queue of people wanting to talk, but yesterday and today they were leaving her alone. She dropped her bag, discarded her clothes and stepped into the shower. And stayed there until the hot water ran out. Dressed in an old tracksuit, she stood in front of her dressing table mirror cursorily combing her hair. It was the same mirror she'd practised her testimony in front of for months, even before she'd known it as testimony. Since the Statement of Claim had arrived, she'd stood here and defended herself, arresting the court with her confident manner, convincing the judge of the rightness of her actions, bringing the trial to an immediate end with the irresistible truth of her declarations.

What a shame the real thing had been so uninspiring. Just a few days ago she had been confident of winning her case. What if now, along with no Patrick, no Emma, no Sandra, no Tony and no Angie, there was also to be no victory? It didn't bear thinking about.

She turned on the TV and watched the early evening news. The ads made her realise she was hungry. She knew from last night when she'd ordered pizza that there was nothing to eat in her kitchen. She was just trying to locate the energy to do something about it when the doorbell rang. It was Tony.

'What are you doing here?' she gulped, nearly falling backwards.

'Delivering your mail.' He was clearly edgy.

'What?' she asked, puzzled.

He handed over the bundle of letters. 'They were sticking out of your letter box as I came past.'

They stood in awkward silence for a few moments. Finally Tony asked if he could come in. As Julia stood back to let him through, she realised how terrible she must look, her face pale and waxy, her eyes receding into their sockets. She blushed as he passed her, his just-showered freshness making her suddenly giddy. Embarrassed, she looked down at the mail in her hand and caught sight of the postcard on top. It was from Emma in Paris; there had been one every day this week. It was brief and jokey, with a happy reference to an old friend she was staying with for a few days. Lots of love, hope you are well.

Julia passed the postcard to Tony and went into the kitchen to pour them both a glass of wine. He could probably do with the refreshment; she could certainly do with the fortification. He still hadn't explained why he was here. They sat at the table and she waited nervously for him to say something. Eventually, he asked if she would like some aspirin for her headache.

It wasn't a question she had expected. 'Is it that obvious?'

'It was inevitable, wasn't it?'

They got some take-away and took it down to the grass near the beach. There was not much of a moon and they sat on a bench near a lamp, Julia selecting the dimmer end. She was grateful that Tony had persuaded her out of the house. It provided a brief distraction from her woes, a different backdrop anyway.

At the same time, she was on high alert, waiting for the cruel clarification of his visit, half-expecting Angie to appear at any moment so that together they could break the news to her. They were probably telling Geoff tonight as well. Since Tony offered no explanation, finally she asked why he'd come.

He was immediately selfconscious. There was no particular reason, although he'd heard things hadn't gone as well for her on the witness stand as they might have. He'd been concerned for her, and thought she could probably do with some company. 'I didn't have much on this week, so I thought I'd come and see how you were.'

Julia briefly wondered why he didn't have much on; his practice was successful and he was usually booked up for months. She asked when he would be going back to Brisbane. He was intending to stay until the weekend, he said, but then he had to go back. It was his turn to have Antonio.

The implications hit Julia. 'You're not staying for me?' she asked sharply. She did not want his pity.

'Not at all,' he assured her quickly, reading her tone. 'I have a few things to attend to in Sydney.'

Of course he did, she thought, suddenly foolish.

They were both silent for a while, then Julia asked how Antonio was. Tony shrugged. Not too bad, considering what he was going through, although he was noticeably less secure and more demanding than previously. And of course he was missing his father. 'Although I sometimes think he misses you more than me,' added Tony. 'He's always asking about Ju-ya.'

They walked home slowly in the dark. As his voice and his fragrance and his quiet strength surrounded her, Julia was sure he must be able to hear her heart, leaping at ribs she had until now thought quite solid. Jerkily she pulled to the far edge of the footpath. Tony did not move closer. Once they reached her house, he declined her offer of a lift to his hotel and they waited together for his taxi under the street light at her gate.

She knew that she had only these few minutes to tell him. Things were going to be awkward for them from now on, and there might never be a time so suitable. She spoke slowly, her gaze trained on the traffic passing the end of her street.

She wanted to thank him for all the help he'd given her at this time. Not just this evening, but the months of support that had gone before. She especially wanted to thank him for making sure she wasn't left to go through her trial by herself. She forced herself to look at him. 'I'm very grateful, Tony.'

Tony held her gaze but said nothing.

Julia wasn't finished. 'Which brings me to the support I gave you during your trial. Rather pitiful in comparison, wouldn't you say?'

'It was a completely different situation, Julia.' He turned away from her, embarrassed.

'Maybe it was and maybe it wasn't. But I wanted to say thank you. And I wanted to say sorry.'

Chapter 48

Julia emerged from the railway station and trudged slowly in the morning rush towards Gianni's Cafe. The first of the defence's medical experts, her colleague Julius Tong, would be giving evidence today, but Julia's mind was far from her trial; she was still thinking about last night. Tony's unexpected arrival had rocked her. She'd only recognised her feelings for him forty-eight hours ago. It would have been nice to have had time to prepare herself before having to face him. But he'd landed on her doorstep, come to comfort her in her misery.

That was Tony – thoughtful and modest. She had to suppress an unprompted comparison with Patrick who, while charming, tended to focus on himself. Like most people. But not Tony.

The evening had been pleasant, but it had been uncomfortable, probably for him as well. For herself, there had been a sense of finally coming home. Only to find tenants in her house. Her gaze had greedily traced the sinews of his long, gentle hands to where they disappeared beneath his jumper. Her contemplation had then shifted to the partly-shadowed skin in the soft hollow of his neck and, from there, been drawn to the movement of his generous mouth as it curled into a smile. And finally, she had come to rest in the deep pools of his kind eyes. And she had been rendered breathless by the familiar but forgotten feelings she had for him.

She thought she'd detected in him as well a hint of remembrance of what they'd once had. Overlaid with regret. But then she'd seen him focus resolutely on his future. The conclusion of the evening had been even more awkward; she'd embarrassed him with her parting apology. He'd darted into the taxi and left without even a wave. No doubt off to see Angie.

As the crowd bustled past, she found she'd stopped walking. Dear, dear Tony, her soul mate, the most wonderful man she'd ever known, the father of her daughter – and of her son. A voice screamed in her mind. Why did it have to be Angie, for God's sake? Why not someone she could compete with? Or at least someone she'd have the consolation of hating? She wondered if this was what it felt like to drown.

Marcia stepped into the warmth of Gianni's, still shivering as she approached the table where Julia now sat, stirring her coffee mindlessly. 'I keep forgetting how cold and miserable the city is,' she said.

'A city of shadows and wind tunnels,' agreed Julia, thankful for Marcia's tact about her red-rimmed eyes. 'An impressive victory of greed over natural advantage, wouldn't you say?'

As Marcia took her seat, Julia demanded to know everything that had been happening at the surgery. The secretary happily obliged, hoping her reports would cheer her friend. Marina Sorensen, the PR doyenne, had been in for a postnatal visit with Sylvie. Her blood pressure was now completely normal, her body back to its pre-pregnancy shape, and her tiny daughter dressed in the most beautiful outfit by Collette Dinnigan.

'I didn't know she did babywear.'

'I think it was a one-off,' confided her secretary.

Jane Steel had finally gone into labour on Monday, five days overdue, and had been badly let down by her uterus. It failed to contract adequately, despite help from oxytocin, and, after ten hours stuck at four centimetres, she had finally agreed to Leo's suggestion of a caesarean. The baby, a boy, was absolutely gorgeous by all accounts, but was also letting her down. He seemed to know nothing about four-hourly feeds.

'And finally,' said Marcia, bursting with the wonderful news, 'Grace Chan is having twins. And everything is going fabulously. I've given her an appointment to see you on the first day you get back.'

How long ago it all seemed, thought Julia curiously, since she was a doctor who saw patients.

Julia and Marcia were already present when Ernestine walked into the court with her team and greeted Tracey. Soon after, Gordon St Jude hurried in and took his place at the bar table. He was the first of the defence team to arrive, which was exceptional. It seemed to Julia that it often took him half an hour to remember where they were up to. There were days she doubted he even knew which case it was. If he was here, it must be ten o'clock.

At that moment, Mabel Appleton preceded Judge Owen into the courtroom. There was still no sign of either Richard or Ming. Richard was sometimes delayed by the other cases he had to coordinate, but Ming was always early. Julia hoped the young barrister wasn't sick. Not now, when she needed her so badly. After the dismal events of the past two days, it might only be Ming who could save her.

As Judge Owen took his place on the bench, Gordon St Jude looked up from his papers. Realising for the first time that he was the only defence lawyer present, he checked his watch, set aside his documents and quickly opened the folder Ming had prepared for the next witness.

Dr Julius Tong had been the director of neonatal services at Royal Eastside Hospital since 1993. It was the biggest unit in the state and he was an acknowledged expert in his field. He had been directly involved in Brendan Edwards' care and a party to the debates between various experts as to what exactly was wrong with him. He disagreed with the view that the child exhibited features consistent with birth asphyxia. The characteristics of his disabilities were simply not typical.

Gordon went straight to one of the weaknesses in their own case. He asked the paediatrician why the diagnosis 'birth asphyxia' appeared on Brendan Edwards' Interim Discharge Summary. In his measured way, the doctor explained that the form had been completed by his colleague, Dr Pauline Menzies. It was her belief that hypoxia during labour was at least partly responsible for the child's condition. Dr Tong disagreed, but since Dr Menzies was the consultant responsible for patient care on the day the child was transferred to Special Care, it was her job to complete the paperwork.

'Who completed the Final Discharge Summary when the child was discharged from the hospital altogether?'

'I did. As director of the service, I complete all Final Discharge Summaries.'

'What was the diagnosis you made?'

'Neurological impairment of unknown cause.'

'That's a bit unsatisfactory, isn't it, Dr Tong?'

It was, agreed the doctor, but if it was the truth then it should be recorded as such. It was far better to have a category of 'unknown cause', and to continue the search, than to ascribe an incorrect cause. Far better for the child, and far better for national health statistics.

Gordon asked Dr Tong to explain why he was unhappy with a diagnosis of birth asphyxia in the case of Brendan Edwards. The expert said that the diagnosis required proof that there was hypoxia and acidosis during labour.

'That's lack of oxygen and a build-up of acid?' clarified the barrister.

'Yes.'

'How do you test for this?'

The best way was to take a sample from the baby's umbilical cord at the time of delivery. 'This tells you exactly what the situation is at the moment of birth.'

'Did you get this sample?'

'No. Dr Kent provided a piece of umbilical cord for this purpose, but it was accidentally discarded.'

'By whom?'

'By our intensive care registrar.'

'Does this happen often, Dr Tong?'

Dr Tong explained that it didn't happen often, thankfully. But
it did sometimes. A baby as sick as Brendan required a lot of
attention. In the process of intubating, providing oxygen, and
transferring a child urgently to neonatal intensive care, the piece
of cord sitting on the resuscitation trolley could be overlooked.
It was an emergency, after all.

'Without the cord sample, Dr Tong, how can you test for acidosis and hypoxia?' asked Gordon St Jude.

'We can collect a sample from the baby himself.'

'And did you do this?'

'Yes.'

'And what did that sample show, Dr Tong?'

'The result was normal.'

'Are you telling the court, Dr Tong, that there was no blood test
evidence of hypoxia and acidosis in the case of Brendan Edwards?'

'That is right.'

'What other features do you look for as evidence of birth
asphyxia?'

'Neurological irritation. Especially seizures within the first
two days, generally within the first twenty-four hours.'

'Did Brendan exhibit these?'

'No. He did develop seizures, but not until the fifth day after
birth.'

'What does this suggest?'

'Another cause for his problem. Possibly an inherited condition or a metabolic disorder. Maybe a viral infection. Even drug
withdrawal. But not hypoxia.'

Ernestine stood and looked at the witness. 'Dr Tong, you said to
Mr St Jude that causes other than hypoxia needed to be considered
with respect to Brendan Edwards' disability and seizures.'

'That's right.'

'Causes such as inherited conditions, metabolic disorders, viral infection and drug withdrawal?' she read from her notes.

'Yes.'

'But you looked for all those things, didn't you, Dr Tong? And found nothing?'

'That doesn't mean that one of them is not responsible. It just means that it is beyond the limits of our current knowledge to ascertain. Which is why my diagnosis was neurological impairment of unknown cause.'

'But you looked and found nothing,' Ernestine repeated.

'Yes.'

'Just like you looked for hypoxia and did not find it.'

'Hypoxia is more readily detectable than the other conditions referred to,' defended the paediatrician.

'But you still looked and didn't find it. Just like you looked for the other causes of disability and didn't find them. Isn't that right, doctor?'

'Well, yes, but –'

He went to clarify the distinction but Ernestine was onto the next question. She asked Dr Tong about the sample he took from baby Brendan to test for hypoxia and acidosis.

'How old was Brendan when you took the sample?'

'About forty minutes.'

'That seems a long time to wait to take such an important sample, doesn't it?'

'The time passes quickly in an emergency, Mrs Hillier. We had transferred Brendan from the labour ward, resuscitated him, stabilised him and put the lines in before we took the first blood sample.'

'And all that time you were giving him oxygen, weren't you?'

'Yes.'

'So you tested blood that had been receiving oxygen for forty minutes and claimed not to find lack of oxygen.' She tried to look disbelieving.

Dr Tong had been expecting the question. It was a common issue in the neonatal intensive care unit. The oxygen level was not the most important measure – the acid and base levels were. Even after forty minutes of oxygen, they would not be back to normal if they had been seriously abnormal at birth.

Ernestine was not put off. She asked if it would be possible for there to be some hypoxia and acidosis present at birth, but for the levels to be back to normal when the baby was tested after forty minutes of oxygen.

Dr Tong conceded quietly that it would be possible. 'But only if the level was mildly abnormal to start with.'

'So your test after forty minutes of oxygen is useless, isn't it?' the barrister continued provocatively. 'It tells us nothing about the level at the moment of birth, does it?'

'That's not entirely true. The level of acidosis required to cause brain damage does not correct itself that quickly.'

'But it does correct, doesn't it? That's why you give the oxygen.'

Gordon was quick to re-examine his witness. 'How often are doctors from your neonatal intensive care unit called to the labour ward to be present at deliveries where there might be some asphyxia, Dr Tong?'

'Several times a day.'

'That often?'

'Yes. Which is one of the reasons we have both a registrar and a resident in the unit twenty-four hours a day. And often a consultant as well.'

'And what is the usual outcome of these deliveries?'

'The babies are fine. Most don't even need to go to the nursery. They can stay with their mothers.'

'So these are false alarms?'

'Not exactly. It's just that the possibility that the baby might be asphyxiated is far more common than the baby actually being asphyxiated.'

'So, how often do you see cases of true birth asphyxia, Dr Tong?'

'Severe asphyxia, once a month, maybe. Lesser degrees, once a week.'

'And how often do you see babies like Brendan Edwards?'

'A handful of times a year.'

'Does birth asphyxia commonly cause the disabilities he has?'

'No. Asphyxia is not generally thought to cause his sort of problems.'

As they broke for lunch, Julia couldn't help noticing Ernestine chatting happily with her team; she clearly considered Dr Tong's concessions to be significant. The plaintiffs' position had improved immeasurably since the weekend, and Ernestine knew it. No doubt she would be looking to see what concessions she could squeeze from the remaining three defence witnesses. And, since the DDO was having trouble keeping its lawyers in the court, you didn't have to be a genius to know Ernestine thought things were looking promising.

Gordon also seemed reasonably happy with the morning and his witness's testimony. Dr Tong had been honest and credible, and had convincingly argued against birth asphyxia as the cause of the child's disabilities. That he was not stridently unbending was a point in his favour.

The defence barrister did not seem happy, however, with the continued patchy presence of his legal team. Richard had turned up some minutes after the examination in chief of Dr Tong began, but Ming was missing for most of the morning, appearing only as the lunch break began. Even then she barely glanced at Gordon, or indeed at anyone, before dragging Richard Tripp out of the courtroom and propelling him rapidly towards the lift.

Julia, peering anxiously after her lawyers, accompanied Julius Tong from the courtroom. She was pleased with her colleague's testimony and grateful that he had appeared for her. But she was also embarrassed that he'd had to become involved in her trial. She thanked him for coming.

'Julia, it was a pleasure to be able to help you. Cases like this have to be defended. Otherwise all the good obstetricians will retire from practice,' he added, nodding wisely and smiling his gentle smile.

Ming was back at Gordon's side at the bar table at two o'clock as the second expert witness for the defence, Francine O'Dwyer, the professor of paediatrics at the University of South-Western Australia, was called. This time it was Richard who was missing, his absence accentuated by the junior counsel's furtive glances at the door.

Gordon took Professor O'Dwyer through her CV. In her early fifties, small and intense with keen blue eyes and a helmet of straight steel-grey hair, she was the author of several textbooks and an expert in childhood neurological disorders. Gordon reviewed with her the available information about Brendan Edwards' first few days of life. He asked about the child's current condition and that at birth, about his first blood gas assessment, his inability to suck, his early and later head ultrasounds, and the occurrence of seizures on day five.

They then discussed his subsequent development. The professor had read Brendan Edwards' entire medical record and had examined the child on two occasions. Her opinion was almost identical to that of Dr Tong. She could not say exactly what his problem was, except that it was unlikely to be related to birth asphyxia.

'How unlikely, professor?'

'Highly unlikely.'

Gordon thanked his witness and sat down.

In every case there were witnesses a barrister would rather not question. Occasionally, if it seemed that an expert's opinion was immutable, counsel actually chose to pass on cross-examination. While this left the expert's testimony unchallenged, sometimes it was the better option. But it looked bad; not so much to a jury, who assumed that there was a good reason for the tactic, as to a judge, who knew the compromise it suggested.

Ernestine could not leave Professor O'Dwyer unchallenged

but was fearful of worsening the situation. She even flirted with the idea of letting Michael cross-examine the expert from Perth. She could then look surprised when he failed to score any points. She wouldn't do it to him, of course, but it had been done to her more than once when she was the junior barrister.

'Professor, you've told the court that you don't know why Brendan Edwards is disabled.'

'That's right. But I don't think that it's an asphyxial injury,' Professor O'Dwyer reiterated before Ernestine could stop her.

'But you don't know for sure, do you?'

'That's what I've said.'

'We have other medical experts who believe that Brendan's disability is related to hypoxia at birth.'

'They are entitled to their opinion, but I believe they are wrong.'

'Is it common for medical experts to disagree about such things?' It was a good question for such a steely witness.

'It is.'

'You're saying it is common for medical experts to disagree?' repeated Ernestine.

'Yes.'

'In that case, one party is right, and one is wrong, professor?'

'Yes.'

'So it could be you that is wrong, could it not?'

Just as Julia was deciding that there was nothing worth watching on television and wishing she had something decent to read, the phone rang. It was Angie, keen to hear how the day had gone. She knew all about the law students and the drama earlier in the week. 'How did your experts get on?'

Julia gave an account. The defence witnesses had been quite good; it was Ming who was the worry. The junior barrister had been in and out all day. Not that there had been a lot for her to do, but the re-examination might have gone better if she had been there to help. And after court, Julia had wanted to speak to her, but she was gone again. Julia was growing very perturbed. There must be a serious problem for Ming to behave so uncharacteristically.

'She's probably chasing up documents,' Angie reasoned.

Julia disagreed. If that's all it was, she'd get Richard and the DDO to do it for her. No, it was more ominous than that. Something was definitely amiss.

'Perhaps she's just picked up some of Gordon St Jude's bad habits,' Angie joked. The groan on the other end of the phone made her abandon that approach. 'I'm sure things will be back to normal tomorrow, Julia.'

'I hope you're right, Angie.' Julia sounded desperate. 'I don't think I could cope with anything else going wrong at this stage.'

They spoke briefly about work. Sylvie had done Julia's public list at Eastside with Angie that afternoon. Everyone had asked again where Julia was. Sylvie told them she wasn't entirely sure, but thought it was a family thing. And that it was nearly sorted out.

'Did she tell them I was spending the next six months in Europe travelling with my daughter?'

'Are you?'

'Only in my dreams,' Julia replied woefully.

Neither spoke for a moment, and Julia suddenly felt ill at ease.

'If you're looking for Tony, he's not here, Angie,' she blurted. 'He's staying at the Pacific.'

'I know. I've spoken to him.'

Of course she had, thought Julia.

'You didn't want him to stay with you?' Angie asked softly.

Julia said she hadn't even considered it. As far as she was concerned, he may as well go back to Brisbane. There was no need for him to be here. Not for her anyway.

Angie did not reply.

'So he's still in Sydney then?' Julia asked nonchalantly. She hadn't spoken to him since last night.

'Yes. But he's going back to Brisbane tomorrow to collect Antonio.' Angie paused. 'And then he's returning to Sydney for the weekend.'

'Oh,' was all Julia could manage. Tony hadn't told her he'd be coming back.

433

Chapter 49

Richard and Ming were alone in the courtroom when Julia arrived early on the Friday morning of the third week of the trial. Both were speaking urgently into their phones, an air of frantic tension shimmering like a halo around them. But at least they were here. Julia's heart turned over as she came closer and heard what they were saying. Something was wrong with one of the last two witnesses, the critical obstetric experts. She found she was almost resigned to it. Another crisis.

She moved away from them and took a seat in the back row of the gallery. She did not want to hear any more.

Ernestine walked in at nine-thirty. While a little weary, the older woman wore an air of quiet confidence which slipped only slightly at the sight of Ming and Richard. Julia figured she'd lain awake half the night working out how to increase the lead she'd opened up over the DDO, how to turn it to victory over the next few days. For that's all that was left of *Edwards v Kent*: a few days. There were only two witnesses remaining: the obstetric experts for the defence. They would spill over into Monday, after which was the summing up by the barristers. It was said that the case would be finished by Tuesday.

At the arrival of the plaintiffs' senior counsel, both Ming and Richard left the courtroom. As they exited, whispering urgently, neither looked at Julia. She was no longer impervious to their unease. A sick feeling rose in her throat.

Gordon St Jude introduced Dr Con Raftos, the first of his two obstetric expert witnesses. The doctor was the chairman of the Continuing Education Committee of the College of Obstetricians, the body responsible for formulating best clinical practice guidelines. Just as importantly, he had a busy practice of his own and was a respected and experienced obstetrician. He was in his mid-forties, plump, swarthy and keenly alert. He had a large scar across his forehead which made him appear rather fiercer than he was. Julia hoped Ernestine would be intimidated.

Gordon took Dr Raftos through Tracey Edwards' pregnancy, discussing her small baby and the tests Dr Kent had ordered.

'Is it easy to detect that a baby is small, Dr Raftos?'

'No it is not. It is one of the hardest things that we as obstetricians have to do.'

'Did Dr Kent demonstrate good clinical practice in detecting that Brendan Edwards was small?'

'She did.'

'Dr Raftos, have you read the medical files of Tracey and Brendan Edwards?'

'I have.'

'In your professional opinion, after fifteen years as a busy obstetrician, why do you think that Brendan Edwards, at two point four kilograms, was so small?'

'Because he was abnormal.'

'Would you like to elaborate?'

'Yes, I would.'

It appeared there were two types of small baby. One was the asymmetrically small baby that resulted from chronic lack of oxygen. The brain's growth was favoured over that of the abdomen, and the baby was typically scrawny but with a normal-sized head. It was the type of poor growth that was more common. The second type was the symmetrically small baby where everything was in proportion. The baby was often perfectly healthy. On the other hand, it could be suffering from an abnormality or have been infected by a damaging virus like rubella.

'Which sort of small baby was Brendan Edwards?'

'Symmetrically small.'

'What conclusion do you draw from this, Dr Raftos?'

'Given what we now know about him, I conclude that Brendan Edwards was small because he was abnormal. And I also conclude that nothing indicates his smallness was due to lack of oxygen. Despite his mother's smoking,' he added pointedly.

'Do you consider that Dr Kent appropriately investigated the baby's smallness?'

'I do.'

'Would a full biophysical profile have added any benefit?'

'I do not believe so. Dr Kent did a large number of tests and these all demonstrated that the baby was small but growing well along the curve.'

Gordon turned momentarily to Ming to see if she had anything further for him to ask at this point. She was missing again. As was Richard. The older lawyer made as if to pick up some papers from the table and continued as if nothing was amiss.

Dr Raftos spoke about foetal wellbeing in labour, confirming earlier testimony that as long as close midwife care was available, continuous CTG monitoring had not been shown to offer a margin of safety over regular intermittent listening with a Doppler.

Gordon deemed this a good point on which to wind up.

'In conclusion then, Dr Raftos, what judgement would you make about Dr Kent's management of the pregnancy and delivery of Tracey Edwards?'

'I would say that it was exemplary.'

In her place at the solicitor's table, Julia let out her held breath. If there was a problem with one of the last witnesses, thank heavens it wasn't Con Raftos. She had needed his endorsement, personally as well as for her defence, needed to hear someone say she was a good doctor. As Ernestine stood for her turn with the expert, Julia felt her body go stiff. Please don't let her shoot him down, don't let her tarnish his evidence. She looked to Ming for support, but the junior barrister was still missing. Julia bit her lip.

The luncheon adjournment was announced and Judge Owen left the court. Julia turned to greet her father, dressed as usual in his one and only suit, but today with a rose in his lapel. She was pleased he had heard Dr Raftos's testimony, and relieved that Ernestine had so far scored few points in cross-examination.

'How are you, Dad?' she asked, leaning over the narrow barrier to kiss him.

'I'm fine, princess.'

'I like the flower,' she added, indicating his lapel.

'That's lucky,' he replied, reaching into a large plastic carry bag on the seat beside him. 'The rest of the bunch are for you. Bought, I'm afraid. Mine won't bloom till November.'

'Oh, Dad, how lovely. Orange roses, my favourites.'

'Are they?' asked the gardener, unsurprised. 'I thought I'd do something special for my last appearance. Apparently it will all be over before next Friday.'

'I certainly hope so,' said Julia, her weariness obvious.

'I'm not sure if I do, princess.' He looked at her cheekily. 'I've enjoyed these little trips to Sydney.'

Julia caught sight of Ming in the lobby, scurrying towards the street, her phone to her ear. She caught up with her between calls. The young lawyer stared at her distractedly, clearly preoccupied and in a terrible hurry. Julia determinedly told her how well Con Raftos was performing, but she knew Ming barely listened. She began to panic. Something was seriously wrong.

'Will Professor Henderson be here after lunch?' she managed to ask as her lawyer's phone rang again.

'No, he won't. There's been a change of plan,' Ming replied, without elaboration. Then her face softened and she touched Julia lightly on the arm. 'I'll tell you about it at two.' With that she disappeared into the crowd.

'Are you staying for the weekend, Dad?' Julia asked, trying not to think of what was going to happen this afternoon. Her father had been uncertain of his plans earlier in the week.

'I think I will, princess. Tony's organised a spot of fishing for us boys again tomorrow.'

'Oh?'

'Yes. I think Angie's bigger boy might join us as well this time,' he continued cheerfully. 'He heard what he missed out on last time.'

'How could anyone resist?'

Ming Tan stood at the bar table, the papers in her hand rustling with the tremor she could not control. 'Judge . . . Owen,' she faltered before the hushed court. The judge leaned forward. She spoke up. 'The defence would like to announce its intention to call a new witness to the stand this afternoon.'

'Is this a witness we have been notified about previously, Ms Tan?' The judge, brow furrowed, looked to Gordon at this point, but the senior counsel, stonily preoccupied with his fingernails, ignored him.

'No, Your Honour,' answered Ming, slowly gaining confidence. 'The witness is someone we did not know had potentially useful information until earlier this week. Information that has only been confirmed in the past twenty-four hours. In fact, he only agreed late yesterday to testify.'

'This is most irregular, Ms Tan.'

'We realise this, Your Honour, but we feel that the information the witness has is crucial to our client's defence.'

Judge Owen turned to the plaintiffs' barristers. 'Mrs Hillier, do you have anything to say before I rule on this?'

438

'I certainly do, Your Honour.' Ernestine rose. A few minutes before she had been briefed by Ms Tan about the nature of the intended new testimony. She knew that if the witness was permitted by Judge Owen, what he had to say would bring about the end of her case and her client's claim. This was not an outcome she would willingly facilitate. She spoke with all the authority her experience and seniority conferred.

'Your Honour, the injury to Brendan Edwards occurred over five years ago. Dr Kent was first notified three years ago of Ms Edwards' intention to seek damages for the injuries sustained by her son. Three years, Your Honour,' she repeated with emphasis. 'Surely three years is ample and sufficient time for the defence to assemble its witnesses. To bring in a new witness at this stage suggests either that they have been cavalier in the preparation of their case, or that this is a tactic of desperation in order to hijack the proceedings in its closing stages.

'It is entirely unacceptable to the plaintiffs that the defence's lack of preparation should be rewarded. Because rewarded is what it will be if they are allowed the advantage of producing a new witness at this stage. Not only is there an unfair advantage, Your Honour, but the introduction of a new defence witness at this point allows the plaintiffs' team no time to properly test the integrity of the testimony. It robs us of the opportunity to assure ourselves of the witness's credibility and to prepare for cross-examination in a thorough fashion.'

Judge Percival Owen nodded. They were the arguments he would have made. And they were compelling. Now was not the time for either side to be introducing witnesses of which the court had not been notified and who had not submitted pre-trial reports. He was inclined to disallow the defence team's request. On the other hand, if there was indeed evidence that would influence the outcome of the trial, then it should be heard. Whichever decision he made, one side would have grounds on which to appeal. But he had to make a decision. He was the judge after all.

'Ms Tan?'

'Yes, Your Honour.'

439

'I will allow you to call the witness, Ms Tan, but be warned. If his testimony is spurious or falls short of your claims, I will withdraw my leave to allow him to appear. Do you understand?'

'Yes, Your Honour.' Ming's tremor eased slightly; the first battle was won. She drew herself up to her full one hundred and fifty centimetres, took a deep breath and quickly scanned the courtroom.

On the plaintiffs' side, the senior and junior counsel sat grimly silent. Behind them, solicitor Louise Craig tried to busy herself sorting papers. Beside her sat Tracey Edwards, tired but calm, as yet unaware of what was about to happen. No one had wanted to tell her.

On the defence side, the gallery was more crowded than it had been throughout the entire trial. When the witness had last night agreed to testify, Ming had immediately rung Sylvie, who'd passed on the news to Angie and Leo and Marcia. And so the whole support team was here.

The only ones who hadn't known what was going to happen until just a few minutes ago were Gordon and Julia.

Ming had tried to tell Gordon; he'd been the first person she'd shared her theory with a few days before. But he'd derided her. Richard had taken her more seriously and, as a reward for her intuition and industry, had said that she could examine the witness; she was the one who knew where all the pieces fell into place, after all. As a result, Gordon now sat angry and silent, though Julia was sure she'd heard him mutter something about making a complaint to the DDO board about how he'd been treated.

As for herself, she was so stunned she feared she might be dreaming. No one had wanted to tell her until now, in case it all went wrong. She leaned forward and hoped she wouldn't wake up as Ming faced Judge Percival Owen and, as loudly as she could, said, 'Your Honour, the defence would like to call to the witness stand Brendan Edwards' father, Mr Brett Halsted.'

As the final witness walked into the courtroom Julia looked instinctively at Tracey, who sat absolutely still, staring straight ahead. When Brett took his place in the witness box, Tracey sagged slightly, the colour draining from her face. The last few months had been awful enough, but Julia knew only too well that the unexpected sight of the man she'd once loved must be unbearable for her.

Julia noticed that Brett didn't look at Tracey either. Now in his thirties, he was a picture of robust manhood, but his manner, today at least, was surly and hostile. Still in the army in Darwin, he had been located just two days ago and compelled to appear. Ming had said she would subpoena him if necessary. He had flown to Sydney this morning and his face told the tale of his coerced presence.

He was asked to identify himself to the court and confirm that he was Brendan Edwards' father. Ming then asked when he'd first learned about the Supreme Court trial of Dr Julia Kent.

'When you rang me on Wednesday,' he replied sharply.

'You knew nothing about it before?'

'Nothing.'

'When was the last time you saw your son, Mr Halsted?'

'On the day he was born.'

'And the last time you spoke to Ms Edwards?'

'Close to five years ago.'

Ming paused and looked at her notes. Not that she needed to. Every detail was etched into her brain.

'Do you have any other children, Mr Halsted?'

'Yes,' he replied, looking down.

'How many other children?'

'One.'

Ming elicited the information that Brett had had a daughter three years before Brendan. Tegan was now eight and living in Perth. She had been the product of a very casual relationship and Brett hadn't even known of the pregnancy until after the child was born and her mother had contacted him.

'Can you tell us about your daughter, Mr Halsted?' Ming continued.

'She's disabled,' he said quietly.

'In what way?'

'Like Brendan.'

'Does she live with her mother?'

'No. She's in a home.'

'Have you seen her?'

'Never.'

Brett's surliness was now gone, supplanted by a dull sadness. Julia sensed Ming's heart go out to him, but the lawyer had to press on.

'Do you believe that the disabilities of Tegan and Brendan are related?' she asked gently.

Brett looked down again. 'Yes. They probably are.'

He told the court that after the birth of Tegan, he'd been apprehensive about having another child, as any parent would be. This anxiety was the reason he'd left for a month in the middle of Tracey's pregnancy. But he'd wanted to be with Tracey and had come back. On returning, he'd sought reassurance from Dr Kent that everything was all right with the baby and been told that it was. As far as could be known.

When Brendan was born, Brett was crushed. While it took everyone else a few weeks to realise the serious and permanent nature of the child's problems, to his father, fearful already, one glance confirmed his dread. And its cause. It was him; he was a monster-maker. For someone who took such care of his body, it was devastating, and he had run away from the problem, determined to ignore it. Until six months ago. Now in a new relationship with someone who wanted children, he could disregard it no longer. He'd seen a doctor who'd referred him to a genetics expert. She'd quickly guessed the problem and had organised comprehensive blood tests to confirm her suspicions.

'Could you tell us why you think your children's problems are connected, Mr Halsted?' asked Ming kindly.

Brett Halsted spoke sombrely as a hushed court strained to listen and Tracey fixed her stare on a piece of fluff on the carpet. There was a problem with a couple of his chromosomes, he said. Small bits of genetic material had been transferred between at least two of them.

'Does this chromosomal problem have a name, Mr Halsted?' asked Ming.

442

Brett shook his head. He'd blocked it all out.

'Would it be called a balanced translocation?'

'That's it.' He gave a bitter laugh. 'A balanced translocation.'

It transpired that Brett himself was in excellent health and had a perfectly normal total amount of genetic material. It was just that some of it was sitting in the wrong place. Problems only arose when he donated chromosomes to his offspring. The material they got was unbalanced. Too much of one of the forty-six chromosomes, too little of another. Or vice versa. The amount of material involved in the translocation was very small, but was evidently critical for neurological development.

Brendan had had chromosome tests when he was born, of course, and they'd been reported as normal. But ordinary chromosome tests were relatively crude and could only detect major changes in chromosome structure. They couldn't pinpoint such tiny alterations as Brett had. There were, however, highly sophisticated and expensive new tests which could.

'And these special chromosome tests revealed your problem?'

'Yes,' replied Brett gloomily.

'Has Tegan been tested?' asked Ming, who had the report before her.

'Yes. She's got an unbalanced translocation. Inherited from me.'

'And Brendan?'

'He hasn't been tested.'

'Why?'

Brett shrank in the witness box. 'I couldn't bring myself to contact Tracey and tell her.'

Julia immediately understood. After Brendan was born, the hospital doctors had asked Tracey whether there was anyone in her own or Brett's family who had a similar problem. When Tracey had asked Brett, he'd scoffed at the idea. It was nothing to do with him, no way.

It was soon after that that he'd transferred to Darwin.

Chapter 50

The doorbell rang. Julia switched her attention from the Saturday papers she was just extricating from their plastic wrap to the kitchen clock. It was a dull morning, not yet eight. Had her father locked himself out? Folding her dressing gown tightly around her, she tiptoed to the front door and peeped through the hole. And shrieked. On the front porch, surrounded by her bags and blowing a kiss to her mother, was Emma.

Julia tugged open the door and flung herself into her daughter's arms. 'What's wrong, Em?' She anxiously scanned her only child. 'Why are you back so soon? Why didn't you tell me you were coming? How did you get from the airport? How long have you been standing here? Is something wrong? Why aren't you in Paris?'

'It's all right, Mum, it's all right. Calm down. Everything's fine.' She smiled. 'I came back to be with you.'

'With me?'

'Yes. When Dad told me things had started to go wrong, I knew I couldn't stay away any longer.'

'Dad?'

'Yes. He phoned me on Tuesday after you fell ill on the witness stand.'

'Tony told you? About the court case?'

'Mum, I've known all along. Ever since it started last year.'

'You have?' That couldn't be right. 'You can't have.'

'I did, Mum. You left some legal papers on the hall-stand one night. I picked them up, thinking they were lecture notes of mine.'

'You didn't say anything, Em.'

'Didn't I?' She smiled indulgently at her mother. 'Neither did you.'

Sitting on the back couch, Julia caught up briefly on Emma's travels before turning to the drama which had brought her daughter home early. After familiarising her with the main characters and the proceedings of the past three weeks, she arrived at the tumultuous developments of yesterday afternoon.

'Wouldn't little Brendan have had chromosome tests when he was born?' Emma recalled her high school biology.

Julia explained the inadequacy of the old tests and the role of the new technology. 'To be honest, Em,' she confessed, 'I'd hardly heard about it until yesterday.'

Emma cheered. 'That's lucky, Mum, the one test you need for your case gets invented just in the nick of time.'

It was lucky, agreed Julia. But even without the test, once it was known that Brendan's father had another child with a similar problem, the case against her would have been hard to maintain.

Emma asked whether all of his children would be like that.

Julia's brow creased sadly. She didn't know the answer to the question, but hoped it wouldn't be the case.

'So how did you find out about him? And Tegan?' Emma was agog with the drama of it all.

Julia paused for a moment, remembering the amazing scene in court. The truth was, she still didn't have a clue. What she did know, however, was that with Ming and Leo and Sylvie on her case, nothing useful to her defence was ever going to get away.

Emma poured a cup of tea for them both. 'So it's all over, Mum? The trial?' Since the last Emma had heard was the awful news from her father earlier in the week, it was hard to believe the turnaround in events.

It wasn't quite finished, Julia explained. Brett's revelation had only come in the last two hours of yesterday. Judge Owen had directed Tracey's legal team to consider its position over the weekend, but even the cautious Richard Tripp thought it would probably be over by Monday.

'Do you think Tracey knew? About Tegan? And Brett's tests?' Emma was very curious.

Julia shook her head. She'd been pondering poor Tracey, remembering how small she'd looked when Brett appeared, how she'd shrunk even further as he gave his testimony. And how she'd seemed to nearly disappear completely as his words cut adrift forever her hopes of bringing Brendan home. 'No, Em, I don't think she knew. She got a bigger shock than I did.'

Just then the front door closed and George appeared.

'Grandpa!' squealed Emma, leaping out of her chair. He was returning from his morning walk; fishing had been put on hold until Tony got back from Brisbane with Antonio.

'Scallywag! What are you doing here?' he asked, as innocently as he could. 'Sick of Europe already?'

Emma pouted. 'I kept waiting for you to join me, Grandpa, but you never showed up. Neither did Mum or Dad. I got lonely and decided to come home.'

'Well, we're glad you did, Em. Although I'm not sure Jason's new girlfriend will be so pleased.' He winked before retreating through the kitchen.

'Grandpa . . .' Emma shouted, on his heels as he ducked down the hallway.

The cupboards were still bare so, keen for a hearty breakfast after his walk, George went to get groceries while Emma headed to the shower in preparation for her surprise visit to Jason. Julia took the opportunity to take the papers back to bed for a while.

She flicked through them avidly, as she had every day for the past three weeks, and was once again relieved to find no item about her trial. She gave a small sigh. With luck, there now never would be.

Emma came in to sit on the bed as she dried her hair.

'So what happened with Patrick, Mum?'

Julia put down the newspaper and silently mulled over her daughter's question. Her understanding of the situation was still evolving. The timing hadn't been great, of course. The court case and her fears about publicity had made her tense and self-absorbed. But even without that, her life hadn't easily accommodated a new relationship, and Patrick hadn't liked that. As well, she probably had shown poor judgement in not telling him much earlier about Tracey Edwards and Madeleine Morgan.

On the other hand, she'd come to accept that Angie also had a point. Patrick had expected too much too soon. If he'd really wanted to be with her, he'd have allowed her the time to make room for him; he knew she was desperate to do it, that she recognised the lack of balance in her life. He'd seen her cut her hours and knew she would cut them further once Leo needed less support. And as for the secrets she'd kept from him, her concealment was partly his doing. He hadn't given her much chance, really.

In the past few days she'd seen something else as well. She had loved Patrick, there was no doubt about that, loved his enthusiasm and his sense of fun and his energy, but she'd been blind about him too. So badly wanting a relationship, so desperately needing to be the object of someone's affections, she'd paid less attention than she might to whether he was right for her. She'd just wanted him to be right.

And that wasn't the only thing she'd come to understand this week. Patrick's abandonment of her had occurred just after Emma left, and therein lay the clue: it was the same time that Tony's phone calls had stopped. The recognition had stolen up on her only slowly but was now as bright as stadium lights. As the weeks had passed and the trial approached, it was the absence of Tony – not Patrick – that had affected her more. At first just a tiny spark, her feelings for her ex-husband, his thoughtful inquiries and gentle advice, had slowly overtaken what she'd felt about her ex-boyfriend. Until, this week, it had combusted.

'Well, Mum?' Emma was still waiting.

'I wasn't what he wanted, Em,' was all Julia said.

'So you won't get back together then?'

'We broke up the week after you left and I haven't seen him since. It's definitely over.'

'Is there anyone else?' Emma was anxious.

'What? Are you kidding?' Julia laughed in spite of herself. Her daughter knew better than anyone that Patrick was the first serious relationship since her divorce and that had taken her seven years. She couldn't honestly imagine she'd have a new boyfriend in just a few weeks. Especially *these* weeks. 'Goodness, Em. One of my lawyers, perhaps? The clerk of the court? Or maybe the judge?'

'It's okay, Mum, I was just asking.' Emma's face relaxed with relief.

After her daughter had gone downstairs to help George in the kitchen, the phone on Julia's bedside table rang. She knew it would be Tony. He and Antonio were in a taxi coming from the airport. Antonio had insisted he call, he said, which the child confirmed in a brief exchange with Ju-ya.

'Where are you going now, Tony?' Julia asked carefully.

'Angie and Geoff have invited us to stay again.'

'I see.' Julia knew he would want to catch up with Angie, but she needed to see him too, before she handed him over forever. She wondered if they might like to call in for breakfast on their way past. Her father was cooking up a storm.

Tony thought it a nice idea. He then hung on the phone for a minute, saying nothing. Julia was likewise silent. She knew what he wanted to hear, but couldn't stop herself from teasing.

'All right,' he said finally, giving up. 'We'll be there soon.'

She could torment him no longer. 'She's here, Tony. She got in an hour ago.'

'Thanks.'

Julia and Tony were alone. Emma had waited for her father and brother to arrive and had then left to see Jason, while George had taken Antonio down to the beach. Julia hadn't seen Tony since Wednesday night, when she'd upset him with her apology. Now, distressed and embarrassed and overwhelmed by his nearness, she found herself prattling. Had his flight been good? Was the traffic bad? Did he think Emma looked well? Wasn't it wonderful of her to come home?

As her tension grew, she ushered him onto the deck. Maybe out here his closeness wouldn't press on her so much. And there'd be more air.

'You must be relieved,' Tony said after a while.

Grabbing the neutral topic, Julia admitted that she was. Relieved and pleased. And in a state of disbelief. It would take her months to get over it, but she might never have recovered if things had gone badly. Which was how they looked only sixty hours before.

Tony nodded in agreement. Tuesday and Wednesday were now the distant past. They sat for a silent moment, looking down to the ocean, powerful and irresistible. Julia knew there was no putting it off, but waited for Tony to tell her at his own pace.

'I've decided to fight for custody,' he said eventually.

She realised she'd been expecting this; Tony wouldn't leave Brisbane if his son was there. She steadied herself for the rest.

'I can't let Cecilia have Antonio. I spend my days dealing with people whose parents messed them up and I can't let it happen to him. It would be different if she was capable of really loving him, but she isn't. In another couple of years, he'll realise it too.'

They sat quietly for a while longer before Tony spoke again. 'If I win custody, I'm thinking of moving back to Sydney.'

Though it was what she'd been expecting him to say next, his indirect avowal of love for Angie hit her hard, and she found the air wasn't enough after all. But she'd made up her mind in the dark hours of this morning and she wasn't going back on her resolution: she would not tell Tony how she felt. It would gain

449

her no benefit, and would only upset him and Angie. And, although it would nearly kill her, she was going to be not only gracious, but also cheerful towards them. They had been extraordinary friends to her and it was her turn to be generous.

A very flat, 'That's great,' was all she managed, as winds of misery gusted away her resolve.

Tony nodded slowly; he was not finished. 'I've been thinking about what you said the other night, Julia, about my trial. I also want to apologise for –'

'It's fine, Tony, fine,' Julia cut in. Barely in control, she'd lose it completely if he said something nice. But he was not to be put off.

'I let you down badly at that time, with Sybilla first and then with my stubbornness over Madeleine. I didn't realise until you left how seriously I'd hurt you; to be quite honest, I'd never anticipated for a minute that your love for me was actually in jeopardy. I obviously didn't give it enough thought, just assumed that what we had was too special not to survive. As soon as I realised what I'd done, I was crazy with remorse. But it was too late.' He turned from her to look at the ocean. 'I've regretted it every day since.'

Julia heard his words but their meaning washed over her. So he had some regrets; who didn't? But once again, he was moving on, carving out a new life, while she continued to drown in the stagnant pool of the old one. Suddenly, she was angry. Didn't he know she needed to hear the truth from him? Why was he sidetracking her? How much more did he think she could take?

'Why are you moving back to Sydney, Tony?'

'I think it's a good idea.'

'Do you want to be near Angie?' There, she'd said it.

'Angie?'

Julia was bewildered at his prevarication; this wasn't like Tony. 'Yes,' she repeated, unable to keep the frustration from her voice. 'Are you coming back to be near Angie?'

Tony's heart quickened as he understood. 'Angie doesn't even know where she's going to be, Julia. She's got some very big decisions ahead of her. And while I'll always be available for her, she's not the reason I'm moving back to Sydney.'

'You're not together, you and Angie?' Julia shifted to the edge of her chair. Any further and she'd upend it.

'What? No, no, of course not. Angie's not ready for a new relationship; she's not even finished with the old one yet.' It was time to say it. 'And I'm in love with someone else.'

Just then the front door shut. It was Emma; Jason had gone to work. She came out tentatively to join her parents, trying to read their mood.

'Have you told her yet, Dad?' she asked quietly.

'I was just getting around to it, Em.'

It was a spontaneous party, always the best kind, and it was at Angie's, the only one who could have fed everyone without fuss. Not that Geoff was home to help her; he'd gone to a work function he apparently couldn't miss and which he hadn't mentioned to Angie until this morning.

Ming and Richard were there, of course. The DDO solicitor had an exciting new brief for the young barrister, which they were already discussing in detail. They were lawyers, after all.

Jennifer Pereira came by for a while. She'd been delivered six weeks prematurely and her son, now home, was doing well. Julia thanked her for finding Ming. 'She was brilliant, Jennifer. Untiring, unorthodox, and unrelenting. I probably wouldn't have won without her. I certainly wouldn't have won if things had been left to old boofhead St Jude.'

Jennifer diplomatically avoided commenting on the senior barrister, but admitted that with the junior, she'd had little choice. Sylvie had threatened to phone her every hour of every day until she found the best bloody junior barrister in Sydney for Julia's case. She was not to go on maternity leave until she did. And Sylvie had kept her word, harassing Jennifer constantly until she had come up with Ming. 'She's a very intimidating woman.' Jennifer looked around furtively as she spoke.

'Thank God for that,' exclaimed Julia. Sylvie had been wonderful in so many other ways as well, as had her other colleague, Leo Steiner. They must be world experts on labour-related neurological injury by now. The DDO should think about using them in other cases.

Shortly after Jennifer left to feed her son, Sylvie arrived bearing flowers from Sandra Steiner's garden. Leo couldn't come, but sent his best wishes.

'How is she?' Julia was overwhelmed by the kindness of her friends.

'She'll die this week, I'm afraid. And he'll die a little bit with her. But he's delighted for you.'

While Sylvie went to get some champagne, Julia smiled at the sight of George and Tony drinking their beers and anticipating the fishing they had planned for the morning. She then laughed out loud as Emma and Jason and Ben and Richie ran past her to hide in easy places so that Antonio, who was looking for them, could squeal with delight when he found them. Over time she noticed that Emma and Jason were hiding in more private places.

After a while Marcia arrived with Patricia and Cynthia and Erica.

'Congratulations, Julia.' They hugged her. 'We've missed you, and so have your patients.' No one mentioned Stephen, whose absence from tonight's gathering spoke for itself, but they had news about Grace Chan and Jane Steel.

'Grace's twins are going well,' related Marcia excitedly. 'And she's looking forward to seeing you next week.'

'And Jane Steel has bunkered down and is refusing to go home from hospital until you come and see her.' Patricia detailed the phone calls she'd received. Jane had been badly mucked around, didn't you know, and she'd had enough. Her doctor had gone missing, her labour had been mismanaged, and now her baby wouldn't feed properly.

'And it isn't just Jane who is suffering,' cut in Marcia. The charge sister had rung the surgery yesterday as well. For the second time. Jane buzzed the midwives constantly, and had managed to exhaust the wisdom and patience of every nurse on the ward. If they couldn't discharge her soon, they'd all be taking stress leave.

'And Jane has a lot of unanswered questions,' added Erica, who'd taken several phone calls as well.

'Which Leo has told her to write down. So that she doesn't forget a single one to ask when you come in,' finished Marcia as they howled with laughter.

After Sylvie and the practice staff had gone, Julia went with Angie out onto the deck. It was cool, but Julia was flushed from the joyful effusion of the past two days.

She turned to Angie. 'I can't thank you enough. I don't know what I would have done without you.'

Angie was humble. 'I was happy to help, and it wasn't much really.'

'It was everything to me,' Julia countered, her voice unexpectedly giving way as she recalled the awful weeks after Emma left and Patrick said he didn't love her any more. She would never have coped without Angie; she'd have starved to death, certainly. And it wasn't as if her friend had been cruising through her own life at the time. 'I'll never forget what you did.'

'You'd have done the same for me,' said Angie simply.

Julia did not trust herself to speak for a short while. Then she asked, 'Did you know Emma knew right from the beginning?'

'Yes.'

'And that she immediately told Tony?'

'Yes.'

'And my father?'

'Yes.'

'So they all knew long before Christmas.' Julia was confused. 'Why didn't you tell me?'

Angie was awkward. 'In the beginning it was because I knew you didn't want to involve them. It was all you could cope with just focusing on the case itself. I thought it would put you under too much pressure if you thought you had to deal with them as well.'

'And later?'

A tiny smile crept around Angie's lips. 'By then it was part of a bigger strategy.'

At least partly subconsciously, Emma had engineered her father's visit at Christmas to finally force Julia and Tony together. She'd grown up a lot in the previous year and become annoyed that her parents, both wonderful people, still didn't see each other. Her ambition did not extend beyond having them on amicable terms. But then it happened. Emerging from his disappointing relationship with Cecilia, the scales dropped from Tony's eyes and he realised he'd never actually stopped loving Julia.

He'd let slip how he felt on his Christmas walk with Emma and she, thrilled by the unanticipated possibility, encouraged him to give it a try. But Tony was too demoralised, both by his own failures and by Julia's love for Patrick. It was his daughter who pushed him to ring all the time and to bring Antonio to meet her mother. Of course Tony felt like a fool, like he'd been wasting his time, when Emma told him in February that Julia now planned to marry Patrick, but his daughter badgered him not to give up, to keep ringing anyway.

'With your trial coming up and Tony losing confidence, it was all we could do to persuade her to still go on her trip,' confessed Angie.

A glint of recognition came into Julia's eyes as she recalled the number of times Emma had suggested she stay. She couldn't keep the shock from her voice. 'You knew all this and didn't tell me?'

Angie admitted that was the case, but it hadn't been her place to say anything. 'At the same time Tony was wanting me to find out how you felt about him.' Angie shrugged hopelessly. 'But I couldn't figure it out.'

This came as no surprise to Julia; she hadn't figured it out herself until a week ago.

'I just knew that you didn't want to talk about him,' Angie continued.

It was Julia's turn to feel awkward. 'Actually, I . . . I thought Tony was in love with you.'

'With me?' Angie asked carefully.

'Yes. You're the most fantastic, gorgeous woman in the world;

why wouldn't I think he loved you? And . . .' Julia was quieter now. 'I thought you felt the same about him. Especially after you went to Brisbane and didn't tell me.'

Angie blushed. She hadn't realised Julia even knew and could see how it must have looked. She'd gone to Brisbane both to get away and to seek Tony's advice about Geoff. As she spoke, just for a nanosecond Julia saw something else flit across Angie's eyes then disappear, and she understood; after all, she'd still been planning to marry Patrick at that time.

The faint echo of regret in Angie's tone confirmed what Julia suspected. 'Once Patrick was off the scene, Tony knew he'd never forgive himself if he didn't try one final time to get you back.'

Julia said nothing and looked into the garden unable to understand why Tony had stopped ringing if that was how he felt, but knowing she couldn't now ask Angie.

Angie guessed anyway. Tony knew how devastated she must be and wanted to give her time to grieve, to make sure she didn't still love Patrick. So he stood back. But he kept himself well informed about everything that was happening to her. 'And he left the last two weeks of your trial free in his calendar, so that he could be here if you needed him.'

'And I told him not to come,' Julia remembered.

'That might have been the end of it for both of you,' said Angie simply. 'He gave up again after that; he'd tried and failed. He figured you were probably still carrying a torch for Patrick, but even if you weren't, it was clear you didn't want anything to do with him.'

Julia was giddy with the near-miss of it all, while Angie's face lit up with happiness for her friend. 'It's a good thing you went to pieces on the witness stand, Julia. It made him realise he couldn't keep away.'

At that moment Tony rounded the corner in the garden below, chasing a delirious Antonio.

'He's the most wonderful man in the world, Julia,' Angie said softly. 'Don't let him go this time.'

Chapter 51

Julia felt a small tug at her pyjama sleeve. She stirred in the early dawn and waited for the urgent whisper she knew it heralded. 'Ju-ya, Ju-ya, come see what I got. What Santa give me.'

She slid out of bed and followed Antonio to the abandoned pillowcase and its delivered booty. Under instruction, she sat on the floor while he scouted among his new toys, proudly demonstrating each one: his tip-truck, and ball, and playing cards and picture book. The truck was the early favourite. 'Play wif me, Ju-ya,' he commanded.

They built a makeshift highway in the kitchen and ferried tomatoes and boiled eggs and peas across the country. Predictably, the occasional chocolate for distribution was lost en route. Finally Antonio released Julia to let her make a cup of tea, and went in search of his father.

As she waited for the kettle to boil, Julia found herself humming with contentment. At the same time, she recognised it might not be such a happy day for others. Tracey, for example, would wish she could wake up on Christmas morning and have

456

her son in the next room as most mothers did. They'd seen a bit of each other since the trial and Julia was relieved that Tracey's initial suspicions of her had dissolved to the point where they were now working together to lobby the government. They wanted it made easier for parents to care for their severely disabled children at home.

Life was such a game of chance, she thought sombrely, her focus now on Leo, who'd be spending the festive season without his beloved wife for the first time in four decades. Although his family, now including his new granddaughter little Sandra, would make sure he was not alone, it would still be a difficult time for him.

Julia called out to Tony that the tea was ready, but there was no response. She could hear him whispering to Antonio down the corridor and tried to guess what plan they were hatching.

Moving to the table with the cups, she wondered how Angie was going; it was her first Christmas in new circumstances as well. Much happier since separating from a flabbergasted and chastened Geoff, she was in the process of buying his half of the house; the boys had chosen to be with her after all. Geoff had been invited for lunch today and would be next Christmas as well. Angie was not one for having kids split between their parents at such a time. But that was as far as it went; there was no way she'd ever be going to back to him. In fact, she seemed to be rather taken with Simon Littlewood, one of the cardiac surgeons she worked with.

Also much happier than last Christmas was Sylvie. Freedom from her mother's chronic disapproval had been liberating for her; moving into a sunny townhouse had helped a lot as well. But it was the confidence she'd gained during the trial that had really seen her come into her own. Julia considered that nothing would hold her back now.

She paused in her stream of thought for a minute; Sylvie was still waiting to hear what she'd decided about giving up obstetrics. The latest annual insurance premium had just been announced: one hundred and thirty thousand dollars, payable on January first. Half of the state's obstetricians had decided to

457

call it a day, including several at Eastside. Julia had one week to make her decision, but she still didn't know what it would be.

While she pondered her career dilemma, Antonio reappeared dragging a small gift-wrapped box in his truck. 'Special divery for you, Ju-ya,' he repeated as instructed.

'Oh?' Expectation coloured her face. She picked up the box then handed it back to Antonio, who wanted the joy of unwrapping it. His interest retreated when he saw what it was.

'Play ball, Daddy,' he said to his father, now smiling in the doorway. Tony said he would play in a minute. But first he had to wish his new wife happy Christmas. They'd been married a week, Julia joking that she'd been planning all along to tie the knot at the end of this year – she'd just had to switch one groom for another. Tony came to where she was still peering into the small box. 'Do you like it?'

'It's beautiful, Tony,' she said, the glow rising over her cheeks. 'I've still got the old one, you know.'

'Do you?' He hadn't seen it. It was one of the reasons he'd bought this one.

'I could never bear to part with it,' she admitted. She'd taken the small diamond cluster out several times recently but put it away again without trying it on; she'd felt strange at the thought of wearing it.

'Save it for Emma. This one is for our new beginning.' He slipped the gorgeous emerald and diamond ring over her wedding finger. Still holding her hand, he sought again the green eyes which had inspired his choice. 'Happy Christmas, Julia.'

Returning his gaze, she wondered how she had ever lived without the irrigation of his love. Without his goodness, his quiet thoughtfulness, his wry, gentle insights. She hadn't realised how withered she'd become until he had reconnected the disused taps one by one, and let his love wash over her once more. Looking into his eyes, her joy was all the more exquisite for its unexpectedness. Who'd have thought she'd be this lucky again?

She reached up to enfold him in a hug. 'Thank you, Tony, for everything. And happy Christmas. Doesn't it seem an eternity since the last one?'

Emma came into the kitchen in the middle of her parents' embrace. 'Come on, Antonio,' she said to her brother, who was bouncing his new ball noisily around Tony and Julia, uncertain why no one was telling him to stop. 'If they can have a big cuddle, so can we.' She picked him up and kissed him noisily, at which point Julia and Tony disentangled one arm each to enlarge their circle and incorporate their children. 'Are we going to have snow on the Christmas tree this year, Dad?' Emma asked with a twinkle. Tony looked at Julia; she'd only just vacuumed the living room. But she nodded happy assent. Of course they'd have snow.

Watching Antonio's exultant face as Tony held him aloft with the talcum powder, Julia couldn't believe how well things had turned out. Ming and Ritzy had resolved the custody problem in a matter of weeks, the resolution centring around the words Curtis (Cecilia's body-builder boyfriend), steroids and life-ban all used in the same sentence. Julia was still amazed that Cecilia had given up this beautiful little boy in return for Ritzy's file on her lover. But, if that was how little she valued Antonio, then it was all the more wonderful that he was now with them. Julia was determined to be at least two mothers to him.

Congregating around their now-speckled tree, they cheered as each present was unwrapped. After only a short while, their glee was disturbed by the phone. It was the hospital. Grace Chan, seven and a half months pregnant with the twins she'd waited ten years to have, had arrived in labour. It was normal for twins to come early and Julia was not concerned. Both babies were well grown and presenting head first. Still, she'd have to go now to make sure everything was ready.

'Sorry,' she sang as she kissed her family goodbye.

'Sure you are, Mum,' winked Emma, who knew her too well not to recognise her excitement. 'Just don't make anyone any promises about next month while you're there. Right?'

Julia and Tony were having all of January off, staying at a little beach house down the coast. Emma would be up and down but George would be there the whole time. He'd already mapped out the best fishing spots and was giving everyone a fishing rod for Christmas. Angie was coming down for a week with her sons. She might even be bringing Simon Littlewood.

'I won't,' vowed Julia to her daughter.

Grace Chan looked up in relief as Julia slid open the door and entered the labour room. 'I'm sorry about your Christmas, Dr Kent. But I'm glad you're here.'

Julia came over to her. She was glad too. If Grace had laboured while she was on leave, one of her partners would have cared for her. After ten years of being Grace's doctor, of sharing the successive frustrations and disappointments, she would have hated to miss out now, when things were finally going to fall into place.

She examined Grace, who was contracting well and nearly fully dilated. She'd had an epidural inserted, routine with twins, and was quite comfortable. The babies were also happy. Finally she was ready for delivery and the room was abuzz with staff. There were two teams of midwives and two paediatric registrars as well as the anaesthetist who'd stayed after the epidural in case he was needed further. Grace's husband, Albert, held his wife's hand, grateful for Dr Kent's warning and the video she'd given them about the birth of twins. Even so, he wished he could sit down.

'You're doing really well,' encouraged Julia as Grace pushed and rested and pushed again. 'I think you'll have the baby with the next contraction.'

The labouring woman's eyes widened with determination, and the head of the baby appeared outside the vagina. 'What is it?' she gasped urgently.

'We'll have to wait and see a bit more to know that,' laughed Julia. 'But it's got a pretty nose.' The midwife, Sally Stevens, nodded as the contraction built. 'A gentle push this time,' coached Julia. Grace complied and, with Albert's assistance, her little daughter was lifted up onto her chest.

While the proud father and one team of staff fussed over the first twin, Julia and Sally turned their attention to the second little Chan. Having originally been head first, it was now lying transversely across the uterus. Sally switched on the ultrasound machine so that Julia could see the exact position. It was going to be easier to bring the baby out as a breech. After warning Grace, she inserted her hand up high inside the uterus and felt for a foot. She grabbed one then lost it; it was slippery inside the bag of waters. She grabbed it again and this time held firm. 'Start the oxytocin, Sally.'

Sally indicated that a contraction was building. Julia turned to Grace. It was time to push again. With the foot now low, Julia ruptured the amniotic sac; the baby's right ankle appeared at the entrance to the vagina. Then the left ankle. Soon the buttocks and genitals arrived – twin two was a boy – followed by the abdomen, chest and neck. Only the head remained. Everyone rested while awaiting the final contraction. Some of the more junior midwives giggled at the view of the headless baby. The birth was nearly over but no one could relax. Especially Julia. She watched Sally's face, willing the contraction to come quickly. Sally nodded triumphantly.

'Okay, Grace,' commanded Julia softly. 'One more push and you'll have him.' With that, Julia eased the baby's head gently over the vaginal skin and lifted him up onto his mother. He was a little stunned by the delivery, but soon realised that if he didn't scream he'd be in trouble. When he started, it sounded as if he'd never stop.

After delivering the placentas and putting in a couple of stitches, Julia went out to the main desk to complete the data entry. She was flushed and exhilarated; Grace was going to call her tiny daughter Julia. Sally and Liz were chatting happily as she approached to thank Sally for her help with Grace's delivery. 'Knowing I had you there made the management of the second twin much easier.'

Sally coloured at the praise and then congratulated Julia on the birth as well. They didn't see many vaginal twins any more. All they seemed to do these days was traipse to the operating theatre for caesareans. Julia commiserated. Modern obstetrics was phasing out midwives. And skilled obstetricians.

The midwives were silent for a minute, glancing anxiously at each other. Finally Liz spoke. 'You're not giving up next week, are you, Dr Kent?' They'd heard she hadn't yet made up her mind.

'What do you think I'm going to do?' Julia asked, having come to a decision only in the past hour.

'Well, you've just gotten married,' said Sally.

'And you've told everyone you're not going to be working so hard any more,' said Liz.

'And it's an obscene amount of money,' said Sally.

'And the hours are impossible,' said Liz.

'So?' Julia was curious about their conclusion.

The midwives looked at each other. 'Well actually, Dr Kent, we think you love it too much to give it away.'

Julia grinned. 'Unfortunately, girls, I think you may be right.'

And she went off to ring Sylvie.

Louise Limerick
Dying for Cake

Life has suddenly taken an unexpected turn for the women in a Brisbane mothers' coffee group. Baby Amy disappears, and her mother, Evelyn, broken and distant in a psychiatric hospital, won't utter a word.

Desperate to find Amy, desperate to understand, the women cope with the loss in their own ways. But Evelyn's withdrawal has altered them irreversibly, and each begins to look for something to satiate the cravings they had not allowed to surface before . . .

Joanna is dying for cake. Clare is longing to paint again. Susan wants to claw back all the time she's lost. Wendy is trying to forget the past. Then there's Evelyn. Nobody knows what Evelyn wants. But how can she not want her baby back?

Dianne Blacklock
Wife for Hire

Sam knew she was a model wife, a prize wife, the kind of wife men secretly wished they had. But now Jeff wanted to leave her for someone else.

All Samantha Driscoll once wanted out of life was to be somebody's wife. She would marry a man called Tod or Brad and she would have two blond children, one boy, one girl.

But instead she married a Jeff, had three children, and he's just confessed to having an affair.

Sam's life purpose crumbles before her eyes, with the words of her mother playing in a continuous loop in her head, 'You've got no one to blame but yourself, Samantha.'

Spurred on by an eclectic bunch of girlfriends and her nutty sister, Max, she finds the job she was born for: *Wife for Hire*. Sam handles the domestic affairs, and acts as personal shopper and social coordinator for many satisfied customers.

But when attractive American businessman Hal Buchanan is added to her client list, Sam soon realises she can organise many things in life, but not her emotions.

Kris Webb and Kathy Wilson
Sacking the Stork

Sophie presumed 'making sacrifices for your children' meant giving up Bloody Marys and champagne for nine months. When she thought about it that is . . .

But then two blue lines appear on her pregnancy test.

How does a baby fit in with a hectic job, a chaotic social life and the absence of Max, the y chromosome in the equation, who has moved to San Francisco?

Support and dubious advice are provided by an unlikely group who gather for a weekly coffee session at the King Street Cafe. It is with Debbie the glamorous man-eater, Andrew the fitness junkie, Anna the disaster prone doctor and Karen the statistically improbable happily married mother of three, that Sophie discovers the ups and downs of motherhood.

And when an unexpected business venture and a new man appear on the scene, it appears that just maybe there is life after a baby.

Written by two sisters who live on opposite sides of the world, *Sacking the Stork* is a novel that tackles the balancing act of motherhood, romance and a career, while managing to be seriously funny.

Sandy Curtis
Deadly Tide

When her father is arrested for murder, Samantha Bretton takes over
as skipper of his fishing trawler, the *Sea Mistress*, determined to clear
his name. Brisbane cop Chayse Jarrett, guilt-ridden by the death of a
young woman on his last assignment, goes undercover on the vessel,
and soon realises that Samantha is hiding something.

Secrets that could implicate her father in more than murder.

Secrets that Chayse becomes reluctant to uncover.

As Chayse and Samantha fight their attraction to each other, the case
takes a sinister twist, and she is forced to relive the horrors of her
past. Then in a night as deadly and unpredictable as the ocean that
threatens his life, Chayse finds new allies, but now faces danger from
old and bitter foes.

Before that night has ended, even enemies will discover that things
are not always as they seem . . .

Praise for Sandy Curtis:

'[*Dance with the Devil*] announced a splendid talent in the competitive
field of crime and suspense and that is confirmed in *Black Ice*.'
GOLD COAST BULLETIN

Ilsa Evans
Spin Cycle

Ever had one of those weeks when you've been soaked, put through the wringer and hung out to dry?

On Monday morning, this twice-divorced mother of three was bemoaning her boring life that left her feeling deflated and unhappy. By the end of the week she wishes that was all she had to worry about.

In the space of seven days her life is picked up and spun around when she discovers her mother's getting married again (for the fourth time), her older sister is pregnant again (for the fifth time), her younger sister lands the perfect boyfriend (who is very fanciable), her sister-in-law is running a brothel, her new next-door neighbour is going to be her ex-ex-husband. Oh, and she's been arrested, her best friend's gone missing and the pets keep dying. All in the same week she sacks her therapist because she thinks she can work it all out for herself. But can she? And how can she work it all out if she doesn't even know what it is she wants to work out?

Jessica Adams
I'm A Believer

'Even complete cynics will fall for the many charms of *I'm A Believer*'
NICK EARLS

'Adams puts a refreshing spin on the boy meets girl scenario, guiding her flawed but likeable hero to the heights of love from the depths of despair'
VOGUE

'Funny, sad, quirky – and very real. Adams has done it again'
MAGGIE ALDERSON

Mark Buckle is one of life's natural sceptics. He's a science teacher who'd rather read Stephen Hawking than his stars and he's highly suspicious of Uri Geller, feng shui, crystals and tarot cards.

Most importantly though, Mark Buckle absolutely, positively, doesn't believe in life after death – until his girlfriend, Catherine, dies in a car crash, and everything changes.

Within days of her death, Mark sees Catherine sitting by his bedside wearing the dressing gown that he packed away for the local charity shop. Then, Mark discovers that they can communicate as well.

By the end of the year, Mark Buckle, super-sceptic, will be a believer – but not before his dead girlfriend finally sorts out his love life for him.

Bunty Avieson
The Affair

It started so innocently. But doesn't everyone say that?

In the opulent rooms of a Sydney specialist, Nina and James Wilde
are waiting. Waiting to learn whether the rare, hereditary condition
that killed James' father will threaten not only James, but also their
much loved son, Luke.

That is just the beginning of Nina's torment.

She has a secret, one that is now a decade old and just as capable of
destroying everything that is most important to her. Memories of
another time and a sweet, passionate love that should never have
happened are haunting Nina. Suddenly her grasp on life and
happiness seems more precarious than she could ever have
anticipated.

Beverley Harper
Shadows in the Grass

Enraged screams filled his head. Deadly shapes bore down. Animal and man driven by one single thought. Kill or be killed. Neither wanted to die.

Falsely accused of a terrible crime, impetuous young aristocrat Lord Dallas Acheson is forced to flee his native Scotland, leaving behind the only woman he has ever loved – Lady Lorna de Iongh. From that day onwards, he must learn to live a different life in a land where danger is an ever-present partner.

Fate takes him to southern Africa and the emerging seaport of Durban, from where he sets off to trade and hunt, seeking his fortune in the little-travelled midlands of Natal and the wilds of Zululand. Tested to the limit, Dallas discovers more than he could have imagined.

Married to a woman he doesn't love, he yearns to abandon the restraints of nineteenth-century society to be with Lorna. And when the Zulu war breaks out, finds himself torn between old and new loyalties, required to be an enemy of the land that is now his true home.

Brimming with the trademark qualities of evocative storytelling and accurate research brought to vivid life, Beverley Harper, author of *Jackal's Dance*, is indeed 'Australia's answer to Wilbur Smith' (AUSTRALIAN GOOD TASTE).

Peter Watt
Papua

Two men, sworn enemies, come face to face on the battlefields of France. When Jack Kelly, a captain in the Australian army, shows compassion towards his prisoner Paul Mann, a brave and high-ranking German officer, an unexpected bond is formed. But neither could imagine how their pasts and futures would become inextricably linked by one place:

Papua.

The Great War is finally over and both soldiers return to their once familiar lives, only to find that in their absences events have changed their respective worlds forever. In Australia, Jack is suddenly alone with a son he does not know and a future filled with uncertainty, while the photograph of a beautiful German woman he has never met fills his thoughts. Meanwhile the Germany that Paul had fought for is vanishing under the influence of an ambitious young man named Adolf Hitler, and he fears for the future of his family.

A new beginning beckons them both in a beautiful but dangerous land where rivers of gold are as legendary as the fearless, cannibalistic tribes, and where fortunes can be made and lost as quickly as a life:

Papua.

A powerful novel from the author of *Cry of the Curlew*, *Shadow of the Osprey* and *Flight of the Eagle*.